Elizabeth Heiter likes ~~~~~ heroines, chilling villa ~~~~~ little romance. Her resea ~~~~~ of serial killers, throug ~~~~~ the FBI Academy's shooting range. Elizabeth graduated from the University of Michigan with a degree in English literature. She's a member of International Thriller Writers and Romance Writers of America. Visit Elizabeth at www.elizabethheiter.com

Regan Black, a *USA TODAY* bestselling author, writes award-winning action-packed novels featuring kick-butt heroines and the sexy heroes who fall in love with them. Raised in the Midwest and California, she and her family, along with their adopted greyhound, two arrogant cats and a quirky finch, reside in the South Carolina Lowcountry, where the rich blend of legend, romance and history fuels her imagination.

ALASKA MOUNTAIN RESCUE

ELIZABETH HEITER

COLTON'S DANGEROUS LIAISON

REGAN BLACK

MILLS & BOON

First Published in Great Britain 2020
by Mills & Boon, an imprint of HarperCollins*Publishers*
1 London Bridge Street, London, SE1 9GF

Alaska Mountain Rescue © 2020 Elizabeth Heiter
Colton's Dangerous Liaison © 2020 Harlequin Books S.A.

Special thanks and acknowledgement are given to Regan Black for her contribution to *The Coltons of Grave Gulch* series.

ISBN: 978-0-263-28319-8

0121

MIX
Paper from
responsible sources
FSC
www.fsc.org
FSC™ C007454

This book is produced from independently certified FSC™ paper to ensure responsible forest management.

For more information visit: www.harpercollins.co.uk/green

Printed and bound in Spain
by CPI, Barcelona

ALASKA
MOUNTAIN
RESCUE

ELIZABETH HEITER

This book is for my new brother and sister, Farris and Lamia, who have made the word *in-law* sound amazing.

Writing a book is often just me, my parrot and my computer. But the process of bringing a book to life takes many! My deepest thanks to my editor, Denise Zaza; my agent, Kevan Lyon; and everyone behind the scenes at Mills & Boon who helped get *Alaska Mountain Rescue* to readers. A special thanks to my family and friends, who are always my biggest cheerleaders: Andrew Gulli, Chris Heiter, Kathryn Merhar, Alan Merhar, Caroline Heiter, Kristen Kobet and Robbie Terman. And a special thanks to my writer pals, who met me virtually or in person to get all the words: Heather Novak, Dana Nussio, Tyler Anne Snell and Janie Crouch.

Chapter One

The whispers started the moment she stepped into town.

"It's *her*. The kidnapped girl. The one from five years ago."

"The one who almost got her real sister killed?"

Alanna tried to ignore the sidelong glances from the two women peering at her from the open door of the grocery store. In a place like Desparre, Alaska, the stares and chatter were likely to bring more people.

Alanna hunched her shoulders, trying to disappear into her heavy coat as she picked up her pace. Still, she felt their accusatory gazes bore into her. The pace of her breathing picked up, sweat breaking out all over her body. This was the side effect of sending the "parents" who'd raised her for fourteen years to jail and then returning to another state, to a family she'd tried so hard to remember but didn't quite fit into anymore. The side effect of spending too long dodging reporters desperate to be the one to break her silence and get the inside story of her abduction.

The voices faded as the women disappeared back into the grocery store, one of a handful of buildings that lined Desparre's small downtown area. It looked so tiny compared to the suburb on the outskirts of Chicago where she'd returned after living in the remote wilderness of Alaska with the family who'd kidnapped her.

Even after being gone for five long years, in many ways, Alaska still felt like home.

Alanna took a deep breath of the crisp, cool air and closed her eyes, letting the familiar sounds and smells and sights calm her. At her side, her St. Bernard, Chance, recognized her method for coping with anxiety and scooted up against her, then promptly sat.

A minute later, the sound of Chance's low, sustained growl made her eyes pop back open.

The St. Bernard was definitely a gentle giant, more likely to thump his tail and wait for a belly rub than go after anyone. But his size and his warning growl never failed to make people who were a little too aggressive back up fast.

In the past, Chance had used that growl on a handful of particularly determined reporters who'd stuck with her for years, following her around and ambushing her at the most unexpected times, seeking a candid photo or a sound bite. Because no matter how much time passed, she was still one of *those* women. A name that had made national headlines. A story she could never outgrow. Today, Chance was using his growl on the police officer who'd somehow managed to get close while her eyes were shut.

His startling blue eyes darted to her dog, then back to her. "Miss, do you need hel—"

The words trailed off as those blue eyes widened slightly. In a face made up of sharp angles and pale skin, his eyes were especially compelling. His tone was less friendly, more suspicious as he said, "Alanna Altier?"

"Morgan," she corrected. The name of her birth family, instead of the family who'd raised her for most of her childhood. After five years, the name Morgan was finally starting to feel less foreign on her lips.

"Morgan," he repeated. His gaze swept the space behind her, as if the woman who'd raised her—who'd helped kidnap her and four other children over the span of eighteen years and then escaped from police custody five days ago—would suddenly appear.

Anxiety started to swell again and Chance scooted even closer, his warm fur pressing against her leg, his big head nuzzling her.

Absently petting him, Alanna kept her eyes on the officer. She didn't recognize him. Not that she would—the Altiers had kept her and her "siblings" far from prying eyes, especially law enforcement eyes. She'd been to town before, but more often she'd stayed home, spending most of her days inside the house she'd helped build. Or in the dozen acres surrounding it that the Altiers owned, a buffer from them and the rest of the world. At times, it had felt like an oasis. At others, it had seemed more like a cage.

The officer's narrowed eyes locked on hers again, unsettling in their singular focus. "I thought you'd moved back to Chicago, with your real family."

It was somewhere between a statement and a question and Alanna tried not to fixate on the word *real*. She loved the Morgans, the parents who'd enveloped her in hugs the moment she'd stepped back through their door, who'd kept all her belongings from when she had disappeared from their lives at five years old. The big brother, who'd stared at her with huge, teary eyes before breaking into a shaky smile and whispering, "I can't believe it. You're finally home." The older sister, who'd traveled across the country on the slimmest of leads, who'd almost died trying to save her.

"I did," Alanna finally answered. "But—"

"But Darcy Altier is back to her old tricks. And you think...what? She's coming back here?"

Darcy Altier. The woman she'd called "Mom" for fourteen years. Alanna had always known she'd been kidnapped, remembered with startling clarity the moment when Julian Altier had yanked her out of her yard in Illinois and into his car. But Darcy and Julian had never harmed her. They'd treated her like their own child, held her when she cried, smiled with her in happy times. They'd loved her. Despite everything else, she knew that.

Over those fourteen years, she'd grown to love them, too. She'd also grown to love the other children the Altiers had kidnapped, her "siblings." She missed all of them with an ache that was hard to explain to anyone, least of all the family who'd waited and searched for her all those years.

"Well?" the officer pressed, shifting so his right side was angled toward her. The side where a gun was holstered at his hip.

Her anxiety ratcheted up again and Chance stood up, stepping slightly forward. Protecting her, the way he'd done since the moment she'd brought him home. He'd been a tiny, emaciated puppy then, who had somehow managed to survive in cruel conditions until he was taken away and eventually ended up in her care. Now, though small for a St. Bernard, he outweighed her by twenty pounds.

Alanna put her hand on his back, pressed down slightly. Telling him to stay put.

"I don't know," Alanna answered, her gaze darting to the police station behind him. She *was* here for Darcy, because from the instant she'd seen the news report about her "mother's" escape, she'd known it deep down. Nowhere had felt like home to any of them the way Alaska had. But she wasn't about to say that to an officer who'd stared at her with barely veiled suspicion since the moment he'd realized who she was.

Seeming to recognize her discomfort, the officer took

a step backward. But he still held the odd angle and she couldn't stop staring at that weapon.

"I think we got off on the wrong foot," he said, the words sounding strangled. "I'm Peter Robak."

Robak. The name floated around in her mind, vaguely familiar, and Alanna tried to place it. Before she could, he was speaking again.

"Why are you back in Desparre, Alanna?"

"I…" She was on a fool's quest. One that would have horrified her family back in Chicago if she'd told them about it in person, instead of in the note she had left. One that had definitely frustrated her boss, when she'd called to let him know she was taking time off in the middle of the work week and wasn't sure when she'd be back.

But who else knew Darcy Altier like she did? It was one thing that Darcy had escaped police custody. Alanna knew the woman belonged in jail, but that didn't mean she liked the idea of the person who'd helped raise her being behind bars. If it had simply been an escape, Alanna would have stayed in Chicago. But when a child had gone missing…

Straightening her shoulders, Alanna told him, "I was actually on my way to the police station."

Peter eyed her with distrust for another minute, then stepped slightly aside. He swept his hand forward, gesturing for her to lead the way.

She felt him close behind her for every step of the short walk into the police station. Opening the door, she led Chance inside with her, not caring how the officers would feel about that. Technically, he was a service dog.

Inside the station, a wall of warm air hit her, reminding Alanna of just how cold it was outside. In her years living here, she'd gotten used to it and when she'd made the trip back, she'd packed appropriately. Yanking the hat off her head and unwinding her scarf, she looked around.

It was a tiny station, with a counter up front and an officer who glanced up, then returned to his paperwork when he saw Peter.

Peter said, "Alanna Alt… Morgan is here. Is the Chief around?" And suddenly the officer looked a lot more interested.

"Hang on a sec," he replied, giving her one last look before he disappeared behind a door marked Police Only.

Alanna planted her feet in a wider stance, tipping her chin up. A trick she'd taught herself to help her feel more confident, more in control. Chance's familiar form pressing against her leg didn't hurt, either.

From a back room, the police chief appeared, leaving the door to the bullpen open behind her. She was young for her position, but strode through the door with a genuine confidence Alanna envied. With the chief's dark hair pulled back into a bun and her expression somehow serious and friendly at the same time, Alanna could see her both putting victims at ease and scaring criminals.

The chief nodded once at Peter, then held out a hand. "How can I help you, Alanna?"

The officer who'd been sitting behind the counter settled back in his seat, this time ignoring his paperwork, unabashedly interested. Another officer stared at them through the open doorway, curiosity on his face. Alanna tried to shut them all out and just focus on the chief. Focus on the reason she'd come all this way, back to a place she thought she'd never see again.

"I…" Clearing her throat, Alanna said, "I'm sure you are already aware that Darcy Altier escaped from custody when she was allowed to go to my fa… Julian Altier's funeral. And that a child went missing a few miles from where she escaped and she's a suspect in the case."

It was a bold, dangerous move, something Alanna had

never felt Darcy was capable of. At least, not until the moment Darcy had picked up a shotgun and fired at Alanna's sister, Kensie, who'd flown to Alaska to try to save her.

Shutting that memory out, Alanna continued, "I think she might come back to Desparre. I want to help you find Darcy." She wanted to help them bring her in safely.

The chief smiled, the expression half pitying and half amused, and Alanna felt her cheeks flush deep red.

The woman reached out and put a hand on Alanna's upper arm. She squeezed gently, as if Alanna was the sheltered, scared nineteen-year-old from five years ago. Back then, officers from a neighboring town had taken her away from the only family she'd known for fourteen years and brought her to the hospital, where her biological sister waited.

Now Alanna was twenty-four, in the process of getting her master's degree and catching up on all the things she hadn't really known she'd missed while she was hidden away in Alaska. But she suddenly felt nineteen again when the chief said, "We appreciate that, but I think we've got it handled."

The chief continued with words of sympathy about the man who'd kidnapped her, who'd been a father to her for so many years. The man who'd been buried five days ago, whose service Alanna had longed to attend, but hadn't, knowing how it would hurt the family who'd missed her since she was five.

Alanna barely heard the words. Instead, she heard the snicker from the officer behind the counter.

Humiliated, Alanna spun back in the direction she'd entered.

The officer who'd brought her into the station—Peter Robak, who she remembered suddenly as someone she'd seen on TV a few years ago, a war reporter who'd almost died covering a hostage release—stood in her way.

He stepped slightly aside as she pushed past him, back into the frigid Alaskan air with Chance at her side, like always. She hurried across the unpaved street toward the truck she'd rented when her plane set down at the closest airport, which was still hours away. Then she stopped, spun back around, and looked up and down the small street. Despite the fact that it was still only midday, it was empty now.

Her St. Bernard stared up at her with his soft brown eyes. Then his head pivoted at the sound of a hawk's call overhead. Chance wasn't used to the vast emptiness of Desparre compared to the suburb outside busy Chicago where they lived.

Right now, there was only a light sprinkling of snow on the Desparre streets. But that could change at any time. Winter came here early, hard and fast. Sometimes, it got hit with enough snow to make leaving Desparre impossible until spring came.

When Chance's gaze returned to hers, there was a question there, as if he was asking, *What are we doing here?*

Being in the police station had made coming back here feel like a big mistake. But somewhere nearby, Darcy and a small child were hiding. Alanna was sure of it. And that child—like some of the "siblings" she'd grown up with— was young enough not to remember his family if they didn't find him in time.

For fourteen years, Alanna had been afraid to speak up, afraid to try to get help. At first, that fear had been because she hadn't known how her abductors would respond. Would they hurt her? Would they kill her? Later, it had been because, despite everything, she loved the Altiers and the four kids she'd called brothers and sisters. She'd become afraid of what would happen to all of them if she tried to sneak away and told anyone the truth.

For the past five years, she'd felt guilty about all of it. Seeing the pain she'd caused her biological parents and siblings Kensie and Flynn, wondering if some of the other kids wouldn't have been kidnapped if she'd spoken up sooner.

She couldn't change the past. But she could change the future.

This time, she wasn't staying silent. She wasn't going home and she wasn't staying out of this investigation, whether the police wanted her help or not.

"We're going to do this," she told Chance. "We're going to find them."

SHE'S GOT A lot of nerve, showing up here," Peter muttered to no one in particular.

As usual, his partner, Tate Emory, heard him. "I don't know. I feel bad for her. Imagine what she's been through. It can't have been easy to write that note and turn in the only family she'd known since she was five years old."

Peter shifted and scowled at his partner, who'd strode over to stand beside him, moving silently. Or maybe Peter just hadn't heard him, since Tate had come up on Peter's left side. The side where his hearing was mostly gone.

Being new to the force, new to policing in general, hadn't been a smooth transition for Peter. Most of the officers here still stared at him like the rookie he was. Worse, he knew plenty of them hadn't wanted him accepted onto the force in the first place because of his hearing disability. Some of them were still trying to push him out.

He'd never felt that from Tate. His partner had only been on the force for five years, just long enough to have been present for Alanna's dramatic rescue.

It had all started with a simple note, left between some money at a general store on the outskirts of Desparre. The note had been as straightforward as it was confusing, since at the time there'd been no indication Alanna was even alive, let alone that her kidnappers had taken other children. *My name is Alanna Morgan, from Chicago. I'm still alive. I'm not the only one.*

The FBI had done a quick investigation and called the note a hoax, yet another dead end in a more than decade-old cold case. But Alanna's sister had believed it, had traveled over three thousand five hundred miles across the country in search of a sister she'd only known for five short years. The rescue had been sensational, making national news and putting the sleepy town of Desparre in a spotlight it desperately wanted to avoid. Now that spotlight might be returning.

Back then, Peter had been overseas, doing something he thought he'd stick with until it was time to retire. The scandal of the kidnapping had caught his attention only because he grew up in Luna, the little town next to Desparre where Alanna had finally been reunited with the sister who'd come to Alaska to find her.

Peter stared at the closed door Alanna had disappeared through, trying not to picture the embarrassment in her eyes. Yeah, he felt sorry for what she'd gone through, but five years had passed. Enough time to create a new life for herself with her real family, people who must have gone through hell thinking she was lost to them forever. She should have been home with them now, not out looking for a kidnapper. Because no matter what she said, he didn't quite believe she was here to put Darcy Altier back behind bars.

Alanna Morgan might have started out as a victim, but now she could choose her path in life. And every nuance in her voice, the flickers of emotion he'd seen in her eyes, told him she was choosing all wrong. She was here for Darcy Altier, all right, but not to get her arrested. To help her hide.

"Why do you think she believes Darcy returned to Desparre?" Tate asked.

Peter shrugged, his gaze still fixed on that closed door. It was a good question. Darcy Altier had been granted furlough to bury her husband, who'd been killed in jail. She'd managed to slip free of her guards and run, but that had been in Oregon, back near the prison. A smart woman would head as far from the site of her original crimes as possible. So why did Alanna think that Darcy was here? Why was *Alanna* here?

"They've been in contact." Peter spoke his thoughts out loud. It was the only logical explanation.

"Seriously?" Tate scoffed. "Alanna's the one who turned her in. You really think Darcy would reach out to her after that?"

Peter turned to look at his partner. Tate was a couple of inches taller than Peter's five-foot-ten-inch frame, his skin and hair a couple of shades darker. From the moment they'd met, Peter had felt a strange kinship with Tate, a sense that both of them had known hardship they didn't speak of, that both of them had a restless desire to move past it.

"This woman raised her since she was five years old," Peter insisted. "Alanna spent most of her childhood with her. I bet she barely remembered her real family. How much do *you* remember from before you were five?"

Tate shrugged. "Enough. Obviously Alanna remembered them or she wouldn't have left a note for them to find her."

"Sure, but then she continued to hide with the people who kidnapped her."

"That's a little harsh. She was nineteen. How much freedom do you think they gave her? You, of all people, should understand—"

Peter let out a humorless laugh. "Understand what? The lengths people will go to in order to protect someone who hurt them?"

That was something he definitely understood. He'd gotten an up-close look at the unnatural attachment a hostage could develop for their captor. That experience had destroyed his career as a war reporter—had destroyed much of the hearing in his left ear, too. There was no chance of recovering his hearing, no surgery or hearing aid that could improve it.

Peter had no doubt that Alanna had a similar unhealthy attachment, that she was suffering from serious delusions about the woman who'd stolen her away from her family. It made her motives questionable. Worse, it made her dangerous.

Tate was shaking his head, but Peter kept going. "You're right. I do understand. Ultimately, it doesn't matter if Alanna has spoken to Darcy or she just knows her well enough to predict her movements. If Darcy is crazy enough to actually come back here, Alanna is the key."

Speaking the words aloud made anticipation swell in his chest and his gaze dart back to the closed door. Alanna *was* the key—and not just to locating a fugitive and solving a kidnapping, but to Desparre's reputation as a quiet, safe place to be left alone. And to Peter's future on the Desparre police force.

"Uh-oh," Tate said. "I know *that* look."

"Alanna is going to lead us to Darcy Altier and the missing kid." He headed for the door, gesturing for his partner to follow. "We're not letting Alanna out of our sight until she does."

Chapter Two

Alanna stared through dense woods at the house where she'd grown up. She'd helped build it on this mountaintop, dragging wood alongside her "siblings" and helping her "parents" lift the framework into place. All those months of hard labor, of watching the house slowly take shape. When it was finally finished, she'd been proud of her home.

Now it looked derelict and empty, snow covering the driveway that no one had bothered to shovel. Likely no one wanted to buy a house built by a pair of kidnappers, once home to five stolen kids.

Once upon a time, she'd stared at it with happiness and love. Now, there was bitterness, too, with the memory of her "mother" and "older brother" firing weapons at Kensie as she risked her life to bring Alanna home.

Alanna swallowed hard as she stepped out of the truck she'd parked at the end of the gravel driveway. Chance bounded out after her, quick despite his size, loving the heavy snowfall in Alaska. He stuck close to her, a faithful companion who needed no leash.

She'd come here straight from the police station, not even bothering to check in to her hotel yet. Now, she wondered if she should have taken a break, given herself a chance to emotionally acclimate to being back here.

Her attention snagged on broken bits of scattered wood. The sign with her "family's" name and a No Trespassing warning had been smashed to pieces.

She bent down and picked up the largest piece, a splintered slab of wood that read Altier. She ran her gloved fingertips over the hand-carved lettering, remembering when Darcy had made it. The urge to take it with her was strong, but what if her family in Chicago saw it? They'd be hurt and full of questions she didn't know how to answer any better now than she had five years ago, despite the degree in psychology she'd earned since coming home. So, instead, she set it carefully back on the snow, tucked her hands in her pockets and strode toward the house. Chance walked beside her, comfortable in the frigid weather that made Chicago seem mild.

It would be foolish for Darcy to come here. But she and Julian had spent so many years running from state to state, never staying long in one place, afraid to draw any attention. In this remote patch of Alaskan wilderness, they'd finally felt like they weren't being chased. They'd been willing to put down roots, trusted that the children they'd raised wouldn't turn them in for kidnapping them from families they either barely remembered or, in the case of Alanna's youngest "siblings," didn't remember at all.

Walking around the edge of the house, her feet sank into deeper snow that dampened her pants just below the knees, where her boots ended. She peered through each of the windows on the ground floor. Nothing. No sign that anyone was inside, no sign that anyone had been here in a long time.

The furniture they'd picked out or built had been moved around—chairs knocked over, drawers hanging open with the contents spilled. All the things she and her "family" had left behind, had never been able to come back to claim.

Alanna rubbed the bare finger where she used to wear a worn ruby ring, an Altier family heirloom that was the only thing she'd taken with her back to Chicago. She'd stopped wearing it when she'd noticed her parents and siblings constantly eyeing it, though they'd never actually come out and asked what it meant to her.

Focusing on the house again, Alanna leaned closer, peering through the windows into the living room, looking for any sign that Darcy had been here recently. The dirt on the wooden floors had faded to a light gray with no new tracks in the dust. It was clearly old, from when a slew of police officers had traipsed through, looking for her "family" five years ago. Back then, they'd already fled, but not far enough, not fast enough. The police had caught up to them.

Alanna squeezed her eyes closed against the memory of a circle of officers training weapons on her "parents" and screaming at them to get down. Of watching Julian and Darcy be flattened to the ground in deep snow, officers' knees pressing hard into their backs as they were cuffed. Of her youngest "siblings" crying and clinging to her. Of her older "brother" scowling, the tension in his body telling her he might do something stupid.

Chance nudged his big head against her thigh, hard enough to almost make her stumble. Her eyes opened, a laugh breaking free despite the pain in her heart. "I know, boy. You don't understand what we're doing here." She sighed, stroking her gloved hand over his soft head. "I used to live here." Her attention drifted to the dense woods behind the house, the steep slope of a mountain that dropped off suddenly. Protection from fears she hadn't totally understood as a child. "I used to be happy here."

The rumble of an engine nearby made Chance's head swivel. Alanna peered around the edge of the house, to-

ward the street. This part of Desparre wasn't on many
maps. Houses were set apart by miles, far from the road
and hard to find if you didn't know where you were going.
They were up higher in the mountains, in an area more
prone to avalanches and deeper snow. Even locals didn't
often come this way without a reason.

Her heart rate picked up as she squinted at the street for
any sign of life beyond the thick trees. Could it be Darcy?
If it was, how would she react to Alanna's presence?

Five years ago, Alanna's older "brother" Johnny had
started talking about wanting to get married. It had put
an ache in Alanna's heart with the realization that she'd
never have any memories with the family she'd tried for
fourteen years to remember. Not unless she acted.

So, she had. When Julian had taken her into some stores
on the outskirts of town, she'd slipped a note into the stack
of bills they'd used to pay. She'd been so afraid Julian
would notice. She hadn't been afraid he'd hurt her—she'd
stopped fearing that long ago. But she *had* been scared of
how he'd react if he found it.

Yes, he'd kidnapped her. There was no way to spin that;
it was just wrong. But he'd loved her. He and Darcy had
raised her; they'd homeschooled her in every subject so
well that when she'd returned and taken her GED, it had
been ridiculously easy. She'd sailed through college, too.
But it hadn't just been academics. They'd taught her to be
self-reliant in the dangerous wilderness, taught her skills
that Kensie and Flynn still shook their heads at with awe.
They'd raised her with love and, as the years went by, she
couldn't stop herself from loving them, too.

Back then, she had been so focused on seeing her birth
family again. She hadn't let herself consider the possible
consequences for the people who'd raised her, or for the
kids she'd called brothers and sisters, who she still missed

desperately. She knew if she'd paused to think about all of that, she never would have done it.

The sound of the vehicle reached her ears again, this time the slow grind of tires over snow that hadn't been packed down yet. Was it Darcy, noticing the unfamiliar truck in the driveway, afraid to approach?

Alanna stepped out from behind the house, hurrying toward the street with Chance bounding after her. He loved the snow, thought it was a game, but she was too anxious to pay much attention. Would Darcy stop if she saw Alanna now? Or would she speed away?

When Alanna reached the street, a dark SUV backed quickly out of view. It was too quickly to decipher who was in the vehicle, but there were two people in the front seat. One thing Alanna knew for sure: it wasn't a child in the passenger seat. It looked like there were two men in the car.

Pinpricks of awareness swept across her arms. The Altiers had built this home in as secluded a spot as they could find. But that seclusion worked both ways. Right now, it meant no one would hear her cry for help.

Back in Chicago, the news stories had called her a hero, had highlighted how it all ended, with her leaving a note for her family to find her. But in Alaska, it was different. In Desparre, she wasn't the girl who'd helped five kids go home to families who missed them. She was the girl who'd put their sleepy, intentionally below-the-radar town on a national stage. She was the girl who'd been hiding in the woods for years, never reaching out for help. Because while the locals might have a live-and-let-live attitude about someone else's business, they also protected their own. If she'd asked, they'd all said, they would have helped her.

In all the years she'd lived in Desparre, she'd never asked. It was pretty clear some of them hated her for it.

"Chance, come on." She tapped her thigh twice, then ran for her truck, the dog close on her heels.

They hopped into the vehicle and then Alanna was speeding in the other direction, away from the strange SUV, away from the downtown. Deeper into the mountains.

"WE SCARED HER OFF." Tate stated the obvious as Alanna and her St. Bernard jumped into their truck and took off at a speed that would normally get them pulled over.

Silently, Peter cursed himself for getting too anxious, getting too close. But he'd been intrigued by the house deep in the wilderness where five kids had been hidden away for years. Like a lot of Alaska, Desparre was known for being a place where people could get lost. Most people were here for legitimate reasons—wanting to run from some tragedy in their life, wanting to recharge in Alaska's wild beauty or even wanting to hide from someone who meant them harm. But Alaska sometimes attracted people for the wrong kind of reasons, too... People like the Altiers.

The house wasn't what he'd been expecting. It was pretty, a log cabin set back in the woods at the crest of a mountain. The isolated location was particularly creepy, though, as he considered the dangerous drop he knew was right behind the house and the dense woods where a family could hide with shotguns. That last part had actually happened when Alanna's real sister had come searching for her and almost died in the process.

When police and the FBI had gone through the house after the Altiers had been arrested, they'd found a stash of forged documents. They'd also found years' worth of family pictures. According to police gossip, the earliest pictures showed obviously distraught kids, but as time went by, that changed. The pictures started to show what looked like a happy family. The most disturbing thing of all, according to one of the Desparre police department's veterans, was how much they'd all looked like a real family. Apparently the Altiers had grabbed kids who looked like they were related. The veteran had confided in Peter that what haunted him most was that if Alanna hadn't left the note, no one would ever look at the seven people living in this house and think for a second they weren't a legitimate family.

To Peter, the scariest part was how that lie still seemed lodged in the mind of the person who had been the least brainwashed, the one who'd ultimately turned the kidnappers in.

Still, rumor had it that the Altiers had learned from their mistakes—when two of the kids they'd kidnapped couldn't forget their real families, they had started abducting younger children. It appeared that Darcy was sticking to that pattern, because police believed she'd grabbed a three-year-old boy not long after she'd escaped custody.

"Let's see where Alanna is headed next," Peter muttered. He was normally good at stakeouts, at making sure no one spotted him or his vehicle in a town full of naturally suspicious residents. It was a skill he'd learned as a reporter, when he'd sometimes go on scouting missions with soldiers. When he'd needed to keep up and keep quiet. But apparently the Altiers had taught Alanna to be hypervigilant and wary of strangers, and to run at the first indication someone might have noticed her.

It was ironic, really, that she still lived by that credo. After being plucked out of her front yard by a stranger as a kid, she should have been hypervigilant in a totally different way. Crowds should have been a source of comfort—more people to notice if something went wrong. Instead, she was still following what she'd been taught by the couple who'd kidnapped her and hidden her away from the world.

All of those things told Peter where her allegiance still lay. It was obvious to him that when it came to a choice between helping bring Darcy in—the line she'd given the police—and helping her escape, she'd choose the latter. Most likely, she'd do it regardless of the cost to others.

His hand was halfway to his left ear before he realized and yanked it back down.

"We need to be objective here," Tate said, somehow sensing what Peter was thinking.

Peter hadn't told Tate about his experiences overseas, but his last assignment as a war reporter was something few people in and around his hometown had missed. It had made national papers—along with a picture of him, blood dripping from his head, a cloud of dust covering his entire body and a stunned look on his face. The cameraman who'd caught the shot had done so seconds before the horrific aftermath of what Peter had just seen, what he'd just experienced. Only later would Peter realize most of the hearing in his left ear was never going to return.

"What we need to do is keep her in our sight," Peter grumbled, following the tire tracks in the loose snow. This far on the outskirts of Desparre, the roads saw minimal traffic. People who lived out this way all had snowmobiles for days when the snow got too deep for driving.

"It didn't look like anyone had been at the Altier house in a long time," Tate continued, unperturbed or indifferent that Peter was annoyed. "Don't you think if Darcy and Alanna had been in touch, Alanna would have known where to go? It seems like she's guessing as much as we are."

"Well, maybe they haven't been in touch. Or maybe

they have and all Alanna knows is that Darcy is coming back to Desparre."

"If Alanna really wanted to help Darcy, why would she stop by the police station and offer us her help? Until she did that, no one was looking for Darcy here."

Peter let up on the gas slightly as Tate's words sank in. The search for the kidnapped boy—and escaped felon Darcy Altier—was making national news, but the search itself was centralized in Oregon. If anyone in law enforcement had reason to think Darcy was coming here, no one at their station seemed to know it.

Peter frowned and pressed down on the gas pedal again, hoping he was still following the right tire tracks but not willing to get within visual distance of Alanna's vehicle. Not willing to risk scaring her off again. She might have left five years ago, but when it came to the most remote part of Desparre, she definitely knew it better than he did.

"Where's she going?" Tate asked, his quiet tone suggesting he was talking to himself more than Peter.

"No idea," Peter answered anyway. "A second meetup point maybe?"

Tate shook his head and Peter could sense he was rolling his eyes. "I know Desparre isn't exactly a hotbed of crime and no one is likely to be missing us right now, but I seriously doubt Alanna Morgan came all this way, knocked on the police's door and gave us a heads-up she thinks Darcy is here, then headed right to her."

"Maybe not," Peter conceded. "But she's obviously searching for Darcy. And no one in Desparre knows her better."

"Okay," Tate agreed. "It still seems unlikely that Darcy would run back to Desparre, but if she *is* here, Alanna has a better shot at finding her than any of us."

"Glad you're seeing it my way," Peter said with a grin

as he wound around another steep bend, taking them farther up the mountain. He cranked up the heater, feeling the temperature dropping as they climbed.

"If Alanna actually does find Darcy, she might need our help," Tate said.

"Why's that?"

"She's the reason Darcy Altier spent the last five years in prison. She's the reason Julian Altier died in prison."

"I don't think we can pin all of that on Alanna." Despite his suspicions about her motives now, she wasn't responsible for their actions or what had happened to them. It must have taken enormous fortitude to eventually turn them in. He had to give her that.

"I'm talking about Darcy's perspective, Peter. Alanna might think the woman who raised her will be happy to see her and will hand over this kid, but honestly? I think she's just as likely to take a shot at Alanna like she did at her sister five years ago."

Peter frowned, the idea of Alanna Morgan facing down a shotgun making him push the gas pedal harder. But when he rounded another bend, the road ended. A big wooden sign half-buried in snow announced it a dead end.

He hit the brakes hard and the SUV skidded to a stop, the four-wheel drive groaning. He glanced around, searching for a trail that snaked off somewhere, but saw nothing. "Where did she go?"

Tate shook his head, a hint of a smile on his lips. "I think she's a lot savvier than we gave her credit for. We lost her."

Chapter Three

"Hey, Chief, have you talked to Colter Hayes lately?" Peter asked as he strode back into the police station's bullpen the next day, Tate on his heels.

Chief Hernandez frowned back at him, disapproval in the lines between her eyebrows.

Peter had met Keara Hernandez when he had applied for the police officer position but knew little about her. In a town where people respected others' right to privacy, she hadn't shared much of her background with her officers. All Peter knew was that she'd come from somewhere in the Lower 48, where she'd been a detective. The move to the remote town of Desparre was a chance for a promotion, sure, but they didn't see much crime here. Undoubtedly, she was running from something—like so many of their civilians—but Peter had found her to be a fair boss. Her one shortcoming was her tendency to cut off ideas she didn't like, shutting them down fast.

He could see it coming before she opened her mouth, so he preempted her with another question. "When's the last time Colter was in Desparre with Alanna's sister?"

Colter Hayes was a Desparre transplant, a soldier who'd seen his entire unit die and decided to spend the rest of his life in the solitude of Desparre. Then he'd met Kensie Morgan and eventually followed her back to Chicago.

But first, he'd helped Kensie track down Alanna—and in the process, uncovered the Altiers' kidnapping scheme.

The chief crossed her arms over her chest, turning to face him from where she'd been standing in front of the station's overworked coffeepot. "I've had some contact with him. He hasn't been back in about a year now. His wife is pregnant. Actually..." Chief Hernandez's eyes lifted upward, then she nodded. "No, by now, they've had the baby. I'm guessing they're pretty busy back in Chicago."

"Because—"

She cut him off with a single dismissive word, spoken with authority. "No, Peter."

Despite the fact that she was only six years older than his twenty-nine years, she said his name the way his mom had when he got in trouble as a boy. It made him feel like a kid and he scowled. He might have way more experience as a reporter than a police officer, but he knew how to follow a lead. And Alanna Morgan was a lead.

"Alanna Morgan was a *victim*," Chief Hernandez said. "It's sad that she can't let go of her past, but it's not our problem. I've talked to the federal agents handling the investigation back in Oregon and there's no reason to suspect Darcy Altier came this way."

"Is there a reason to suspect she went anywhere else?"

Chief Hernandez gave him an exasperated sigh, her gaze darting once to Tate, who stayed silent, then back to Peter. "What is this fixation with the Altiers? I didn't assign you to look into this. Alanna is on a mission for herself, Peter. She probably feels guilty for everything that happened, even if it wasn't her fault. She wants to help, but she's out here guessing. It's our job to make sure she's safe while she's here. But she's not a lead worth following. Leave her alone."

"What if she's right?"

"I already—"

"Alanna didn't fly all this way for nothing. Sure, maybe she does feel guilty, but if she thought Darcy was still in Oregon, wouldn't she go there?"

"Peter, this woman isn't law enforcement. She doesn't have any insight into this case that we don't."

"She does have insight into Darcy Altier that we don't," Tate contributed.

Peter glanced at his partner, who was leaning against the wall, looking unruffled by the argument with the chief. But Tate didn't feel as strongly about Alanna being a lead. He definitely didn't have as much to prove as Peter.

Giving him a quick nod of thanks for the support, Peter turned back to the chief. "Maybe Darcy Altier isn't here. But maybe she's on her way. I've read through the case information and Desparre is the only place the couple stayed for more than a year. Darcy got comfortable here. If anywhere is home to her, it's our town."

Chief Hernandez's forehead creased and her eyes narrowed, like she was thinking over his argument. Then she shook her head. "Whatever we don't know about the Altiers' motivations or mindsets, we can say this—those kids felt loved. The Altiers raised them like they were really their own children. That couple created a makeshift family for themselves. She and her husband got away with it for eighteen years, from the time they kidnapped that first boy until they were caught. They're not stupid. They know their house was searched and ultimately seized. She's not coming back here, Peter. And I won't waste your time—or Tate's time—following Alanna Morgan around."

"This isn't five years ago, Chief," Peter insisted. He thought of Alanna racing to the street to get a look at his SUV back at the Altier cabin. The expectation on her face, the hope that had shifted into wariness as he'd reversed at high speed.

Alanna believed the woman she'd called mom for fourteen years was returning to Desparre. That meant Peter believed it, too.

"That image of a happy family was all an illusion," Peter reminded her. "I'm not saying they didn't love those kids, in their own messed-up way. But Darcy and Julian made Desparre their hideout. In the end, this place destroyed them. Darcy spent five years in jail. Her husband died there. She watched all her 'kids' being taken away. This time around, do you really think she'd repeat those mistakes?"

The chief's arms dropped from where they'd been crossed over her chest for most of the conversation. Reluctant interest sparked in her eyes. "Wouldn't coming back to Desparre be a mistake, then?"

"That assumes she's thinking straight. She could be operating on pure emotion. Wanting what she had, where she had it. Or wanting something else, something stronger. Maybe this time, her goal isn't to steal herself a new family."

"Except she's already started one, with that little three-year-old boy in Oregon," Tate argued. But even he had pushed away from the wall and stepped closer, looking more interested in the conversation.

"Maybe the plan isn't to start a new family with this little boy. After all, where's the rest of Darcy's 'family'? Dead. Or back with their real families. Maybe this time, she's out to prove something."

"What?" Chief Hernandez asked, but the question was less hostile now.

"That she can outwit us all. Maybe Alanna's right, in a

way. Maybe Darcy is coming back here to get revenge on us. The town that gave her up."

Chief Hernandez's lips twisted upward in the corners, but she was nodding slowly. "Except it wasn't really Desparre who turned Darcy in. It was Alanna."

"Exactly," Peter said. "Which means if Alanna isn't in on Darcy's escape, she might be a target."

Tate stepped a little closer. "So, you think we need to keep following her, to keep her safe?" he asked, probably assuming this was Peter's roundabout way to keep chasing that lead.

"Sure," Peter said. "That's one reason to keep following her."

"What's the other?" Chief Hernandez asked, eyes narrowing like she already knew the answer.

"She's our bait to catch a kidnapper."

"Alanna?" The high-pitched voice gained volume and then a hand gripped Alanna's arm hard. "Alanna Morgan?"

Reluctantly, Alanna turned to face the woman with long blond hair and perfect makeup who'd stopped her as she and Chance stepped out of their truck in the parking lot of Jasper's General Store. The store where Alanna had left her fateful note five years ago.

"I thought it was you," the woman said, her voice too cheery, her eyes too bright. Her breath swirled between them in the cold, doing nothing to obscure the raw ambition in her gaze.

No doubt about it. She might not have a microphone or a camera crew, but she was a reporter.

Alanna had been here for twenty-four hours and already a reporter had found her.

From the way Chance let out a low rumble—not quite

a growl, but not friendly—when she reached her hand toward Alanna, he knew it, too.

The woman withdrew her hand quickly, her too-huge smile slipping just a bit, and Alanna felt herself being transported back five years.

The flight home had seemed to take forever. She'd been heading to a suburb outside of Chicago, to a home she'd never seen because her parents had long since moved out of the place where she'd been kidnapped in the front yard. Clutching Kensie's hand too hard on the turbulent flight, having never been on an airplane before. Nerves churning her stomach as she prepared to greet parents and a brother she hadn't seen in fourteen long years.

The drive from the airport to her parents' house, where she'd soon be living, had gone by in a blur but the moments afterward were the ones Alanna would never forget. She'd expected her parents and brother, had known their extended family was waiting to give them a private reunion first. They didn't want to overwhelm her, they said.

But she hadn't expected the reporters. The news vans had made it nearly impossible for their driver to pull up to the house. The bursts of light from camera flashes going off all around her had made it hard to see. The reporters and their crews had pushed in on her from all sides, making her feel claustrophobic. Their questions screamed at her from all directions. *What's it like being home after all these years? Do you remember your real family? Did the Altiers hurt you? Why did you leave that note? Why didn't you come forward sooner?*

Trying to shake off the memories, Alanna leveled the woman with a hard stare and pulled her arm free. "No comment."

Five years ago, Kensie had snapped those words at the reporters, pulled Alanna protectively into the crook of her arm and propelled her forward into the respective quiet of the house. Inside, Alanna had immediately been folded into hugs by her parents, while her teary-eyed older brother stared at her in wonder.

Of course she'd known they would have changed in fourteen years. Just as she'd changed from a curly-haired five-year-old into a young woman.

Still, it had been a shock to see the streaks of gray in her mother's dark hair, the worry lines on her father's forehead and at the corners of his eyes. The scents of her father's aftershave and her mother's perfume had swirled around her, subtle but still making her eyes water—she was used to the outdoorsy scents of the Altiers when they hugged her. Her parents had looked older than their years. Alanna had been struck with the guilt of realizing it was probably from having their youngest child ripped out of their lives, from the years of searching and always coming up empty.

Then there was Flynn, standing stock-still, his lips trembling as his tears started to spill at the corners of his eyes. It had been hard to reconcile the twenty-three-year-old man staring at her with the nine-year-old brother she remembered. He'd been thinner than she'd expected and there was something desperate in his gaze she realized only later had come from years of bad decisions and addictions he'd fought hard to break. He had started when he was a teenager, feeling neglected by parents who'd been constantly looking for the daughter they'd lost, forgetting the two children they still had left.

All of it, ultimately leading back to her. To all the small moments over the years that were chances she might have had to reach out sooner, but hadn't taken. There hadn't been a lot, but she'd definitely had opportunities. In the beginning, she'd been far too afraid to take them. As she grew up, as she grew to love the family she lived with, she'd been scared of what it would mean for all of them.

In the early years with the Altiers, she used to squeeze her eyes closed tight and hold the images of her family in her mind, desperate not to lose them. As she'd grown, those images had blurred around the edges. Memories had faded, leaving behind only vague images and the feeling of having once been loved by a totally different family. With fourteen years between them missing, the home-coming she'd expected to be joyous had been happy but awkward. At that moment, the idea of rebuilding a life she barely remembered with a family she'd only known as a young child had seemed overwhelming.

"Are you sure?"

The reporter's voice cut through her memories and Alanna realized she'd frozen in the parking lot while the woman stared at her quizzically.

As Alanna's gaze refocused, the woman rushed on, "No one's ever really told your side of the story. What it was like to say goodbye to four kids you'd considered your broth-ers and sisters. What it was like to go home to a family you hadn't seen since you were five. I can do that for you."

Alanna's gut clenched at the reporter's insight, but she shook her head and turned away, rushing for the store with Chance keeping pace. She didn't take a full breath again until she was inside with the door closed behind her.

Here, at least, things looked the same. She'd been in-side Jasper's General Store only a few times over the years they'd lived in Desparre. The Altiers had feared someone would recognize her, even years later and so many thou-sands of miles from where she'd been kidnapped. But as time went on, she'd eventually been given more freedom.

Trailing her hands over the rusting metal shelves filled with household staples, Alanna walked slowly toward the counter where an old man sat. The owner, Jasper. The man Julian had asked her to hand over the money to for their groceries. The man who'd unknowingly taken the note within her stack of cash.

He stood as she approached, recognition in his deep brown eyes. His gaze flicked once to Chance, walking happily along beside her, then returned to her. "Alanna Morgan."

"Hi." She stuffed her gloved hands into the pockets in her coat. "I was wondering—you knew my... Julian Altier once. Did you know Darcy?"

Jasper had a reputation for being cranky and unapproachable, and as he came around the counter, his pace was slow but determined. But when he stopped in front of her, there was compassion in his gaze and sadness in his voice. "I didn't really know either of them. I'd only seen Julian a few times over the years. I'm sorry I never noticed anything wrong. I wasn't even sure how that note got into my stack of cash."

Alanna shook her head, squeezed the hand he'd reached toward her. "It's not your fault. Even when I handed over the money and the note, I didn't act like anything was wrong." In some ways, nothing had been wrong. In others, everything had been.

"So you wouldn't recognize Darcy if she came through here?"

His eyes narrowed, making more lines crease his weather-worn skin. "I'd recognize her now, of course, with all the media coverage. But back then? I don't know. She might have come through here with Julian before, once or twice over the years. Hard to say."

"But not recently?" Alanna pressed, trying not to get discouraged.

"No way. People around here would know her now. We'd turn her in."

He said it like it was exactly what Alanna would want to hear, but her shoulders dropped. Maybe the police were right. The people in Desparre felt betrayed by Julian and Darcy, were angry with all the negative attention the couple had brought them. If there was any place Darcy would be recognized quickly, it was an insular town that promised anonymity but recognized and distrusted anyone who didn't live here.

"Thanks," Alanna said, her voice coming out in a squeak. She saw Jasper's lips twist in sympathy as she spun toward the door.

"Come on, Chance," she said as her St. Bernard lagged slightly behind, probably wondering what they were doing.

She'd been a fool to come here, to think she could make a difference. A fool to think that Darcy would return to the place that had once made her most happy, instead of doing what she'd been truly doing all along: running.

Alanna had been a fool to risk the bonds she'd spent five years rebuilding with her family to chase after her kidnapper.

Shame and anger filled her as she pushed the door open a little too hard, almost slamming into someone.

The "sorry" died on her lips as the person on the other side caught the door and flung it the rest of the way open.

Then he was filling the doorway with his scowl, the gaze of his too-blue eyes drilling into her. Peter Robak. The cop who thought she was in cahoots with Darcy.

Only after she'd slipped away from the SUV following her yesterday—making a quick turn onto a wide path not meant as a road—had she realized who was chasing her. Not a threat like she'd imagined, a pair of men who'd spotted a woman all by herself in an isolated area. But police officers who thought she was little better than a criminal.

"You can stop following me around now," she snapped

at him, taking an aggressive step forward despite knowing it was a bad idea to get inside a cop's personal space. But the fear she'd felt yesterday shifted into fury now. The shame and guilt and frustration felt better channeling outward than inward. "I'm finished here, okay? You can leave me alone."

From the corner of her eye, she saw Peter's partner—the other man in the SUV yesterday. Surprise was on his face, his hand dropping away from his weapon as if he'd reached for it when he saw someone rush toward Peter, then changed his mind when he saw it was just her. Just a foolish woman chasing a past that was better left alone.

"You're leaving?" he asked.

But it was Peter's words that drew all of her attention: "You were right."

Dread dropped into her stomach. "Right about what?" Was Darcy here after all? Had someone spotted her?

People here were often armed, ready to protect their own when help could be far away. The residents understood that Desparre usually attracted people who just wanted solitude, but that it could also attract those trying to escape something they'd done, something that had the law chasing them. Had one of those people seen Darcy and taken aim? Had the police arrested her? "What happened?"

Peter frowned at her, studying her like he was trying to unravel all of her secrets, all of the years she had spent happily living with a pair of kidnappers, then turning them in one day. "Darcy's not in Desparre. Not yet. But I think she's on her way."

"What? Why?"

A slight smile twisted one side of his lips, but there was nothing happy about it. "We know she's headed in this direction from Oregon."

"Why?" Alanna pressed, every second she stood there

waiting to understand adding to her anxiety, making her stomach churn and her breathing turn shallow.

Chance let out a low whine and nudged her with his nose.

She put a hand on his head, stroking his fur to assure him she was okay, even if it wasn't true.

"She was spotted in Canada today. They didn't catch her, but now this has become an international chase, Alanna."

Alanna sensed Peter's partner stepping closer, as if he planned to intervene in whatever Peter was going to say next, but she couldn't take her gaze off Peter.

He stared back at her, his uncompromising expression only cracking as he said, "Darcy kidnapped another kid today."

Chapter Four

"What's Darcy's endgame?"

Peter's words were angry and suddenly he was the one getting into her personal space.

Alanna backed up a step and Chance pushed his way between her and the police officer, using his size and St. Bernard strength as a warning.

"Chance," Alanna said, tugging his collar just enough to let him know he should back up, too. But her mind was still trying to get a grip on the words Peter had spoken a moment ago.

Darcy was partway between where she'd escaped custody and Desparre. Now she had two kidnapped kids with her instead of one.

"It makes no sense."

She didn't realize she'd spoken the words out loud until Peter asked, "What? How many kids does this woman have to kidnap before you see her as a threat, as a criminal?"

Anger made her heat up underneath her winter gear and she could feel the flush rising to her cheeks.

"Peter," his partner said, his voice quiet but firm. "Go easy."

Then he stuck a hand toward her. "I'm Officer Tate Emory. I was in the police station yesterday when you came in to offer your help. We'd like to take you up on that."

He was the officer she'd noticed watching her exchange with the chief from the bullpen yesterday. Her eyes narrowed as she looked from him to Peter. "Why? Because now you know I can lose you when you follow me around?"

Tate's lips twitched, like he was holding back amusement.

Peter took a step closer. "Because it's the right thing to do." His tone was less raw anger now, more accusatory, as if daring her to say she *wouldn't* help the police.

The police had scoffed at her offer before. Then they had two officers follow her around like she was a criminal. And now?

She wasn't sure how Darcy would feel seeing her again. But she figured the woman was way more likely to let her get close if she was alone than if she had a pair of police officers trailing her every move. Especially police officers Alanna didn't trust.

Peter might say helping them was the right thing to do, but how could she believe they'd do what was right when the time came? Would they trust her to talk Darcy into turning herself in, into turning over the kids she'd kidnapped, rather than run or fight? She doubted it.

"I think you ought to leave her alone."

The voice came from behind her. When Alanna glanced over her shoulder, she saw Jasper scowling at the cops, his arms crossed over his chest.

She gave him a thankful, shaky smile before Tate drew her attention again.

"Look, we should have been up front with you," he said, giving Peter a glare that clearly said *go easy.* "We didn't have any reason to believe Darcy was coming here before. Now we do. And you have insight into the places she knows in and around Desparre. You have insight into her as a person. You can help us bring those kids home to their families."

She stared back at him, at the guileless look on his face, and saw something else there. Not the distrust Peter broadcasted whenever he spoke to her, but pity.

Averting her gaze, she felt a familiar discomfort well up. The feel of too many eyes on her, all evaluating, all judging. Not just reporters, but also all the people who read or watched their stories. To this day, she still got mail from some of them, letters of encouragement or morbid curiosity or misplaced anger.

She was sick of all of it.

Forcing her gaze back up, she told both officers, "I was wrong. I don't think I can help you. But if I find anything, I'll let you know."

She wasn't sure if the last words were a lie or not.

"Alanna—"

Peter stepped closer still, despite Chance angled protectively in front of her.

Chance let out another low warning growl, but Peter only glanced at him, seemingly unconcerned. Apparently he recognized that the St. Bernard wouldn't hurt anyone unless they were a real threat to her.

"This isn't like Darcy," Alanna admitted, the words breaking free before she'd even realized she thought them.

It was true. The Altiers had gone years between grabbing kids. Abducting two within a few days, while on the run from the law, was reckless.

Was Darcy trying to create a brand-new, ready-made family? Did she want to re-create what she'd had with Alanna and her "siblings"? Had she simply snapped from the grief of her husband's death, after years being locked away, after losing the kids she'd raised?

It was possible. And yet, something didn't seem right. It didn't seem like Darcy at all.

"Are we sure she's the one who took those kids?" Alanna looked from Peter to Tate, trying to read the truth in their eyes because she wasn't sure she'd hear it from their lips.

The pity intensified on Tate's face, in the way his lips crumpled, in the tilt of his head.

Peter just looked exasperated. "What do you think? That someone else is following her—an escaped fugitive— and they just happen to be doing what she did for eighteen years? Really?"

"No," Alanna said softly, because it sounded ridiculous. Obviously it was Darcy. But if she was acting this out of character, even if Alanna could find her, would she be able to get through to her? Would she be able to change anything? Or was coming here a total waste of time?

THE DOOR TO their old home had been left unlocked. It opened with a hard shove, groaning in a way that told Alanna no one had been through in a long time. She slipped underneath the faded yellow tape that had probably once read Do Not Cross but had become illegible over five Alaskan winters.

Her heart began to pound as she stepped over the threshold and a thousand memories hit her at once. Darcy and Julian sitting side by side, holding hands on the blue couch Darcy had upholstered herself. Alanna's older "brother" Johnny staring at the chessboard in the corner, contemplating his next move in a long-running game with Julian. Her younger "siblings" Sydney and Drew sitting cross-legged on the floor, teaching their youngest "sister" Valerie to make a pair of snowshoes.

After Darcy and Julian had been arrested, Johnny had

stared at her with disbelief and confusion. In all the years since, he'd refused to speak to her. Five years of Alanna's letters had been returned unopened. Yet at least once a year, Alanna still tried.

Sydney, three years younger than Alanna and the "sibling" she'd always felt closest to, had tried to keep in touch. In the beginning, she and Alanna had spoken on the phone almost nightly. Slowly, though, the frequency of those calls had decreased, until now Alanna only heard from her every few weeks.

Alanna stomped her feet on the heavy rug still lining the entryway as Chance pushed his way in beside her, knocking free one end of the police tape. The broken tape immediately blew outward, dancing in the wind. Alanna shut the door behind it, closing out the frigid wind and falling snow.

Beside her, Chance did a full-body shake, sending melted snow everywhere. Then he walked into the main room as if he'd been there a hundred times and settled in front of the dark fireplace. It was as if he knew this place had once been her home and he felt at home here, too.

She followed more slowly, each step farther into the house feeling as if she was stepping backward in time. As she ran her hand over the soft, worn blanket on the corner of the sofa, she could picture Drew and Valerie curled underneath it, one on each end of the couch, their toes meeting in the middle.

She'd tried to keep in touch with them, too, but their parents had cut off all contact when they'd gone home. Drew would turn eighteen next year, which meant Alanna could try again. But Valerie was only eleven. By the time she was an adult, how much of her time with Alanna would she remember? Valerie had been six when the Altier "family" had been broken apart—only a year older than

Alanna when she'd been kidnapped. Had her memories of Alanna already blurred around the edges, the same way Alanna's had of the Morgans over the years?

The "siblings" she'd spent the majority of her childhood with were now scattered across the country, no two in the same state. Her video chats with Sydney were the closest she'd come to seeing any of them since that day when police had stopped their car and screamed at her "parents" to get out.

Alanna blinked back tears that suddenly flooded her vision. She wasn't here to wallow in regrets or wonder if she'd made the right choice five years ago. She was here for clues.

It had been two days since Darcy was spotted in northern Canada, since she'd grabbed another young child, this time a two-year-old girl. According to news reports, there had been no confirmed sightings of her since.

Two days ago, after talking to Peter and Tate, Alanna had been ready to head home. Yesterday, she'd even packed her small suitcase and looked for flights. She'd finally picked up one of the calls from her sister Kensie, promising she'd be heading home on Saturday. Instead, today, she'd texted Kensie that she was staying a little longer. She might not be able to talk Darcy down as she'd planned, but she could still help. If anyone could find Darcy now, it was Alanna.

The problem was, if Darcy was speeding back to Alaska, kidnapping more kids along the way, it meant five years in prison had definitely changed her. But not in the way Alanna had expected.

Throughout her childhood, Alanna had always seen Darcy as the "parent" who was the dreamer. Easily distracted, always lost in her own thoughts, she had a million ideas but rarely the initiative to see them all through. It was Julian who took her ideas and made them reality.

All through the house were examples of the way her "parents" had fit together, worked together. The fireplace, for instance, with its border of colorful tiles, had started as an idea Darcy had sketched out to resemble the aurora borealis at night. But it was Julian who'd purchased those tiles, taught all of them to affix them to the fireplace. Darcy had envisioned the extra room toward the back of the house as a place to homeschool and Julian had found schoolbooks for all of them. Then, of course, there were the kidnappings.

Alanna hugged her arms around herself, cold despite being out of the wind and snow. But the heat was off in the house, her breath making cloud puffs in the air.

One of the clearest memories she had—the memory that still woke her in the middle of the night—was that moment when Julian had reached out from his car and yanked her inside. Darcy had been at the wheel, speeding away dangerously as Alanna yelped in surprise and fright, squirming to look out the rear window. She had watched Kensie get smaller in the distance, even as her sister ran after their vehicle, screaming for help.

When Alanna was taken, the Altiers had already had Johnny for four years. Even then, Johnny had barely remembered his birth family and he'd already adjusted to living with the Altiers. The four of them had moved constantly in those early years, never staying in one place too long.

Alanna had only been five years old then, totally reliant on three people she didn't trust. Peter was probably right that being so dependent on them from such a young age had helped forge a deeper connection. Slowly, Alanna's fear and hatred had shifted. Her "parents" and "brother" had worn her down with love and caring. As guilty as she'd felt about it, she'd started to care for them, too.

By the time they'd grabbed Sydney, Alanna hadn't forgotten the Morgans. But she'd felt like she had a new family.

That was when she'd learned how the kidnappings worked. Darcy and Julian always talked about wanting a big family, but apparently Darcy couldn't get pregnant. Every few years, Darcy would see a kid—one who looked like an Altier—and felt as if the child was already hers. Then Julian would make it a reality.

Darcy doing the kidnappings without Julian seemed so counter to the way her "mother" worked. Alanna had come here thinking she could talk some sense into her, make her realize her actions were emotional and unethical. But abducting *two* kids, in such a short span of time? It meant Darcy was different now, that she was taking on both hers and Julian's past parental roles. It meant she wasn't the person Alanna remembered.

When Alanna was a child, she'd always been able to talk Darcy into things to make her happy. One more story at bedtime. A warmer pair of boots so she could spend more time playing in the snow. A later bedtime so she could stay up reading or playing games with her "siblings." But now? With everything that had changed while Darcy was in jail? Would Alanna be able to interrupt Darcy's plan?

Shutting out the memories along with worries of what would happen if she *did* find Darcy, Alanna took a deep breath and looked around the room. Chance had gotten up without her noticing and was standing next to her, staring up at her with those dark brown eyes. A string of drool in the corner of his droopy mouth nearly stretched to the wooden floor and made Alanna smile.

She stroked his soft fur, then said, "Let's get to work."

His head swiveled, as if taking in the small front room and asking, *Doing what?*

"We're looking for somewhere else Darcy could hide," Alanna told him.

He tilted his head at her, making the drool break free, and Alanna laughed. It loosened the tension in her chest, was the impetus she needed to get moving.

Five years ago, when Kensie had shown up at their house searching for her, Darcy and Julian had bundled all the kids quickly into the car and fled. Alanna had initially thought they were going back to what they'd done years ago, skipping from state to state, hiding. Then she'd learned Julian had a specific hiding place in mind and it was nearby. They'd never made it, though, because the police had caught up to them. As far as Alanna knew, other property owned by the Altiers—in their name or some other name—had never been uncovered. But that didn't mean it didn't exist.

If Darcy was returning to Desparre, it was unlikely she'd come back to the cabin. That was too dangerous. But some other hiding spot her husband had scoped out years ago that police and the FBI had never uncovered? That seemed reasonable.

Alanna didn't know where it was. But there had to be a clue in this cabin. She walked from room to room slowly, her gaze lighting on every object, all the pieces of their lives that had been left behind. She picked up old books, looked through cupboards now littered with rodent droppings and then retraced her steps, trying to see it all anew.

Two hours later, she held a small piece of paper in her hand. She'd found it taped to the inside cover of one of Darcy's old drawing books. If the police had found it five years ago, apparently they hadn't thought anything of the random symbols. But they meant something to Alanna: a goofy code she and her "siblings" had created one particularly frigid winter when they'd all been stuck inside for two weeks. Darcy had encouraged them, laughing as they'd constructed what they thought was a tightly encrypted cipher. Translated, the symbols in Darcy's book were a series of latitudes and longitudes. Coordinates.

Alanna stared at the list, five places she knew in her gut were hiding spots. Then she looked over at Chance. "Let's start at the top."

Chance must have felt the mix of excitement and anxiety in her words because he got to his feet quickly and chased her to the door. When she flung it open, her excitement transitioned immediately to dread.

The snow that had been falling slowly for the past few hours had picked up intensity, racing faster for the ground, piling on top of the foot and a half's worth that had already come down over the past two days. Alanna squinted at the gray sky, then at the truck she'd rented. It was built for off-roading in the Alaskan terrain. But there was no rental vehicle hardy enough for the furious climate Desparre could spawn.

In November, conditions could turn dangerous fast. Alanna checked the weather app on her phone, which indicated that the snow was supposed to stop before the top of the hour, only a few minutes away. As if she'd willed it, when she looked back up, the speed of the falling snow had decreased, the snowflakes seeming to shrink in size.

"I think we can do it," she told Chance, glancing again at the paper in her hand. According to her navigation app, the first location was less than half an hour's drive. And she'd spent years in the unpredictable Desparre weather, understood how to take care of herself in it.

Chance bolted out the door, bounding in circles in the fresh snow before coming to a stop by the back door of the truck. He glanced back at her, as if to say, *What are you waiting for?*

She hurried after him, slower in the heavy snow, and opened the truck door for him.

Chance leaped into the back seat, bringing snow with him and making Alanna wish she'd brought more towels.

She ran to the front, turning the heat up to high as soon as she was inside. Tucking the paper into the inside pocket of her coat, she eased the truck carefully out of the driveway, happy to see that the snowfall was slowing even more.

Still, the roads near the cabin were unpaved. The town didn't bother to clear them and the people who lived out this way all had snowmobiles for when winter got too tough for even their all-weather vehicles. So, Alanna drove slowly and carefully, following in other tire tracks where she could. She headed farther away from Desparre, but down the mountain this time, on roads that wound around massive old trees.

It was the route they'd been on five years ago, when the police had caught up to them.

Snow shot out from beneath the tires, fluffy stuff that would have been perfect for building snowmen. Luckily, there was no ice underneath it. On one side of her, the mountain continued upward; on the other was the cliff edge.

She gripped the wheel tightly, slightly less confident after five years of living near Chicago, with their milder winters, snow removal services, far-reaching cell towers and easy access to help. She glanced in her rearview mirror at Chance, lying across the back seat, but his head up, watching out the window. He met her gaze in the mirror, trusting, and she wondered if she was making a mistake.

But when she glanced at her navigation app, she realized she'd driven farther than she'd expected. The snow had stopped falling from the sky, but every once and a while, a big hunk of it slid off a tree branch, startling her as it plopped onto the windshield. She was close now. Her heart rate picked up in anticipation of finding the hideout Julian had probably built, at the possibility of finding Darcy there now.

Then she rounded a corner and swore as she stomped on the brake. The truck swerved slightly in the snow and Alanna clutched the wheel harder, angling away from the steep drop to her right.

Ahead of her, the road was blocked. A pile of snow higher than the front of her truck covered the entire road to the edge of the mountain. She couldn't tell how far it went, but as she leaned forward and glanced up through her windshield, she could tell why it had fallen. Avalanche.

"Guess we'll have to move on to the next spot," she told Chance, but just as quickly, she decided to put that plan on hold. Where there'd been one avalanche, there could be another. Best to get away from the mountain and hope the snow melted.

She backed the truck up slowly, carefully as she got ready to round the bend again backward, since there was no room to turn around. But the tires slid on her anyway, and she overcorrected, more afraid of the drop-off than bumping the other side of the mountain. Except when her rear bumper hit the rock, the truck also slid into a rut. When she hit the gas again, the wheels spun, but the truck wouldn't go anywhere.

Cursing, Alanna pulled her hood over her head and hopped out of the truck to grab the shovel from the back. As soon as she stepped outside, a fierce shiver rushed through her body at the force of the wind. And as she opened the back door, Chance leaped out.

"No!" She made a grab for his collar even as he spun

back toward her, but a noise overhead made her look up. A rumbling like thunder, but far too close. An avalanche.

Years of living in Alaska rushed back to her, as she stared at the mountaintop, instantly seeing the path of the snow. It would probably miss her if she backed away fast enough. But it was definitely going to take her truck. And Chance, standing too close to it…

She grabbed for him just as the wall of snow rushed downward, sweeping him up with it. Then her arms closed around him, just under his front legs. She clung tight, even as the snow slammed into her, hard and fast, shoving them both toward the edge of the mountain.

Chapter Five

Alanna Morgan knew something.

Peter had been following her around half the day. Unlike when he'd last followed her around with Tate three days ago, he was alone today. Saturday was his day off. Unfortunately, that meant he was in his personal vehicle instead of the police SUV. Although his truck could handle the Desparre winters, his police vehicle was equipped for anything. As Alanna headed farther away from Desparre, taking dangerous back roads down the mountain like she'd driven them a million times, Peter's knuckles went white gripping his steering wheel.

He'd grown up on the other side of the mountain, in an area almost as prone to crazy weather as Desparre. But the town of Luna—where his parents and older siblings lived still—was much flatter. They occasionally got nasty avalanches off this side of the mountain, but being at a lower altitude usually meant slightly fewer dangers. It definitely meant easier driving.

Since joining the Desparre police department last year, he'd been up on this mountain a few times, usually doing welfare checks. He'd driven it in far worse weather than this, but he'd never done it while chasing after a former victim, potential new accomplice or possible target. He'd never done it while trailing someone who seemed to know too well how to lose a tail.

Right now, she had good reason to try to lose him. Judging by the excitement on her face when she'd finally left the Altiers' cabin, she'd found something inside it. And the chances that she hadn't spotted him seemed low. So, when she rounded another corner and he heard snow crunching hard, as if she'd slammed the brakes, he eased off the side of the road and waited.

When her truck door slammed, he cursed and wedged his door open against the side of the mountain so he could climb awkwardly out of his vehicle. Better she stride over here, furious and ready for an argument than hide somewhere again while he drove past, clueless. But then she yelled "No!" and almost immediately—as if she'd been yelling at the mountain and it didn't want to listen—an ominous crash and boom signaled an oncoming avalanche.

His heart gave a quick, painful thud and then he was running toward her, rounding the corner before he could fully think it through.

Snow rushed downward from far above, a furious waterfall of white, slowing slightly along the road before it tumbled over the other side. There was a groan of metal over the rush of snow, only the top of Alanna's truck visible as it flipped sideways, then disappeared over the edge of the mountain.

Dread, anger and grief hit him unexpectedly hard. But he didn't have time to linger on it, because there she was, outside the vehicle, just a flash of her red coat in the flurry of snow.

He darted toward her and his left boot slid on the spilling snow, almost taking him down, sucking him under. He looked up quickly and saw that the avalanche was slow-

ing, the end in sight way above him. But that flash of red
was too close to the edge.

Fear threatened to freeze him in place, but he gritted
his teeth and changed his angle, moving toward the edge
of the mountain, toward a big old tree withstanding the
onslaught of snow. Wrapping an arm and a leg around it,
Peter reached out with his free hand, blindly now, since
that flash of red had been overrun by snow.

Somehow, he grabbed her—or at least he hoped it was
her. Cursing the thick gloves that made it hard to get a
good grip, he clung to the edge of material. Then the snow
yanked him forward, the pull hard and unrelenting, tear-
ing at the socket in his shoulder.

The momentum ripped him around the front of the tree
and the right side of his body burned with the contact.
He clung to his quarry tighter, squeezing his left hand as
tightly as he could, praying the coat wouldn't rip right out
of his hand and take Alanna with it.

The snow shifted, taking a slight turn over the edge
of the mountain, probably catching on the trees there. It
pushed him back toward the big tree, easing the screaming pain in his shoulder and letting him get a better grip.

Suddenly, there she was, rising up on the curve of snow.
First came her bright red coat, then a swash of long, dark,
wet hair. Then her face, both too starkly pale and too bright
red in places as she gasped for air.

"Your hand," he croaked, his voice lost beneath the still-
thundering snow. He prayed she'd hear him, grab his arm
and pull herself toward him.

If she replied, he couldn't hear it with his bad ear facing her. Instead, she tried to angle her body toward him in
the snow and he saw both her arms wrapped underneath
the front legs of her enormous dog. The St. Bernard was
scrabbling for purchase with his huge paws and was ac-

tually managing to get a little traction, moving them both closer to Peter.

But then the last rush of snow swooped down and both of them disappeared underneath it.

Peter took a huge breath and squeezed his eyes shut as the snow claimed him, too.

SHE WAS SUFFOCATING.

The world around her finally stopped moving, but where had she landed? Had she tumbled over the edge of the mountain and managed to get wedged between some trees? Or was she still on the edge of the road, where one wrong move would send her flying over it?

She tried to move her fingers and felt Chance squirm in her arms. Tears pricked her eyes with the relief that he was still with her, still alive. But when she opened her eyes, there was only darkness. And cold like she'd never experienced.

The avalanche had buried them both. But how deeply?

She shifted along with Chance, not moving her arms from around his belly, not wanting him to go too far. Hoping there was a pocket of air, she finally had to open her mouth and gulp in a breath. There was a pocket, but it felt too little for both her and Chance, especially as her lungs demanded more, more, more.

Keeping one hand locked around Chance, she thrust the other upward, hoping to encounter fresh air. But there was only more snow. Was she really reaching up? Or had she been spun around so she thought down was up?

Don't panic, she reminded herself as her heart started thudding faster. She thrust her arm the other way, and this time she felt hard ground. At least, she thought so. Which meant escape was above her. But was it through a few feet of loosely packed snow, just above where her fingers could reach, or twelve feet deep and pressing down hard? Would movement help her get to safety or shift the weight of the snow so it crushed them both?

Her collapsible snow shovel was in her truck, which was probably buried under the snow with her. By the time she'd heard the telltale *whomp* of snow breaking free that signaled an oncoming avalanche, it had been too late. She should have known better; she never should have been out here in this weather. And now Chance, who'd suffered so much as a tiny puppy, who'd been her constant, loyal companion for the past two years, would probably die with her.

Stop it, she commanded herself. She needed to find a way out for both of them. For Peter, too?

Had she imagined seeing him at the edge of the avalanche in those brief moments when the snow had shifted and let her suck in a desperate lungful of air before it pulled her under again? Had she imagined his hand reaching out, yanking her backward, even as the avalanche tried to throw her forward, over the edge of the mountain? She reached behind her, felt a hand clutching her coat and her heart gave a hard thump.

He'd tried to save her. He didn't even like her, but he'd tried to save her life. Had it cost him his own?

The fingers locked in her coat weren't moving. She tried to scoot toward him, tried to urge Chance to come with her. She moved slowly, terrified of triggering more snow that might crush them, not sure how close they were to the edge of the mountain.

But as she slid toward Peter, Chance broke free from her grasp. She fumbled for him, her hands grasping nothing but snow, feeling clumsy in the cold.

"Chance!" As she gasped his name, she sucked in snow and more fell, closing the gap between her and her dog. She stretched her arms farther, but couldn't find him.

Panic took hold, squeezing her lungs tight as she turned her head and spit out the snow, trying to get more air. She found another pocket of it, but it felt stuffy, like it was already emptying of oxygen, and she tried to take shallow breaths. Reaching behind her, she tugged lightly on Peter's arm and he moved. But she couldn't tell if it was just gravity or if he was okay.

"Chance!" she tried again, even as she heard him moving away from her. Was he headed toward the edge of the mountain? She was too turned around to tell. Even if he managed to get free of the snow, would he fall over the edge?

Holding in a sob—for her dog, for herself, for Peter—Alanna shifted again, sliding closer to Peter. She tried calling for Chance again, but she couldn't hear him anymore. She yelled louder, even as she wondered if she was doing the right thing. Maybe Chance could get free of the snow and save himself, at least.

Now, she had to try to do the same for her and Peter. As she scooted backward toward him through the heavy snow, his hand moved again, this time sliding down to grab her arm. Relief made more tears fill her eyes, but she blinked them back fast, not wanting them to freeze on her face.

She wasn't shivering so much anymore. Either she was adjusting to the cold or—more likely—she was starting to face hypothermia.

"We have to get out of here," she told Peter, even as the tiny pocket of air in front of her collapsed and more snow crashed down on her.

The weight felt crushing, the sudden lack of oxygen making her panic. She swung her arms out, trying to find a new pocket of air.

Then something scratched against her leg, a frantic

pawing that got faster as she instinctively jerked away. Chance! He was trying to save her.

He was behind her now. Did that mean he'd somehow dug free of the avalanche? Alanna moved her legs, trying to help him free her. She grabbed Peter's hand as Chance suddenly took her ankle in his mouth and tugged.

She slid backward about a foot, snow crushing her even more, making her lungs and chest hurt. Then Chance's paws were up near her head and the snow in front of her face suddenly broke away, giving her precious air as the weight on her eased. She scooted toward him, trying to pull Peter with her, but Chance had already turned away from her.

He had started digging frantically beside her and soon Peter's torso and head emerged from the snow. Peter dropped her hand, somehow pulling himself forward, and then he and Chance were digging her the rest of the way out, dragging her free of the snow.

Struggling to her knees, Alanna threw shaky arms around Chance's back as she stared at the huge pile of snow. It was as tall as a house in the middle. Somehow, she, Peter and Chance had been at the edge of the avalanche, where it wasn't as high, where it hadn't smashed down hard enough to crush their bones or suffocate them. Her truck was gone, either buried under it or tossed over the side of the mountain, crashed somewhere below.

But she was alive. Chance was alive. And Peter was alive. That was all that mattered.

She stumbled to her feet and the bitter wind sliced through her wet clothes. Her teeth started chattering as Peter grabbed her hand.

"Come on. My truck's around the corner. We have to warm up."

As she stumbled after him, Chance at her side, Alanna

realized his truck was far enough away that he could have avoided the avalanche altogether. He'd run toward it to save her, even though he didn't like her, even though he seemed to think she might be in cahoots with a kidnapper.

He didn't trust her. She didn't trust him, either. But he'd risked his life for her, which meant he was a good person. They might not agree on how to go about it, but they had the same ultimate goal: to save the kids Darcy had kidnapped.

They rounded the bend and Peter held open the door to his truck, waiting for her and Chance, his face a bright, unnatural red from the cold.

She slowed and he urged, "Come on, Alanna. Hurry."

"I want to work together," she blurted.

"What?"

It didn't matter what they thought of each other. She'd figure out a way to convince Peter that he needed to bring Darcy in carefully, peacefully. He had resources she didn't, like access to whatever the Desparre police learned from other law enforcement. But she had resources he needed, too, and an insight into Darcy's mindset that he'd never figure out without her.

They'd be stronger together.

"Let's work together to find Darcy and save those kids."

He stared at her a minute, something pensive in his brilliant blue eyes, then he nodded. "Deal. Now get in the truck."

Chapter Six

It was amazing they'd lived through the avalanche.

He wasn't sure he could handle another minute out in this cold. Instead of running around to the driver's side and trying to wedge the door open so close to the upward slant of the mountain, Peter clambered into his truck behind Alanna and Chance. His limbs were clumsy from the cold. He slammed the door shut behind him, pressing awkwardly against the dog until Chance leaped into the back to get out of the way. Then, Alanna scooted into the driver's seat, giving him a little space.

He'd left the truck running with the heat blasting, but he could barely feel it now. He turned it up all the way, then yanked off his sopping wet gloves. He reached up to take off his hat and discovered it was gone. His short hair was iced over and when he ran his hand through it, ice and water flew across the seat. Thrusting his hands in front of the heater, he glanced at Alanna, who'd slumped against the seat and closed her eyes.

"Come on," he told her and started unzipping her thick coat, which was definitely made for an Alaskan winter but not for getting buried in an avalanche. His fingers felt too big, swollen beyond their normal size and clumsy. But at least he could feel them, the stinging pain assuring him the nerves still worked.

"What are you doing?" she demanded, but the question had no heat. Her eyes opened, then drifted closed again.

"We've got to get out of these wet clothes," he muttered, running his tongue over his lip, which was way past chapped and split open as he spoke. "Come on," he said again, and this time, Chance pitched in.

The St. Bernard pressed his big head through the space between the seats and grabbed Alanna's sleeve with his mouth, tugging on it until she opened her eyes again.

She turned toward him sluggishly. "You okay, Chance?"

"He saved us," Peter said, giving the dog a quick pat on the head. "I guess he knows St. Bernards are snow rescue dogs."

Chance let go of Alanna's coat long enough to give a brief bark, which made Peter laugh and startled Alanna, finally seeming to focus her.

"It's so cold," she said, trying to tug the zipper back up on her coat.

"Nope." Peter ignored the squelch of his own uncomfortable, freezing clothes as he shifted to get closer to her. He yanked her gloves off and tossed them on the floor behind them, then awkwardly pulled off her coat. At least she could feel the cold. Her hands were bright red, which was definitely better than being unnaturally white, but they both needed to warm up fast.

Grunting at the uncomfortable angle and his aching body, he leaned over her and unlaced her boots, tugging them off her feet. Then came her thick socks. Her toes were too white and he rubbed them for a minute, then shoved her feet underneath the floor heaters.

When he came back up, she was shivering. A good sign.

"Get the rest of your clothes off," he said, slipping out of his own coat and dumping it on the floor behind him, careful not to drop it on Chance.

"Sorry, buddy," he said, leaning over the dog as he grabbed the stack of blankets he always kept in the vehicle in case of an emergency. Getting stalled out in Desparre could mean death if you weren't prepared.

He set most of the stack between him and Alanna, then tossed one over Chance, rubbing down the dog's back to dry some of the dampness.

Realizing Alanna was just staring at him, he yanked off his sweater and snapped, "Hurry up."

She flushed, a different shade of red flooding along her cheeks and neck, and quickly averted her gaze.

She was only five years younger than him, but he suddenly felt much older. He'd been inside war zones for years, lost most of the hearing in one ear and experienced huge change to his professional and personal life as a result. And her?

He realized he was still staring at her as she tried to cover herself with one of the blankets and shimmy out of her soaking jeans at the same time, so he turned the other way. Then he yanked off his boots and socks, sighing as the blast of heat hit his bare toes.

She'd been kidnapped at five years old and, if news reports could be believed, she'd lived a pretty sheltered life with the Altiers. What had her life been like since she'd returned home to Chicago? Had her real family smothered her, too, afraid to let her out of their sight again? Had she ever ventured out on her own before this?

Resisting the urge to glance at her again, he yanked off the rest of his clothes, shivering as the hot air hit his wet skin. There wasn't much space in the passenger seat, but he managed to get the itchy wool blanket wrapped all the way around him. Then he closed his eyes and let the warmth inside the truck seep into him.

Alanna was on his bad ear's side, but in the close confines of the truck, it didn't matter. All too easily, he could hear her moving around, presumably still in the process of undressing. He squeezed his eyes more tightly shut, suddenly picturing the paleness of her skin, the long, lean legs that had been encased in jeans earlier. Things he had no business imagining.

When the noise finally stopped, he asked tightly, "You covered?"

"Yes."

He opened his eyes, trying not to actually glance at her. But he couldn't help himself.

She was wrapped tightly in the dark wool blanket, covered up to her chin with her drenched hair draped over the front of the blanket and sticking to the seat behind her. Her cheeks were still a patchy red, but it was the bright red of standing outside in Alaska too long, not from embarrassment or shyness.

"You okay?" he asked, staring into her deep brown eyes. It suddenly hit him how beautiful she was.

He hadn't noticed it before, not really. He'd been far too busy trying to figure out how she'd gone from kidnap victim to accomplice, enabler and defender of criminals.

But she wasn't out here, risking her life, just for Darcy. She was here for those kids, too, kids she probably identified with because she'd once been in exactly their position. She had to be.

One of her hands slipped free from the mounds of wool and squeezed his arm. "Thank you for coming after me."

"It's lucky I happened to be following you around." As soon as the words were out of his mouth, he regretted them, but she laughed.

"Yeah, I guess so."

"Did you mean what you said earlier? About working together to find those kids?"

Tiny lines appeared between her graceful eyebrows. "Of course."

He leaned closer to her, glancing at the gas gauge, and relaxed when he saw that they still had plenty in the tank. They could sit here and warm up a little bit longer. Then again...

He leaned over her, angling so he was looking upward out the window. Being parked around the bend from where the avalanche had hit was a safer spot. The mountain above didn't come down at quite the same sharp angle. It was less prone to avalanches. Still, if the snow above was unstable, he didn't want to sit here and discover he was wrong.

Alanna had squeezed against the back of her seat and he could practically feel her holding her breath until he sat back and put some distance between them.

"We should probably move."

She twisted in her seat, giving him a glance of bare shoulder as she smiled at Chance, who'd shaken free of the blanket and lay down on the back seat, looking far more relaxed than he should have after digging them out of an avalanche.

"You okay, Chance?"

Her dog lifted his big head, strained forward and licked her cheek.

"Guess so," she said, laughing as she turned forward again. She squirmed inside the blanket until she had it wrapped around her more like a towel, her arms and shoulders bare. Then she twisted and tucked it around her knees and gripped the wheel. "I'm not running around the truck to change seats and I think climbing over each other will be a disaster. So, how about I drive?"

He blinked back at her, suddenly conjuring an image of the two of them tangled together, wool blankets awkwardly between them and nothing else. "You drive and I'll direct. Let's go to my house and figure out a plan."

She stared at him a long minute, the air suddenly tense between them, until finally she gave a short nod and shifted the truck into Drive. She made a careful turn and they headed back up the mountain, past the Altiers' old home, and then downward again, back to Desparre's downtown.

With every mile, he snuck glances at her, her hands tense on the wheel, her hair slowly drying and curling slightly against the wool blanket. She seemed more serious in profile, older somehow, and Peter wondered which Alanna was the real one.

The woman who'd held tight to her dog, even at the risk of being tossed over the edge of the mountain by the avalanche? Who'd offered to help the police catch someone she obviously still cared about? Who'd blushed when he stripped his sweater off, even when she should have been more concerned about her own physical well-being?

Or was she the person who'd defended the couple who'd kidnapped her? Still the child who'd been molded by two kidnappers, who'd had her emotions manipulated for so long that her loyalty would always lie in the wrong place?

By keeping her close, he could keep her safe. But would he just be putting himself back in the same position he had two years ago, risking his own safety for someone who was beyond saving?

ALANNA MORGAN LOOKED good in his house, looked good in his clothes.

Peter scowled at the ridiculous thought as he handed her a steaming cup of coffee and settled on the chair across from her, Chance on the floor between them. He'd started a fire as soon as they'd walked through the door. Now it was blazing, almost too hot, but it felt good after being buried in the snow. He took a long sip of his coffee, making a mental note to grab their clothes from his truck soon and toss them all in the dryer. The sooner she was back in her own clothes, the better it would be for his focus.

He still had his suspicions about Alanna, still wondered how much he could trust her, but now sympathy was mixed in with those other emotions. She had to be carrying so many conflicting feelings about her past, about Darcy, about her future. He knew that territory well, and he wanted to reassure her that she could make it through just as he had done.

The drive to his house had been quiet. All of Alanna's attention had been on navigating the Alaskan roads and she'd handled them better than most of the locals. It reminded him of something else he'd heard through the rumor mill: the Altiers had taught the kids they'd kidnapped all kinds of survival skills. He knew she could lose a tail better than most police officers. Still, when it came to searching for Darcy, she'd acted with emotion rather than intellect. Both he and Alanna should have known those back mountain roads could be dangerous, and still, they'd persisted.

Was it a mistake to bring her here? A mistake to let her get too close? Because even though she might help him find Darcy and those kids, Alanna was still a threat, too. Maybe not intentionally, but when it came right down to it, who would she choose to help? Those kids and a police officer she'd just met, or a woman who'd raised her for most of her life?

Right now she was glancing around his home with open curiosity. It was cozy in a definably Alaskan way, with big windows that showcased the wilderness outside, exposed wooden beams and huge, open living spaces. She took in the long row of black-and-white photographs on one wall. They were images from his time overseas, mostly inside war zones. Images his family always complained about when they came over, images they'd pushed him to take down as his nieces and nephews started asking about them. Images he still kept up so he'd never forget. There was only one photo he'd never hung, one that had appeared in newspapers across the country. He touched his bad ear, scowled when he realized what he was doing and refocused on Alanna.

She frowned slightly at the photos, then turned her gaze out the window as he studied her.

Five years ago, he'd been too caught up in his own life to pay a lot of attention to a group of kids, ages six to twenty-three, rescued from kidnappers so near his hometown. But when he'd first come home, feeling totally adrift and with no idea what he'd do with the rest of his life, he'd read a lot about the story. He'd scoffed at statements made by the victims saying they'd been loved and well-treated. But admittedly, he'd been biased by his own experiences. He still was.

"Tell me about life with the Altiers."

She shifted to face him, her suspicion of his motives all over her face. Still, she answered softly, earnestly, "I don't know why she's doing this, but Darcy would never hurt those kids."

"She already has," Peter snapped, regretting the words as he spoke them but unable to call them back. "She kidnapped them. Don't you remember how that felt?" Way to get beyond his own biases. "I'm sorry." He sighed, not wanting to tell her about his own past but wondering if that was the best way to reach her.

Before he could, she set down her coffee and leaned toward him. Chance's head popped up, glancing between them, obviously sensing the tension. "I do remember. I still have nightmares about it sometimes. I know you don't understand how I can—" she took an audible breath, then stared him straight in the eyes as she finished "—love them."

"I do understand that." Or at least, he understood that she *thought* what she felt was love, instead of a complicated mix of fear and dependency, multiplied over fourteen years. "The attachment you can develop for someone who holds you against your will is real. It can be necessary for survival and then it gets ingrained. It's—"

Her snort of disbelief cut him off. She looked offended when she replied, "I got a psychology degree after I left Alaska. I understand why you think that's what's happening here, but don't forget—I'm the one who turned them in. They both went to jail because I left that note. My... Julian *died* because of me."

Peter frowned, scooting to the edge of his seat, wanting to reach for her hand across the coffee table and assure her that none of it was her fault. But he'd done that once before in his life as a war reporter, and it was amazing he'd come out of that situation with only lost hearing.

She squeezed her eyes briefly shut, then continued, "I know what they did was wrong. I think *they* know what they did was wrong. But I lived almost my whole childhood with that family. They were the ones who held me when I cried, who made me laugh with their silly jokes, who cheered for me when I accomplished something. The only thing they ever did to hurt me was take me from my family."

"Isn't that enough?" Peter asked, straining to keep his voice neutral.

"That's how my family feels," Alanna said, her hands clasping together so tightly that her knuckles went white.

"But how much do you remember from before you were five? If you'd gone to live with someone else for most of your childhood, how many memories would you have of your family before that?"

Probably sensing her distress, Chance stood and went to her, plopping his big head in her lap and making a brief smile spread across her lips. It faded as soon as Peter spoke.

"You're telling me you hardly remembered your family?" He tried to imagine that, being ripped from his family as a kindergartener by two people who then called themselves his parents, who treated him well and raised him with love. An ache twisted in his heart at the idea. Worse, he could suddenly picture it, could understand why she'd grown to love them and probably forgot more and more of life with her real family as the years went on.

"I remembered enough," Alanna answered, her voice softer now, as if she knew she was getting through to him. "But sometimes, love is irrational. And sometimes years of good actions start to outweigh one bad one, no matter how terrible that moment was."

"And still, you turned them in. Why?" What had changed after fourteen years to make her write that note?

"I didn't want to go the rest of my life without ever knowing the parents I vaguely remembered, the sister and brother I'd had."

Something passed over her face, a wave of sadness that told him she'd sacrificed a lot to fulfill that wish. More than just the loss of two people who'd acted like her parents most of her childhood, but also four other kids she'd loved as siblings. Four other kids who, from all accounts, had also felt loved in that household. Who probably missed Alanna as much as she missed them.

"Have you seen Darcy and Julian since they went to jail?"

She stiffened, straightened in a way that made his internal lie detector go off.

"No."

"But you've talked to them?" he guessed.

"No."

Was she lying? He couldn't tell. But if she wasn't... "Alanna, you need to be careful. I know Darcy and Julian loved you once. But you did turn them in. You said what Darcy's doing now makes no sense. Maybe she changed in prison."

He frowned, knowing that in terms of the investigation, it was a mistake to say any more, but he needed her to recognize the threat against her, to keep herself safe, too. She'd agreed to work with him, but theirs was a tentative truce, at best. She didn't trust him any more than he trusted her, even if he was beginning to sympathize with her. Even if he was starting to like her as a person.

That was a mistake, too, but one he couldn't seem to help. These days, it was his job to risk his life to protect others, even if they put him in danger.

He touched his bad ear again, watched her gaze narrow as she followed his movement.

"Darcy would never hurt me," Alanna said, but her voice lacked confidence.

"You can't know that," Peter insisted. "So, let's make a deal. You want to work together to find those kids? I'm in. But I'm law enforcement, so you're going to let me keep you safe. No more going off on your own to search for her. We stick together from here on out. Deal?"

She looked ready to argue, but after a long moment, she simply nodded.

"Now, where were you going today?"

"I think I have some ideas about where Darcy might go. Julian had backup hiding spots."

Anger flooded through him at the realization that she'd kept this to herself. She'd been gunning for one of those hiding spots and if he hadn't been following her, that information would have been lost. Those kids might have been lost. Maybe for fourteen long years, like she had been. Maybe longer.

This time, he held his anger inside and asked, "Where are these hiding spots?"

Panic rushed over her face and she leaped to her feet, making Chance jump up, too. The pair of them ran to his garage, and Alanna yanked open the back door of his truck, climbing inside as he caught up to them.

When Chance tried to climb in with her, Alanna put up a hand. "Stay, Chance."

The St. Bernard promptly sat, but he looked back at Peter as if to say, *Can't I go, too?*

"We're not going anywhere, Chance," Peter told him as Alanna climbed back out, unzipping an interior pocket of her bright red coat.

The coat was still sopping wet and so was the small piece of paper she pulled out of the pocket.

She unfolded it with infinite care, then swore as she looked back up at him, dismay in her eyes. "It's gone."

"What's gone?"

"The list of locations I found at the house. All the places Darcy might be hiding."

Chapter Seven

"I can't believe it's gone," Alanna said, staring at the little scrap of paper. She hadn't been able to toss it in the trash, even after putting it under a blow-dryer confirmed that all the pencil marks were lost.

Peter sat next to her, taking the smaller spot on the couch to her left instead of the bigger space to her right. "You read the list, right? Maybe if you think about it, you can recall some of the places?"

The heat from his body warmed her still-cold legs and she tried not to fixate on his closeness. It was just residual embarrassment from stripping out of her clothes in his car. Even covered by a blanket, it had been awkward. She'd had to use a lot of willpower not to glance his way as he'd stripped off his clothes—thank goodness he'd eventually wrapped a blanket around himself.

The memory made her hyperaware of the shocking blue of his eyes, the sharp lines of his face and the lean power of his build. He wasn't traditionally handsome, but there was something compelling about him. Maybe it was part of what had made him a good war reporter, the ability to project such intensity that it made it hard to look away.

"Alanna?" Peter pressed.

"I read the list. But it was coordinates, latitude and longitude, and it was in code."

"Code? Are you serious?"

"A silly code. My sis—the other kids and I made it up one winter when we had a bad storm and we were stuck inside. It was just a game, but we left codes for each other all over the house for a week." She shrugged at the interest in his gaze, remembering how much fun they'd had running around the house to find coded clues like a scavenger hunt. "My par—the Altiers got in on the game, too. I'd forgotten all about it until I saw this list."

"It sounds like a good time."

His tone was hesitant, speculative, and Alanna held in a sigh. Reporters—at least reporters actively chasing a story—got right to the point. But once anyone else would realize her history, they'd just pick at the edges. They'd ask sideways questions, looking for insight and pretending to understand, before they announced, "But these people *kidnapped* you." As if she didn't know.

Usually, for Alanna, that was the beginning of the end. It was too awkward to try to convince people that she'd been loved, that she'd loved in return. More awkward still to feel like she had to justify it. It was easier to break ties, keep to herself.

When she'd gone back to Chicago, she'd ventured outside her comfort zone with school and volunteer work. But after an initial burst of interest by anyone with the remotest connection to the Morgans, she'd found herself becoming more and more isolated socially. Kensie and Colter, Alanna's new brother-in-law, had decided something had to be done. Alanna had connected with Colter's dog, Rebel, a former Marine Combat Tracker Dog who had been as good for Alanna's anxiety as Colter's PTSD. So they'd found her a dog of her own, rescuing Chance to give to her.

She smiled at the St. Bernard who'd been so little two years ago, a victim of such cruelty that the vets weren't even sure he would survive. Now, still small for his breed, he was a total gentle giant. And he'd definitely rescued her as much as she'd rescued him.

At her smile, Chance pushed his way between the couch and the coffee table to drop his head in her lap. She stroked his head as she told Peter, "Drew and Valerie, the youngest kids, didn't remember their real families at all. They had no idea they were kidnapped. And we—Johnny, Sydney, and I—didn't tell them because they were so young and because honestly, we hardly remembered our own families. How do you break that to someone? Especially when they're happy?"

"Sydney was the one who remembered her family best, right? She was a few years younger than you?"

Alanna eyed him. "You've done your research."

He flinched, actually looking a little ashamed. "I read up on it when I came back home—to what used to be my home—two years ago. I lived on the other side of the mountain, in Luna, where you were reunited with your sister. When you showed up in Desparre this week…"

"You read through all the news reports again?"

He nodded, not quite meeting her gaze.

The coverage in Desparre hadn't been the most flattering, especially after time went on and reporters looked for a new angle to keep the story alive. They'd all seen her as that new angle. She might have turned the Altiers in, but the real story was how she *hadn't* spoken up for fourteen years.

"No wonder you acted like you already knew and disliked me as soon as you heard my name."

The Morgans had tried to keep the negative coverage from her at first. She'd been getting her GED and applying to college then, trying to get out into the world and reenter her life from fourteen years earlier. But she hadn't been able to stop herself from seeking out the news coverage on herself and the rest of the "family" she'd left behind.

"Hey." Peter's voice was soft, his eyebrows lowered as he put his hand over her free one.

She froze, her other hand stalling in Chance's fur, as his long fingers threaded through hers. The unexpected contact made her skin tingle.

"I didn't dislike you as soon as I knew who you were. I just—"

"Distrusted me?"

"Yes."

She hadn't expected him to admit it. Even though she'd already known it was true, the quiet word seemed to leave a physical mark on her chest. She slid her hand free and glanced away, hoping he hadn't seen that he'd hurt her.

She looked back just as quickly, tired of having to explain herself, tired of being judged by what people read in newspapers about her past instead of by who she was or her actions now. "Everyone thinks they would have gotten help right away, that they would have spent all those years hating the people who'd raised them. But if you haven't lived it—"

"I'm not judging you."

"No?"

Chance lifted his head from her lap at her sarcastic tone. "Do you know why my fa… Julian was killed in jail?" Peter frowned, gave a brief shake of his head.

"He was protecting a twenty-year-old kid who was being preyed on sexually. The predator stabbed Julian in the chest sixteen times for it." She choked on the last words, imagining the man who'd raised her being cornered, brutally attacked and dying on a filthy prison floor.

Peter reached for her and his intent to pull her into a hug was as clear as the confusion in his eyes. He was struggling to reconcile his idea of a child kidnapper with a man who'd risk his life to protect someone he barely knew.

She blocked his hug with a hand to his chest, resisting the urge to fist her hand into his sweatshirt and yank him toward her. To accept his hug along with the friendship he offered. Friendship she still couldn't tell was real or fake.

Standing, she swallowed back the tears that threatened every time she thought about the report the prison had issued. "I think I should go."

He stood, too, but slowly, caution in his expression. "I'm sorry. You're right. I have no idea what your life was like. All I know about the Altiers is what I've read in the papers or a law enforcement bulletin. I know better than anyone how those things can spin a story. But I spent years in war zones and I also know this—no one is one hundred percent good or bad. Everyone lives in gray areas, making right decisions one day and wrong ones the next. Sometimes the way we think of people is based on what side of the line the majority of those decisions lie. Sometimes, it's based on a single, dramatic incident."

His hand twitched upward, the way she'd seen it do before, and she had a sudden realization. He had his own single, dramatic incident. "What happened?"

He stared at her a long moment, not even pretending to misunderstand, before he nodded and sank back onto the couch.

Chance moved his head to Peter's leg, offering his quiet support in a way Alanna had seen him do hundreds of times at the nonprofit where she worked. From the very beginning, when she'd had him certified as a therapy dog so she could bring him to work with her, he'd had a sense of who needed him most.

"I was a war reporter," Peter said, and she nodded, having seen his bylines a time or two. Mostly, she remembered his name from an incident a few years ago, with a picture that had made national headlines: Peter, less fit than he was now, wearing a helmet and covered in sand and blood, one hand to his ear and an expression of horror and disbelief etched on his face.

"You were covering some kind of hostage release," she said, realizing that must have been the incident.

"It was supposed to be smooth and simple. I'd been in far more dangerous situations. The military had brought the ransom money. We were just tagging along—my camera guy and me—to catch the exchange. The hostage-takers hadn't covered their faces—they didn't think they could be identified or they didn't care. The CIA sent one of their officers to make the exchange. She was supposed to walk halfway and leave the money. Then the hostage would walk to us and the hostage-takers would pick up the money and leave. Well, they did take the money and leave."

Peter's hand went halfway to his left ear, then he set it on Chance's head instead, slowly petting the big dog.

"The hostage had been captive for almost six months. She'd watched the other two people who'd been kidnapped with her get killed. We thought she'd be running toward us. But the closer she got, I could see…"

He trailed off, his brows furrowed and his gaze on the wall of photographs across the room.

"What?" Alanna prompted softly.

"I've been to a few hostage exchanges before, where they're expected to go smoothly and our country wants a little good press. Sometimes, the hostages look terrified that something is going to go wrong at any second and they'll be yanked back into the hell they'd been living. Other times, they're crying with relief that it's finally over. And occasionally, they seem like they're not even aware of what's happening. Not this hostage. She was…calm, focused. Stoic, even."

His hand stalled on Chance's head and Alanna set her hand carefully on top of his, offering silent support the way he had for her. The same way she might at work with a survivor or a family member she'd gotten to know over months of visits.

He met her gaze briefly, a hint of a smile twitching on the edge of his lips. Then he looked back at his photos. "I was standing closest when the explosion went off."

Even though she'd seen the photos, had known he'd been close to an explosion, she still gasped at the idea of him being nearest to a bomb. Her fingers clenched reflexively over his. Chance's head tipped up, his attention bouncing to her, then back to Peter.

Alanna tried to remember the details of the article she'd read two years ago, but all she could recall were the details of the photo. Of Peter's face, dripping with blood. Back then, it had been a horrible sight, but now, knowing Peter made every detail more painful. She felt an ache in her chest thinking about what he'd experienced. "What happened? The hostage-takers threw a bomb during the rescue?"

He gave a humorless laugh, his gaze focused on her once more, all his intensity and cynicism directed at her. "They didn't throw anything. It was strapped to the hostage. She set it off herself when she got close to us."

Tension bloomed between them as she stared back at him. Suddenly, it all made sense. His instant distrust of her, his insistence that she must be working with Darcy. He thought she was just like the hostage who'd almost killed him: willing to do whatever it took to help someone she should have wanted behind bars, at the expense of anyone else. As that realization dawned, Peter said softly, "I quit my job after that. I'd wanted to be a reporter my whole life, but after that moment, I never wanted to go into another war zone. I sat around for a good six months, then saw a job posting for a police officer. This hostage almost destroyed that dream, too. The police have strict fitness and health requirements, and with the extent of my hearing loss... They only took me because they were desperate for officers."

His hand went up again, and this time, he did touch his left ear. "I lost most of the hearing in this ear in the explosion."

Alanna's heart gave a sudden, painful ache. He thought she was the same as that woman who, in the face of rescue, had destroyed herself and tried to take out everyone around her in the process. No wonder Peter didn't trust her.

He was never going to trust her.

ALANNA WAS SILENT in the passenger seat as Peter drove her and Chance in his truck the long way around the base of the mountain the next day. They were headed for Luna. Five years ago, Luna police had stopped the Altiers and arrested them. They'd loaded her and her "siblings" into a police car and driven them to the Luna hospital to be checked out. It was the last place she'd seen any of the people she'd called family for most of her childhood.

Last night, Peter had asked if she wanted to go there, to get checked out at the hospital after being trapped in that avalanche. But she had no desire to go back to that hospital, to those memories. And besides still feeling cold and being exhausted, she'd been okay. The worst of it was calling her rental company to let them know what had happened to their truck.

The fastest way to get to Luna was actually to drive up into the mountain and then back down. But after the avalanche yesterday, that wasn't happening. So, she and Peter had spent an awkward hour and a half in his truck. They had at least another hour to go before they made it to the far side of town, where Alanna thought one of Julian's hideouts might be.

She'd spent a long time last night trying to decode the old cipher she and her "siblings" had created, without much luck. But in the morning, she'd had an epiphany about one of them. Hopefully, she was right, because she'd convinced Peter to trust her and come along without notifying his department.

There was a new tension between them since he'd admitted what had happened to him. The uncomfortable silence was worse than sleeping in Peter's guest bedroom, hearing him move around one room over. Smelling like his soap and shampoo, and knowing he hadn't insisted she stay at his place because of the roads, like he'd claimed. The truth was, he didn't trust her not to go off on her own, even though she'd promised she wouldn't.

She squeezed her hands tightly together and said, "Maybe that woman didn't blow herself up. Maybe the explosive had a remote detonator."

"No," Peter replied, not even sounding surprised to hear the suggestion after an hour and a half of near-silence. "There was an investigation. She set it off herself."

"Well, you don't know what they told her. Maybe she felt like she had no choice. Maybe they threatened to kill her family if she didn't do it. I've heard that more than once from victims of violent crime. The person who did it threatens someone they love if they ever talk. After the things they've suffered, the victim believes it. This could be a more extreme version."

"Maybe," Peter agreed. He glanced her way, looking

intrigued, and she realized that he didn't know what she did for a living.

"I work for a nonprofit back home." Calling anywhere *home* besides Desparre still felt strange, especially now that she was back in Alaska, but it was true. Chicago had become her home now.

The thought wiggled around in her brain, bittersweet. Maybe she was truly starting to let go of the people she'd loved most of her life.

Her parents, Kensie, Colter and Flynn had all worked hard to bring her into their lives, to show her how much they loved her. There was still so much missing, so many memories with them she'd never be able to have, but she'd never stopped loving them, either.

Shaking off her musings for another time, Alanna said, "The nonprofit works with victims of violent crime."

"You're a therapist?" He sounded surprised.

"No. It's not that kind of place. We do have support groups, and I've gotten Chance certified as a therapy dog so he can come and sit with people. But we also help people navigate the legal system, act as an intermediary with police when necessary and help them transition back to their regular life. Technically, my job is as a case manager, so I help identify what people need when they first come to us."

"Why did you choose violent crime?"

She darted a glance at him, expecting to see suspicion on his face. When most people heard about her past and her career choice, they assumed she'd been harmed during her years with the Altiers, despite her insistence otherwise.

"I guess I just…" She sighed, wishing it was something she knew how to put in words. "When I came home, I got a lot of attention. All these people I didn't know wanted to help me. They meant well, even if it made me anxious to have them come up to me and ask for details, looking like they just wanted a good story. But in some ways, it was a good thing. The fact that we were all found after so many years inspired a pair of ex-cops who lived near me to start a cold case club. They've solved a dozen cases since then."

Peter nodded, his gaze catching hers briefly before he looked back out the front windshield. The road had been cleared yesterday, but had a new dusting of snow from the morning. "You're doing it out of guilt."

She frowned. "Not guilt—"

"I don't mean it in a bad way. Just—I get it. You feel like these other people who had it worse than you should be getting the attention, the resources, you did."

"Sort of." She fidgeted in her seat, uncomfortable sharing this but somehow feeling he'd empathize. No one else had understood it quite so well. "I also understand how confusing it is to try to fit back into your normal life. I don't identify with the way most of these people have been harmed. But I understand some of it. My case got a lot of press, so most of them recognize my name. They tell me it makes them feel more connected to me, because I've personally experienced some of it. And I like helping people."

"You're a good person."

There was such honesty in his voice, mixed with just a hint of surprise, that Alanna wasn't sure what to say. Her "thanks" was delayed and too quiet.

Peter shrugged, giving her a little grin that sent a flutter of awareness through her. "Don't thank me. That's all on you."

She felt herself grin in response and the tension that had filled the truck since they'd sat together at his breakfast table this morning finally eased. Even Chance seemed to feel it, scooting forward and shoving his head through the space between the seats.

Alanna stroked his silky fur as she stared at Peter's profile. She had a sudden vision of the first moment he'd approached her four days ago, the way he'd angled his body, making his weapon more visible. But his right side wasn't just where he kept his gun; it was also the side with his good ear. He'd done it so he could hear her better, not to intimidate her.

Maybe there were other things she was misinterpreting, too. Yes, he'd admitted he hadn't trusted her when he'd met her. But he'd let her stay in his house. He'd called in to work this morning and she'd overheard him telling someone he was running a lead today and would be late for his Sunday shift. He hadn't mentioned her involvement.

It was the deal they'd struck. She'd share the location she thought she'd figured out from the ruined list and they'd check it out, just the two of them.

So far, he was keeping up his end of the bargain. She had her doubts that he would continue to do so if they actually found Darcy, but this seemed to be the best way forward.

She'd insisted on secrecy because she'd feared if police showed up, it would escalate everything and Darcy might do something stupid. Alanna's gut clenched at the memory of Darcy and Johnny shooting at Kensie five years ago. If the police were there this time, they would see the kidnapper lifting a weapon as a legitimate reason to open fire in return. Her concern had been that Darcy would end up getting herself killed.

But suddenly, she was struck with a totally different worry.

If it was just her and Darcy, Alanna wanted to believe she could talk some sense into the woman who'd raised her since she was five years old. She wanted to believe that if Peter's presence threatened Darcy, Alanna standing in front of him would keep him safe. But was that realistic?

Or was she fooling herself?

As Peter met her gaze again, giving her a quick, genuine smile, she tried to smile back.

He was prickly, and she still wasn't totally sure where she stood with him. But he was smart and capable and he'd run to save her when he could have just as easily stepped back and saved himself from that avalanche. From the moment he'd wrapped his fingers in her coat and held on even as the snow threatened to send them both over a mountain, she'd started to care about him. Probably more than she should.

If she was wrong about Darcy, was she risking Peter's life by bringing him with her?

Chapter Eight

Peter stared at Alanna across the tiny wooden table in the overcrowded coffee shop in downtown Luna. She was back in the jeans and light purple sweater she'd been wearing yesterday, but he couldn't stop picturing her the way she'd looked last night in his too-large sweatpants and long-sleeved T-shirt.

She flushed at his stare, redirecting her gaze to the steaming cup of coffee in her hands. At her side, Chance sat patiently, his size making him look like her protector.

The coffee shop had been here since he was a teenager and he'd spent hours in front of the fireplace over the years. Playing board games from the stack the owners always kept on hand or reading a book from the shelves on the far wall. With a first date or a long-term girlfriend. With family or a group of friends. Or, in those first six months after coming home, feeling adrift and unsure of what the rest of his life held, by himself.

They were less than twenty minutes from the location Alanna thought she'd identified from the Altiers' coded list. Peter had told her he wanted to stop here to take a break from driving, to rest a little before a possible confrontation with Darcy. The truth was, he needed to give his fellow officers a chance to catch up.

He'd called in to the station that morning, giving the

story he and Alanna had agreed upon: he was running a long-shot lead and would let them know how it panned out. She'd been just around the corner, listening in, not realizing he could see her reflection in the mirror across the hall.

When she'd slipped back down the hall, he'd quickly texted Tate with the real story. He felt guilty about it—and Tate had also reminded him that technically, the Desparre police department had no jurisdiction here. But he trusted his partner. He didn't know the Luna officers. He had no idea what Darcy would do if she was cornered, but he wanted to make sure Alanna was safe.

Still, he didn't like betraying her trust.

A few days ago, that wouldn't have mattered to him. He would have considered it a necessary lie for the possibility of rescuing those kids. Now, after the things she'd shared about her life with the Altiers, he understood why her loyalty was conflicted. For the first time in two years, he even sympathized with the woman who'd killed herself— and almost killed him—when she'd been on the verge of being rescued.

He'd always pitied her. But there'd been too much anger for more than that. Peter had always assumed the hostage had been brainwashed, that she'd hit that detonator to protect the terrorists who had taken her. Maybe he'd been wrong. Maybe she'd done it to protect her family, because after nearly six months of being terrorized, she could see no other option.

"What are you thinking?" Alanna asked.

When he blinked and refocused, he realized she was staring at him with an expression that said too many emotions had been obvious on his face.

"You're nothing like I expected," he blurted. From all the headlines, all the newspaper stories, he'd expected a conflicted, confused woman who'd grown up isolated and brainwashed, who'd come to Desparre for her own agenda.

A hesitant smile turned up her lips, warmed her deep brown eyes. "I assume that's a good thing?"

He was attracted to her. The realization slammed into him with an intensity that made him slump back in his chair. It wasn't just her long, silky hair, those plump lips or the secrets in the depths of her eyes. He'd seen too much as a reporter, on both sides of the camera, to really care about that anymore. It was the integrity of her character, the way she tried to do right by everyone, whether they deserved it or not. It was the way she'd clung to Chance in that avalanche, even when letting him go might have been safer for her. It was the way she challenged Peter at every turn, made him rethink his assumptions about everything.

"What?" she asked, sounding concerned as she leaned toward him, put her hand over his.

"Peter!"

What terrible timing. Peter slowly swiveled in his chair to find his parents standing behind him, both holding take-out cups of coffee. His father was looking at Alanna curiously. His mother was smiling at him in a way that told him she'd totally misunderstood what was happening.

"Mom, Dad." He stood, hugged them both and then gestured to Alanna, who was also standing. "This is Alanna."

When Chance gave a short bark, attracting attention from nearby customers, Peter laughed and added, "And this big guy is Chance."

The St. Bernard wagged his tail at the introduction and Peter's mom scratched his ears as his dad shook Alanna's hand.

"Do you live in Luna, Alanna?" his mom asked, giving him a quick grin she probably thought was subtle.

He wanted to laugh and roll his eyes at the same time.

Getting him to move back to Luna was a dream she was unwilling to give up on, even now that he'd lived and worked in Desparre for a year.

"Actually, I live in Chicago."

His mom's brow furrowed, then she breathed, "You're Alanna Morgan, aren't you?" Before Alanna could answer, she looked at Peter with concern in her eyes. "This isn't another story, is it?"

"No, Mom." He shook his head at Alanna for emphasis, but she didn't seem worried by the question, just uncomfortable that his mom had recognized her.

His mom seemed to realize it, too, because she smiled again and said, "Well, we're just off to a movie. You two have a nice time."

"Come by for dinner soon," his dad said as they headed for the door.

"They're nice," Alanna said.

"They're still upset I've moved to Desparre. They thought when I finally gave up being a reporter, I'd come home to Luna like my brothers and sister."

She leaned toward him. "You've got siblings?"

Peter glanced at the front of the shop and saw his mom grinning back at him before she slipped out the door. He realized that she might have incorrectly thought this was a date, but in some ways, it felt like one.

"Three," he replied, shifting his full attention back to Alanna, suddenly wishing they could both shake free of their past baggage, of their reasons for being here together right now. Wishing it was really a date. But he could pretend it was, if only for a few minutes, to buy time. "Two older brothers and one older sister. They've all got kids and they all live in Luna. My parents keep hoping I'll follow their lead."

Alanna smiled, sipping her coffee. "That's nice."

He shrugged. "It's a nice idea." But he'd always been restless, always wanted to get out and see the world, do something that got his blood moving, that made a difference. For five years, he'd done it as a reporter. Since he'd returned to Alaska, he'd discovered that being a police officer filled that need. He'd never been able to understand how the rest of his family didn't have the same restlessness.

"You wouldn't ever move back to Luna?"

"Probably not. Don't get me wrong—I love my family. But it's not like there are tons of opportunities in Luna. They're lucky I got the police officer spot nearby."

"Well, it's close until Desparre gets a particularly bad snow and you can't get over here for months," she said, reminding him that she knew Desparre at least as well as he did.

"When I was a reporter, sometimes they wouldn't see me for six months at a time."

"It's got to be hard for them. First, you're in war zones and now you're a police officer, potentially under fire at any given moment." She looked a little queasy at the idea.

"My grandparents moved here from Czechoslovakia— back when that's what it was called. During the Czech uprising in 1968, when the Soviets sent in half a million tanks and troops, they fled. At first, they thought they'd stick around, be part of the protests. But they didn't like living among so many tanks, the constant unspoken threat of violence. Ultimately they decided they had to get out— about three hundred thousand people there felt the same way. My grandparents said they came here because they just wanted to be left alone. I grew up hearing their stories and the stories they'd been told by *their* parents about what their country was like at the time of the Nazi invasion."

Alanna nodded slowly, probably thrown by his change

of topic. "I don't blame them for wanting to live peacefully, quietly, after all of that."

"Yeah, I guess," Peter said. His parents had wanted the
same thing and so did his siblings. "But I always felt like it
was in my blood to get out there and witness conflict. To
record it for history and, hopefully, help prevent us from
repeating it." He shrugged, suddenly embarrassed by how
naive he sounded.

She reached across the table and put her hand on his.
"I understand that, too."

She understood because in her own way, she'd chosen a
similar path. They were both in professions to help others.

He smiled back at her, realizing how natural it felt to
be sitting in this coffee shop with her, their hands stacked
together. If this *had* been a date, if she was someone he'd
met who lived in Desparre or Luna, he'd already be planning to ask her out again.

His smile faded. If she was right, if they found Darcy
hiding in Luna, it would all be over. Alanna would return
home and he'd never see her again.

From the moment they'd set foot in Alaska, Darcy and Julian had loved the mountains. So Alanna wasn't surprised
when Peter slowed the truck near the location she'd identified and it was at the base of the mountain they'd driven
on last night.

When they'd settled in Desparre, Darcy and Julian had
built their home at the edge of the mountaintop, with the
natural protection of a steep slope at their back. Here, apparently, they'd done the same thing in reverse. Only this
time, there was just Darcy.

The cabin was much smaller than the one in Desparre.
It looked like a single-room shack and if anyone drove
close enough to see it through the trees, it seemed deserted.

Alanna's shoulders dropped as she peered through the windshield. "What if I'm wrong?" There had been four other locations on that list, but although she'd tried to recall the other symbols and decode them, nothing she'd worked out in the little notebook Peter had given her made sense yet. She wasn't sure it ever would.

Peter's hands were resting lightly on the wheel, but there was an excitement in his gaze that told her how much he loved chasing leads. "What's the likelihood that there'd be a cabin at the exact longitude and latitude you decoded?"

He was right about that. Like a lot of Alaska, the towns of Desparre and Luna were more open land than homes or businesses. Her discouragement turned to anxiety. "Maybe I should go up to the door alone. If she's there, I might be able to talk her into giving herself up."

"We agreed we'd go together," Peter replied, then turned into the driveway.

"If she's here, you're going to scare her o—"

The words died on her lips as the cabin's front door opened and Darcy stepped halfway through the threshold, backlit by a light inside that had been blocked by the heavy curtains on the windows.

Shock jolted through Alanna. She'd come all the way to Alaska to find Darcy, but after five years, on some level, she'd never expected to see her again. All the letters Darcy and Julian had sent from prison had gone unanswered, mostly because Alanna knew how much it would hurt her biological parents for her to respond, how badly they needed her to make a clean break. She couldn't bring herself to cut off her "siblings," so she'd made the choice to cut off Darcy and Julian. Every letter had been returned, unopened.

All these years later, it still physically hurt to wonder what Darcy and Julian had written her. Had they been let-

ters of remorse, letters of love? Or had their love turned
to hate over the note she had written and left in Jasper's
General Store in an attempt to go home to the Morgans?

Darcy had been sentenced to sixty-two years in prison
without the possibility of parole. Julian had gotten sixty-
three years, and if he hadn't been killed in prison, he would
still have died there. Since the moment she'd chosen not
to communicate with them, Alanna had hardened herself
to the idea of never seeing Darcy or Julian again. In so
many ways, it had felt like the right thing to do, the only
thing she *could* do. A penance she had to make for fourteen years of silence.

The Darcy in front of her was thinner, her hair almost
entirely gray and lackluster. Her once stick-straight posture was now slumped, defeated. Every day she'd spent in
prison seemed to show in the new lines on her face.

Alanna couldn't take her gaze off Darcy as she climbed
out of Peter's truck and took a step up the driveway. Behind
her, she heard Chance leap over the seat and out the door.

Across the thirty feet separating them, Darcy's eyes
seemed to widen comically, then her gaze darted right.
Toward Peter. Her eyes narrowed, her lips twisting into
an angry scowl. When she stepped fully outside, there
was a pistol tucked into her belt at her hip and a shotgun
clutched in her hand.

It was a nightmare right out of her memory. Five years
seemed to disappear, and instead of Peter beside her, it was
Kensie, who had found her after so many years lost. She
could see Darcy lifting that shotgun and firing at the truck
where Kensie and Colter sat. Alanna heard the echoes of
her own screams from back then in her ears as she threw
her hands wide and ran toward Darcy.

This time, although Darcy's gaze kept darting toward
Peter—and then toward the street, like she expected

backup to come flying in, sirens blaring, at any second—she never lifted her gun. Instead, as Alanna got closer, slowing to a walk until she stood still a few feet away, Darcy shook her head and whispered, "*Why?*"

Up close, the lines on Darcy's face were even more pronounced, the dark circles under her eyes more hollow. Anger lurked just underneath the hurt that flashed in her eyes. The pain and betrayal she felt were as obvious in her voice as the tears she was trying to blink back. "*Why?*" she demanded again, this time almost a scream.

Chance stepped up beside Alanna and she reached for him fast, put a steadying hand on his head to assure him she wasn't in danger.

Darcy's gaze shifted to Chance and her lips shifted into a strange semblance of a smile, an echo of what it had once been. Too quickly, it dropped away. "When you were little, you always wanted a dog." She looked back at Alanna, blinking rapidly. "Guess you got everything you wanted."

Then somehow Peter was beside her, his hand gripping her arm too hard, keeping her in place. His other hand was on the butt of his weapon. "We just want the kids. That's it. You hand them over and we walk away."

Darcy did little more than smirk at Peter's offer, her hand shifting on the shotgun with an ease that told Alanna she might look older and weaker, but Darcy still had an unexpected strength. Then her gaze was back on Alanna.

"Who is this? Why is he here?"

"He's my friend, Peter," Alanna said, glad that it was common in Alaska for people to carry weapons. It didn't immediately mark him as law enforcement. "He drove me out here."

"How did you find me?"

"This is where we were headed five years ago, isn't it?" Alanna asked instead of answering.

Darcy's slight nod, as if she couldn't stop herself from responding, was enough to tell Alanna it was true.

Her own anger flared up, the unfairness of it all, the blame she felt from all directions no matter what choices she made. "And then what was the plan? To keep running, go back to what we did when I was little?"

"We wouldn't have needed to do that if you hadn't left that note. We were good to you. We *loved* you." Darcy shook her head, as if she still didn't understand it.

Alanna's gut clenched at Darcy's use of the past tense, but as much as it hurt, this moment wasn't about her. It was about those two kids who had to be in the cabin behind Darcy, probably terrified and confused like Alanna had been in those early days with the Altiers.

"There was another family out there who loved me, too." On some level, Darcy had to know what she'd done was wrong. Didn't she? "How do you think it felt, knowing I'd never get to see them again?"

Something flashed in Darcy's eyes, some mix of guilt and sorrow that was gone so fast Alanna wondered if she'd imagined it. Then Darcy's attention veered left, into the woods at the base of the mountain. Was that where she'd hidden her vehicle? Was she thinking about making a run for it?

"Please," Alanna whispered. "It's not too late to do the right thing."

A spasm of emotion passed over Darcy's face and for a moment, Alanna thought she'd gotten through to her. Then Darcy swung the shotgun up, past Alanna and Peter, high over the woods to her left.

Alanna's hand darted out to grab Peter, to prevent him from pulling his own weapon. What was Darcy doing? Trying to scare them? Had she lost her mind when she'd lost her "kids"?

The *boom boom boom* of the shotgun firing repeatedly echoed, followed by a louder, heavier rumble that made Alanna's heart seem to drop to her stomach. She recognized that sound, had felt the weight of the snow burying her only yesterday.

Her gaze traveled up the side of the mountain, to the weak spot where Darcy had aimed, an overhang of snow that was now rushing downward. It was far enough away that it was unlikely to reach them, so Peter's scream to *watch out* startled her, made her jump.

Then, suddenly, everything around her was noise and motion.

Peter raced toward the oncoming snow, Chance at his heels, as shapes emerged from behind the trees, people trying to escape the avalanche. People who shouldn't have been there at all. People who weren't moving fast enough.

Darcy's gaze lingered on Alanna for a drawn-out moment, then she darted the other way, back into the cabin, slamming the door behind her.

Alanna glanced toward Peter and Chance and the police officers who'd been hiding in the woods, who were being overrun by the snow. Then she glanced back at the cabin, where Darcy was hiding with two young children.

And she made her choice.

Chapter Nine

For the second time in two days, Peter was running toward an avalanche.

He'd lived in Alaska for most of his life and managed to never get caught up in one before this past week. Like most people who lived this far north, he had a healthy respect for the power of nature but he'd always taken precautions, so he'd never feared it. The way his heart was thundering in his chest now, that had changed.

This time, he wasn't in any real danger of being buried in it. The snow had already stopped falling from above and the rush through the woods was slowing. That was both good and bad. The trees acting as a natural blockade for some of the snow meant it wouldn't spill over to the cabin, where he assumed those kids were being held. But it also meant more of it was piled higher in the exact location he'd last spotted his fellow officers. Including his partner.

"Tate!" he yelled. Now that the thundering of snow was quieting, his voice echoed along the mountain base, taunting him with the lack of response.

He slowed to a stop before he reached the snow, realizing he should have run to his truck instead to grab the collapsible snow shovel most people who lived in these parts always carried. He spun back even as Chance raced past him, right into the snow.

His call for Alanna to grab his shovel died on his lips. He scanned the area around the cabin. But there were only woods and an empty driveway. She must have followed Darcy inside.

Pain clamped in his chest as he glanced back to the snow, where Chance was frantically digging, then over to the silent cabin. He ran back the way he'd come, heading for his truck and shovel.

He had to pray that Alanna was right and Darcy wouldn't hurt her. He had to pray that Alanna would be able to talk Darcy into handing over the kids without hurting anyone.

There was no mistaking that the woman still loved Alanna like a daughter. It was equally obvious that she felt deeply betrayed and probably blamed Alanna for the years she'd spent in jail, maybe even for her husband's death. Peter could imagine things going shockingly well, that he might turn back and see Alanna ushering out two relieved kids and a sobbing Darcy. Or he might hear a series of shotgun blasts and then Darcy fleeing for safety alone.

Right now he had to trust that Alanna was right. That the love Darcy still felt for her was stronger than the hate. That the education in psychology Alanna had earned and her experience working with vulnerable people would have taught her how to navigate such a volatile situation. One thing he did know: Darcy hadn't fired that shotgun at him before because Alanna had called him her friend. If he burst through that cabin door as an officer, Darcy would shoot.

Alanna had a chance. But his teammates didn't. No way could Chance dig all of them out alone before someone suffocated.

Peter holstered his gun, grabbing his shovel and dialing his phone as he ran. "Chief," he huffed when Chief Her-

nandez answered, "I need help out here fast. Avalanche."
He didn't wait for her response, just tucked his phone back
in his pocket and started digging beside Chance.

The big dog had already uncovered the legs of an officer
who was facedown. "Good boy, Chance," said Peter. The
dog gave a quick bark, then left Peter to finish digging the
man out. He bounded a few feet over and started digging
again, his big paws sending snow flying, his strong nose
right on target as another pair of boots appeared.

"Come on," Peter muttered, trading the shovel for his
thinly gloved hands as he got close to the man's face. The
fact that he hadn't moved the whole time Peter and Chance
had been digging him out was a bad sign, but as Peter
swept snow off the back of his head, he suddenly groaned
and rolled partway over.

Charlie Quinn was a longtime member of the force,
someone Peter had overheard more than once complaining about working with "the pity-hire who can't hear." But
when Peter had asked for backup, he'd shown up without
complaint.

"You okay?" Peter asked, helping him to a sitting position.

Charlie put a shaky hand to his head, nodding.

"More help is coming," Peter told him, leaving him
there so he could go dig out the next officer Chance had
found.

As soon as Peter got there, Chance gave him an en-
couraging *woof* and was off again, sniffing his way to a
new spot.

"You're amazing," Peter breathed as he paused a second to watch the St. Bernard. Then he looked back at the
partly uncovered officer in front of him and went to work.
His hands, arms, and even his face stung as he shoveled

snow aside and the cold seeped into him. Finally, he shoved enough snow away to identify the officer.

This wasn't Tate either, but Nate Dreymond. He was the second-newest officer on the force, a twenty-year-old who'd been hired six months before Peter. He was already moving around, flailing and trying to get free of the snow.

"I've got you," Peter said, dropping the shovel and pushing a heavy pile of snow off the young officer, who broke free of the rest covering him so fast and hard that he knocked Peter over.

Nate was gasping, tears and snot mixed with the snow he was raking off his face with bare fingers so pale Peter knew he couldn't feel them.

"Be careful," Peter said, pulling Nate's hands free to reveal he'd scraped up his own face. "Go over there." He pointed toward Charlie. "Help get him into my truck. The heat is on."

As Nate stumbled that way, unsteady on his feet, Peter warned, "There might still be an armed fugitive in the cabin."

Nate didn't show any sign of hearing him, but Charlie looked up sharply, his hand already on the butt of his pistol. He nodded confidently at Peter, pushing to his feet with a grunt. Then the two of them were leaning on each other and moving toward the truck.

Peter spun away from them again, trudging after Chance, the snow up way past the top of his boots now. He was soaked almost to his hips, the cold making him shiver violently. Ignoring it, he took over from Chance's latest dig and the dog was off again, toward an area of snow that was moving, someone clearly fighting to get free.

Yet again, the man Peter finished digging out wasn't Tate. It was Lorenzo Riera, another veteran. As soon as he was freed enough from the snow to speak, he demanded, "Rook?" It was his nickname for Nate, who was his partner.

"He's okay," Peter assured him, glancing over at where Chance was digging away, praying his own partner was under there. How many officers had come to back him up today? How many were hurt right now because of a decision he'd made?

"Peter!"

Peter glanced back as a police SUV screeched to a halt at the edge of the woods, windows down and Chief Hernandez steering one-handed as she leaned partway out the window. The fact that she'd gotten here so fast meant she must have already been out somewhere on the edges of Desparre on a call.

"Status!" she demanded.

"We've got three dug out," Peter called back. "Not sure how many more officers were out here. Presumably Darcy Altier is still in the cabin, armed, with the kids and now Alanna."

The chief was scowling as she slammed the SUV door shut. She had her weapon out of the holster before the door was closed and she nodded at the two officers who stepped out of the back of the vehicle, both in bulletproof vests and helmets.

"Luna police are sending backup. The state police sniper and hostage negotiator are both on another call. We're going to have to breach."

"No!" Peter took two steps toward her, then glanced back at Chance, still digging.

The big dog looked over at him once, let out a long howl, then went back to work.

"Just wait," Peter begged Chief Hernandez. "Give Alanna a chance."

As he pivoted toward Chance and whoever was still buried in the snow, Lorenzo stumbled over next to him to help.

"It's just Tate left. That must be him."

Peter fell to his knees next to Chance, not even bothering to run back for the shovel he'd dropped. He started digging with his hands, shoving snow away from Tate, who'd been moving before but wasn't any longer.

When an arm fell free, Peter tugged on it, trying to pull Tate out of the snow. His head appeared and while Lorenzo and Chance continued to dig around the rest of him, Peter cleared snow off his face.

Tate looked abnormally pale and his lips had a bluish tinge, but when Peter leaned close to listen for his breathing, Tate gasped in a large breath. Lorenzo cleared a big chunk of snow off his back and Peter helped pull Tate to his feet.

"We should have stayed on the road instead of hiding in the woods," Tate choked out, which made Lorenzo let out a relieved laugh.

Peter threw his arms around his friend, hugging him tight. Then he dropped to his knees and hugged Chance. "Good boy," he whispered, and got a big, slobbery kiss on the cheek in return.

Standing, he told Tate, "Now we need to get Alanna out of that cabin safely."

The look on his partner's face—one of dread and sorrow—made him spin to face the cabin.

Sam Jennings and Max Becker—the two officers who'd arrived in vests with the chief—were breaching the front door of the cabin, sending it right off the hinges with a powerful blow from a battering ram.

Peter's "*wait!*" was lost beneath the *boom* of the flash-bang tossed through the threshold. As white light exploded behind the curtained windows, the two officers rushed inside.

Even though he knew it was too late, Peter started running. His heart pounded harder than it had for his first raid. Every freezing-cold intake of breath seemed to seize his lungs.

A flash-bang was disorienting—basically a stun grenade that rendered your eyes and ears useless. When used on civilians, they dropped their weapons to cover their eyes or ears. By the time they figured out what was happening, they were being shoved to the ground by tactical officers.

But the Desparre police force rarely used them, and they didn't have a tactical unit. All they had were regular officers who received special tactical and weapons training each month in case an emergency unraveled too quickly to wait for state police or the FBI. Five years in war zones had taught Peter that sometimes it didn't matter what weapons or tactics were used. With a determined-enough opponent, impossible odds suddenly became possible.

He didn't know a lot about Darcy Altier beyond what he'd read and what Alanna had told him. But he'd witnessed her state of mind. She was volatile, desperate, prone to big swings of emotion. And right now she had three hostages who might be between her and the officers who'd rushed inside blind.

Chief Hernandez was moving, arms spread wide, to block him from rushing into the house. Peter paused, unsure whether to race around her or run right through her.

Then Sam and Max emerged from the cabin, looking grim and shaking their heads.

Peter choked on the sudden emotion that rushed up his throat, then he was pushing the chief aside and running into the cabin.

He waved his hands around to clear the smoke, expecting to see all of them—Alanna, Darcy and the two kids—dead on the floor. But there was nothing but an abandoned shotgun on the floor.

He glanced around, wondering if he'd missed another room, but there were no doors except the open one leading out the back. Darcy and the kids were gone.

So was Alanna.

Chapter Ten

"Follow their footsteps," Chief Hernandez ordered, already out in front with her weapon raised.

Peter hurried up beside her, insisting, "We need to be careful. We have to assume Darcy is holding the kids. She dropped the shotgun, but she still has a pistol. Alanna is probably trying to talk her down."

Chief Hernandez gave him a look full of disappointment and disbelief, then motioned for Sam and Max to catch up.

They were tracking two fresh sets of footsteps that led away from the back door of the cabin, with stride distances that indicated the people who made them had been running. The tracks led through the woods in the opposite direction of where the officers had been buried under snow. Back in the direction of downtown Luna. But before that, they would hit a road that might take them toward Desparre or farther north into even more remote parts of the state.

There'd been no vehicle in the driveway, no garage. Had Darcy hidden it at the edge of the woods, near the road, so the cabin would look deserted? That was logical.

Peter put on a burst of speed, panting with exertion that would make his gun hand shake if he caught up to Darcy and she swung her pistol his way. He passed Chief Hernandez, Sam and Max, ignoring his boss's curse and shout to wait. If they hadn't already left, if Alanna was with them, Peter wanted to reach them first.

Darting around trees, Peter's gaze shifted back and forth from the footsteps in the snow to the area in front of him, hoping he wouldn't misjudge a step, run right into a tree and knock himself out. He slowed as the road became visible and then skidded to a stop at its edge, where the footsteps ended and deep tire indents marked the spot where a vehicle had once sat.

They were gone.

A big chunk of snow fell off a tree overhead onto his head, sliding down his face and inside the back of his coat. He wiped it away just as the chief caught up to him.

"This was a total disaster." Holstering her weapon, Chief Hernandez got in his face—not an easy task, since she was a good four inches shorter.

Still, Peter straightened and clamped his jaw shut. He knew better than to piss off the chief—at least any more than he already had.

"When I tell you to wait, you *wait*." She poked a finger at his chest, fury in her gaze. "You're *my* responsibility, Robak. We're not a big police force, but we're a team. If you want to be part of it, you need to act like it."

She strode past him, heading down the road back toward the cabin. Sam and Max followed her. Sam gave him an apologetic glance; Max ignored him entirely.

Peter's shoulders slumped and a shiver racked his body as the cold and exhaustion hit. His jeans and gloves were completely soaked through and the snow that had dripped down the back of his coat was uncomfortable. He looked once more down the road, then followed his fellow officers.

Had Alanna *chosen* to get in that vehicle with Darcy? Or had she been forced inside?

He frowned as he glanced at the ground in front of him.

Was that an extra set of footprints he was seeing? Had someone else come back this way? Had Alanna chased Darcy, been unable to catch her before she took off in her vehicle, then returned to the cabin?

He hurried to catch up to Chief Hernandez Sam, and Max, noticed them frowning at the extra footprints, too. The chief even had her weapon out again.

The walk back to the cabin didn't take long—it was a straight line compared to the curved, roundabout route through the woods. But the frigid wind picked up and made him shiver harder, made it seem much farther than it really was. When they finally arrived, Tate was shivering by the road. Chance stood next to him, pressed up against his side as if trying to warm him.

"Did Alanna come back this way?" Peter asked. "And why are you out here? Why didn't you warm up in my truck?" Peter glanced around, realized it wasn't there and asked, "Did some of the officers take it back? Is everyone okay?" Was Alanna okay? Where was she?

"Everyone's fine," Tate said, his teeth actually chattering. "But it's not us who took the truck."

"What do you mean?"

"Apparently, while you were still digging me out and the chief was busy watching the front of the cabin, Alanna ran back from the road and took it."

Peter frowned, realizing that Darcy had been gone long before they'd tried to track her through the woods. That meant Alanna had been climbing into his truck instead of running into the snow to help him pull out Tate.

Tate shivered harder, wrapping his arms around himself. "Nate and Charlie said she was alone. I guess they thought it was okay, since she'd been on your side the last time they saw her."

"She's still on my side," Peter said, although suddenly, he wasn't sure.

Chief Hernandez shook her head and holstered her weapon, heading past them toward her vehicle. Sam and Max followed.

Peter just continued to stare at his partner, trying to understand. Why would Alanna come back here but not wait for him? Why would she take his truck but not explain herself to any of the officers?

At least she was okay. She wasn't a hostage. She wasn't dead.

But if she'd taken his truck, she was trying to chase Darcy down alone.

"We need to catch up to her," he told Tate. "She could be in trouble."

"Right now, we all need to warm up and change or we won't be good for anything." Tate stroked Chance's head with hands that shook. "Since Alanna took off, maybe we can make Chance here our K-9 representative."

Tate had been trying to convince the chief they needed a K-9 unit for as long as Peter had known him. The chief had always countered that the department barely had enough money to pay for officers and their training, let alone add dogs to the mix. Maybe today would change her mind.

Chance looked up at Tate, then over at Peter, as if asking where Alanna was.

"We'll find her, boy," Peter told him.

"Robak! Emory! Get over here," the chief called from inside her SUV. The rest of the officers were already crammed inside. "I'm driving you to the spot the other vehicles were hidden before this unsuccessful raid."

Peter felt himself jerk at the term *raid*. The plan had been for the other officers to be backup, in case things went south. Not for them to jump into action from the outset. Hadn't it?

He glanced sideways at Tate, wondering if anyone else had noticed the slipup. Or if his partner would look guilty for hiding the true nature of their "help." But Tate was just striding toward the SUV, looking miserable.

Still, his fellow officers had hidden in the woods. They'd obviously waited while Peter and Alanna tried to talk Darcy down. Maybe a raid had been a last resort if the negotiation soured. Or maybe they would have run straight in if it had been clear they could get to the kids safely.

"No one who was in the avalanche is driving." The chief looked Peter over as he, Tate and Chance joined her, then added, "Not you, either, Robak."

He took her point. Everyone who'd been buried in the snow—and him, since he'd been hip-deep in it, digging men out—were soaked and freezing. Although all he felt was miserably cold, the rest of the team might have had their core temperatures drop enough to make driving dangerous.

Last night, even after waiting until they'd warmed up some, Alanna had still been violently shaking as she'd navigated those mountain roads. Thinking about her made him anxious to get moving and he yanked open the back door.

Tate's eyebrows raised as they saw how crowded it already was. "I don't think we're getting two more men and a St. Bernard in there. Why don't you come back for us?"

The chief scowled at him, then the back seat, then finally nodded. "We'll be fast. The vehicles are less than a mile away. I want everyone who was in the avalanche checked out at the hospital."

When most of the officers grumbled, she snapped, "No arguments." Then the back door was slammed shut and the SUV was off, kicking up snow.

"Were you planning to surround me, Darcy and Alanna no matter what?" Peter demanded as soon as they were alone.

Tate turned to him, his lips still tinged blue, his face still too pale. "Are you kidding? Look what just happened here, man. *Your backup* hid and waited for your signal. Did you even see us out there?"

When Peter shook his head, Tate continued. "Yet somehow, Darcy knew. How do you think that happened?"

Anger heated him. He knew the rest of the team had already been thinking it. But he and Tate weren't just partners; they were friends. Tate should have trusted his judgment. "You're insinuating that Alanna tipped her off?"

Chance glanced from him to Tate, as if waiting for the reply, too.

Tate sighed, shaking his head. "She *stole* your truck. Why do you think she did that? Maybe she was trying to slow you down so you couldn't catch up to Darcy and she's mad you brought backup. Or she's been talking to Darcy from the start and she couldn't shake you, so she just brought you along and told Darcy what was going down."

Peter took an aggressive step forward and Chance, sitting between them, got to his feet, looking wary. The dog nudged his arm, as if telling him to calm down.

Peter absently pet Chance, trying to reassure him as he snapped at Tate, "Alanna didn't even know you'd be here. What happened to you thinking Alanna was genuine, that she was trying to help us?"

"Maybe she was," Tate replied, not looking at all threatened by Peter invading his personal space. "But maybe she had second thoughts. Let's be honest here. You cut her out by calling us in secretly. But that doesn't mean she didn't figure out what you were doing. Was she ever alone? Did she ever have a chance to warn Darcy before

you two came out here? She probably didn't expect Darcy
to shoot at us, but—"

"Alanna would *never* tip off Darcy. She'd never put
those kids in danger."

"Wouldn't they have been in less danger if she'd told
the police what she knew as soon as she found those locations? You have to admit it—she still loves Darcy. She's
still trying to protect her. What happened to *you* thinking
she had some warped loyalty to her kidnappers?"

"I got to know her," Peter said softly, backing up a step
as his shoulders slumped. If even Tate didn't believe in Alanna now, what would happen if they caught up to Darcy
and Alanna was with her?

Tate nodded, the anger on his face softening as he stared
at Peter. "You care about her." It was a statement rather
than a question. "But look around here. She took your
truck. She hasn't tried to contact you. She even left her
dog." He gestured to Chance, who whined and lay on the
snowy ground.

"She's not coming back."

CHANCE LOOKED UP from the spot he'd claimed on the floor
of the Desparre police station and gave a low whine.

They hadn't heard from Alanna in five hours and Peter
definitely wasn't the only one feeling anxious over it. He
leaned down and petted the St. Bernard to comfort him.

"He really shouldn't be in here," Chief Hernandez said,
but she sighed and petted him, too.

The chief couldn't be too stern with the dog who'd just
saved half her force from an avalanche. The same couldn't
be said of the way she was treating him. *Furious* was
an understatement. He wasn't sure if it was because he'd
tried to outpace them in the woods to reach Alanna first

or because of everything that had gone wrong the moment they'd driven up to that tiny cabin.

She straightened and peered over his shoulder at his computer. "Any luck?"

Since they'd returned to the station, he'd been trying to figure out the other locations Darcy might have gone. Last night, he'd given Alanna a tiny notebook to jot down whatever she could remember of the list she'd found at the cabin. She'd spent over an hour writing things down and crossing them out until she'd finally gone to bed. While she'd slept, he'd slipped into the guest room and snagged the notebook off the side table.

He'd tried not to look at her at all, feeling like he was invading her privacy, but he hadn't been able to stop himself. The sheets had been twisted beneath her, her long hair tangled around her face, her eyes moving rapidly underneath her eyelids as she dreamed. Was she reliving the avalanche, he'd wondered? Dreaming of her past? Or worrying about Darcy and those kids?

In that moment, he'd had the absurd desire to curl up with her and chase away her nightmares. Then Chance had walked over and Peter had realized the big dog had been watching him from the floor beside Alanna's bed. He'd given the dog a quick pet, told him everything was fine and gone into the other room to copy the contents of the notebook.

The mix of odd symbols, numbers and blank lines—where presumably Alanna had been trying to remember what she'd seen—hadn't meant much to him last night. They didn't mean much more now. She'd translated some of the code, but not enough.

He shook his head. "Sorry."

"Luna police haven't had a single sighting."

Apparently they'd been notified about what was happening less than five minutes after Peter had contacted Tate. It made sense; the cabin was in Luna PD's jurisdiction. But it still bothered him that so quickly after he'd called for backup, it seemed like everyone knew what was going on. It made him wonder if there was some other reason Darcy had been tipped off, like she'd spotted Luna patrols driving by too often before the Desparre team had arrived.

Still, once the Desparre officers had headed to the hospital after the avalanche, Luna's had swept in. Their PD had set up roadblocks to search for Darcy. Although no one had mentioned it to him, Peter suspected they'd been told to stop Alanna, too. He hadn't protested. He would have been happy if they'd held her, prevented her from catching up to Darcy on her own.

By now, Alanna was either still following Darcy in his truck or she'd lost her and was back to following the list of coordinates. Peter refused to consider the other possibility: that she'd caught up to Darcy and the woman had hurt her.

Peter stared down at the notes he'd taken from Alanna's room. The truth was, he had a couple of guesses, coordinates he'd worked out based on what she'd written. But that was all they were—guesses that could be dead-on or hundreds of miles off course.

His chief narrowed her eyes at him, like she knew what he was thinking and wanted the specifics anyway. Before he could admit he had some possibilities, she told him, "According to the hospital, all of the officers are okay. Most of them are heading back to the station now."

"*Most* of them?"

"They're hanging onto Tate a bit longer. His core body temperature was a little low when he came in and they don't want to take any chances."

Peter swore and Chance came over to drop his head onto

Peter's lap. Absently stroking the dog's fur, Peter realized how much Chance relaxed him, eased his worry over his partner and Alanna.

Chief Hernandez looked from him to the St. Bernard and back again. "Luna PD isn't too happy with how everything shook out today. I think they're wishing they'd said no to our request to handle it. They think it's time to put out a message to the public, enlist their help."

"Okay," Peter said slowly. "But I thought we were holding off on that in case it escalated things."

"It's been five hours," the chief reminded him. "Darcy got through our checkpoints, probably before we even had them up. If Alanna hasn't been in contact by now, she's not going to be."

"Maybe she can't. Her phone could have—"

"Peter." She said his name with a sigh and a tone of finality. "When Darcy fired into that mountain, Alanna made a choice. She *left* all those officers, including you."

"She went after the kids! She—"

"If she was on our side, we would have heard from her by now." Chief Hernandez put up a hand, as if to forestall the argument she knew was coming. "Maybe she's in trouble. Maybe she's already dead."

Chance whined and got to his feet. Peter's insides twisted until he felt himself hunch over from the pain of it.

"I'm sorry," the chief said. "You've gotten too close to this. At this point, we have to consider Alanna an accessory to kidnapping."

Peter jerked to a standing position, knocking his chair backward and making Chance step sideways out of the way. "She'd never actually *help* Darcy get away with those kids!" No matter how much he loved that woman, that would never happen.

"Peter, look around. Your partner is in the hospital and Alanna left her dog behind. She's gone."

"She's coming back. She'd never leave Chance. She hung on to him in an avalanche!"

"I'm sorry," Chief Hernandez repeated. "But it's time. We're going public with this and we're naming Alanna, too."

She gave him one last look, full of apology and residual anger and just a hint of distrust. Then she disappeared into her office and Peter sank back into his chair.

Chance promptly nuzzled up against him with so much force it pushed the chair backward, his whine a half growl, half cry.

"I know, boy," Peter whispered. "This is bad."

He stared at the chief's closed office door, then over at the few other officers in the station, who were studiously ignoring him. He blew out a long breath and stood. "Come on, boy."

Grabbing his coat, Peter strode for the door, trying not to run. Chance stayed right on his heels. With every step, he could feel the new career he'd fought so hard for slipping away.

But did he really have a choice? Alanna wasn't guilty. And he couldn't let her get hurt because she was trying to make amends for something that wasn't her fault.

It was time to break ranks. It was time to search for Alanna on his own.

Chapter Eleven

Maybe Darcy hadn't been as guilty as Alanna had feared.

Not that she was totally innocent. She'd escaped from law enforcement, fled across the country to hide. But for the first time, Alanna wondered if Darcy had been incorrectly blamed.

Had she really kidnapped those kids?

Alanna stared at the cell phone she'd been holding for the past ten minutes, at Peter's direct contact that he'd entered yesterday. She was sitting in his truck, the truck she'd *stolen*, with the engine running in a tiny back alley on the outskirts of Desparre as the sun began to set.

Five years ago, in the process of trying to find her, Kensie had run into trouble with a criminal. Alanna had first seen her in this alley, from the rearview window of a car as it drove away. For the second time in her life, she'd watched her big sister screaming for her, but in the alley, it had been Kensie who was in trouble. Until her sister had appeared at the cabin, Alanna had thought Kensie had been killed here. Things had turned out okay then, but would they now?

Her phone had rung repeatedly for the past five hours, Peter's name lighting up on her screen. When the first call came in, she'd been on Darcy's tail, too scared to take her eyes off the vehicle for a second. She'd caught up to it a few miles away from the cabin. She hadn't actually been able to see Darcy inside it, but the way the vehicle was speeding, taking corners much too fast, who else could it be?

An hour later, after she'd lost the vehicle—at that point not even sure it was Darcy she'd been chasing—she'd thought about calling Peter. But she hadn't been ready to admit defeat yet. And she'd been terrified to learn what happened to the officers who'd been buried under that avalanche.

When the snow had first started rushing down that mountainside, she'd considered staying for about ten seconds. Peter had already been running toward it, Chance outpacing him. She'd known Chance would be better help digging people out than she would. Darcy had been right in front of her, running back into the cabin, ready to grab those kids and make them disappear again. At least, that was what she'd thought.

Alanna had felt like she was those kids' only shot. She couldn't let Darcy take them again.

Now here she was. Alone. No Darcy. No kids. Afraid to learn what had happened at that cabin.

Setting the phone next to her, Alanna flipped on the radio to a local station. Would this debacle have made the news?

"...officers are doing fine," the host was saying and Alanna relaxed against her seat, grabbing her phone to call Peter, to check on Chance and apologize for all of it. Tell Peter what she'd discovered.

She'd been so sure she could talk some sense into Darcy. Of course, maybe she would have been able to if there hadn't been officers hiding in the woods, signaling to Darcy that Alanna had already betrayed her.

She couldn't totally trust Peter. Not even now, after they'd seemed to connect on such a personal level back at his house. The realization hurt. A lot. But it wasn't the most important thing right now.

Alaska wasn't her home anymore. Soon enough, she'd be back in Chicago, Peter a distant memory. Right now, though, she needed his help. Maybe if she was lucky, if she was right, he could help her prove that Darcy wasn't a kidnapper at all. At least not anymore.

"Be on the lookout for escaped convict Darcy Altier," the radio host continued. "If you see her, contact police immediately. She is armed and dangerous. Police are also looking for her accomplice, Alanna Morgan. In case you don't remember the name, Alanna was one of five children kidnapped by Darcy Altier and her husband nearly twenty years ago. She—"

Alanna flipped the radio off, dropping her phone. The police had named her as an *accomplice*? After she'd told them where to find Darcy? After she'd run into that cabin, trying to rescue those kids, all without any police help?

And after what she'd found…

Darcy had been running out the back door. Alone.

At first, Alanna had thought she'd lucked out. That Darcy had decided to run and leave the kids behind, avoid putting them in the middle of a standoff.

But a quick search of the one-room cabin had shown Alanna that wasn't the case. Darcy didn't *have* the kids. Maybe she'd never had the kids.

Unfortunately, kidnappings happened all the time. An escaped convict—especially one who'd been in jail for a series of kidnappings—in close enough proximity to a new case would be an obvious suspect. Then, when another kid went missing in a part of Canada that was along a potential route Darcy could take to return to Desparre? Maybe that had been enough to cinch the investigation and Darcy had been innocent all along. This time, anyway.

Alanna would never know unless she found her. It was more obvious than ever that she couldn't trust the police, couldn't trust Peter.

She needed to do this alone.

"IT's BETTER TO ask forgiveness than permission, right, boy?" Peter asked Chance as he sped them along the icy back streets of Desparre.

Chance's head swiveled in the passenger seat and the look in his eyes suggested he had doubts.

Since Alanna had his truck, Peter had taken his police vehicle. He wasn't sure how long he had before the chief noticed his absence and grew suspicious. Before she called him up and demanded he return to the station. Before he faced serious trouble for ignoring her orders.

Of course, she could track the police vehicle, too, have his fellow officers chase him down. But Peter hadn't had time to find something else. At this point, he was looking at insubordination at best, aiding and abetting a fugitive at worst. What was one borrowed police vehicle in comparison?

Even if he could get away without any charges being brought against him, he was probably finished in Desparre. He'd gotten the job because the department was desperate. Dozens of other applications around the state—even the country—had shown him how fast most police stations would eliminate him without an interview because of his hearing loss.

Unless there was drastic change, his career as a police officer was over. The idea made him nauseous.

Police academy had been brutal. He'd thought he was in good shape before he started, but he'd discovered that traipsing alongside soldiers in war zones hadn't prepared him for the full physicality of chasing suspects for long stretches. It hadn't prepared him for actually carrying his own weapon and learning not to flinch at the sound of it firing, which was just a little too similar to the *boom* of the explosion that had changed his life. It hadn't prepared him for all the small adaptations he had to make just to be sure his bad ear didn't put him or his fellow officers at increased risk.

He'd stuck it out, through the bruises and the flashbacks. He'd even worked through the bullying from an instructor who didn't approve of Desparre PD bending their applicant rules to get another recruit willing to live in their remote town. The guy thought Desparre PD was unnecessarily endangering him—and that Peter could endanger his future colleagues by not being up to the job.

He'd worked hard to be a good officer, to make sure his disability didn't impact his effectiveness. The day he'd graduated from the academy and gotten the official go-ahead to become a Desparre PD rookie, he'd felt a sense of accomplishment and joy headier than his first assignment as a war reporter.

Today he was throwing it all away.

Still, he didn't turn around. No way could he just follow orders when those orders were putting Alanna at risk. No, the only shot he had at saving the career he'd grown to love so much was to bring in Darcy and save those kids.

At least he had an idea where to start. Sure, it was an idea based half on coordinates Alanna had decoded from her memory of the symbols she'd seen, half on guesswork. He had filled in the blanks, considering what else made sense based on the numbers she had and satellite images of the area. But guesswork was better than nothing. It was better than sitting in that station, waiting to hear that police officers in some other town had surrounded Darcy and Alanna. That they'd considered both women dangerous and were willing to sacrifice them in order to save two kidnapped children. That they'd shot first, asked questions later.

The very idea of anyone training a weapon on Alanna made him punch down harder on the gas. The first location he'd worked out wasn't nearby. It was in the total opposite direction of the cabin in Luna, in a town even tinier than Desparre. A place that didn't even have their own police force. It seemed like the best option for his quarry.

After all, there was no way to know how long he could run these leads alone before his fellow officers surrounded his car and demanded he stand down. Demanded he hand over his weapon and his badge.

As if sensing his thoughts, Chance let out a sudden *woof* that startled Peter into jerking the wheel. Chance was jolted in the seat and Peter righted the car on the slippery ice. "I know, boy. You're my backup today."

Alanna had told him how the St. Bernard had been rescued from a cruel owner as a puppy, how she'd gotten him certified as a therapy dog so she could bring him with her to work. It was as much to help her own anxiety as it was to help the trauma survivors she worked with, she'd said. Chance had known exactly when to comfort him at the police station, even when to support Tate out in the cold by the cabin; it was clear he was a damn good therapy dog. And given the way he'd raced into action during the avalanche, he probably would have made a good police dog, too.

"We'll find her," Peter told him, hoping it was true.

Chance whined softly, turning his attention out the front windshield. The dog seemed as desperate to find Alanna as Peter.

And he *was* desperate. There was no other word for it. Four days ago, he would have scoffed at the idea that he could come to trust Alanna Morgan, let alone that he would care for her so much. But at his house, they'd connected. It had lifted a weight off him to be able to open up about his past. And he'd come to admire her fortitude after everything she'd experienced. If she lived in Alaska, if she wasn't part of an ongoing case, he'd already be pursuing her romantically. The idea felt ridiculous and yet it made him yearn for something he hadn't realized was missing from his life.

Maybe it wasn't Alanna. Maybe it was just time for him to think about finding someone to settle down with, like all his older siblings. Have some kids, make a real home. Take down those pictures from war zones on his walls and move forward. Except how could he do that if he didn't even have a job?

He shook off the worries he couldn't be distracted by right now and slowed as he approached the coordinates he'd mapped out. He'd looked up the location online, zoomed in and seen what might have been a cabin. Perhaps it was a hiding spot for a desperate couple who'd known one day their crimes could catch up to them. Who'd suspected they would eventually be on the run again.

Adrenaline shot through him as he drove slowly past. It was hard to tell now that the sun was down, but up close, he realized there *was* a cabin. Tiny and tucked away from the street behind more woods, it looked a lot like the place in Luna from this afternoon. It was a well-built log cabin, similar in style to the house where the Altiers had lived in Desparre, the one they'd built by hand. Could Julian have built this place himself, too? Peter could see light through the windows.

This time he didn't slow down, didn't pull into the driveway. He drove right past and parked down the road where his vehicle wouldn't be visible from the cabin.

For one crazy second, he considered calling for backup. But even though he and Tate had developed a strong friendship outside of work, he couldn't ask his friend to risk his career. Besides, Peter didn't even know if Tate was out of the hospital yet. And there was no one else he'd trust to protect Alanna no matter what they saw, no matter what happened.

"It's you and me, boy," he told Chance, his breath puffing in front of him as he stepped out of the vehicle. His boots broke through a top layer of ice with a noisy crunch, then sank down into more than a foot of snow beneath. He hoped he wasn't making a mistake letting the dog come, but he couldn't just leave him in the SUV, hidden out here in the woods. What would happen if Peter was killed and no one knew he was here?

Chance leaped out of the vehicle, sticking close and moving silently. His big body was hunched over, the fur on his back raised, like he was stalking something. Like he knew exactly what they were doing and he, too, was willing to risk everything for Alanna.

"Be careful," Peter whispered, simultaneously hoping that the dog understood and that Darcy wouldn't hurt Alanna's pet.

Chance glanced at him once, then looked back toward the cabin. The dog was focused and slinking forward as if he knew Alanna was in there.

Hoping he was right, Peter unholstered his pistol and crept slowly along beside Chance, toward the home. He moved from the cover of one tree to the next, cursing the wind that whistled past his ears as it limited his hearing even further. The snow was deeper here than it had been in Luna and the damp cold seeping through his jeans above the tops of his boots made him shiver. But at least the icy top layer was more melted here, his boots making a quieter *crunch* each time they broke through.

A shadow moved behind the curtains in one of the windows and Peter's pulse jumped. It didn't mean he'd found them, but *someone* was home.

He scanned the area and spotted something on the far side of the cabin, a brief reflection of light in the moonlight. Squinting at it, he realized with a start that it was his truck. Alanna was here.

Creeping closer, he reached the edge of the woods, then made a run for the side of the cabin, staying in a crouch. Chance raced along beside him, reaching the cabin first. But he waited for Peter, giving him a look that seemed to ask, *What's the plan?*

Flattening himself against the side of the cabin, Peter peered at the window, hoping for a gap in the curtains. There was nothing to see, so he tapped his thigh for Chance to follow and slunk to the back of the dwelling. He wasn't worried about Chance barking. The dog was well-trained and seemed to sense the need to stay silent.

The windows here were the same, but just like the last cabin, there was a back door. For a building this small, it didn't really need more than one entrance. Unless someone needed an easy escape route.

Peter tested the handle, expecting it to be locked. But it moved under his hand and he froze, hoping no one inside had seen it. For a moment, indecision gripped him, made all his muscles tense. Then he eased the door slowly open, angling his weapon so he could lead with it.

Though it probably wouldn't help; doorways were one of the most dangerous places for police officers. You didn't know what was on the other side, and the only way to find out if someone was standing there waiting with their own weapon drawn was to open the door and go inside.

He'd trained for this, Peter reminded himself. Sure, if he was here officially, he'd have a partner. But someone would still have to go through first. In police academy, you learned a simple series of steps to get you inside and out of a doorway as fast as possible. You learned the exact sequence your gun hand and your attention should move to eliminate any threats before they could eliminate you. Still, none of that changed the fact that dying as you came through a doorway was far too common for police officers.

He weighed calling out "police," but thought it too risky. If Darcy was holding Alanna and the children, he could put them in jeopardy by alerting her to his presence.

He glanced sideways at Chance, who was waiting in a crouched stance as if he planned to bound in after Peter, and held up a hand, telling the dog to wait. Then he steadied his gun hand, ignored the senses-dimming staccato of his heartbeat and pushed the door wide.

The tiny kitchen he stepped into was empty, but beyond an open doorway, he could hear voices. One of them belonged to Alanna.

"I *believed* in you," she was saying, the hurt palpable in her words. "After all this time, I really thought that if I could just talk to you, make you understand, that you'd—"

"What?" Darcy interrupted, the volume of her own anger and hurt dwarfing Alanna's. "Turn myself in? Go back to jail? *Die there*, like your father did?"

"That's the thing," Alanna said, her tone sad but strong. "As much as you wanted to be, as much as I loved you both, you weren't my parents. And—"

Darcy made a sound that was half furious screech, half wounded cry.

This wasn't going anywhere good. Peter darted around the doorway, handgun raised, hoping to find Darcy distracted and across the room from Alanna.

Before he'd fully entered the room, though, Darcy spun toward him, her own pistol raised.

"You shouldn't have come here," Darcy spat.

Peter aimed his gun at her head—instead of her center mass, like he'd been taught. He did a quick visual sweep—Alanna across the room, unarmed, her hands up in the air as if she'd been trying to calm Darcy down. But Alanna wasn't his problem right now.

It was the little boy on the floor, clutching Darcy's leg and staring at him wide-eyed. It was the little girl held in the crook of Darcy's arm, silent tears running down her face as Darcy used her as a human shield.

Chapter Twelve

"Please, just put the gun down," Alanna begged.

"Him again!" Darcy snapped. "What happened to all your promises that it was just the two of us talking? It's always lies with you, isn't it?"

Alanna swallowed the desire to snap back, to argue about who was lying to who. She'd never seen Darcy like this. All her life, Darcy had been full of smiles and ideas and plans she couldn't always see through. She was flighty and occasionally depressed, but she was always patient with the kids she'd called hers.

When Alanna had entered the second cabin in Luna, she'd been amazed. She'd thought it was a sign that things were about to go right. That even though Darcy had escaped from prison, she hadn't returned to kidnapping. That there was a chance to end it all peacefully.

She'd been so wrong.

Maybe Julian's death had unhinged Darcy. Or maybe Alanna had only seen what she'd wanted to see all those years she'd lived with her. Maybe Peter had been right and she'd been brainwashed by a pair of kidnappers.

"She didn't know I was coming," Peter said, his voice calm and soft as Chance walked slowly into the cabin behind him and came to a stop at his side.

The dog's gaze moved from Alanna to the kids, then back to Peter, as if awaiting instructions.

Tension knotted tighter in Alanna's chest. How had Peter found them? Why would he bring Chance into this?

She tried to tell him with her eyes to stay out of it, to let her try to reach Darcy. Her gaze darted to the kids, the small girl in Darcy's arms with dark, curly hair that reminded Alanna so much of herself as a child. The little boy clutching Darcy's leg with the deep brown eyes and the short dark hair. Both of them could have easily passed as Altiers.

"Do you know how much I miss you?" Darcy asked, her voice breaking as Alanna's gaze returned to hers. "Do you know how much I miss all of you? Do you know what it was like to have my kids ripped away from me?"

"I'm—" Alanna started.

"Do you know how badly it hurt to know it was *you* who set it all in motion? What it feels like to have you tell me I'm not your mom?" She let out a humorless laugh. "I know I'm not your mom. Not legally. I…" She shook her head, staring through Alanna now, her brow furrowed like she was peering into the past.

"I could never have kids," Darcy admitted softly. She tipped her head against the child in her arms and the little girl hugged her neck.

She obviously felt safe with Darcy, despite everything. It was what Alanna had felt right from the start, too. Irrational, maybe, but she'd instinctively known she was loved.

A surge of hope hit, a gut feeling that she could still reach Darcy, still talk her into ending this peacefully. Because no matter what else might have changed, the Darcy she'd known for fourteen years was still in there. A Darcy who would never hurt kids she'd decided were hers. But

Peter... If Darcy thought he was a threat, she'd fire at him the way she'd shot at Kensie all those years ago.

She hadn't done it when she could have at the cabin in Luna, a tiny voice whispered in the back of her mind. It was a voice Alanna couldn't trust, a voice that had been born from her past life. Still, it was a past life where Darcy had raised her to be strong, had hugged her every night before bed, had greeted her every morning with love.

"I'm sorry," Alanna said.

"My family never understood me," Darcy continued, not seeming to notice Peter as he shifted just slightly to angle his good ear toward her. His weapon, too.

Chance moved too, surprisingly stealthy for such a big dog, sticking to Peter's side as if they were a team with a shared plan.

Praying that Peter would just wait, that Chance wouldn't think she was in trouble and try coming to her rescue, Alanna nodded encouragingly at Darcy. She'd never met anyone from Darcy or Julian's families. When she was younger, it hadn't occurred to her to wonder why. When she was older, she'd assumed it was because of the kidnappings, because of the Altiers' constant reminders that it was the seven of them against the world. But maybe they'd been estranged long before that.

"They were all overachievers, every one of them. They couldn't stand failure," Darcy said. "Me? I had so much trouble learning. But Julian always accepted me just as I was. When we got married, I wanted our life to be so different from the way I'd grown up. We always talked about having a big family, raising them differently. So when we couldn't have kids, I was devastated. We tried to adopt. A little boy, the age Johnny would have been then. It was such a long process and we finally got to the end of it. He was supposed to come home with us over the weekend. Then that Friday, the adoption fell through. He went back to his biological family. They were drug addicts, in and out of rehab, in and out of prison, but somehow they convinced a judge they should get one more chance to be parents."

The sadness and loss on her face shifted to anger. "Four weeks later, he was dead. Killed in a house fire his parents had set while they were high. And we just couldn't do it. We couldn't go through it again. We gave up on adoption."

"So you took Johnny?" Alanna recalled what she'd read about his abduction in the papers years later. "From the park when his mom was distracted, right?"

"She wasn't even watching him," Darcy said, a new light in her eyes, the spark of a past joy. "Julian said it had been easy to pick him off the swings and bring him home to me. Johnny didn't even cry. It was like he wanted to come to us, like it was meant to be. But afterward…" She frowned, shook her head, glanced at Peter.

Her eyes narrowed and Alanna was sure she'd noticed that Peter was just slightly closer, that Chance was edging closer, too. "Afterward?" Alanna pressed.

"It was such a mix of emotions," Darcy said, happiness back in her eyes. "Probably what it feels like right after you've given birth to a child. Elation like you've never felt, but fear, too. Almost terror, really. And the guilt…" She leaned into the little girl she held and her gun hand, still aimed at Peter, shook a little.

She'd always known it was wrong. Alanna had wondered for years whether Darcy and Julian had felt any regret for taking her and her "siblings." If Darcy had felt guilty then, surely the guilt was intensified now, knowing that the kids who'd gone home to their families had missed them for years.

If she had any regret, felt any guilt, then Alanna could

still reach her. She took a step forward, her hand out toward Darcy.

"A few years later, when we saw you…"

Alanna froze and her heart seemed to contract. It was a moment she remembered so distinctly and yet she'd never known how they'd picked her, or why.

"The first time I saw you, I just *knew*. You looked so much like I did as a child, but it was more than that. I just felt it, deep inside, that you were meant to be my daughter." Her eyes glassed over with unshed tears. "I still feel that, Alanna."

Alanna took another step closer until she could almost touch Darcy, almost reach out and push the gun down. "In some ways, I'll always be your daughter." The words were shaky with emotion, because they were true.

The smile Alanna had seen every day of her childhood blossomed on Darcy's face and the woman's rigid arm loosened, the gun angling downward, away from Peter.

Alanna slid forward just a tiny bit more. "But the Morgans weren't drug addicts. They loved me. They spent so many years searching for me. They were even called into more than one morgue for identifications that turned out not to be me."

The smile slid from Darcy's face. Alanna could see the guilt there as her "mom" glanced down at the little boy still hugging tightly to her leg.

"My older sister almost died trying to find me. My older brother turned to drugs and alcohol and anything else he could find because losing me tore my family apart. They didn't deserve that," Alanna said, sliding forward again. Just one more step…

"I know," Darcy whispered.

Hope erupted inside Alanna, a happiness that she hadn't been wrong about Darcy; that even though the woman had kidnapped her, there was still good in her, still reasons why Alanna had grown to love her.

Darcy was still a criminal. Once she returned to jail, Alanna would have to consider whether to see her again. She'd stolen the childhood Alanna had been meant to have. And yet, that fact didn't erase the fourteen years of love, the happy childhood Darcy and Julian *had* given her. It didn't change the fact that even though Alanna had gone home to the Morgans, even though she didn't regret it, she still loved Darcy, too.

Maybe that was something Alanna needed to stop feeling guilty about.

"You have to let these kids go," Alanna said.

Darcy's face immediately shuttered, the hand holding the gun shaking.

Alanna stepped closer, put her hand on the top of the pistol and said, "You know it's the right thing to do. Please."

The weapon shook violently underneath Alanna's hand, the fight happening within Darcy written all over her face. Then her shoulders slumped and Alanna smiled gently, knowing she'd won.

The sudden grumble of an old car engine from somewhere nearby startled her, made Chance let out a soft *woof.*

In an instant, the indecision on Darcy's face was gone, replaced by an angry determination as she took a fast step backward. The little boy stumbled along with her, the little girl lifting her head as Darcy stiffened her arm and leveled her gun on Peter.

"Don't," Peter warned softly. "I'm a trained police officer. My aim is better than yours."

Betrayal flashed across Darcy's face, but she didn't glance Alanna's way this time. Instead she stared directly at Peter, the guilt in her voice shifting to anger. "You want to find out? You're a bigger target than I am. At this distance, I could be a terrible shot and still kill you. You want to risk being slightly off your mark and hitting my girl?"

Chance let out a low growl, took a slow step forward with his front paw.

Alanna held up a hand and he froze. She didn't dare look at Peter.

She had no idea what Peter's training was like, how accurate a shot he was. She doubted he'd fire unless he had to with the little girl in Darcy's arms.

But five years ago, Darcy had fired at Kensie. And she hadn't aimed to wound.

Darcy's head tipped back slightly, her lips tightening as if she'd made a decision, and panic took hold of Alanna.

She leaped in between them, spreading her arms wide.

"Alanna!" Peter yelled, a mix of anger and fear in his voice as he shifted sideways and she moved with him. "Get out of the way!"

Alanna didn't take her gaze off of Darcy.

A ghost of a smile lifted one corner of Darcy's mouth, a sad understanding look in her eyes, before she spun and escaped out the front door with the little girl.

"CHANCE, STAY!" ALANNA yelled as she practically body-slammed Peter.

Peter slid his finger off the trigger, bracing himself to absorb her weight so he wouldn't get knocked to the ground. "What are you doing? She's getting away!"

"She could kill you!" The panic in Alanna's voice was unmistakable, the desperation clear in the surprising strength of her grip as she wrapped her arms around his waist and hung on.

He swore, angling his gun away from her as he tried to push her away with his free hand. Alanna was a lot stronger than she looked, with lean muscle in her arms and legs and a good knowledge of leverage that she used to her advantage.

He glanced at the closed door. "If she gets away now, how will we find her? She's got a child!"

"Darcy won't hurt her, but she'll hurt you," Alanna said, her fingers digging into him, her desperation dangerous.

He didn't want to hurt Alanna. But the cough and sputter of a car's engine followed by the squeal of tires made him swear. "I'm sorry," he said, and twisted her arm as if he was going to push her to the ground and arrest her. The move broke her grip on him, prevented her from twisting back. Then he pushed her away and darted for the door, hoping he wasn't too late to stop Darcy.

Alanna ran after him and he spun back, holding his pistol away from his body, afraid it would accidentally fire as she grappled him. But she wasn't coming for him this time.

She reached for the little boy Darcy had left behind, who'd been crying since the melee had started and now ran toward the door, too, to follow the woman who'd kidnapped him.

Chance got there first, blocking the boy's way and plopping onto the floor. He knocked the boy down with him, but instead of crying harder, the little boy wrapped his arms around the big dog and buried his head in Chance's fur.

Alanna sighed, then looked up at Peter, fear and regret in her eyes.

She had to know he wouldn't hurt Darcy unless there was no other choice, didn't she? He wanted to reassure her that everything would be okay, but it wasn't a promise he could make, so he just broke eye contact and took off out the door.

The yard seemed empty, moonlight filtering through the towering trees and iced-over snow. But there were a lot of places to hide and no guarantee the engine he'd heard was actually Darcy's. Would she have been able to get into a vehicle that fast? He hadn't seen any other vehicles except his own truck when he'd arrived. The trees here were thick; there probably wasn't enough space to hide a vehicle except close to the road.

His heart thudded too fast as he tried to focus on any sound that didn't belong, any movement in his peripheral vision. But the woods were too dark, the diminished hearing in his left ear made worse by the stress of knowing Darcy could be hunkered down behind a nearby tree, taking careful aim at him.

A crunch that could have been someone stepping through the icy snow made him swivel his head right, toward the direction of his parked police vehicle. He squinted through the darkness, trying to spot any movement, then a quiet *snap* from the left made his head swivel. Animals? Darcy sneaking up on him, ready to eliminate the only other person with a weapon?

If he was shot in these woods, what would Alanna do? Rush out and try to help him while Darcy took aim at her, took her revenge for Alanna's betrayal, and then disappeared with both kids?

Furious to be in this position, Peter backed slowly toward the cabin, slipping inside. He shut the door, holstered his weapon and pulled out his phone.

"What happened?" Alanna demanded from where she was crouched on the floor, her arms around both Chance and the little boy.

"I can't see anything. Do you know where she parked?"

Alanna shook her head. "I didn't see a vehicle."

He pulled Chief Hernandez up on his phone, but Alanna was by his side, gripping his arm, before he could hit Call.

"What are you doing?" She sounded panicked, like she was still thinking with emotion instead of logic.

For a few brief moments, he'd thought her raw emotion and honesty were what would change Darcy's mind and end this whole thing peacefully. But that time had passed. Now they needed logic. And manpower.

He pulled his hand free and did the thing he should have done from the start. "We need backup."

When Chief Hernandez answered the phone, he gave her a quick rundown of their location and status, then turned back to Alanna.

She was staring wide-eyed at him, the shock on her face mixed with grief.

Knowing she'd just lost a piece of her childhood, he squeezed her hand gently as he told her, "Lock the door behind me. Stay here with the boy and Chance."

Chance stood at his name, took a step toward Peter, then looked at the closed door. As if he was ready to run out with Peter or stand between a threat and Alanna.

"Good boy, Chance," he said, then looked sternly at Alanna. "Don't let anyone in except the Desparre PD."

He didn't mention that they considered her an accomplice and might arrest her when they arrived. He and Alanna would have to deal with that if it happened. Instead, he let go of her hand and turned for the door when her fingers latched onto his arm again. When he turned back, there was regret on her face.

"Back at the other cabin, when I chased after her, I was so sure I could catch her. I thought if it was just the two of us, I could talk her down."

"I know," Peter said, peeling her fingers away. He pulled out his weapon again, glancing at her before he moved to slip out the door. The pink flush of emotion across her pale cheeks and the sadness in her dark eyes were a split-second image he knew would stick with him long after she was gone.

He'd risked his career for her. Risked his life for her. He had no regrets about that, but he'd still been wrong tonight.

If he'd let his team in on what he was doing, he would have had backup right now. There would have been a team waiting outside the cabin, ready to surround Darcy and talk her down, or follow at a distance until they could bring in reinforcements to take her out and protect the little girl.

Instead, Darcy was gone again. He and Alanna had the boy, but what about the little girl?

Peter forced himself not to look back at Alanna, at the sorrow and regret in her eyes. He closed the door behind him, his eyes slowly adjusting to the darkness. He hoped it wasn't already too late, but his gut told him it was.

He'd sacrificed his job thinking he was doing the right thing for everyone, Alanna in particular. But had his mistake just cost a little girl the chance to grow up with her real family?

Chapter Thirteen

The subtle *clack clack clack* of metal against metal echoed through the woods and Peter froze, his arms tense as they supported his pistol. The noise was coming from his right, in the direction of where he'd parked.

In an instant, he realized what it was. The sound of someone trying to open the door to his police SUV. He didn't pause to wonder why Darcy would be trying to get into his vehicle instead of racing for her own. He just started running.

The deeper he went into the woods, the icier the top layer of snow got, crunching as he set each foot down, trying to suck his boots off as he lifted them back up. His breath puffed out in front of him in frigid blasts of air, his lungs feeling every degree that had dropped in the past few hours, every moment he'd spent earlier today digging his friends out of the snow.

As he got closer to the SUV, he slowed, knowing his heavy footsteps in the snow were telegraphing his approach. He couldn't hear Darcy anymore. But was it because she'd gone silent, listening to his approach and trying to line him up in her sights in the darkness? Or just because his hearing wasn't good enough to make out the soft noise of her slinking away over his own footsteps?

He ducked against the shelter of a big tree trunk just

before the *boom* of a gun rang out. The muzzle flash told him she was standing behind his vehicle, using it as cover.

His heart thumped at the near miss, then with a realization. Darcy had run the wrong way out of the cabin. Unless he'd totally missed it, there was no other vehicle out this way. She must have left her car in the other direction. To get to it, she'd have to slip past him. Instead of taking the risk, she'd tried to take his vehicle.

He didn't need to rush her now, try to get close through the threat of more bullets. He just needed to pin her there, prevent her from flanking him and returning to her own vehicle. Then he could wait her out, because the rest of his team was on their way. With sirens and lights, they should arrive in less than ten minutes.

Sliding farther behind the tree trunk, Peter squeezed his eyes shut and focused on his hearing. He angled his good ear toward the vehicle, straining to hear any sound that would indicate Darcy was on the move. But he heard nothing.

The muzzle flash had left a temporary mark on his retinas and he waited, listening, until it went away. Then he opened his eyes again and shapes that had been indistinct before became identifiable. A stray branch, broken and dangling from the tree in front of him. Holes in the snow, distinctly paw-shaped, where Chance had stalked alongside him on the way to the cabin. Bigger holes where his boots had broken through in his frantic rush to get to Alanna.

Peter leaned slightly around the edge of the tree, leading with his gun, because if his eyes had started to adjust to the darkness, surely Darcy's had, too.

There was nothing. No top of her head peeking over the vehicle, no outstretched hand clutching a pistol, shifting to take aim. No crying little girl, cold and afraid.

A curse formed on his lips as he turned his head, angling his right side the other way to listen for Darcy. Had she given up on her vehicle to head deeper into the woods? Or maybe she had just kept going past his car and to the road, hoping to hitch a ride from someone who didn't recognize her? Was she able to move through the snow more quietly than he could, his hearing loss too great to detect her?

He didn't hear her. But suddenly, he heard sirens, approaching fast.

Then Darcy was racing away from his vehicle, desperation in the extended length of her strides, in the way the child was clutched in her arms.

She held the girl tight with both hands, Peter realized. It meant she didn't have a hand free to aim and fire.

He moved away from the protection of the tree to pursue her. He was taller than her, with longer strides, and he was quickly closing the gap between them. But he couldn't fire without risking the girl, so he holstered his gun.

Darcy glanced back, saw him gaining and put on a new burst of speed.

It wasn't going to be enough, though, and she must have known it, because she halted suddenly, spinning toward him, her arms shifting to juggle the girl and pull her gun.

He leaped toward her, going for her gun hand. He grabbed it before her finger could slip under the trigger guard and then he was tossing the weapon aside, twisting her arm up and back.

She yelped and the girl, still caught in her other arm, started to cry.

"Hand her over," Peter demanded. Then the sirens were suddenly on top of them, the flashing blue and red lights sweeping over Darcy's face and illuminating the tears there, too.

Chief Hernandez and Tate were running through the

woods to meet them, weapons out. Peter felt a wash of relief to see his partner had been discharged from the hospital.

"She's unarmed," he yelled, even though as he said it, he realized he couldn't be sure she didn't have another weapon on her.

Still, he had a hard grip on her arm, had it twisted at such an angle that there was no way for her to move it without causing a break. If she wanted to go for a weapon, she'd have to drop the child. Staring at her now, at her tear-filled eyes, wide and panicked, he knew she wouldn't do it. Because even as she shook her head at the approaching cops, she made soothing *shh* noises under her breath to the child, slightly rocking her. Trying to comfort her.

"Hand her over," Peter repeated, softer this time, as the chief stepped forward, holstering her weapon and holding out her arms. "It will be okay. We'll take care of her. I promise."

Then he heard the crunching of ice behind him, the sound of someone dashing toward them.

Tate shifted his weapon up and over, then returned his aim to Darcy.

Peter glanced over his shoulder and cursed as he saw that it was Alanna. Chance and the boy weren't with her, which meant she'd left them in the cabin. She'd probably heard the sirens, heard him yell to his teammates that Darcy wasn't armed anymore.

Darcy's gaze locked on Alanna and guilt flashed across her face before she dipped her head. Then her shoulders slumped. She stretched her arm with the girl in it toward Chief Hernandez.

The girl clung to Darcy's neck and Chief Hernandez peeled her arms free, tried to soothe her as she cried. The chief stepped backward, unzipping her coat and tucking the child into it as she nodded at Peter.

He grabbed Darcy's other hand and handcuffed her. Then he pushed her against a tree trunk and moved her legs slightly apart with his foot so he could pat her down for additional weapons. "I tossed a pistol that way," he told Tate, gesturing with the jerk of his head the area where he'd knocked it away from Darcy.

Alanna reached them just as he'd confirmed Darcy didn't have any other weapons on her. Alanna was panting from exertion, her gaze darting to Tate, to the pistol he still held as he swept the discarded one out of the snow, and tucked it into his belt.

Peter's partner didn't train his weapon at Alanna, but as he straightened, he locked eyes with her, ready to take action if she rushed to help Darcy.

"She's no threat," Peter told Tate, hoping it was true. "The boy is in the cabin with Chance."

His partner gave him a tense nod.

Peter had definitely destroyed some trust tonight.

"Why did you run?" Alanna demanded, her focus entirely on Darcy. She stepped forward, getting too close, and Peter forced Darcy backward, toward the police car.

Tate holstered his gun and stepped in front of her, preventing Alanna from getting any closer to Darcy.

Chief Hernandez told Peter, "Put Darcy in my vehicle. You'll bring the kids back to the station. Take Tate with you." Her words were clipped and angry, telling Peter there was a reckoning to come.

Peter nodded and pushed Darcy toward the open door of the police vehicle at the edge of the road.

Alanna's voice trailed after them, gaining volume as she demanded over and over, *"Why? Why? Why?"*

Darcy didn't respond, didn't look back once as Peter put her in the SUV and slammed the door shut.

Then he turned back to the scene behind him. He took

in Chief Hernandez smoothing her hand over the girl's hair, whispering quiet words as the girl stared up at her, her tears slowly drying. His gaze skipped to his partner next. Tate stood in front of Alanna, feet braced hip-width apart as if he expected he'd need to forcibly stop her from chasing after them. And then there was Alanna herself, frozen in place, her lips still parted from her last screamed question. The pain on her face was hard to see, but at least their chase was over.

Her methods might not have been ideal, but she'd helped them find Darcy. Ultimately, she was the reason they'd been able to rescue these kids. Without her knowledge of Darcy and how to decode symbols that had looked like nonsense to whoever had gone through the Altiers' home years ago, they never would have found this place.

The kids would be reunited with their families now. Alanna could go home to the family who'd waited so long for her return.

It was where she belonged. Back in Chicago, a town he'd never visited, never wanted to.

He belonged in Desparre, fighting for a job that had given him back his passion. For a team he'd grown to respect, a partnership that had become a friendship. A calling that spoke to him even more than being a reporter. A job that now might be beyond saving.

He hadn't even known Alanna for a full week and they'd spent most of that time at odds. He'd broken her trust by calling in his team at the cabin in Luna. She'd broken his by going after Darcy alone after the woman had caused an avalanche. But he had the sense that Alanna understood his actions, as he did hers. After everything they'd been through, he felt a connection to her that was undeniable.

It had been fast, and yet, he couldn't imagine her leaving. Couldn't imagine losing something he'd only just begun to realize he wanted in his life.

Chapter Fourteen

Alanna drove slowly through downtown Desparre, taking in the snow-lined streets bracketed by a handful of buildings, looking like a postcard for peace and solitude. She was in a new rental car; her forgiving rental company had apparently lost other vehicles to avalanches. And yes, maybe they'd also been angling for juicy details of the new kidnappings from the mouth of someone whose involvement was still a mystery.

The police had given a statement to the press first thing this morning. Alanna had watched it in the darkness of her hotel room after a fitful night of sleeplessness. They'd announced Darcy's arrest and the rescue of the kids. When reporters demanded to know whether Alanna was still at large, the police chief had briskly shared that Alanna was no longer a person of interest, that she hadn't been involved in the kidnappings. Then she'd left the podium, ignoring the reporters' follow-up questions.

Technically, Alanna had been cleared of any wrongdoing. But she knew how this worked. The lack of details meant reporters would be clamoring to talk to her again. They'd start showing up on her doorstep, using creative methods to get into her building, asking invasive questions about her life and her emotions.

After watching the press conference, it had taken another hour for Alanna to get up the courage to leave the hotel and drive into town. But she wanted to see Desparre once more before she went home. She needed to make one stop before she drove to the airport and left Alaska behind, probably for good.

When she'd lived in Desparre, she'd only seen the downtown's main street from the back seat of a car. The Altiers had deemed it too risky to let her or her "siblings" walk around the more populated parts of Desparre, even if "more populated" meant seeing a dozen people.

The small town was beautiful, comforting. It was similar to the smaller section of streets nearer to the cabin where they'd lived, where she *had* been allowed to walk around sometimes. In a lot of ways, Desparre still felt more like her home than Chicago.

But it wasn't. And it was time to leave again.

Five years ago, when she'd stepped onto that plane with Kensie, she'd been terrified of what the future held. Terrified to leave behind everything she'd known for most of her life. But deep down, she'd known she'd done the right thing. This time, she wasn't so sure.

Yes, the kids were safe. But would it have happened sooner if she'd been more open with the police?

From the passenger seat, Chance leaned over and nudged her arm with his wet nose.

When she glanced at him with a fond smile, he gave her a forceful *woof*, like he knew what was going on in her mind and wanted her to forgive herself.

Darcy was back behind bars. This time, the woman who'd raised her had refused to see *her*. The children she'd kidnapped had been taken to the hospital to be evaluated. Their parents were flying in to be with them, joyous reunions that would get the reporters clamoring again.

They were safe. And they were young enough, the extent of their kidnappings short enough that they wouldn't attract the same kind of sustained media attention she'd faced.

There was nothing left for her here, no more guilt-ridden mission to fulfill. No reason to remain in Desparre any longer. If Darcy wouldn't see her, after everything that had happened, maybe that was for the best. And yet, Alanna felt unsettled, as if she still had unfinished business.

One last apology, she reminded herself, pulling into the parking lot alongside the Desparre police station. One last goodbye.

As if he could read her mind—and didn't like it— Chance gave a soft whine as she opened the door.

"I'm going to miss him, too," she whispered softly, realizing what was causing her anxiety. It wasn't the awkward apology, the thought of all those judging eyes inside the station. She was expecting that; she'd had practice dealing with it. No matter what the official line was, Alanna knew most of the police force was angry with her. For her part in leading them to the site where Darcy had started the avalanche. For going off on her own afterward. For whatever role she'd played in Peter's decision to come to her aid alone.

None of those things were making her heart beat too fast, making dread lodge in her chest. It was the thought of never seeing Peter again.

"We have to do it," she told Chance, forcing herself to get out of the car. She was grateful there weren't any reporters camped out at the police station like they'd been at her hotel; she had needed to slip out the service entrance. But why would there be? They wouldn't expect her to come here.

She owed the whole station an apology. Her intentions

might have been good, but when they'd come to help, someone she loved had tried to kill them.

She owed Peter an apology most of all. Even though they had never really been anything except reluctant partners in a search for a kidnapper, it felt like they'd created a friendship. It felt like they'd been on the path to something more.

Chance leaped out of the car to follow her up to the police station the way he'd done the first day she'd returned to Desparre. Had it only been five days ago?

When they'd arrived, his tail had been wagging at the adventure. He'd strode along beside her, then raced off briefly to pounce in the fluffy snow before returning to her side.

Today, his tail faced downward and even his chin was angled to the ground. Either he was catching her mood or he was sad to be leaving this place, too.

"We'll be home soon," she tried to reassure him. "You'll get to play with Rebel."

At the mention of Kensie and Colter's dog, Chance's tail gave a quick wag, but then he was staring ahead again, intent and serious.

Alanna took a deep breath and closed her eyes, trying to relax. But her usual method for coping with anxiety didn't work. Instead, she pictured Peter's face, in turns furious, betrayed and understanding. She could almost feel his long fingers sliding through hers, offering comfort, even as distrust flickered in his eyes.

What might have happened between them if she had a reason to stay longer? If she'd come here for a different purpose entirely? If they were both different people, him without the trauma of standing too close to a hostage who'd blown herself up, her without the baggage of growing up with people who'd kidnapped her?

Maybe nothing. Maybe it was their pasts that had drawn them together, made them both understanding and wary of one another. Maybe the same thing that had created the spark between them would have ultimately destroyed it.

"I guess I'll never know," Alanna whispered, pushing open the door to the station.

The moment she was led into the bullpen where the officers worked, a dozen gazes flicked her way, started to turn back, then fixated on her. Angry, suspicious gazes from officers who'd dug their way out of an avalanche yesterday. Officers who, at minimum, thought she'd wanted a kidnapper to get away and at worst, thought she'd been helping Darcy all along.

"I'm sorry," Alanna said, her voice creaking out, little more than a whisper. She cleared her throat and repeated the words, louder. "I came here because I wanted to help. I came here because I thought I knew Darcy. I thought I understood what she'd do and how I could get through to her. I never wanted anyone to be hurt because of me."

When the officers just continued to stare at her, none of them making a move to accept her apology, heat pricked her cheeks and she ducked her head.

Then Tate was beside her, kindness in his eyes and in the hand he put on her arm. "It's okay, Alanna. It wasn't your fault. We all know that now." He shot a quick glance at his fellow officers, who grumbled agreement and went back to their work. "Besides," Tate added as he bent down to rub Chance's ears, "you brought along a snow rescue dog."

She gave him a grateful smile as Chance thumped his tail.

Tate stood again, looking more serious. "You should come with me, though." He headed through the station, toward the back, where she'd never been.

"I was actually hoping to talk to Peter," Alanna said, as she and Chance hurried after him. "I wanted to say goodbye."

"There's someone who wants to talk to you first." He gestured to the closed conference room door ahead of him.

Was Darcy in there? Had she agreed to talk to her after all? But why? And why would the police agree to it?

Or maybe it was the kids? Or their parents, wanting to know how to help them recover from the trauma of being kidnapped?

Even though it was part of what she did for a living, this was too personal. She was still too conflicted to offer the support they needed.

She shook her head, backed up a step, but then Tate pushed the door open for her.

On the other side of it, the police chief and Peter glanced her way. Then Kensie and Colter were there, hugging her, almost squashing baby Elysia between them.

Yet again, Kensie had flown across the country for her. This time, she'd brought her husband, five-month-old baby and their dog, too. She'd always been willing to do anything to protect Alanna. From the moment she'd wrapped her in a hug in Luna's hospital five years ago, Alanna had discovered her big sister always seemed to know exactly what she needed.

Rebel and Chance barked greetings to each other as Alanna breathed, "What are you doing here?"

"What are *you* doing here, sis?" Kensie asked her with a troubled gaze as she leaned back. "Why didn't you call us? We'd have come with you."

Peter looked at the police chief and said, "Let's give them have some privacy." The chief nodded and they left the room, keeping the door ajar.

In a quick burst, Alanna gave her sister and brother-in-law the short, ugly version of what had happened with Darcy.

Kensie stared at her a long moment, then asked, "What about the cop?" She nodded toward Peter in the other room.

Alanna glanced at him and blurted, "I owe him an apology." Kensie and her husband shared a smile over her head.

Then Colter announced, "Kensie and I came here to bring you home, Alanna. But I think we're going to spend the night at my cabin. We haven't been there in more than a year. I want to show the place to Miss Elysia here." He took his daughter from Kensie, bounced her in his arms and mumbled baby talk to her, then added, "It'll give you time to make that apology."

"But—" Alanna gestured to Peter, staring at her from beyond the conference room with his usual intensity, and Kensie took her hand.

"This time, when you come home, I don't want you to have any regrets, Alanna."

"I didn't—"

"It wasn't fair of us to think you'd want to leave this whole life behind, just walk away from everyone."

"You didn't," Alanna interrupted. "You encouraged me to stay in touch with Sydney and Johnny. You tried to help convince Drew's and Valerie's parents to let me talk to them. You've always supported me."

"But I should have understood how hard it was for you to leave the people who'd raised you, too," Kensie said. When Alanna tried to protest again, she pressed on. "You did a good thing, coming here to help find those kids. I know you're upset about how it all went down, but that's not your fault. And I can see that you found something else while you were here."

Alanna flushed and tried not to glance at Peter as Kensie winked and added, "Big sisters always know."

"It's not what you think," Alanna tried to explain. Her connection with Peter was forged from a situation that had ended. It would break as soon as she stepped on that plane.

"Maybe, maybe not," Kensie said, finality in her voice, a big sister tone Alanna had always secretly loved. "But years later, I don't want you thinking 'I should have, could have…' So, Colter is right."

"Happens sometimes," Colter interjected, making faces at Elysia as she squirmed and giggled.

Kensie rolled her eyes at her husband, then hugged Alanna once more. "Don't do it here. Go see him after work. Talk. Just be honest and at least then, whatever happens, you can move forward. Okay?"

Alanna nodded, unable to stop herself from glancing at Peter, who'd been staring at her as if he knew he was the subject of their conversation.

ALANNA STARED AT the house in front of her, at the light shining through the curtains, the shadow moving inside. Her engine was still running as she debated whether she could go through with it.

Alanna could hear her sister's voice in her head from this morning, telling her she needed closure.

She'd never be able to have closure with Julian. The same was probably true of Darcy now, as well. It was too late to change either of those things. But she could find closure with Peter.

It had seemed like a good idea to go to Peter's house when Kensie had suggested it this morning. But ten hours later, she was having doubts.

Woof! Woof!

Chance's bark startled her and made the curtains part in the house's window.

"*Chance*," she chided as Peter stepped outside, wearing just jeans and a long-sleeved T-shirt in the frigid weather.

Alanna turned off the engine and got out of her car, an apology already on her lips as Chance leaped out after her.

"Come on," Peter said, cutting off her apology and turning back for the house, his expression inscrutable. "It's cold out here."

Chance bounded up alongside him, accepting Peter's ruffling of the fur on his head before he jumped up the stairs and into the house.

Alanna followed a little more slowly, nerves building.

When she stepped inside, he helped her out of her thick winter coat, silent but not taking his gaze from hers. This singular focus made her flush and then he smiled.

His default expression was always so serious: his lips pressed together, his gaze steady, the sharp lines of his face making him seem even more intense. His was the face of a police officer. But his smile was a little bit crooked, a little bit shy. It made him seem younger, more approachable. It charmed her.

When he smiled, she could imagine walking beside him, tentatively slipping her hand into his. She could envision the giddy nervousness of a first date, the sweetness of a first kiss and then the smile on his face giving way to a thrilling intensity as he lay with her in front of the fireplace.

Awareness flickered in his eyes, then he stepped back, giving her more space than she wanted. "Let's sit by the fire." He headed that way, tapping his leg, calling, "You, too, Chance."

Her St. Bernard hurried after Peter, tail wagging. When Peter sat on the couch, Chance lay at his feet.

Alanna settled awkwardly a few feet away, angled toward him. She twisted her hands together, trying to remember the words she'd planned out on the drive to his house. But they wouldn't come and she turned away, her attention snagging on the bare wall across from her.

"You took down the pictures," she said.

"It's going to make my family happy. They're going to ask what prompted such a big change." His hand skimmed hers, then he shifted closer until they were sharing a seat. "I've been focusing on the wrong things. You taught me that."

"What? I did? How?"

The smile was back, amused now, less self-conscious. But those bright blue eyes were still laser-locked on hers, practically hypnotic. "You've had to make a lot of hard choices. Pretty much everyone around you—all these people who love you—they expect something from you. I see you trying to do right by all of them. I see you putting your own needs last. And honestly, with all the reasons you have to hate some of the people involved, you always seem to choose love."

Alanna shook her head, blew out the breath she'd been holding. Was that really how he saw her? She wished it were true. "I try to be fair to everyone, but it doesn't always work. It feels like I let people down a lot."

"You don't—"

"I let you down," she interrupted, flipping her hand over to squeeze his, trying not to fixate on how perfectly his hand seemed to fit with hers. "I owe you an apology. I shouldn't have run off without telling you where I was going. I shouldn't have forced you to make a decision that would hurt your career."

"I made my choice," he said, confirming what she'd suspected—his career as a police officer was in danger. "And I'd do it again." He lifted her hand, his breath dancing over her skin as he whispered, "If only we didn't live across the country..." Then he pressed his lips to her knuckles.

It was the briefest touch, but it made her skin tingle and her whole body warm.

"I wish..." Her voice came out so soft she wondered if he could even hear it.

He shifted even closer, pressed against her from knee to shoulder. "What?"

When she'd lived in Desparre, she'd been sheltered, isolated. She'd barely had the opportunity to talk to people outside of her own home. She'd certainly never dated.

When she'd returned to Chicago, Kensie had encouraged her to get out, meet people, join activities. She'd dated sporadically, but it had always felt awkward, tinged with a voyeuristic curiosity about her kidnapping on their part. She'd never developed a real connection with any of them.

Sitting next to Peter felt natural. It felt like she was supposed to be here. And now she was leaving again.

She didn't realize a tear had spilled from one eye until Peter swiped it away. His warm hand stayed on her face, turning to cup her cheek, stroke down the length of her neck. All the while, he never took his eyes from hers.

She couldn't seem to get a full breath as he leaned closer, so slowly, and his lips finally grazed hers. Then suddenly her free hand was clutching the front of his T-shirt and the fingers he had been resting on her collarbone moved into her hair. He took her upper lip between his, brushed his tongue against the seam of her mouth.

Pulling him toward her, she wrapped her arms around his back and held on tight, leaning into his kiss, demanding more. She didn't want to think about tomorrow, didn't want to think about leaving. She only wanted Peter, for as long as they had together.

He groaned, the sound somewhere between frustration

and need, and then she was in a controlled fall until her back hit the couch cushions, her feet still dangling on the floor. Peter angled over her, his weight on his elbows as his lips met hers again, his kisses still unhurried even as she arched up toward him.

She slid her hands down his back, pulling him toward her, thrilling in the sudden contact as he lowered his weight more fully onto her, as she shifted so her whole body was underneath him. Running her hands through his hair, over his shoulders, she fused her lips to his. The world around her seemed to fade away until all she could think of, all she could feel, was *Peter*.

The phone vibrating in her pocket startled her, made her jerk. She yanked it out of her pocket, ready to toss it on the floor, when she saw the name on the caller ID. Kensie knew she'd come here tonight, probably knew she wouldn't want any interruptions. So why was she calling now?

As she squirmed to sit up, Peter moved off of her but stroked her hand.

Her voice was breathless as she answered, "Hello?" She cringed at how she sounded.

"Alanna?" Kensie's panicked voice made Alanna's head clear fast.

"What's wrong?"

Her older sister, who'd risked her life to find Alanna five years ago and come to her aid once again, burst into tears. "She's gone!" Her words were garbled over the tears as she rushed on. "Someone came into the cabin. Elysia was sleeping. Now, she's just gone. Alanna, she's been kidnapped!"

Chapter Fifteen

"How is this possible?" Alanna paced in front of the fire, her skin still flushed from their embrace, her lips still slightly swollen from his kisses. With panic all over her face, she spun to face him. "How?"

"I don't know." Peter stood, used his free hand to pull her against his chest as he listened to the officer on the other end of the phone. "Are you sure?" he asked the officer, then swore.

"Well?" Alanna demanded.

Peter shook his head. "Darcy is still behind bars. They just confirmed it. She didn't escape again."

"And?"

"And nothing. She's not saying a word."

Alanna hurried across the room and picked up her coat, fumbling as she tried to get it on. Chance raced after her, barked once, then looked back at Peter.

He followed and grabbed the coat out of her hand. "Just hold on, okay? Let's not waste time driving around. Let's figure out what's going on here."

"This can't be a coincidence," Alanna said, her voice too high-pitched, panic in every shaky movement.

"I know." He pulled her back into his arms, held on tight. "I know. We'll find her."

He felt tension all through her body and wished he could

rewind to five minutes ago, before Elysia had been abducted out of the Hayeses' cabin a mere twenty feet from her sleeping parents. Back to Alanna breathless and kissing him, back to a time when nothing else mattered.

He'd been expecting her at his doorstep, had known an apology was coming. He'd planned to cut it off to let her know how she'd impacted his life. He hadn't planned to tell her that he'd developed complicated feelings for her. He definitely hadn't expected anything to happen between them.

Now none of it could matter. Because somehow, from behind bars, Darcy Altier had orchestrated the abduction of Alanna's niece. "It could be a copycat," he theorized out loud. Maybe Darcy's media attention had spurred someone else into action.

"Really? Another kidnapper?" Alanna squirmed free of his tight hold just enough to look up at him from within the circle of his arms, her expression skeptical.

She was only a few inches shorter than him, and he was tempted to lean down slightly and kiss her forehead. He ignored the urge and agreed with her. "Probably not. But Julian is dead. Darcy's been in jail for five years. How likely is it that she managed to find a new partner while she was on her way here from Oregon?"

"There's no way," Alanna said, pulling away from him and starting to pace again, her hands curled into fists. "Maybe Darcy paid someone? I mean, it's Elysia." Her voice cracked and she swiped a hand over her eyes. "Darcy is trying to hurt me because I turned her in five years ago, because I came after her again. I should have stayed home. I should have made sure Kensie stayed home. I can't believe Darcy would do this! I can't believe—"

Peter pulled her back against him just as Chance ran

over and pressed against her side, nudging her with his big head. "It's not your fault."

"Of course it's my fault!"

"Alanna—"

"Let's not argue about this." She spun in his arms to face him, staring up at him with desperation and trust. A trust he probably hadn't earned. "Let's just figure out how to find my niece."

"We will," he promised, praying he could keep his word.

To find Elysia, he had to figure out if Darcy had contacted someone. Who would help her? According to the station, Darcy hadn't made a single call since she'd been arrested yesterday. Maybe someone had acted without her needing to ask? Maybe they'd seen the news and taken their own revenge.

But who?

"Could it be someone she met in jail back in Oregon?" he asked. It was an odd thing to consider, but it definitely happened.

"Wouldn't that person still be in jail?" Alanna was obviously not following his trail of thinking.

"I mean, someone who visited her. You know those women who marry men on death row? Or marry murderers while they're still in jail, then move in with them when they get released? It happens with female inmates and male civilians, too."

Alanna shook her head. "Darcy was already married. Julian—"

"Was in jail, too. They were separated, in two different prisons. Maybe someone started visiting her. Even if she wasn't interested, maybe they followed the news. They could have followed her here. Maybe it was their way of trying to win her over. Stranger things have happened."

Alanna looked skeptical, but it was the best idea he

had. It made a lot more sense if it was someone who'd visited Darcy, who'd schemed with her. Someone whose trust she'd earned, someone who'd do anything to make her happy.

No matter what Alanna thought about Darcy and Julian's relationship, these were people who'd spent nearly two decades with kids they'd kidnapped. They were both capable of manipulation. Maybe someone desperate and lonely had visited Darcy in prison and she'd seen an opportunity. Then, when she'd managed to escape, he'd followed her here and taken revenge when she'd gone back to jail.

That actually seemed possible. No matter what Peter thought of Darcy's actions, he'd seen the love for Alanna in her eyes. He could absolutely picture her kidnapping kids she didn't know, trying to re-create what she and Julian had once had. But he wasn't sure he could imagine her intentionally hurting Alanna by having her niece kidnapped by someone else.

It wasn't her MO. Whatever messed up psychology had allowed her to rationalize kidnapping children, she'd grabbed them with the intent of raising them. This was different. Elysia's kidnapping seemed malicious, angry, driven by revenge.

"I'm going to talk to the US Marshals she got away from back in Oregon," he told Alanna. "They've probably already looked into who visited her in prison. Hopefully they'll share that info with me. Otherwise, I'll try the prison."

Pulling out his phone again, he looked up the number for one of the US marshals who'd accompanied Darcy to Julian's burial. He'd spoken to the agent a few days ago to give her a heads-up that he thought Darcy could be in Alaska. At the time, she'd seemed overworked and over-stressed and seriously doubtful that Darcy had made it so far north so fast.

When she picked up now and he explained the situation, there was a long pause. Then she admitted, "We can't be sure about this, but it's possible Darcy had help escaping us at Julian's burial."

Peter swallowed back words of frustration that he hadn't heard about this the first time he'd called. "Who?"

"We don't know. We don't even know if he was in on it. At the time, we assumed it was a coincidence. But given what you're telling me now, maybe we should have looked at it more closely. The distraction he caused, right when he caused it... He left right after, with the rest of the crowd. We never tracked him down."

"It's what gave Darcy a chance to run?" Peter guessed, as Alanna tilted her head close to his, listening in.

"Yeah."

"You have a description?"

"It was a man. Younger than her. Probably white."

Peter let out a noise that sounded like a laugh, but was all frustration. "That's it?"

"It was drizzling. He was wearing a dark raincoat. He wasn't particularly close to us and he wasn't our priority. There was a big crowd there, gawkers and press, plus mourners from another burial service nearby. He was in the wind immediately."

"Okay." Peter sighed, then said, "A little girl is missing. We think it's connected to Darcy. Do you know *anything* else about this guy that could help?"

"I'm sorry."

"Did you look into who visited her in prison?"

"Of course. But no one visited her. We confirmed with the prison that she received mail, but following procedure, they didn't read it. And whatever she received wasn't in her cell after her escape."

"What about phone calls?"

"Nope. She requested to have all the kids she abducted on her approved contact list, if you can believe it, but obviously, that was denied."

"Thanks." When he hung up, he saw how tightly Alanna's lips were pursed together, how her eyes were twitching like she was holding back tears. "I'm going to call my department. Whoever Darcy is working with, she had to contact that person somehow. If it was via mail, maybe one of her cell mates knows who was writing her. We'll find him. In the meantime, let's—"

The buzzing of his phone cut him off. He answered and told his partner, "Tate, I was just about to call you. Alanna's niece—"

"Has been kidnapped. Colter Hayes called us twenty minutes ago. You need to get in to the station right now."

"We're trying to run down leads," Peter told him, squeezing the hand Alanna had placed in his, watching her wipe away tears. "I think—"

"I've got a lead. I need you here right now," Tate interrupted, then hung up.

THE MOON WAS an ominous sliver in an angry gray sky when Peter whipped his truck into the Desparre PD parking lot.

Alanna leaped out as he put the vehicle in Park, Chance chasing after her. She raced across the lot to the station's door, sliding on a patch of ice and pinwheeling her arms until she regained her balance. Her frustration at the lack of information had grown unbearable on the way over. All Peter had told her after hanging up with Tate was that there was a lead.

Peter didn't live that far from the station—less than ten

minutes at the near-dangerous speeds he'd been driving. But she'd felt every one of those minutes like they were hours. Elysia was out there somewhere, at the mercy of a stranger.

Alanna had never felt a joy quite like the day she'd gone to the hospital to meet her niece. She'd spent years agonizing over her choice to leave behind "siblings" she'd loved, so she could return to siblings she'd missed but who'd become vague memories. But that first moment she'd held Elysia in her arms, she'd been so overcome with love, she'd nearly burst into tears. That moment had been worth every doubt, every ounce of guilt she'd tried to psychoanalyze away.

Now Elysia was in danger. And it was because of her.

Yanking the door to the police station open, Alanna nearly stumbled as Chance raced in past her, barking a greeting that was returned immediately. Rebel was here. Which meant Kensie and Colter were, too.

The door marked Police Only was propped open and Chance bolted through it. Even though she knew Kensie and Colter would never blame her, Alanna's steps faltered. Her anxiety ratcheted up, but then Kensie was running toward her. Colter hurried after his wife, his gait uneven as he leaned on the cane he rarely used, his wartime injury obviously acting up. Before Peter had even finished slipping through the door behind her, Kensie and Colter had their arms around Alanna, a family hug that reminded her how much she'd missed in all her years away. Chance doubled back, running circles around Colter and Kensie's Malinois-German Shepherd, until the two of them pushed their way into the circle.

A short burst of anxious laughter broke through her threatening tears as Alanna pulled out of the tight embrace.

She saw the panic and desperation on Kensie and Colter's faces and a sob burst free. "I'm sorry."

"Don't," Colter snapped, something deadly coming into his eyes that might have been his war face. "It's not your fault. We need to focus on getting her back, not on regrets."

Alanna nodded, swiping away the tears that had spilled despite her best efforts. "What do we know?"

At the question, Tate appeared, frowning as his eyes skimmed down the top page in a big stack of paper. "Not what we expected."

"What does that mean?" Alanna demanded, tired of all the cryptic information.

"Let's go sit in the conference room." Tate nodded briefly at Peter, then spun back the way he'd come.

Alanna hurried after him, alongside her sister, brother-in-law, Peter and the two dogs. Together, they all crammed into the little conference room and then Tate announced, "The parents of those two kidnapped kids arrived late this evening." He glanced at his watch and then amended his statement. "Technically, yesterday. Once they saw their kids, we sat down and talked to them about what happened."

"I'm sorry," Kensie interrupted, her hand clutched tight in her husband's, her eyes and nose bright red like she'd been crying fiercely not long ago. "What does this have to do with Elysia? Do you have any leads on where she is?"

Tate set the stack of papers on the table, rubbed the side of his hand against his forehead like he was exhausted. "We all assumed Darcy had kidnapped those kids."

"What?" The floor seemed to move underneath her and Alanna flung her hand out to steady herself on something. Before she could grip anything, Peter was holding her arm, keeping her upright.

"She *did* kidnap them, didn't she?" She looked from

Tate to Peter and back again. "She had those kids at the cabin…" Or did she? They'd obviously been at the second cabin, but at the first one, Alanna had only seen her run out the door. Where were the kids then?

"It sounds like she was involved," Tate said, "but…" He glanced at them, leaning against the wall, holding onto each other, the dogs positioned in front as if standing guard. "Why don't you all sit?"

"Just tell us," Colter demanded, his arm tight around Kensie's shoulders. "What's going on?"

"According to the kids, Darcy didn't grab either of them. The little boy said it was a man, much younger than Darcy, who kidnapped them and brought them back to Darcy."

"I've been in touch with the Marshals who were watching her in Oregon," Peter jumped in. "It sounds like this could be the same person who helped her escape at the burial. We need to talk to the prison, try and see if we can figure out who was writing her there. She must have met someone through letters, convinced him to help her escape."

Was that really what had happened? Or was the answer much simpler? Alanna felt herself sway as Tate continued.

"Apparently, when you caught up to Darcy and the kids at the second cabin, this man was out. When you found her at the first one, he'd already taken the kids to the second location. Both times, he had their vehicle. Darcy had needed to start that avalanche so she could slip away and wait somewhere for this guy to pick her up. It's why she didn't have anywhere to go at the second cabin. Darcy was supposed to erase all traces of them and then call to get picked up again."

"Did they mention a name? Have we pressed Darcy on who it is?" Peter asked. "Or I can call the prison right now, light a fire under them, so that they—"

"You don't need to do that," Alanna said. "I know who it is." She looked at Kensie and Colter, shaking her head in disbelief, ashamed that it hadn't occurred to her before now that Darcy might have had help.

Darcy might see a child from a distance that she wanted, that she believed should have been her child. But it had always been Julian who'd made it happen. With Julian out of the picture, there was only one person Alanna could think of who would try to piece together a new family for Darcy.

"It was my older 'brother,' Johnny."

Chapter Sixteen

"Johnny is the kidnapper," Tate confirmed. When Kensie gasped and looked to Alanna, Tate said, "We don't have a recent photo of Johnny, but we showed the kids a picture from when he was rescued five years ago and they confirmed it was him."

"Why?" Kensie asked Alanna. She was flushed with panic and clutching Colter, whose expression had morphed into a fury Alanna had never seen before. "Why would he kidnap those kids? And why would he take Elysia?"

"He's—" Alanna choked on a sob, then took a deep breath to get control of herself. Focusing on all the mistakes she'd made, worrying about all the worst-case scenarios for her niece wasn't going to help right now. She needed to focus on what had happened to turn Johnny into a kidnapper. Maybe that would help them figure out where he was now and how to stop him.

"He was the first one the Altiers kidnapped," Alanna said, trying to work it out in her mind at the same time she tried to explain to everyone else. "He was five years old. As we grew up, he remembered his family, but barely."

"He refused to talk to you once you came to Chicago. He…" Lines appeared between Kensie's eyebrows as she squinted into the distance, into a memory. "He's the one who shot at me and Colter at the cabin five years ago, isn't he? That was him with the gun?"

Alanna nodded, wishing she could make it untrue. Wishing she could have gotten through to Darcy enough to get her to admit that Johnny was involved.

"He won't hurt Elysia," she blurted. Whatever Johnny had become, he'd never harm a child. Right now it felt like the only thing in her life she knew for certain.

"Alanna," Colter said, judgment and barely contained anger in his voice. "I know he was your big brother for a long time, but—"

"I'm not trying to make excuses for him." She cut Colter off, even though the thought of Johnny doing any of this made her chest hurt so bad she wanted to double over. He might not be her blood, but he *was* still her big brother. When she'd first been kidnapped, feeling terrified and alone, he had comforted her. He'd promised to always look out for her, look after her. He'd said they were brother and sister now and that would never change.

Except if he'd kidnapped Elysia, it *had* changed. There was nothing random about it. While the idea of Darcy grabbing Alanna's niece for revenge had seemed out of character, Alanna could imagine Johnny doing it far too easily.

The truth was, everything between them had changed five years ago. From the moment she'd left that note and brought the scrutiny of the FBI, Johnny's brotherly love had turned into confusion and then hate. When Kensie and Colter had tried to rescue her, Johnny had seen Darcy pick up a weapon, so he'd done the same. He hadn't spoken to her since that moment when the Altiers had been arrested, and he'd barely spoken to the rest of their "siblings," either.

"Drew's and Valerie's parents won't let them talk to any

of us. Johnny won't talk to me, so he's only been in contact with Sydney since that day. Sydney said…"

Alanna frowned, wishing she'd tried harder to reach out to Johnny, found a way to get through to him. But every phone call had gone unanswered. Even her emails and letters had never gotten a response. Over the years, she'd all but stopped trying, reducing her attempts to a few letters a year she knew he'd never read.

If she hadn't given up on him, would it have come to this?

"*What*?" Kensie pushed, tears and anger mixing in her voice.

Alanna tried to focus. "Sydney said Johnny moved back to Alaska. When his birth family came to get him, he was already twenty-three. Initially, he went home with them to Colorado, but apparently it never felt like home to him. The last time Sydney and I talked about Johnny, she said he barely spoke to his birth family anymore. I think they gave up trying to build a relationship with him, because he didn't want one."

For Johnny, the Altiers had become his only family. When she'd left the note to tell the world she was still alive, she'd destroyed that family. From then on, he'd essentially been all alone.

"So this kid—man, since he's twenty-eight now—learned Julian had been killed. He was devastated, but saw it as his opportunity to help Darcy escape," Peter said, thinking quickly. "He went to Oregon for the burial, but also to create a distraction and help Darcy get free. They traveled to Alaska together and presumably hatched a plan to kidnap kids along the way. Or maybe they planned the kidnappings before that, when he wrote to her in prison, as soon as they learned Darcy was granted furlough for the burial."

"I think the recent kidnappings were spur-of-the-moment," Alanna said, remembering how Darcy had spoken of seeing her as a child and just *knowing*. She pictured those two kids in the cabin, so similar to the way she and Johnny had once looked. "I think Darcy saw a kid and felt a connection, felt like the child should have been hers. Then Johnny made it happen, like Julian used to do."

She flushed, realizing the one piece of information she'd held back five years ago suddenly mattered now. "Johnny knew how to do it because…" She squeezed her eyes shut, hating that her "brother" had been involved at all, wondering if he'd ever really had a chance to return to a normal life. Wishing she'd tried harder to help him.

"Why?" Colter asked, stepping closer. His dog, Rebel, who'd been in war zones with him as a Combat Tracker Dog, stuck close to his side, knowing when Colter needed him.

"When they kidnapped me and Johnny, they saw an opportunity and took it. But with all the other kids, they *created* opportunities. Darcy and Julian saw Sydney at a playground and they had Johnny lure her around a corner from where her parents were sitting, so they could grab her."

"*What*?" Kensie blurted, looking horrified but also distrustful, as if she wondered what else Alanna had kept from her. "You never told me that."

"It wasn't in the police reports, either," Tate said, his narrowed gaze on her.

To his credit, Peter kept holding her hand. She was afraid to look at his expression as she tried to explain. "Johnny was only thirteen when that happened. Did he really have a choice? I didn't want Johnny to get in trouble because he did what the people he'd called his parents since he was five told him to do. I didn't want him to get charged."

"He was a minor," Peter said softly. "He wouldn't have been charged." When she looked at him, her misery probably clear in her eyes, he asked, "That's not all he did, is it? What about Valerie and Drew?"

She could feel all eyes on her again, and she forced herself to look at Kensie and Colter. "For those abductions, Julian asked Johnny to distract the parents, pretend he needed help while Julian grabbed the kids." She ducked her head as Kensie and Colter stared back at her, disappointment and disbelief all over their faces. "I didn't know about it until after the fact," she added as if it mattered.

Ultimately, when she'd known anything related to kidnappings didn't really matter, did it? It's what Peter had been getting at the first time he'd met her. Yes, she'd been a kid, but she'd had fourteen long years when she could have spoken up, when she could have stopped this.

"He was older then," Tate said when she went quiet. "He would have been seventeen with Drew and twenty-one with Valerie. An adult."

"Yes," Alanna admitted. "But he was a victim, too. They took him when he was five years old and raised him with love, but also raised him to be theirs. He reacted to it differently than the rest of us, maybe because when they kidnapped him, he didn't have anyone to reassure him, like the rest of us did." It had been *Johnny* who'd first gotten through to her, comforted her, made her feel safe when her whole world was turned upside down. He'd done the same for Sydney, Drew and Valerie.

"None of this was ever his choice. Drew and Valerie, they didn't remember their families, but the rest of us— we felt torn between these lives we sort of remembered and the life we had, the family who loved us." She swiped more tears away, begging Kensie to understand. "I'm so sorry. If I'd ever thought—"

"You were trying to protect someone you loved. I understand why you didn't tell." Kensie's voice sounded understanding, but her hands were fisted, betrayal in the depths of her eyes.

"I'm so sorry," Alanna repeated, but it felt like she was talking into a void, like it was already far too late. She'd tried so hard to do right by everyone and in the end, maybe she'd done right by no one.

Peter squeezed her hand, but she didn't look at him, didn't want to see the judgment there, too.

"So, what's the dynamic *now*?" Tate asked when the silence dragged on too long. "Who's in charge? Darcy? Now that she's behind bars again, Johnny is after revenge, right?" His gaze skipped to Colter and Kensie and he grimaced as he looked back at her. "What does that mean for Elysia? You said he'd never hurt her, didn't you? So what's his endgame?"

Alanna looked around the room, at four pairs of eyes all staring at her, waiting for an answer. It was an answer she didn't have.

He'd been right from the beginning.

Peter stared at Alanna, who was trying so hard to hold it together, and remembered the distrust and suspicion he'd felt when he'd realized who she was. Had that only been six days ago?

Despite everything that had happened since then, he'd been right. He just hadn't been right about Alanna.

When this all started, he would have felt vindicated that his theory wasn't illogical. He'd believed from the very beginning that the kidnapper could be someone who'd been kidnapped and raised by the Altiers, who'd bonded so closely to them, he was now willing to do whatever it took to protect them. It wasn't unusual. Feigning loyalty to stay safe in the beginning could easily shift over time into a warped need to protect the very people who'd kidnapped you. But Alanna hadn't been the one afflicted. Her "brother" had been.

Alanna remembered Johnny as a vulnerable and confused boy, and it was messing with her perception. Peter saw the truth: Johnny was dangerous to them all.

Peter should have felt sorry for him, but instead, it took him back to that war zone, covered in blood and sand and knowing everything he'd worked for as a reporter was over in an instant. He could feel his hand twitching, a strong desire to touch his bad ear. Ignoring it, he tried to focus on what he'd just learned and what it meant for the investigation.

Johnny had been the one kidnapping kids all along. Regardless of Darcy's involvement—which was identifying a kid she wanted—Johnny had actually taken action. What else was he capable of? And how far would he go to get back at Alanna for what he perceived as the ways she'd done him wrong?

He squeezed Alanna's hand tighter, not wanting her to get close enough to Johnny to ever find out.

Across the room, Tate's gaze dropped to their linked hands, then up to Peter's face. Tate's lips pursed slightly—assessing or judging, Peter couldn't be sure. Right now, as much as he liked his partner and valued his opinion, Peter didn't really care. His job was already in jeopardy. The fact that they'd called him at all, that they were letting him in on the investigation, probably had more to do with his proximity to Alanna than their belief in him as an officer.

After the debacle at the cabin, the chief had told him to take a few days off. He'd only been at the station yesterday because the chief had called him in to give him a serious dressing-down. He was lucky she hadn't immediately demanded he hand over his badge and gun. But he knew that wasn't the end of it. She'd all but told him she was still deciding if he had a future on the force.

He had a reckoning coming at the Desparre PD. He didn't want to think about it, couldn't afford the distraction of worrying what it meant for his future, for the very way he'd come to identify himself. Right now, his sole focus had to be on finding Alanna's niece. And on keeping Alanna safe in the process.

It was his job, but it had become more than that. Whatever his connection to Alanna meant, however long it was destined to last, he couldn't let her down now. Not with so much of her happiness at stake. Because if her niece *wasn't* okay, Alanna would never be okay again, either.

"What do you think Johnny was trying to do?" he asked Alanna, tugging on her hand until she turned to face him, forcing her to shut out the stress of her family's reactions and focus on what she knew about her so-called brother. "When he was grabbing those kids Darcy pointed out, are you sure that's how it happened?"

Alanna squinted at him questioningly, her free hand absently stroking Chance's fur. Her loyal dog scooted closer, lending support, as she asked, "What do you mean?"

"Didn't you say that you decided to reach out with that note five years ago because Johnny had met someone, started talking about getting married? Is there any chance he was grabbing these kids for himself, that maybe Darcy being there just gave him the courage to do it? What about this woman he wanted to marry? Who was she?"

Alanna shrugged. "I barely remember her. Darcy and Julian trusted Johnny more than the rest of us, gave him more freedom because they said he'd earned it. He met a woman when he was in town and thought it was love at first sight. Darcy and Julian were skeptical and warned him about keeping the family's secrets, but he started dating her. Once the truth came out and our faces were all over the papers, she wanted nothing to do with him."

"So, you don't think he's trying to build his own family? That grabbing Elysia was just a way to do it and get revenge at the same time?" It might be the best option, the version of events that made it most likely Johnny would take care of Elysia rather than kill her.

"No." Alanna's near-tears of a few minutes ago had turned into something hard and determined. "I think he wanted to re-create the family he had."

"But that was never going to happen," Peter said.

"No. He won't talk to me. Drew's and Valerie's parents won't let him talk to them—and from what I've heard in news reports, they're always watched over. That just leaves Sydney. She talks to him every few months, but growing up, she was the one who remembered her birth family best. The Altiers grabbed her when she was six—older than the rest of us were when we were kidnapped. She's the one that Darcy and Julian always worried would say something and put the 'family' in danger. Besides, she's twenty-one now. She's going to college. She has her own life. It's pretty different from our isolated existence in Desparre. She told me more than once that she'd never come back here. I'm sure she said the same to Johnny."

"So, he decided to find new siblings?" Tate asked, getting Alanna back on track.

"That'd be my guess."

"And then you showed up," Tate said. "You ruined his plan, so he snatched Elysia."

Peter frowned, wondering if his partner was right. Maybe it was enough for Johnny to know Alanna was suffering. But his gut told him otherwise. Everything Alanna had said about Johnny suggested he'd been deeply damaged by his experience growing up, that he had the psychology of someone who would misdirect all their anger and rage at the easiest available target. What good was rage like that if the target didn't know who was hurting her?

Peter looked at Colter and Kensie. "Did you see Johnny at the cabin? Did he leave any indication that it was him? Some kind of message for Alanna?"

"Elysia was in her crib in the back room," Colter said. "Kensie and I had fallen asleep by the fire. We woke up because Rebel was going wild, trying to get into the bedroom. She might technically be a senior dog, but she still thinks like she's military. We ran back there and found it was locked. I was scared to kick the door in with Elysia in there, so I ran around outside. I found the window open." His jaw tightened, his lips turning inward. "Our daughter was gone."

"You didn't see anything? Not in the backyard or in the room? No note?" Tate pressed.

"If we had, don't you think we would have told you by now?" Colter snapped. He ran a hand through his dark blond hair, making it stick up. "Sorry. My daughter is five months old. We've just—" He choked on a sob, then finished, "I'm trying to hold it together here, but we have to find her."

Tate nodded, his expression saying he'd been in this room before with scared parents. He looked back at Alanna, and Peter was suddenly glad of Tate's extra years on the force, of his background as a police officer in a bigger city before he'd come to Desparre. "Are we waiting for a ransom note here, Alanna?"

Alanna shook her head, frustration and exhaustion on her face. "I don't know." Then that frustration morphed into angry determination. "But I know who does. I want to talk to Darcy."

Chapter Seventeen

"I don't understand you at all," Darcy said, staring at her from across the table inside the Desparre PD's claustrophobic interrogation room.

Tate and Peter had brought Alanna here, insisted that Darcy had to remain cuffed and then left them alone to talk. Of course, *alone* was a relative term. Alanna's gaze darted to the camera mounted in the corner. Whatever was said in here, Peter and Tate were watching. She didn't know who else from the department was with them.

Darcy looked even worse than she had at the cabin. Her shoulders were slumped inward and the lines pulling at the edges of her mouth and eyes seemed even more pronounced.

"I'm not sure I understand you, either," Alanna said, clutching her hands tightly together underneath the table, trying to keep her tone even, keep the anger and blame out of her voice. Darcy knew her better than most people on the planet; it was unlikely she'd be fooled.

"You let me go at the cabin," Darcy said, real confusion in her eyes. "You stood in front of me, gave me an opportunity to escape."

Alanna tensed, resisted the urge to glance at the camera surely recording every word spoken in this room. That hadn't been her reasoning at all, but she clamped her lips together, let Darcy continue. She'd rather fight an accomplice charge than risk angering Darcy, risk losing the chance to find out where Johnny had taken Elysia.

"So, why did you bring police in the first place? Why did you turn us in all those years ago? It's like you're two different people, Alanna." A humorless smile flitted across her face, before morphing into a scowl. "I should have realized it sooner, I guess. You're torn between two worlds. I saw it over the years when you were growing up, this far off look you'd get on your face, like you were dreaming about the family you'd been born to, instead of the one you were meant to be a part of. I thought you'd grown out of it before you wrote that note. After all those years, we thought we could trust you."

This again? Alanna fought down her frustration. The guilt she'd seen in Darcy's gaze, in her words, when Alanna had told her how her kidnapping had affected the Morgans, already seemed forgotten. Right now, seeing Darcy wasn't about getting an apology. It wasn't about getting closure on her past. The fact was, she'd probably never fully have it. That was something she needed to manage. And it was something she *could* manage, with her degree in psychology and her job helping others overcome worse trauma.

What she *did* need was for Darcy to understand the hurt she'd caused. She needed to understand the further hurt she'd cause if she let Elysia stay with Johnny. It was the only way Alanna had a shot at getting Darcy to choose Alanna's happiness over that of the man she still called her son, the man who still called her Mom.

Alanna folded her arms in front of her on the table, leaned in.

Before she could speak, Darcy asked softly, "What happened to your ring?"

Alanna's hands twitched, her wish to keep them hidden under the table too late. Darcy had given her a worn ruby ring when she was sixteen years old. It was a family heirloom Darcy had worn most of Alanna's childhood. Alanna hadn't taken it off for three years. It was the only thing she'd taken with her when she'd left Alaska besides the clothes she'd been wearing the day police had split apart the "family."

The Morgans had all stared curiously at it when they didn't think she would notice, but they waited for her open up to them at her own speed. She hadn't wanted to hurt them, hadn't wanted to admit that she missed Darcy and Jullan, that the ring felt like her final connection to them. Instead she'd taken it off, placed it carefully at the bottom of a drawer and hadn't put it on since.

"It's safe," Alanna said. "I still have it." She slid her hands back under the table, tried to get the conversation back on track. "You thought you could trust me? Well, you said you loved me. You said you wanted to raise me to be strong and happy."

The offense was as obvious on Darcy's face as it was in her voice when she insisted, "I do. I did."

Alanna leaned toward her again, closing the space between them, letting Darcy see the hurt and fear on her face. "Then why would you let Johnny take my niece?"

Darcy's mouth dropped open into a small *O*. She shook her head slightly, her brow furrowed, but she didn't quite meet Alanna's gaze.

"You didn't know?" Alanna demanded, not sure if the confusion on Darcy's face was feigned or real. Hope started to replace the fear that talking to Darcy was too much of a long shot. If she really hadn't known, she'd be more likely to help Elysia. But would she be able to? Would she know how to get through to Johnny?

"I— No. That wasn't part of the plan. I didn't even know your niece was here. Heck, I didn't even know you *had* a niece. It's not like you talk to me anymore." She scowled, then gave a quick, hard shake of her head. Her voice was sad and lost when she continued, "We just wanted what we had before. We weren't trying to hurt you. We weren't trying to hurt anyone."

"But you know you did, right?" Alanna asked softly, willing Darcy to look at her, to face what she'd done. "Just like you knew what you'd done to all of our families. You tried not to think about it, tried to convince yourself the families you stole from would all be fine, that the kids you ripped away from them were happy. But deep down, you knew. You *knew* it was wrong."

Tears filled Darcy's eyes and she blinked rapidly, clearing them away. She started to reach her hand out, then looked at the cuffs keeping them locked together and faltered.

Alanna leaned farther across the table, closing her hand over the top of Darcy's linked hands, hoping she wouldn't fixate on the missing ring again. Not that many years ago, Darcy's hands had been smooth and soft, deceivingly small for how strong she was. Those hands had picked Alanna up hundreds—thousands?—of times as a child. They'd sewn her clothes and helped her build a desk for her studies. They'd wiped away her tears and wrapped around her in loving hugs that Alanna still missed.

Now those same hands felt paper-thin, dry and rough. They looked older, too, as if she'd aged twenty years in prison instead of five.

The guilt that was never far beneath the surface bubbled up. Normally, Alanna reminded herself that she had no reason to feel guilty, that she'd done the right thing. This time, she let Darcy see all of her conflicted emotions, hoped it would help Darcy admit to some of her own.

"Please," Alanna whispered. "Elysia is only five months old. Johnny doesn't know how to take care of a baby that young. Not alone. And my sister deserves to get her child back. Kensie has been through enough."

"I…" Darcy's cheek twitched, her lips twisting downward. Her gaze skipped away from Alanna.

"Johnny still has a chance to make a normal life for himself."

Was it true? Alanna didn't really know. Not only because he'd certainly be facing charges for helping a prisoner escape and kidnapping three children, but also because everything that had happened in the past week proved he was more damaged by their upbringing than Alanna had ever realized.

Still, there was one thing she knew for sure. Turning himself in, handing Elysia over unharmed, was the only chance he had.

Darcy looked up at her, eyes narrowed and unreadable.

"Please help me find them," Alanna begged, squeezing Darcy's hands under hers.

Darcy ripped her hands away and turned her gaze to the ground, but not before Alanna saw the regret there. "You're lying to me. I'm not going to help you relegate Johnny to the same life I've had, the life Julian had. I love my son."

She looked up at Alanna once more, finality in the hardness of her eyes, the clenched line of her jaw. "Goodbye, Alanna."

SHE'D FAILED.

Alanna stood outside the interrogation room, her whole body too heavy with dread to move. Even knowing that Peter and Tate had surely already seen everything over the camera feed, Alanna didn't want to face them. More than that, she didn't want to face Kensie and Colter, didn't want to have to admit that their best lead to find Elysia was gone.

The finality in Darcy's goodbye had brought tears to Alanna's eyes. Just as quickly, she'd blinked them away, vowing never to shed another tear over Darcy or Julian Altier.

Yes, they'd raised her with love. But ultimately, everything they'd done had been selfish.

Five years ago, Alanna thought she'd taken a huge step in regaining control over her own life. But maybe she'd just been living in limbo, stuck between two worlds, between two families.

Now, finally, she was picking sides. But she'd done it much too late.

Taking a deep breath to control her anxiety, wishing she had Chance beside her, Alanna forced herself to move back toward the station's bullpen, toward Kensie and Colter.

As soon as she rounded the corner, there they were, crowding around her, fear and hope in their eyes that quickly turned to disappointment when they saw Alanna's face.

Kensie swallowed hard and clutched her husband's hand. Then she reached for Alanna's hand, too, always the big sister, even when Alanna didn't deserve it. "We'll find another way," she croaked, but her voice was full of fear. "The police are already combing the woods around our cabin, looking for trails. They'll find something."

Chance, obviously sensing Alanna's distress, pushed his way through the crowd until he was beside her, his big head nudging her arm. Rebel hurried over, too, slipping in between, so she could press up against Colter and Kensie at the same time.

Alanna stroked her dog's fur, letting his calming presence relax her too-rapid heartbeat. She looked past her family to Peter and Tate, who were standing a few steps away.

Peter stared back at her with sympathy in his eyes, no obvious sign of the distrust he had to be feeling after all of the things Darcy had said about her. Beside him, Tate looked more pensive, but Alanna was surprised to see that he didn't seem angry or distrustful, either.

"What Darcy said—"

Peter stepped closer, cutting her off. "You did your best. I'm sorry she let you down."

She blinked back at him and for half a second, it felt like it was just the two of them in that station. She could see in his eyes that he understood, that he hadn't ever believed she was trying to let Darcy go. A smile trembled on her lips, remembering his frustration in that moment back in the cabin and knowing he'd chosen to believe her.

It faded just as fast as reality rushed back in. Elysia was still missing. Without Darcy's help, how would they find Johnny? Without Darcy's help, how did Johnny expect to care for a newborn while he was on the run?

"He never planned to," she realized aloud.

"What?" Kensie asked, leaning closer, probably recognizing the excitement in Alanna's voice.

"Without Darcy, Johnny's not trying to re-create a family anymore. He's looking for revenge."

Kensie and Colter shared a worried glance, maybe because they'd already decided Johnny had grabbed Elysia out of revenge. They were probably worried it meant Johnny saw Elysia as expendable.

It was more than simple revenge, though. Darcy was all highs and lows, lots of excitement followed by periods of depression. But she always acted with love, even when it was misguided. And until now, she'd stood by all of her "children," no matter what. Johnny followed her lead when it came to his mood swings, but his emotions were always all or nothing. Love or hate. Once the pendulum swung, it was hard to send it back.

He'd treated her like his best friend growing up, the little sister he was so happy to have by his side no matter what. When she'd left that note, all that love had twisted into fury. There was no in-between for him.

If Johnny had given up on rebuilding a family, then his entire goal was revenge. It meant Tate had been right when he'd asked what use revenge was if she didn't know it was Johnny. But with the kids rescued, of course they'd eventually figure out it was him. What Johnny needed her to know now was how to find him. What he needed was a reason to make her come. He'd found the reason. And she knew where to go.

Johnny had returned to where it had all started. He was at their cabin in Desparre.

Chapter Eighteen

"Why are we out here?" Tate demanded, zipping his coat up to his chin.

Alanna looked around the circle of people she'd hustled out of the station and into the snow. Kensie and Colter had Rebel between them, and the dog looked as curious as her owners in the darkened parking lot. Peter stood beside her, absently petting Chance and waiting for her to speak, his narrowed eyes telling her he already suspected what was coming.

When she'd told them all she needed to go outside for some fresh air, she'd hoped Tate would stay inside. Some part of her had hoped Peter would, too. Because if either of them refused to go along with her plan, her niece could be in more danger.

"Maybe you should go in and warm up," Alanna suggested, trying to sound sincere.

"You figured out where they are, didn't you?" Tate demanded.

"What?" Kensie gasped, clutching her hand. "Really?"

Alanna stared back at the big sister who looked so much like her and nodded. "I think so. But…" Her gaze darted to Peter and Tate. "Johnny understands the Alaskan wilderness the way Darcy does. We grew up learning to shoot in case of trespassers or a rogue bear. Despite my carelessness a few days ago, we were taught how to spot signs of a potential avalanche. We learned how to use the wilderness to our advantage."

"Like firing at an overhang of snow and burying a team of police officers who thought they were well hidden?" Tate stared, assessing her like he was still trying to determine if the people who'd raised her were that in tune with their surroundings or she'd somehow given away their presence.

"Johnny was better than any of us," Alanna continued, ignoring the unspoken question—Tate was either going to have to trust her or she wasn't letting him in on her plan. "I can't have officers trying to surround him. Not with Elysia in the way."

Peter took her hand. "We'll be more careful about—"

"No." She turned toward him, Kensie's desperate face in her peripheral vision. "What I said before, about Johnny looking for revenge? I'm the one he thinks did him wrong."

"We're not going to let him hurt you," Colter hissed.

His loyalty brought tears to her eyes and she nodded a quick thanks to the brother-in-law who'd risked his life for her before he'd even known her to help Kensie bring her home. "I don't think he will. He's not trying to just lure me close enough to shoot me. He spent the past five years ignoring me. This is his way of reaching out."

Kensie let out a huffed breath, then leaned into her husband over Rebel.

Alanna kept her eyes locked on Peter, willing him to believe her, praying he'd have enough trust left with Tate to keep his partner quiet, too. "He wants to talk."

"Talk?" Peter asked, eyebrows raised. "And then what?"

"I know Johnny," she said instead of answering. "If we give him the opportunity to take me instead of Elysia, he'll jump at that deal."

"There's a better way than trying to make a trade," Peter insisted.

"Aren't we getting ahead of ourselves?" Tate asked. "Where is he keeping Elysia? Let's do some surveillance. We can—"

"You'll never get close to him," Alanna insisted. "But I can. I can go there and convince him to leave her behind. I just have to go with him."

"What?" Kensie stepped forward and Rebel did, too, giving a sharp bark in response to Kensie's distress. Kensie grabbed Alanna's arm, turning her so they were face-to-face. "I don't want to lose you again."

"You won't," Alanna said, forcing herself not to blink or shift her gaze. "He hates me right now, but I'm still his family. As long as I don't betray him by bringing the police, he'll go with me. He'll leave Elysia. I *know* he will."

"Alanna." Her name sounded like a sigh as Peter moved so he was in her line of sight, too. "You can't know how anyone from the Altier 'family' is going to respond anymore. Things have changed."

"You saw what happened in that cabin," she told Peter. "Darcy turned her weapon on you, but she ran instead of risking that she'd hit me. After everything that happened, Johnny is still her son. He'll do the same."

Kensie and Colter shared a worried glance and Peter's gaze lifted to Tate's, his forehead crinkled with doubt. Tate gave a short, hard nod and Alanna felt her whole body relax.

They believed her. They'd follow her plan. She let herself smile, because she knew it could work. Johnny had only grabbed Elysia to get back at her. He'd never hurt a baby. But no way did he want to raise one all alone.

"You can still go inside," Peter told Tate softly. "You don't know anything. You don't have to be a part of this."

Tate shook his head, the expression on his face a mix of anger and determination. "We've come this far because Alanna could predict what Darcy would do. If Johnny knows this place half as well as she does, he could disappear way too easily." His gaze darted to Kensie and Colter and then back to his partner. "Our department is good, but situations like this need one of two things—a good hostage negotiator or a full-time tactical team." He looked at Alanna. "I'll bet on our hostage negotiator."

"Thank you," she whispered. Then she took a deep breath and looked at her big sister. "He's at the cabin where we used to live. He must be. It's the only place he can be sure I'd know to look. I'll go up there and get in the car with him. We'll drive away and leave Elysia there. That way, he can be sure anyone coming after us will go into the cabin first. He's good at watching for tails. He'll see if anyone follows us."

"What happens if it doesn't work?" Peter demanded. "What happens if he tries to run with both of you?"

"I won't do it." Understanding that Johnny would probably be armed and there might be a situation where she had no choice, Alanna added, "If I have to get in the car with both of them, I'll signal you. Then you stop the car. Otherwise, you go in the cabin and get Elysia."

"What about you?" Kensie asked.

"Once we're far enough away, Johnny and I will talk things through. I doubt I'll be able to get him to turn himself in. But he'll know I won't stay with him forever, just like I didn't stay with the Altiers forever. He'll have to let me go."

They all stared back at her with worried expressions and she insisted, "I told you, he won't hurt me. He might take a while to let me go, true. Then he'll be a fugitive, because I can't bring him in if he doesn't want to go. But I'll be okay. I promise."

Chance whined, shoved his big head against her arm a few times, like he was begging her to be honest.

She stroked his fur and kept her expression even. Darcy would have been able to see through it, but the woman had raised her. Kensie had only known her for ten years, five of them as a little child and five as a woman torn between two worlds. But no longer. Today she was going to prove where she belonged.

If she didn't live through it, then at least she'd die looking after her niece the way Kensie had looked after her.

THIS WAS THEIR best shot.

Peter believed it, but he didn't like it. If this were any other case, he'd bring in his team. He'd trust them to do their jobs better than a group of civilians. Proceeding by the book would have meant officers surrounding the cabin, bringing in a state SWAT team if they had time. It meant keeping higher-ups abreast of every single movement of the operation. It meant Alanna would stay safely outside, far away from danger.

As much as he wanted that last part, Alanna was right. They wouldn't have captured Darcy without her. Darcy and her husband had taught Johnny how to shoot, how to hide, how to fight. Right now, sending Alanna into danger was their best shot at getting Elysia back to her parents safely.

Since Kensie and Colter hadn't immediately nixed Alanna's plan, they knew it was true, too. From the way they were staring at each other—fear, hope and helplessness all over their faces—they didn't like it any better than he did.

Of course, they didn't have to do it completely Alanna's way.

Her plan was probably going to save Elysia's life. But

it was probably also going to destroy what was left of Peter's career. It would take down Tate with him.

Thinking about either of those things put a pain in Peter's chest, but Tate knew what he'd agreed to, understood what was at stake. If it meant giving Alanna the life she deserved with the people who loved her, the way it should have been all along, Peter could accept giving up what he'd only recently discovered was his life's calling.

What he wasn't willing to do was risk Alanna's life.

She could be right. She knew Johnny best, knew what he was capable of and, hopefully, where he'd draw the line. Whatever their sins, the Altier "family" had loved each other. But love that had turned into hate was dangerous. It was unpredictable.

They could trade Alanna for Elysia, make sure the infant was safe. But they needed a backup plan, needed something to trade Alanna for, too. Peter wasn't willing to risk Johnny driving off with her and having her disappear again from everyone who loved her.

Peter's family could really annoy him sometimes. His parents still treated him like a teenager. Their encounter with Alanna at the coffee shop hadn't been the first time they'd seen him around town with someone, assumed he was on a date and told the woman how badly he needed to settle down. His siblings weren't much better. They were all older than him, all happily married with kids and certain that what they had was all that was missing from Peter's life. That if he would only hurry up and find the right woman, settle down and make a couple of babies, he'd forget all about the reporter job he'd left behind, forget how hard he'd fought over the past year to be accepted at the Desparre PD as an equal, rather than a possible liability.

No matter how little he sometimes felt they understood

him, they loved him. They supported him. And he'd gotten their support his entire life.

Alanna deserved the same thing. She deserved to watch her niece grow up safe and happy and surrounded by her real family.

If he was being honest with himself, she made him see what his family was always insisting he needed. If she lived in Alaska, he could imagine dating her, could imagine one day marrying her and making babies, little miniature versions of her, maybe with his eyes.

It wasn't meant to be. But he wasn't going to let Johnny decide her future. Even if it couldn't be with him, Alanna deserved to have her own babies and watch them grow up safe and happy, too, surrounded by the family that had waited and searched for her for fourteen long years.

"I have a plan, too," he announced, making everyone's head swivel his way. Even Rebel and Chance looked up at him expectantly.

"Colter and Kensie, you should drive Alanna back to my place. Drop the dogs off there and wait for my call. Then Alanna should take her rental and you two should follow at a distance."

Chance and Rebel looked from him to Colter and Alanna, as if waiting for their reply. When there wasn't an immediate rebuttal, Chance barked and Rebel followed suit, like they didn't approve of the plan.

"Sorry," Peter told the dogs, as a smile broke free, the first one he'd felt since they'd gotten the call from Kensie. "But you two need to stay home this time." He looked at Tate. "I'm going to tell the chief that Alanna has good reason to suspect the baby is at the first cabin we went to, the one where Darcy started the avalanche. I want you to go there with them, keep them looking. Keep them out of the way."

Tate shook his head. "I know what you're doing. You want to keep me out of trouble, hopefully save my career. But it doesn't matter. If you pursue this on your own and I looked the other way, it's the same thing as going with you. Face it. I'm in this. I'm with you."

"I want you to make sure the police go. I want you to make sure they're out of the way long enough for us to pull this off."

Tate crossed his arms over his chest. "Where exactly am I supposed to say *you* went?"

"Tell them I'm going to make sure Alanna and her sister don't try to get to Johnny first."

Tate shook his head. "You're trying to make things better for me and I appreciate it. But do you really think the chief will believe that I didn't know what was really happening? It would be better if I came with you. What if you need backup?"

"We'll be okay." He wasn't sure it was true, but this was about more than just doing whatever he could to salvage Tate's career. It was also about getting his partner out of the way. Because trying to take down a criminal without backup or following procedure was one thing. But what the rest of his plan entailed? Not even the closest partner would agree to it.

"I really don't think—"

"It's the best way," Peter insisted, knowing he needed to put this in motion fast before he thought better of it, too. He headed for the door, then pivoted back toward Alanna, Kensie and Colter, who were all standing immobile, like they hadn't absorbed his plan yet.

"Get moving," he told them. "Then wait at my place until you get my call that the rest of the department has cleared out. I want them far enough away that if anyone calls them to a situation at the old Altier place, they won't be able to respond quickly. But I also want to do this now, while it's still dark. Hopefully give us some element of surprise and keep Johnny off-balance."

His gut knotted at how badly this could all backfire and he tried to ignore all his training, all his common sense screaming this was a mistake. "Go," he insisted again, and finally Colter and Kensie nodded, heading for their trucks.

Rebel followed, but Alanna stayed where she was. She shook her head mutely at him, studying him too closely like she knew he wasn't telling her everything.

He wasn't going to give her time to figure it out. Moving in close, he looped an arm around her waist, pulled her to him and kissed her.

Her arms slid around his neck and she half leaned, half fell into him as Chance gave a sharp bark. Then she was kissing him back, the desperation in those kisses telling him that what he'd planned was necessary.

She pulled back first, stared at him a long minute, then spun and hurried to the truck where Kensie and Colter waited. Chance barked at him once more, then bolted after her.

"Let's do this," Peter told Tate, passing his partner and reaching for the door to the station.

Tate put a hand on his arm. "What are you really planning?"

"Trust me, it's better if you don't know." He yanked open the door and went inside before Tate could argue.

Then he was running toward the chief, pasting a frantic look on his face that wasn't completely feigned.

She was on her feet and met him before he made it halfway there. They met in the middle of the bullpen, all eyes on them. Chief Hernandez looked from him to Tate. "What's happening?"

"Alanna and her sister and brother-in-law just took off," Tate said.

"I told them they could leave their dogs at my place and get some rest, then come back to the station. I said we'd call if we had any updates," Peter jumped in, not wanting Tate too involved in the lie. "I think they are going to drop the dogs off, but I don't think they plan to stay there."

The chief's eyes narrowed. "Why not?"

"I overheard Alanna telling Kensie and Colter that she thinks Johnny took Elysia to the cabin over in Luna, where Darcy started the avalanche."

"Why does she think that?" Chief Hernandez asked. "I saw the conversation between Darcy and Alanna. Darcy never said anything about that cabin."

"Alanna spent fourteen years with that woman," Peter said. "She can read between the lines better than we can. Look, she might be wrong. But do we want to risk it? We need to go out there. Actually…"

The chief's narrowed eyes shifted into a scowl. "Actually, what?"

"I should go to my place, see if I can keep them there, keep them out of the way. I might be able to get Alanna to listen."

"I'll go with the team," Tate said. "I don't know what Darcy said to Alanna, but she seemed convinced they'd be at that cabin. We need to go now."

Peter swore inwardly at Tate's addition, because it made him part of the lie, rather than someone who'd trusted the wrong partner. But Tate's word seemed to be enough, because suddenly Chief Hernandez was nodding and waving her arms for the rest of the officers to gear up.

As they raced to the equipment room to gather the heavier weapons and protective gear, Peter ran out to his SUV and whipped out of the lot in the direction of his

house. Around the corner, he turned off his lights and
parked. He slipped out of the vehicle and pressed himself
against the corner of the grocery store, waiting until the
last police vehicle raced out of the parking lot.

Then he made one quick phone call, before he ran back
to the station. He used his key card to get in the rear entrance, knowing there'd be an officer who'd stayed behind.
They couldn't leave the station totally empty, not with a
prisoner in a cell at the back.

Hopefully, that officer wouldn't check on Darcy for a
while.

Peter ignored the voice in his head screaming at him.
Yes, he was about to break the law. Yes, it was against everything he believed in. But he couldn't think of any other
way to ensure the woman he loved wasn't heading will-
ingly toward her own death.

The woman he loved. The words rang in his head, ridiculous after such a short time knowing her, yet they felt
all too real.

He'd worry about it later.

Slipping the cell keys from their drawer, Peter unlocked
the only occupied cell inside the Desparre station.

Darcy stared at him, unmoving even as he yanked open
the door.

"Let's go," Peter said, striding inside and pulling her
to her feet.

She resisted, staring up at him suspiciously.

"You want *both* your son and daughter to still be alive
by morning?" he demanded.

She stopped digging her feet in and allowed him to lead
her as he whispered, "You're my backup plan."

Chapter Nineteen

A prisoner was handcuffed in the seat beside him; one he'd broken out of her cell. If his plan worked, she'd be back behind bars soon—and there was a decent chance he'd be headed there himself.

The whole thing sounded ridiculous, even in his head. When he'd first met Alanna, he'd seen her as his chance to finally find acceptance at the Desparre PD. Instead, he'd lied to the whole department and committed a crime inside his own station. How had this become his life?

Peter tried not to think too hard about the consequences as he maneuvered up the slick mountain roads toward a cabin well hidden in the woods that he'd only visited once before. Of course, his passenger knew the route from memory.

As soon as he'd gotten Darcy clear of the Desparre police station, he'd hustled her down the dark sidewalk around the corner to his truck, praying no shop owner was watching from behind darkened windows. Then he'd slapped handcuffs on her and pushed her into the passenger seat of his vehicle.

For a brief moment, he'd considered cutting Alanna out entirely, just driving Darcy up to the cabin and trying to make the trade directly for the baby. But he'd reconsidered before he'd reached the base of the mountain. It would be too hard to manage it all alone. The safest thing for Elysia was to get her completely away from the line of fire. At least with Alanna, she could walk toward him. How would he hold a baby while keeping his gun trained on Johnny? Even cuffed, there was no way to predict what Darcy might try. And while Johnny probably didn't actually want to raise the baby, Darcy might.

Besides, Alanna had asked him to trust her. Maybe she'd be able to get through to Johnny and end the whole thing peacefully. Maybe he'd even be able to slip Darcy back into her jail cell without anyone noticing she'd been gone.

Yeah, and maybe he'd still have a job come daylight.

Still, there was a chance. Somewhere on the road ahead of him, Kensie and Colter were driving up in one vehicle and Alanna in another. Alanna was supposed to text them all once she'd reached the cabin, then wait for their confirmation before she went to the door.

Once Alanna left with Johnny, he would follow. Kensie and Colter were going to get the baby and take her to safety. When he'd called to tell them to get moving, he'd gotten Colter off Speaker. The man had a leg injury he'd sustained as a marine that had never fully healed, but he still had a military mentality. If needed, Colter had promised to get his wife and child down the mountain, then come back up with a weapon and possibly Rebel. While her specialty had been tracking bomb-makers and she was long retired, she'd been military, too. Peter had worked with enough soldiers to know: once military, always military.

Peter hoped he wouldn't need them, but he did feel slight relief at the idea of having backup if everything went sideways. Overseas, the deadliest thing he'd carried had been a pen. But he'd been with soldiers, who'd been armed and ready to protect. Now on the force, he worked with a partner. But right at this moment, he'd never felt more alone. And it might be Alanna's life on the line.

"You're in love with my daughter, aren't you?"

It was the first time Darcy had spoken since she'd let him pull her silently out of the station and into his truck. She hadn't even protested when he'd handcuffed her.

He glanced briefly at her, remembering the harsh words she'd spoken to Alanna in the interrogation room. "If you still think of Alanna as your daughter, then you'll help me convince Johnny to let her go and take you instead."

"So, that's your plan. I figured it had something to do with my son. I didn't think you actually planned to let me go, though. You must really love her if you're willing to break the law. Or have you always been a crooked cop?"

He darted another glance at her, trying not to show how her words stung. Her opinion of him didn't really matter. But he did wonder what she thought of their chances of getting both Elysia and Alanna out of there safely.

She just stared back at him, a mix of curiosity, distrust and anticipation on her face.

If this went sideways, he'd have to worry about more than just going to jail. If he couldn't find a way to stop Darcy and Johnny after he got Alanna to safety, he'd be letting two child kidnappers go free. He had no doubts she and Johnny would start up right where they'd left off.

A ball of dread filled his stomach and twisted angrily. Peter clutched the wheel harder as the icy dirt roads beneath him became even more rough; this was an area that the town's snowplows didn't go. Anyone who lived up the mountain was tough. They lived at the mercy of the Alaskan wilderness and they always had a backup plan, too.

Peter darted one last glance at Darcy, hoping she'd be worth enough to Johnny that he'd give up his dreams of revenge. Hoping he didn't have his own plan that would leave all of them at his mercy.

The phone in his cup holder buzzed, startling Peter, and he glanced at it. *Alanna.* She'd arrived and was waiting for their go-ahead. Less than a minute later, Colter texted that he was in place, hidden off the side of the road. They were just waiting for Peter.

He hit the gas and his wheels spun out slightly. As he righted the vehicle, Darcy warned, "Don't drive us off the side of the road now. Not when we're so close."

She sounded too calm, like this had been her plan instead of his, and he tried not to let it worry him.

Then they were near the top of the mountain, still deep in the woods, as the first rays of morning sunrise started to filter through the trees. In theory, there weren't many routes off this mountain, just the main roads that snaked their way up and down, and they were sometimes impassable. But Alanna had lost him up here less than a week ago and if she could do it, so could Johnny.

He pulled the truck off the side of the road, far enough away that Johnny wouldn't be able to see him from the cabin. Then he took a deep breath and sent a group text. I'm here. Be careful.

I'm going in, Alanna responded.

From where he was positioned, Peter could see the very end of the Altiers driveway. He watched as Alanna's rental pulled in and then disappeared up toward the house. Now all he could do was wait.

Time seemed to stretch out forever and Peter couldn't stop his fingers from tapping a nervous beat against the steering wheel. Beside him, Darcy kept craning in her seat, trying to get a glimpse of the house. But it wouldn't happen. Alanna had told him exactly where to wait to stay out of view from the house.

Maybe he should go in. In theory, he'd be able to hear a gunshot from here, but a gun wasn't the only way to kill someone. Alanna was fairly tall for a woman and much stronger than her thin frame suggested, but he'd seen pictures of Johnny from five years ago. The man was six feet tall, even back then, and made up of all lean muscle. Plus, he was full of rage.

Peter glanced at the clock, then at his phone again. Ten minutes and no word. It was too long.

He was just reaching for the gear shift when an engine started up. The *clunk clunk* was familiar and Peter realized it was the same sound he'd heard at the last cabin. He mentally flashed back to that moment. Alanna had been getting through to Darcy. He'd seen the decision flash across her face, the recognition that it was time to stop running. Then that car had driven by—the old engine sounds grumbling—and she'd changed her mind. Johnny must have been driving up to get her.

Peter shook the memory clear as an old sedan backed down the drive. He grabbed the binoculars he'd stuck in his truck when he'd tracked Alanna on his day off and peered through them as the vehicle backed onto the street.

Johnny was in the car, but he was in the passenger seat. He glanced around, paranoia in his eyes but a smile on his face. He held a pistol, pointed toward the occupant of the driver's seat.

Peter glanced right and saw Alanna behind the wheel, her jaw clenched tight. As she stopped in the street, she gave an unmistakable triple nod of her head: the signal that Elysia had been left behind. Then the car shot forward, racing out of sight.

Peter held his breath as another vehicle pulled into the Altier cabin driveway. Peter backed into the street, then braced his foot on the brake, waiting.

"Come on, come on, come on," he muttered as Darcy demanded, "What are you doing? Follow them! Follow Johnny and Alanna! When I was caught, he ditched his phone to be safe. I don't have a way to get a hold of him anymore. Hurry!"

Every instinct he had demanded he pick his foot up off the brake and stomp down on the gas, catch up to Johnny and Alanna before she drove right off the mountain and the two of them disappeared. But he'd promised.

"Come on!"

At his shout, Darcy jerked in her seat but went quiet.

Then his phone buzzed with a message from Colter. *We've got Elysia.*

Peter shifted into Drive and stomped on the gas, making the back of his vehicle fishtail as snow sprayed out behind him. Then he and Darcy were off, racing down the mountain, hoping to catch up to Johnny and Alanna.

THIS ANGRY, SNARLING man holding a gun to her head as she drove was the "brother" who'd once carried her half a mile through the snow when she'd twisted her ankle playing. The brother who'd wiped her tears away when he'd caught her crying over missing the family she'd been taken from. The brother who'd told her he couldn't wait to watch her dancing at his wedding.

Every time the old sedan hit a bump on the potholed road down the mountain, Alanna grimaced, hoping Johnny's finger wasn't on the trigger.

Her plan had worked. She'd walked up to the front door and Johnny had opened it before she could even knock. He'd held the gun on her, then glanced past her at the driveway. When she'd offered to go with him if he left Elysia behind, he'd scoffed. Then he'd stared at her a long moment, nodded his head and let her look in on a sleeping Elysia, content in an old crib.

"I know you're not here alone. They try to come for me and I'll take you out first, you got that, Alanna?" he'd asked.

The coldness in his tone had dried up her mouth and all she could do was nod.

"Then let's go," he'd said, ushering her out the door. "I don't need the baby. And I'd never hurt her anyway. But you and I have a score to settle."

That had been five minutes ago. Hopefully by now, Elysia was cradled in Kensie's arms, on her way back to her parents' cabin.

Since then, Johnny had just looked over at her and demanded, "Are the cops coming?"

Alanna had shaken her head and stared back at him, feeling truthful, because the only cop around was Peter. And he wasn't coming until Elysia was safe. Even then, he'd have to catch up to them.

Johnny had always been able to read her. Maybe because he was older or he'd known her for so long, he'd always been able to tell when she was lying. This time, he'd just smiled and ordered her to head down the primary road off the mountain.

"I never wanted to hurt you, Johnny," she whispered, the fear she felt coming through in her voice.

He snorted, not moving the pistol away from her head. "Well, you sure screwed that up."

She darted a glance at him, taking in the new lines just visible across his forehead and the harsh line of his jaw, now shaded with dark stubble, that had still looked boyish five years ago. At twenty-three, there'd been something sad and pensive if you looked close enough into his eyes, but he had usually worn a smile on his face. Now there was nothing but anger.

An ache filled her chest, knowing her note had ripped his life apart and he hadn't been able to put together a newer, better one. Sadness followed, regret that she hadn't tried a note years earlier, back before Darcy and Julian had asked Johnny to lure Sydney away from a playground. Back when it might have made a difference to the life of the older "brother" she'd adored for so long.

Was the person she loved even in there anymore? Or had all the good in him been warped and destroyed?

She swiped at the tears that suddenly blinded her and Johnny snapped, "You don't get to cry. You caused this. You caused all of this."

She shook her head, wishing she could pull the car over, that they could just talk like old times. "Johnny—"

"Didn't you love us at all?" he asked, his voice suddenly softer, more uncertain, like the boy she remembered.

The boy she'd hugged tight while he shook with suppressed tears after Sydney had first come to live with them, had cried and slapped him, telling him she hated him. The boy whose skinned knees she'd helped bandage after he'd fallen on the roof they'd been building, skidding halfway down the side before catching himself. The boy she'd tried to keep up with when he took her snowshoeing through the woods.

"I've never stopped loving you," Alanna said, letting her foot lift off the gas a little, slowing their dangerous speed down the treacherous road.

He snorted. "That's a lie." But he lowered the pistol slightly away from her head and there was less fury in his tone.

The Johnny she remembered was still in there somewhere.

Her heart rate picked up, hope sparking through the fear. "There's another way, Johnny." She spoke fast, not wanting him to cut her off. "It doesn't have to be like this. It should never have been like this. But I still love you. You're still my brother."

"And what about our mother? What about our *father*?" He lifted the pistol again and when she looked over, she saw the tears glistening in his eyes.

"I didn't want any of that. But you know what they did was wrong. What they made *you* do was wrong."

"They looked after us," Johnny said, but there was a tremor in his voice, as if he was trying to convince himself it was true.

She could get through to him. She just needed a little time.

Alanna lifted her foot a tiny bit more off the gas. She didn't know what the next stage in his plan was, but if she could stretch out this trip, where she had his undivided attention, then maybe she'd have enough time to get through to him. Convince him to put the gun down and turn himself in.

Her gaze darted to the rearview mirror and she pushed down on the gas again. She'd started out at dangerous speeds, speeds someone not familiar with the mountain roads probably wouldn't be able to match. But Peter was coming for her. She needed to stay far enough in front of him that she could talk Johnny down, but not so far that he'd lose her if she was wrong.

She loved Johnny. Despite the things he'd done, he'd been a victim once, too. He deserved the chance to rehabilitate, the chance to start a real life for himself. One that hadn't been built from lies, where he was surrounded by people who loved him without stipulations, who'd support him as he rebuilt something better for himself.

Still, if he refused to take this chance, she wasn't willing to give up her own life for him. She deserved a chance to really start over, too. She wanted to be fully honest with her parents, Kensie and Flynn, about how conflicted she'd felt for the past five years. She wanted the chance to travel to Kansas to see Sydney in person again. To talk to Drew's and Valerie's parents, explain that she didn't want to relive the past with their kids, but to build a future where they were still a part of her family, too.

And she deserved a chance to tell Peter how much he'd come to mean to her over the past week. If she survived this last drive with Johnny, she was heading home to Chicago. Three thousand five hundred miles was too far to build a romantic relationship. But it wasn't too far to build a friendship. It was less than she wanted, but it was better than losing him.

Before she could fight for Peter, she had to convince Johnny that everything he believed about Darcy and Julian was wrong, that everything he believed about her was wrong. She took a deep breath, then said, "They *did* look after us. But they stole from us, too. They stole our chance to grow up with other people who loved us."

He made another sound of disbelief, but it was quieter this time and the gun was lowering again.

"I met your parents, you know."

Back at the hospital in Luna, five years ago, Johnny's parents had shown up, tearful and excited to see their son again, just as she'd been ready to leave for Chicago. She'd shyly said hello and his mom had squeezed her arm and whispered, "Your parents are going to be overjoyed." Then she'd looked at her husband and added, "We couldn't even believe this was real."

"You did?" Johnny asked.

His gun was on his lap now, his expression a mix of suspicion and anger. But beneath it all, there was interest. Beneath it all, there was still hope.

Still a chance.

"Yes," Alanna said, her hand twitching to take his.

Then suddenly a truck flew out in front of her from a side road, making her slam on the brakes. Her head flew forward, the seat belt painful across her chest. The back end of the sedan fishtailed wildly, the vehicle not equipped to handle this kind of terrain. They continued to skid downward and she pushed the brake harder as the ABS activated, praying she wasn't about to crash into the vehicle stopped in front of her.

Peter's vehicle.

The car kept moving and Alanna heard herself scream, even though she didn't remember opening her mouth. Somehow the car finally stopped, with only a soft screech of metal as the front end scraped the side of Peter's truck.

Then everything seemed to happen at once. Peter scrambled out of his truck as Johnny's hand fisted in her coat, his other hand unhooking her belt. Then she was being pulled across the front seats, her body bumping every surface, surely creating bruises everywhere as she tried to help herself along. Suddenly she was outside the car, Johnny's hand still rough on her biceps, his pistol against the side of her head.

Across from her, Peter stood with his own hostage. Darcy's hands were cuffed in front of her, but the woman actually looked serene, a half smile on her face as Peter shouted, "I've got a trade for you, Johnny. Alanna for Darcy."

Chapter Twenty

Peter had destroyed his career trying to save her.

Alanna swallowed back tears as she stared at him standing behind Darcy, his gaze steady on Johnny, his finger resting above the trigger guard on his pistol.

The metal of the pistol barrel against her own head felt cold even in the ambient Alaskan temperatures. Johnny stood behind her, using her as a human shield, his grip painful on her upper arm, his angry breaths puffing against the top of her head.

She'd almost gotten through to him. But just like with Darcy, in the end, she hadn't been able to reach him. Not in time.

"Johnny—"

"Shut up," he snapped. Then louder, to Peter, he yelled, "What's to stop me from shooting you and taking them both?"

Alanna flinched, trying to twist in his grip despite the gun to her head. "No!"

"I'm a trained police officer," Peter said, his voice calm and steady. "You could miss and hit your mother. I won't miss."

She felt Johnny jerk at Peter's words, felt her own heart thud harder at the threat, at the idea of watching her older brother die right beside her.

"Your sister taught me something, Johnny. She taught me that love is stronger than hate. I know what you're feeling right now. You feel betrayed. You're angry with Alanna. But you still love her, just like she loves you."

"I don—" Johnny started.

"She doesn't want to go with you. She risked her life to protect her niece. You're her older brother. It's *your* job to protect *her*. It's your job to make sure she's happy. Let her go. You can take Darcy. The two of you can disappear. It's not right and you know it, but you can do it. Just let Alanna go. Please."

Johnny's hand loosened slightly on her arm and Alanna stared at Peter and the stoic determination on his face. It was probably all Johnny saw: a trained police officer who wasn't afraid, who'd be willing to shoot two kidnappers to save someone.

But she saw past that to the fear in his bright blue eyes. And she knew shooting Johnny would be his very last resort, something he'd only do if Johnny's finger started depressing the trigger on the gun to her head. She knew it was because she loved Johnny.

"Do it, Johnny," Darcy said. "Let Alanna go."

Alanna's gaze skipped to Darcy, saw the exhaustion on her face, the regret that said maybe she'd finally realized how many lives she'd hurt.

The hand squeezing her biceps released and the metal barrel against her head moved, redirecting to point toward Peter.

"Alanna, come here," Peter said, his gaze still entirely focused on Johnny as he let go of Darcy.

Alanna took a hesitant step forward, afraid any quick movement would startle someone, would make a nervous finger twitch against a trigger. Then she took another, her legs wobbly as Darcy moved past her in the other direction.

Darcy's gaze swung to her for the briefest moment, skimming over her face as if she was memorizing it. A sad smile flitted over her lips, then she mouthed something that might have been "Sorry."

Alanna took another step and then Peter's hand was on her arm, shoving her behind him as Darcy ran to the sedan and jumped in the driver's seat.

Johnny's gun stayed steady on Peter as he screamed, "Give me the key to the handcuffs!"

Peter tossed them over, his gun never moving off target.

Johnny caught them one-handed and jumped into the passenger seat. Then the sedan sputtered, the wheels spitting snow as Darcy, still handcuffed, maneuvered it around them.

Peter kept his weapon trained on Johnny and Johnny held his pistol in kind until the car was out of sight. Then Peter holstered his weapon and spun around, yanking her into his arms so hard she could barely breathe.

"I've got her," he said and it took her a moment to realize he'd pulled out his phone and was talking into it. After a short pause, he said, "Hurry. Darcy and Johnny are on their way down the mountain. They'll get off the main road now that I have Alanna, but we're close to the bottom. Come pick her up. I'm going after them."

As he hung up the phone and pulled back so he could look at her, Alanna asked, "How did you—"

"Darcy showed me a side road to get in front of Johnny's car. Colter and Kensie are only a few minutes behind us. They're coming to get you. I'm going after Johnny and Darcy. I've got to call in backup—I sent them all the way to Luna, but they might have figured out by now that it was a misdirect."

"Peter, you shouldn't have—"

"Don't worry. You're more important than a job."

Before she could reply, his lips crashed down onto hers. His kisses felt desperate, frantic, relieved.

She barely had time to wind her arms around his neck and kiss him back before he was pulling free. He smiled briefly at her, touched her cheek with his gloved hand and said, "I'll do what I can to bring them in safely."

Colter's truck raced up beside them and Peter jumped in his own vehicle. He waved a quick goodbye and then he was off.

Alanna stared after him until she couldn't see his truck anymore, then turned toward Colter and Kensie with tears in her eyes.

Was someone she loved still going to die today?

ALANNA WAS SAFE. But there were two kidnappers on the loose and it was Peter's fault.

The law said so, but so did Peter's conscience. He had a shot at catching up to them alone, at getting Darcy back behind bars before anyone at the station realized what had happened, but it was a long one. He'd be more likely to capture Darcy and Johnny with help.

He didn't call Tate as he maneuvered down the slippery mountain roads, scanning any bisecting road for signs of Johnny's car. He didn't want Tate implicated any more than he already was. Instead, Peter called Chief Hernandez directly.

"Where the hell are you?" the chief demanded, her voice a tight hiss. "And where is Darcy Altier?"

"You're back at the station?"

"Heading there right now. I got a call from Sam, who was stationed in the front."

"We have Elysia Hayes. She's safe. But Alanna traded herself for Elysia and I—"

"You traded Darcy for Alanna." There was no surprise

in Chief Hernandez's voice, just a quiet fury that told him unquestionably that his career was unsalvageable.

The grief tightened his chest, made it hard to breathe, but he forced it to the back of his mind. "I'm almost at the bottom of the mountain on the Desparre side, trying to catch up to Darcy and Johnny. They're in an old mustard-colored sedan. Plates are muddied and unreadable, but you'll hear the car before you see it."

"You'd better hope like hell we find it," Chief Hernandez said. "For your sake and your partner's."

"Tate had nothing—" he started, but the chief hung up before he could finish.

Silently cursing Tate for jumping into the middle of his lie, even if it had helped sell it, Peter pushed his truck harder. Hopefully he wouldn't pass Johnny and Darcy right by as he hurried to the base of the mountain. Because once they got onto flat ground, they had more options, more ways to disappear. Darcy and Julian had stayed under the radar for eighteen years. Even once police had suspected she was in Desparre, even with her face so well-known from the media coverage, Darcy had still managed to avoid them. She'd probably still be at large if it weren't for Alanna. If Darcy and Johnny got off this mountain, he'd probably lose them forever.

Then he heard it. An old engine turning over and over, but not catching.

Peter hit the brakes hard, certain they'd heard him, too. He eased his truck slowly forward, inching toward the break in the forest ahead that suggested a side street.

Before he reached it, he stopped the truck. He left it running as he climbed out. Maybe it would give him a slight element of surprise if they thought he was still creeping forward in his vehicle instead of on foot. He texted a quick location to Chief Hernandez, then messaged Colter, too, telling him not to come any closer until help arrived. Then Peter slid his pistol from his holster, hoping Johnny didn't already have a bead on him through the dense trees.

He couldn't see the car yet and suddenly, he couldn't hear it anymore, either. They knew he was here.

Hurry up, he willed his team as he slid against the closest tree, moving cautiously forward. He couldn't wait for them, couldn't risk letting Johnny and Darcy get away again.

Johnny's voice rang out. "I'm a better shot than you give me credit for."

Peter froze, pressed harder against the tree as he scanned his surroundings. Could Johnny see him or was he hoping Peter would respond, give away his location?

"I'm afraid I'm going to need your truck," Johnny said as Peter twisted his head, trying to use his good ear to pinpoint the man's location. "Toss me the keys and I'll let *you* walk away. Otherwise, I'm going to have to take them off you."

He was straight ahead. Probably Darcy was too, although Peter couldn't rule out that she actually held the weapon. Johnny could be distracting him so Darcy could flank him and put a bullet in his head.

Except as Peter crept sideways, darting to the tree beside and slightly ahead of him, there was Johnny. He was scanning the forest, too, his attention mainly focused near Peter's still-running truck. Darcy was beside him, her hand on his arm.

As Peter lined the sight of his pistol on Johnny's center mass, Darcy's whisper carried through the woods. "It's over. You can't shoot him. Your sister loves him."

The weapon in his hands gave a violent shake before Peter righted it again, Darcy's words ringing in his ears. Why would she say that? Had Alanna said something to her when Peter hadn't been with her, made some calculated comment meant to help protect him that wasn't actually true? Or was it possible that Alanna was falling for him the way he was falling for her?

"We have to get out of here," Johnny whispered to her. "I'm not letting you go back to jail."

Darcy's hand pushed down on Johnny's arm, forcing his weapon to lower. "I don't want to go back, either. But I'm not letting you *kill* someone."

Johnny wrenched his arm free, lifting the weapon again, scanning the woods. But the expression on his face was conflicted.

Then sirens sounded, approaching quickly, and Johnny's pistol whipped in their direction.

If he fired at the police officers, they'd shoot back. Just like Peter, they were trained to shoot to kill.

This was Alanna's brother. And she still loved him.

Peter stepped out from behind the tree, keeping his weapon centered on Johnny. "Put it down. Please."

Johnny swiveled toward him, sighting his pistol on Peter's face, his gun hand shaking.

"Johnny, this is the moment that defines the rest of your life. If you fire that weapon, my team *has* to shoot you. Please don't make them tell Alanna you died here today. She loves you. She still wants a relationship with you. You still have a life ahead of you. *Please*."

The sirens ended as the police vehicles came to hard stop. Officers jumped out, using the doors as shields.

"Hang on," Peter yelled. "Just wait! He's putting it down. Right, Johnny?"

Peter stepped forward and lowered his weapon, knowing the team had Johnny in their sights. "Please. Please."

"It's over, Johnny," Darcy whispered.

Johnny glanced at her, then lowered his arm and tossed his gun in the snow.

Then Peter's team was swarming the woods, pushing both Johnny and Darcy against the cars, frisking and cuffing them. Tate was with them, but he stayed back at the edge of the woods, his expression pained as he stared at Peter.

The fact that Tate was here right now meant at least his partner's job was safe. But his expression told Peter everything he needed to know about his own. He looked right and suddenly Chief Hernandez was beside him, hand out.

"Give me your weapon, Robak."

Even knowing it was coming, the request hurt. With shaking hands, Peter unholstered his gun and handed it to the chief. He didn't make her ask for his badge and just handed that over silently, too.

She gave a sharp nod over his shoulder and then Charlie Quinn was behind him, yanking his arms behind his back.

The sound of the handcuffs snapping over his wrists echoed in the woods and then Chief Hernandez shook her head. "You're under arrest, Peter."

Epilogue

Three weeks ago, when those handcuffs had closed over his wrists, Peter had felt the life he'd worked so hard for slipping out of his grasp forever. He'd glanced over at Tate through the trees, grateful that his friend wasn't facing the same treatment.

He'd spent a week in the Desparre jail. He'd asked his family not to come see him and told Tate not to let Alanna back to the cells, either. The last time she saw him wasn't going to be through the bars of a jail cell. At least that way, when she climbed aboard the airplane with Kensie and Colter, her last memory of him would be the kiss they'd shared.

He'd been sure his arrest would make the news. There'd be no way to hide it from her. But he hadn't wanted her to see him, to try to help. Hadn't wanted to give her one more thing to feel guilty over when it had been his decision. And he'd do it again. Even if it hadn't turned out okay in the end.

Now Peter handed over his ID at the tiny airport a few hours outside of Desparre. The next flight to Chicago left in two hours. Along with the three legs of the flight and the layovers in between, that meant he'd land in Chicago eighteen hours from now. Maybe in that time, he'd figure out exactly what he was going to say.

Alanna had called the station a few times over the past few weeks, trying to get through to him, presumably not knowing the outcome of his arrest, since the chief had actually kept it out of the press. Alanna had even managed to dig up Tate's number and had Colter call Chief Hernandez. He'd asked them all to just pass on that he would be fine, without giving any specifics. He didn't want to give her false hope, didn't want to open the lines of communication if he was going to spend the next five to ten years behind bars. Didn't want to say anything at all until he was one hundred percent sure.

Nodding his thanks to the clerk who handed back his card and took his luggage, Peter headed to security, which was light as usual. It was a small airport, mostly jumper flights in and out of Fairbanks.

After passing through the X-ray machine, he went straight for the big window to stare out at the vast snowy expanse that represented Alaska to him. He'd be back, of course. His whole family lived here. When he had told them about his plans, they'd all looked at him like he was out of his mind and then erupted with arguments. Until his mom had simply held up a hand to silence everyone. Staring straight at him, she'd asked, "Are you sure?" When he'd nodded, she'd smiled sadly and said, "I expect you back here every two months, minimum. Got it?"

With the promise secured, he'd headed home and packed enough for a month. Hopefully in that time, he'd know.

Taking a deep breath, he turned his back on the openness of Alaska that he loved.

Then a loud bark made his head swivel and there was Chance, bounding toward him through the airport.

"What the—" Peter knelt down as Chance reached him and almost got knocked over for his trouble. "Easy, boy." He hugged the dog, looking over his head. "Where's Alanna?"

Then he spotted her, rounding the corner at a run, her rolling luggage making a *thunk thunk thunk* sound, her long dark hair trailing behind her.

He stood, running to meet her with Chance on his heels.

She skidded to a stop and he did, too, a foot away from her. Chance plowed in between them, walking through and back, punctuating each turn with a bark.

"Chance, relax," Alanna admonished, then stared up at Peter. "What are you doing here?"

"What are *you* doing here? Didn't you go home weeks ago?"

She settled her luggage next to her, slapped her hands on her hips. "Yes, when Colter and Kensie insisted there was no talking any sense into you, that you were never going to see me." Her eyes watered over, then she blinked the moisture away. "Why did you do that?"

He reached out, taking her hand. "I didn't know what my future held. I didn't want to tie you to it."

"I was already tied to it. It was my fault—"

"That's just it," he cut her off. "It wasn't your fault. And I don't want us to be connected by obligation."

She stared at him a long moment, then asked, "What happened? Last I heard, you'd been arrested."

"I was. But Tate talked the chief into filing things differently. *A police decision without proper documentation*, is I think how he framed it. That's not exactly how it ended up, but he saved me jail time."

Her shoulders relaxed, a smile lighting up her face. "So, your job is okay?"

"No." The smile faded and he squeezed her hand a little tighter, feeling awkward reaching across the space between them, but not willing to get any closer. Not yet. "I'll never be a police officer again."

This time, the tears did spill over. "Peter, I'm so sorry. I never—"

"Don't you dare apologize. It hurt, but it's not the first time I've left behind a job I loved. At least this time, it was a conscious decision. I knew what was on the line when I broke Darcy out. I got more than I deserved, because Tate is a damn good friend and Chief Hernandez can be nicer than she seems. And now…"

"Now what?"

He took a deep breath, suddenly nervous and very aware of how much he'd needed those eighteen hours to figure out what he was going to say to her. "I took a new job. It's a trial period, but I'm going back to reporting."

"Oh." Alanna's fingers twitched in his. "Back into a war zone?"

"No. I'm going to cover crime. With my background as a police officer and a reporter, they thought I'd be the perfect fit. It's not exactly where I thought I'd be right now, but I'm glad. I'm hoping you'll be happy about it, too."

"Well, yes. I'm sorry you can't be a cop anymore and I wish… Well, I'm glad you've found something else that excites you." She glanced down at their linked hands. "Peter, look, I came back here because I couldn't take all the silence. No matter what, I had to see you. I know we didn't have long together, but I…" She took a visible breath and Chance nudged up against her, as if to say, *Spit it out*, then sat at her side. "In the time we spent together, I've developed feelings for you. I want to see where that goes."

"Alanna—"

"Just hear me out." She stepped closer, almost close enough to kiss. "I know a cross-country relationship won't be easy. But I miss Alaska. I want to visit more. And I think you'd like Chicago. I really do. If we each travel to one another a few times a year, I really think—"

"Alanna, stop."

She looked at her feet, then back up at him. "I know you care for me, Peter. I—"

"I love you," he said, cutting her off. "I know it's fast. Too fast, maybe. But it's there and it's real and I'm not letting it go." He took a step closer, until he *could* kiss her if he just leaned down. "I'm not letting *you* go. I do want to travel back and forth a bit—my family insists on it, actually—but the job is in Chicago."

Her mouth dropped open and she just stared at him.

"I know you need to be there," he said softly. "It's right that you should get time with the family you were denied for so long. You deserve that. And I want to be where you are."

She continued to stare until he let out a nervous laugh. "Too much? I know—"

Before he could finish the sentence, she was up on her tiptoes, falling against him, her arms around his neck and her lips on his.

When she finally pulled free, her cheeks flushed and her eyes sparkling, she whispered, "I love you, too, Peter."

Then Chance pushed his way in between them and Alanna laughed.

Peter took hold of her luggage and her hand, then spun back toward the entrance.

Alanna hurried to keep up. "Where are we going?"

"I'm thinking back to my place. I'm hanging on to it for when we visit here. What do you say we stay here for a few days, then head home to Chicago?"

She stopped abruptly, making him pause, too. "Home to Chicago." She smiled, grabbing hold of him for one more kiss. "I like the sound of that."

* * * * *

COLTON'S DANGEROUS LIAISON

REGAN BLACK

For Mark, my personal hero and partner through everything. Here's to the next thirty years!

Chapter One

Melissa Colton studied the ebb and flow of hundreds of guests enjoying the lively wedding reception. She recognized nearly every face. Friends and family, most of them local to Grave Gulch, the vast majority tied to the city's police department, of which Melissa was chief. It was refreshing to see the people she cared for so much cut loose and celebrate the occasion.

At twenty-two, Mary, the newly minted Mrs. Edwin Suzuki, made a stunning bride in her winter-white gown that highlighted her petite form perfectly. She wore her long, dark hair down tonight, and it spilled in artful waves over her shoulders. Such a contrast to the dark blue uniform she wore while working as the front-desk clerk at the Grave Gulch Police Department. The entire department was happy for Mary, though they would miss her while she was away on her honeymoon.

Mary and Edwin were practically glowing as they danced and visited with their guests. And why not? Surrounded by loved ones, today marked the beginning of a bright future for the newlyweds.

She'd confided to Melissa the plan to spend the wedding night here at the bridal suite of the Grave Gulch Hotel. Tomorrow they'd travel to whatever tropical destination Edwin had chosen, well away from the typically bitter cold of Michigan in January.

When—*if*—Melissa married, she envisioned a summertime event. This beautiful historic hotel could work, if they held the ceremony outside in one of the lush courtyards full of summer color. They'd host the reception on the grassy bluff where she and her currently imaginary groom and all their friends would enjoy the extended twilight and stars winking into view over Lake Michigan.

And in pondering that wispy future, she realized suddenly she was missing the magic of this moment. Right here, tonight, the couple radiated pure happiness in the grand ballroom that had been decorated like a winter wonderland. Boughs of sparkling, silver-dusted evergreens and ivy twined with soft blush roses, and pops of deep red berries framed the arched windows and doors, and decorated each table.

Out on the dance floor, Melissa spotted her plus-one, Martin Tate, having a blast with another woman and resisted another little pang of envy. Oh, not of the woman he was with, just the romance of the occasion.

But the timing that was right for Mary and Edwin wasn't right for everyone.

Melissa had been twenty-two during her rookie year as a police officer. A husband and family were the furthest things from her mind then. Fourteen years later, she'd earned her post as the chief of police and took great pride in the accomplishment. Though she had no regrets, a little balance between a fabulous career and what amounted to a pitiful personal life would be nice. Edwin and Mary were utterly lost in each other and the mutual devotion was so beautiful. Had she missed her window for a husband and family entirely?

Martin was a prime illustration. He was a local, successful handyman and she'd been invested in their relationship right up to the day he'd dumped her. She'd thought they were fine, while apparently, he'd grown frustrated with coming in second to her job, weary of her changing plans or bailing on dates due to one emergency or two others. She was thankful they'd salvaged their friendship, though, or she would've arrived to the reception alone.

This was a silly time for a pity party and she had to work to shake it off, find a better distraction. With a mental chuckle, she wished Martin better luck with his new dance partner. Melissa didn't regret the hard work or any of the tough choices that had carried her to her current position as chief of police. Events like this just left the door open for doubts to creep in and push at her from every angle. From the newlyweds to the happily married couples to the children, ranging from toddlers to teens, it seemed every exuberant person served as a reminder of what she didn't have...which she'd recently felt a deep longing to have.

No husband or children. No partner to wake up next to or unwind with at the end of the day. No one willing to share a meal, no round-faced baby to rock to sleep or a little one to chase around the playground. She'd all but given up on finding a man willing to exchange vows and build a family with her. She'd never trade her job for anything—and it came with too much baggage.

She sipped the sparkling punch and smiled as the music changed to a Frank Sinatra ballad. At the center of the dance floor, the bride stepped into her groom's embrace. They shared a sweet kiss and started to sway. All around them, others paired up as Sinatra's voice cast a romantic spell.

Melissa swallowed the lump in her throat, searching for any other place to focus her attention. Would her natural ambition be as all-consuming had she been in any other career? It was a question she'd asked herself more frequently, knowing she didn't want to settle for a solitary life. She wanted it all: the satisfying work *and* the loving, messy family. The self-help books and gurus claimed she could have everything, others said she could have it, but not all at once, and still more experts touted that a definitive choice had to be made. She still wasn't sure which view was right.

A fresh awareness stung the back of her throat. Right here and now, she'd choose family. A surprise, considering her badge was wedged into her tiny purse alongside her cell phone and a lipstick.

In the aisle between a row of tables and the dance floor, her cousin Desiree Colton, and her eighteen-month-old son, Danny, danced with Melissa's older brother, Clarke. The trio was laughing and Melissa grinned as she crossed the room to join them. Seeing her, Danny dashed her way and she scooped up the toddler. Kissing his nose, Melissa spun them in a circle while he giggled. The sound was so addictive, the pure joy on his handsome little face so uplifting. She drank it in, giving him another spin before nudging him back to his mom.

She and Desiree had always been close, but since Danny's birth, they'd spent even more time together. Though Melissa was aware it wasn't all smooth sailing, Desiree managed single motherhood with such devotion and grace that Melissa often wondered if she couldn't have it all, that maybe she could manage at least one child.

Of course, when she'd confided in Desiree, her cousin had pointed out that she was a part-time sketch artist and had schedule flexibility. Meanwhile, Melissa had a full-time job that was far more demanding. Having a baby on her own would mean leaning heavily on the help of her parents, who had active lives of their own, as well as finding an affordable nanny willing to take over no matter when a call came through.

Enough of the litany of what-ifs, she scolded herself, stepping outside into the winter garden for a moment. She wasn't here to wallow; she was here to celebrate Mary and Edwin.

With the music drifting softly behind her, she walked along the cleared path. White lights were strung overhead, turning the fresh snow to a blanket of diamonds. Heaters had been strategically placed along the walkway to prevent anyone from catching a chill. Silk floral arrangements, in deference to the season, echoed the colors and textures of Mary's bridal bouquet. It almost made Melissa rethink her ideal summer wedding.

Refreshed, she headed back inside, pausing at the beverage station for another glass of punch. Several guests were enjoying the open bar, but Melissa had a rule about drinking in public. Other than a single beer at the annual department picnic, she didn't indulge. She put stock in being ready for anything. A young man, wearing the black shirt, slacks and shoes of the hotel catering uniform, walked up to the station to collect the dirty glassware.

"Victor Hadley?" Melissa asked. When he turned

and smiled, her entire mood lifted. "Wow. It's good to see you."

"Look, Chief. No handcuffs," he joked, parting his hands. Tall, bordering on skinny, he hadn't quite outgrown that sharp-elbow-and-knee teenager stage yet.

Victor was the grandson of one of her mother's friends. Melissa had met him when he was fifteen, after he'd been arrested for shoplifting. She'd worked with the store owners, arresting officers and Victor to negotiate a lengthy and strict community-service penalty rather than bring formal charges against him. Once his year of community service had been completed, she'd spoken with several local leaders to get him interviews for various jobs he could work around his high-school schedule. He'd been working here at the hotel quite happily, based on what she heard, ever since his first day.

"Mr. Ruiz," Victor said, referring to the hotel owner, "is amazing. He sat in on my last personnel review."

"You're kidding." The idea of the wealthy hotelier with a reputation for serial dating giving any attention to a kid from the wrong side of the tracks shocked her.

"No. It was cool. Intimidating, but cool," he added. "He asked about my interests here and what I had planned after graduation."

She smothered another wave of surprise. "You want to own hotels?"

Victor laughed. "Not really. Wouldn't mind running a kitchen, though."

"Seriously?"

He nodded. "Someday." Excitement shone in his gaze. "Long way from here to there. I have so much to learn. Mr. Ruiz added me to an apprentice program, though."

"That's wonderful," Melissa said. Though she wanted

to catch up further, she didn't want to impede his work. "I can't wait to hear more as you progress. If you ever need a taste-tester, come by the station."

He laughed again as he carted away the dirty glassware, leaving her with a satisfied mood boost. Success stories within the community were one of the high points of her career. Antonio Ruiz was a well-respected businessman and invaluable asset in the city. He seemed to hire talented staffers in every area of his hotel operation. Victor's situation was just one example. Mary, during the wedding planning, had mentioned time and again how professional and streamlined the entire process had been, from the first tour to the final walk-through before her big day.

Melissa appreciated the business acumen that brought tourists to the hotel, but she never would've guessed that the strikingly handsome owner had a heart inclined to guide teens with a knack for getting into trouble. It was an appealing, heartwarming discovery, though it didn't make Antonio her type. He escorted a new date to every event and she was looking for commitment. When she had time to look at all. "You look pensive."

She turned toward the familiar voice and gave one of her younger brothers, Travis, a warm smile. "In a good way," she promised. "Are you enjoying yourself?"

"I am," he replied. A highly successful businessman, he was the founder and co-CEO of Colton Plastics. Somehow Travis hadn't gravitated to law enforcement, or a profession connected to it, like the rest of them.

"Why aren't you out on the dance floor?" She peered around his shoulder, making it obvious she was looking for his date.

"Up-tempo isn't my thing." He raised a bottle of beer

to his lips. "You know it's better if I don't put lives at risk with my two left feet," he said with a wink.

"Left feet or not, you know what Mom would say about making sure everyone is having a good time." Even as she said it, she scanned the reception, impressed that no one seemed to be hovering at the fringes of the action or looking left out. Guests who weren't on the dance floor seemed happily engaged in conversations.

"Why do you think I'm standing with you?" Travis said pointedly.

"Was I really the only one alone?" That brushed up too closely to her earlier melancholy.

"That's how it looked to me, Chief," he teased.

"Stop," she said, chuckling at the tone. She was fortunate to have her family's full support in her career with the GGPD. Aside from the requisite sibling jokes, her parents and brothers made it clear they were proud of her accomplishments. "Don't worry about me," she assured him. "I'm having a great time."

"Glad to hear it. Is that legal?" He tipped his head toward their youngest brother, Stanton, who was doing the twist with a bunch of other guests.

Her laughter was cut short by a shout and frantic movement at the tables on the other side of the room. "Danny!" Desiree yelled urgently, pitching her voice over the music and voices.

Her cousin dropped out of Melissa's sight for a moment, likely looking under a table. When she popped back into view, the color had leached from her face and her panic was clear as Melissa rushed across the room.

"Danny! Where are you?" she shouted again. Her long curly hair was in disarray from her searching and her frantic plea filled the room as people quieted and the music stopped. She hurried toward the long curtains framing the tall windows. "Danny!" she screamed. "Mel!" She grabbed Melissa's arm, her grip brutal with her anguish. "You have to help me. I can't find him. Oh, God. Help me find him."

"I will. We will," Melissa said, sliding seamlessly into her professional role even while her heart hammered in her chest. She raised her hand, signaling for everyone's attention. "Folks, it seems Danny has wandered off. He's only eighteen months old." She described his clothing and directed the officers in attendance to systematically search the garden, the anteroom and the hallways. "Show me where you last saw him," she said to Desiree as everyone joined in the effort to find the little boy.

Desiree guided her to the table where they'd been seated for the reception. All around them guests shook their heads, but kept looking. There was no sign of Danny, other than the stylish tote Desiree carried with his necessities.

The officers Melissa had sent into the courtyard and the hallway returned. "No luck?" she asked.

"None."

Melissa steeled herself for the next step, striving to maintain the stoic appearance of a responding officer when she was breaking apart with panic inside. She quickly assigned officers to comb the streets around the hotel and then she called the station.

She nudged her cousin into a chair while she waited for an answer. "Find something with his scent, please," she said gently. Tears streamed down Desiree's face as she clutched the tote. "We'll find him," Melissa promised again. "Just pull out a shirt or his favorite blanket or something."

The GGPD had two K-9 officers, one specializing in tracking and one in suspect apprehension. She wanted them both on scene immediately. Fortunately, Officer Brett Shea and his tracking specialist partner, a female black Labrador named Ember, were at the station. He promised to call Officer Coleman and his German shepherd partner, Bear, on the way to the hotel.

Although fighting her own emotions, Melissa felt marginally better already. "The K-9 teams are on the way," she said. A flicker of hope flashed across Desiree's face. The officers and their partners had earned excellent reputations in the region for helping on a variety of cases.

With one hand on her cousin's trembling shoulder, all Melissa could do now was hang on and trust in her officers to pick up a lead on Danny.

FROM HIS OFFICE on the second floor, Antonio Ruiz, owner of the Grave Gulch Hotel, tried to ignore the wedding reception going strong in the main ballroom. Oh, he couldn't hear the music or happy voices, couldn't see the celebration unless he went to the security office and watched through the cameras. But he knew it was happening. It was the first big event of the year and normally by now he would've checked in with the staff to make sure things were running smoothly. Sometimes, depending on the occasion, he dropped in on guests and thanked them for choosing his hotel.

Not tonight.

He had no intention of going anywhere close to that ballroom. He was sure the vast majority of the GGPD was down there. Although he valued their role in the community, the police were not his favorite people these days, not even the intelligent, pretty redhead who served as the chief. As a major property owner, it was smart to maintain a good rapport with law enforcement. Up until six months ago, he would've claimed that bond was as strong and healthy here as it was at his other locations around the country.

Not anymore.

Grave Gulch was home and it stung more than a little that the police department had let him down when he'd needed them to step up and take action. Last summer, he'd reported a harrowing incident involving a fellow businessman he'd considered a new friend, Drew Orr.

Antonio rubbed at his temples. It was done; he should be over it. The situation had been a near miss all around. Thankfully, he'd learned Orr's business values and strategies didn't line up with his *before* he'd signed the proposed contract for a multiproperty deal here in town. Though Orr had been good at hiding his shady nature, Antonio eventually saw through the act. Orr was the type of investor who gave them all a bad name. The man viewed bribes as one more cost of doing business and had a shocking willingness to cut corners on construction.

As if that ever worked.

This time last year, he cut all ties with Orr, never expecting to see him again. But in July, the man had shown up out of the blue with blood on his hand, muttering about having killed his girlfriend. He'd claimed she cheated on him, so he'd attacked her and buried the body in a remote corner of Grave Gulch Park. Claimed a lot of things that sounded like rambling excuses to Antonio's ears. He'd urged Orr to go to the police, but the man had run off. Worried some piece of the story might be true, he'd gone straight over to the GGPD and reported the incident.

What had they done about it?

Not nearly enough. Granted, he wasn't a cop, but from his perspective their investigation had been seriously lacking. In his business experience, weak teams reflected the leadership. Sure, they'd found the body and questioned Orr, but they hadn't seen any sign of blood on him and nothing connected him to the crime.

In fact, Orr had fed them some story about jealousy and reputation that had the police taking a hard look at Antonio for the murder. He was furious but he should have expected it of the man after learning how willing he'd been to blur the lines to serve his own interests.

He had a solid alibi, since he'd been helping out an elderly neighbor with yard work that afternoon, but the entire mess only reinforced Antonio's long-held intention to remain as independent as possible. In business and his personal life.

Although hosting weddings at his hotel was lucrative and a consistent boost to the bottom line, this was one contract he'd been tempted to override with a rejection. Fortunately, his business sense and community spirit trumped his temptation to be petty. Just because the GGPD lacked professionalism didn't mean he had to stoop to their level.

Someone knocked rapidly and the door swung open before he could issue an invitation.

"Mr. Ruiz, there's an emergency," Victor said, breathless.

For a split second, Antonio just stared. He surged up from his chair. "Tell me on the way."

"A little boy is missing from the wedding reception," Victor began as they jogged for the stairs.

Antonio listened, dread mounting, as the situation of the missing toddler was laid out for him. There was nothing worse than losing a child—at any age, in any manner. "How long?"

Victor shrugged. "Maybe fifteen minutes. Chief Colton has a search started. I heard someone mention a tracking dog."

"Good." Approaching the ballroom, he slowed his steps, refusing to add to the chaos and panic. But the expansive room was almost quiet and he found GGPD Chief Melissa Colton at the center, taking reports and giving orders. She wasn't in uniform, but she was definitely in charge.

"Tell security to start looking for anyone leaving this room. Tell them to go back thirty minutes."

"Yes, sir." Victor took off at a run, but Antonio couldn't focus on that lapse right now.

He walked in and her gaze locked on him. Almost as if she'd sensed a newcomer invading her domain. Her department's weak response had disappointed him when he'd reported Orr. Tonight, however, she projected fearless strength, competence and confidence.

He wanted to pause and drink her in. Though he often saw her classic oval face and blue eyes unframed because she wore her hair in a ponytail or bun while working, she looked different tonight. Her beautiful red hair was swept up and back in a sleek, formal twist, with a few curled tendrils softly framing her face. Someone had done her eyes in a way that made them look bigger, and brighter than ever. Or maybe that was the crisis. Her skin looked as silky as fresh cream, her throat and shoulders shown to perfection by the forest-green dress she wore.

He couldn't recall ever seeing her out of uniform before. Certainly never in a dress that emphasized every supple curve of her lovely body. This was probably the worst time to register that she wasn't just pretty, she was an absolute knockout.

"Chief Colton," he said, extending a hand. "Victor told me we have a situation. How can I help you find the boy?"

"I appreciate the offer," she began. "Your security office was my next stop."

"I have them searching for anyone leaving the reception in the past thirty minutes."

Her chin dipped in acknowledgment. For a moment, he could've sworn her eyes filled with tears. He braced for waterworks, then she blinked and her gaze was as clear and steady as her voice.

"We're searching for Danny Colton. Eighteen months old. Last seen right here, approximately fifteen minutes ago." She turned the cell phone in her hands and showed him a picture of the little guy.

"Please send that to the hotel security's email address." He spelled out the address when she was ready and watched her hit Send. "Do you need more searchers?"

"My officers are working the area," she replied. She paused, her nostrils flaring. "Creating a search grid," she continued when she had control again. "Our K-9 officers will be on-site any minute. Most everyone in the room is local or federal law enforcement." Her auburn eyebrows flexed. "I have no idea who managed a kidnapping under our noses."

It seemed the embarrassment was holding her other emotions in check, but there was a deeply personal panic just under that cool exterior.

He considered himself a businessman, but dealing with people was his real specialty. His expansive success in the hospitality industry was due to his gift for reading guests, as well as his teams. Early on he discovered an innate ability to recognize the specific talents of his staff members. He loved matching the right person to a role where they could thrive. Every year, he headed up training sessions to teach his employees how to anticipate guest needs. The consistent rave reviews from guests spoke to their expertise. "I have surveillance cameras all around the property," he said. It was a fact she should remember after he'd shared surveillance footage of Orr's last visit to the hotel six months ago. "We can review all the angles in the security office."

She hesitated, her gaze sliding to the woman seated at the table, the only person not actively searching. "This is my cousin, Desiree Colton, Danny's mother."

Antonio crouched in front of the distraught mother. "We will do everything possible to find your son. You'd be surprised how many fun places there are to hide in a hotel. With your permission, I'll borrow Melissa for a few—"

"Melissa!"

Antonio stood up as two men came barreling across the room. He recognized both Clarke Colton and Ken Maxwell from previous professional visits to the hotel. Clarke, Melissa's brother, was a private investigator. Ken, a wedding videographer, was one of the best around when it came to capturing every priceless moment for the bride and groom.

"Have you found him?" Desiree asked, swiping tears from her cheeks.

Clarke gave Desiree's shoulder a squeeze. "We might have a lead," he said, his hesitant tone indicating extreme caution. "It's progress."

He tipped his head, indicating Melissa should step aside with him. "You need to see this."

Melissa soothed Desiree before joining Clarke and Ken at the next table. Antonio followed so he could see what they'd found, as well.

Melissa gave him a sharp look over her shoulder. "What are you doing?"

"Observing. If there's a face or good angle of exit, I'll know just which cameras to ask my security team to focus on."

"Right." She turned her attention to the other men. "Show me."

With the four of them crowded around his camera, Ken tapped the screen and the video clip played, showing a small face peeking around the side of a woman.

"That's Danny," she whispered.

His little face was visible just long enough to leave no doubt. The abductor's back was to the camera; she wore a navy blue dress, and a fancy hat. The video didn't show her shoes, but it seemed either the weight of the toddler or something else was putting some stress on her stride.

Antonio immediately put the images in context. The videographer had been across the room when he'd inadvertently caught the kidnapper's exit through the side door of the ballroom. He made a mental note of the 6:13 p.m. time stamp in the corner of the screen and then asked, "How many children Danny's age are here tonight?"

"Only Danny," Clarke answered. "He's the youngest."

Melissa directed the videographer to enlarge the images as best he could. "I'm sure that's a woman," she said. "Navy dress, stylish spectator hat. I don't remember seeing that hat at the ceremony. Can't see her hair color. Do you have another angle?" she asked Ken.

The man shook his head. "I'll keep looking for her among the arrivals."

"I have more views," Antonio volunteered. He nearly backed up a step under the combined weight of desperate gazes from Melissa and Clarke. "More tools, too. We might find her face as she entered the hotel or the reception."

"Yes, please," Melissa said. "Clarke, coordinate with Troy and keep searching. He can run point while I'm with Mr. Ruiz."

They all gave a start when her phone chimed with an alert. The color drained from Melissa's face as she read whatever had appeared on her screen.

"What is it?" Clarke asked.

"G-get Troy," she replied, her voice hoarse.

She swayed as Clarke rushed off and Antonio guided her to a chair. "Take a minute," he said. "Just breathe." He sent Desiree a reassuring smile before returning his attention to the chief. "Look at me." He paused, waiting until those blue eyes met his. "The boy's mother is watching your every move."

"I know." Though she whispered, her voice cracked.

"Then stay tough," he said. "Show me the message."

"No." Those soft tendrils swayed as she shook her head. "This is police business."

His gaze scanned the room. People were either searching for the child or on their phones. The place would be overrun with reporters any minute now, thanks to the

miracle of social media. The brewing publicity nightmare wasn't ideal, but it paled in comparison to the missing child.

"It's a ransom demand?"

"Not your business," she insisted, clutching the phone
tightly in her hands.

Before he could argue, Clarke and the man who must
have been Troy arrived. Desiree rose and threw herself
into his arms. "Shh," Troy soothed her. "We'll find him,
sis. It's going to be all right."

"I—I—" Desiree hiccuped and he eased her back
into the chair. "He was just here one minute and gone
the next."

Troy offered her a few more assurances and then ex-
tricated himself to join Antonio and Melissa. The chief
stood up, reclaiming her professional distance and authority. He wished he could so easily dispense with the sympathy twisting his heart. The ache of his own losses, the
wife and child taken too soon, never left him completely.

"We have a ransom message." Melissa tapped her
phone and a few seconds later, Clarke and Troy checked
their devices.

As they lamented the message's untraceable source,
Antonio peeked at Clarke's screen.

You'll get the kid back when you figure out how there
is indisputable evidence that Everleigh Emerson murdered her husband when she is completely innocent.
Her trial is a sham. Exonerate Everleigh, get the boy
back. That simple.

Clearly he wasn't the only person in town with opinions and doubts about the GGPD. The kidnapper had to

be desperate to cast a spotlight on an injustice if they'd resorted to kidnapping a baby with strong ties to the department.

He looked up from the message to find Melissa glaring at him. "That implies the boy isn't on hotel property any longer," Antonio stated, getting nods of confirmation from the others. "We can verify that no one dressed like that made it to the elevators or stairs or anywhere else inside. My events manager will speak with the bride and groom about how to proceed with the reception, and I can open a conference room for you to work from, if you want to stay on-site."

"We do," Melissa said. "This is our best chance of picking up a lead."

Her laser-blue gaze shifted to the others. "Troy, Clarke, find out more about Everleigh Emerson, anything about her case, where her relatives are. Find a motive. I'll go with Mr. Ruiz. With luck, hotel surveillance will give us more information about the woman in the navy blue dress."

Antonio extended his arm toward the main door. "This way." Her efficiency impressed him and gave him hope that mother and son would be reunited.

He didn't speak, as he was unwilling to risk being overheard as they moved swiftly from the ballroom, through the central lobby and past the registration desk to the security office at the back of the hotel. Her heels clicked on the marble floor and her dress swished softly with every stride. Though he'd interacted with Melissa frequently at various community events, he didn't recall smelling the enticing fragrance she was wearing before tonight. She smelled like lilies and moonlight.

Which was a ridiculous distraction while a mother wept for her son.

Pressing his access card to the panel near the door, he greeted the two men on duty in front of the array of monitors. "We've just cued up the wedding and reception arrivals, sir."

"Thank you," Antonio said. "Any sign of the woman or child outside the hotel?"

"Not so far."

"All right. Give us the room," he directed, ushering Melissa to one of the vacated chairs.

He didn't care for this rush of awareness of her as a woman. She was a cop. The head of a department he didn't have much faith in right now. He hoped, for the family's sake, though, that this search ended happily for everyone.

"Don't feel like you have to hold back." She leaned forward, her gaze already scanning the various images. "I know you don't like me," she said.

"That's not how I'd put it," he said, hedging. He found her outrageously attractive this evening. Honestly, he'd *always* found her attractive, and also off-limits, especially after the fiasco over the summer. "I don't care for the recent lapses in your department. Based on that ransom note, it sounds as if others share my view."

Her lips flattened into a stern line. "Is that supposed to be an attempt at diplomacy?"

"Yes." He turned his attention to the monitors, looking for any sign of the woman in the hat leaving the hotel with the boy. "You seem to care a great deal for Danny."

"I love that little guy as if he were my own," she admitted. A frown pleated her auburn eyebrows as she studied the videos cycling. "Desiree is a single mom.

He's her entire world." She pointed to a camera in the winter garden they'd created for the wedding. "There."

The woman hurried away, the hat blocking the only potential view of her face. Melissa swore.

He followed the route through his cameras, but the woman had been smart about her exit with the child. She must have visited the hotel before to get a sense of where the cameras were. It gave him something to think about.

"He isn't wailing or trying to get away from her. The little guy falls in love with anyone who smiles at him these days," Melissa murmured. "I can't believe that woman is someone familiar to him."

"Why not?" he queried.

"Off the top of my head, I can't think of anyone familiar to Danny who is also this invested in Everleigh Emerson's innocence."

The Emerson case was all over the news and on the front page of every paper since the trial began. Everleigh, a local barmaid, had allegedly cheated on her estranged husband, Fritz. Then she apparently had killed him with a paperweight during an argument over divorce.

Using the controls like a pro, Melissa rewound the few seconds of video in the winter garden. "I do *not* recognize that outfit at all."

"Here." He switched two monitors in the middle of the setup to show the arrival of wedding guests. "Let's see if we can pinpoint her arrival for the ceremony."

"Reception," Melissa suggested. "The ceremony was a small service. I'm absolutely certain no one with that hat was at the ceremony."

"All right." Antonio adjusted the timing of his search. Within minutes, they found her. "Here," he said, pointing.

Again, Melissa leaned closer to the displays and this

time her knee bumped against his. The pleasant simmer from the inadvertent contact surprised him.

"Damn. Between the hat and the other guests, her face is blocked. You'd think the hat would've made it harder to tuck in close," she said. "She knew what she was doing."

"Seems so," Antonio agreed.

She reached for her phone and made swift notes in some app. "Clearly, she cares about Everleigh. That narrows the suspect pool quite a bit." She looked up at him then, her blue eyes deep with a desperate intensity. "Can you show me to the conference room you set up for my team, please?"

"Absolutely." The sooner he got her out of this small space, the better. Those eyes of hers drew him in, tempted him to offer more comfort than practical assistance. That was a dangerous line he didn't dare cross.

The desk phone rang and he checked the monitors instinctively, braced for more trouble. "Ruiz," he answered.

His event manager gave him an update. "Thanks. I'll pass that along," he said, replacing the handset. "The reception is winding down," he told Melissa. "The bride and groom are saying their farewells while the staff creates to-go boxes for everyone with food and cake."

"I'm sure they appreciate that."

"Sounds like a friend is keeping the boy's mother company so you can focus on the search," he added, escorting her from the security surveillance room. "I've also been warned that the media is gathering," he added. "We're keeping them outside and offering no comment."

He'd been tempted to keep the presence of the press to himself, but a child was at risk. This wasn't the time to let her walk into a media circus just to be petty. In the hallway outside the conference room on loan to the GGPD, he paused, giving in to that strange and persistent need to comfort her. "Good luck, Chief Colton."

Then he walked away, hoping they wouldn't cross paths again anytime soon. She was temptation, pure and simple, and challenged his resolve to steer clear of anything with the potential for an emotional entanglement.

Chapter Two

Melissa took a breath, helpless to keep her gaze off Antonio as he walked away. The man rattled her. Always had. He was only a few years older than her, but she'd always admired his commanding presence in any environment. Oh, he was tall and lean, too, and she found him sinfully handsome with his perfectly styled dark hair and sharp-edged short beard. His unfailing self-confidence only added more depth to his overall appeal. She doubted Antonio Ruiz had ever experienced an insecure moment in his life.

She wasn't sure what cologne he wore and, since its scent was practically addictive, she would never dare ask. The strength in his hand, his voice, when he'd helped her through that terrifying moment when the ransom message had come in… He'd kept her from an embarrassing breakdown. That had been categorically chivalrous. Kind. She hadn't expected kindness, not from the man who made no secret of how little faith he had in the GGPD.

From a layman's perspective, she could understand his frustration with her department. He'd reported a murder and had expected justice, especially after the body had been found. But contrary to Antonio's statement, they didn't have anything tying Orr to the crime. Worse, Antonio had been a suspect himself for a short time as the GGPD worked the case. Good police work meant following every lead, even those that turned out to be bogus.

Although she didn't appreciate his nosing into confidential aspects like the specifics of the ransom note, they definitely needed his resources and assistance. Preparing the initial aspects of the search here on-site saved them valuable time when every second counted.

So why was she out here, musing over Antonio, when they had a baby to find?

She walked into the conference room, hoping her team had a list of suspects started.

Troy—who was a GGPD detective, her cousin and Danny's uncle—gave her a hopeful look from his seat on the far side of the big oval table in the middle of the room. "Tell me you have a face or potential ID to go on."

"I wish." She rubbed at the tension gripping the back of her neck. "We found the woman in the navy blue dress and that hat as she entered tonight, but her face was obscured. She came through the front doors with a crowd of reception guests, but I'm not exactly sure where she waited for her moment. Did anyone in the reception remember seeing her?"

"No," Troy replied. "So far, it doesn't look like she spent any time in the ballroom. I've questioned the guests closest to Desiree's table, based on the wedding videographer's footage."

"Anyone recognize her or the hat?"

"No," Troy repeated. He scrubbed a hand over his short black hair. His hazel eyes were haunted and she knew he wanted to turn the city upside down until they found his nephew. "I'm only guessing, but it makes sense that she might have joined the reception when the dinner buffet opened."

"Lots of movement, more distractions," Melissa agreed, thinking it through. "And less than a half hour later, she scoops up Danny and heads straight for the garden."

"He wasn't crying."

"I know. That worries me," she admitted. As a part-time sketch artist, Desiree was often in the police station. Everyone on the force had probably met Danny at one time or another and he was an outgoing child who didn't seem to have any fear of new faces. Did someone inside the GGPD have an issue with the Fritz Emerson murder case? "Any progress on the ransom message?"

"Nothing beyond the wording of the message. Full words and punctuation strikes me as someone over twenty-five." He pressed the heels of his hands to his eyes, defeated. Looking up, he said, "I'd be surprised if the phone is even in one piece anymore."

That was the trend for criminals. Burner phone, blocked number, disposed of after immediate contact. It didn't narrow the suspect pool at all.

"Chief?"

She turned toward her cousin, Grace Colton, a brand-new cop on the GGPD roster. "You have something?"

"I called Mason County Prison and verified Everleigh is in her cell. No visitors since the start of the trial."

"Good work. Thanks." She looked around the room. "All right. Female and over twenty-five is a starting point. Give me what you have on Everleigh Emerson's relatives. Let's clear them one by one. Female first."

She was tempted to step out of her heels, but she

couldn't run around barefoot. "Where's Clarke?" Maybe he could swing by her house and pick up a change of clothes for her.

"He went to find the public defender, following that mention in the ransom note, to dig into the evidence against Everleigh."

"Good." Spotting a stack of notepads with the hotel logo and a pile of matching pens, she chose one of each and sat down with Troy. Making notes as Troy reviewed the list with her, she got a good picture of Everleigh's potential support system.

She felt every second ticking down, and worried that the kidnapper was taking Danny farther out of their reach, or worse. Tapping the pen to her palm, she tried to breathe through the crushing pressure. This wasn't just any case. And when she found the kidnapper, she'd...

"Do you need to go home?" Troy asked.

Melissa went still at the suggestion, remembering she had a responsibility to her officers and the community to be objective. "I should ask you the same thing, seeing that you're a closer relative than I am."

"I'm not leaving this to anyone else."

"Then we work it together."

She looked up when Officer Shea and his black Lab Ember came in. "Chief," Shea began, frustration tightening his features. "Danny's trail goes from the reception straight to the parking lot and ends. We can't pick up anything helpful beyond that." Ember tilted her head, ears perked as she waited for a new command. "We did a sweep of the interior of the hotel, but there's no indication he's here."

Melissa ignored the wrenching pain in her heart— she'd been so hopeful. "You've done plenty." They knew where Danny wasn't, which saved time and angst. "Thank you both." She reminded herself that the kidnapper was female and that likely meant better odds for Danny. When the K-9 team left, she turned back to Troy. "Any chance we're missing a motive?"

He scowled at his notes. "Like what?"

"Do you think the mention of the Emerson case is a diversion tactic?"

He looked at the ransom message someone had printed out while she'd been with Antonio in the security office. "No. The message was too personal, in my opinion. Too emotional."

She agreed, but she needed to avoid any tunnel vision that could mislead them and delay Danny's rescue. They *would* find him; she couldn't entertain any other outcome. Those few minutes skimming video with Antonio had threatened her confidence. His concern that her department wasn't up to the task was palpable. He wasn't the first person to be upset with her department and he wouldn't be the last. People didn't understand that GGPD's investigations were rarely cut-and-dried and cases weren't solved in the convenient span of an hour-long television show.

She had good, devoted people in her department. Having worked her way up the chain of command, she'd known most of them for several years. They were passionate about their work, but still only human. Mistakes happened because people weren't perfect. They needed to be perfect tonight.

"Start sending units out," she told Sergeant Brad Joseph. He'd loosened his tie and unbuttoned the collar of his shirt. His suit coat was draped over the back of a chair. "Park teams of two at each of the addresses that

Detective Colton gives you. Report only," she added. "I don't want anyone to engage unless they are sure the child is in imminent danger." The stout man picked up his phone and got to work.

Melissa reminded herself that overall, the GGPD had a superb success rate with most cases, from misdemeanors to felonies.

Then there were cases like the Wendy Paxton murder. Cases that became convoluted and troubling and remained unsolved. Antonio had come into the station and reported that Drew Orr allegedly admitted to having killed his girlfriend, Wendy. The GGPD had found the body a few miles away on a remote hiking trail in the county park just north of his hotel. The case had gone cold, despite Antonio's report and a thorough investigation. The security cameras in the park showed Orr and Wendy entering the park in his car that day, matching his statement, but the light and angle made it impossible to tell if she had been with him when the car exited the park. Naturally, Orr was the prime suspect and they'd tried to punch holes in his alibi, but it had held up. The department had been hoping for something helpful from the forensics team, but when the lab finished the evaluation, none of the DNA evidence at the scene connected Orr to the crime. The whole situation still bothered Melissa.

Please don't let Danny become one of those cases.

The Paxton family still wanted justice for Wendy. Melissa did, too. It was hard to ignore that a killer had gotten away with the crime. Antonio was right to be frustrated with the GGPD over the lack of results in the Paxton case and with Orr's intentionally misleading allegations. He didn't seem to understand they'd worked it by the book, even following up on Orr's assertion during questioning that Antonio was the killer. The lean, sexy hotelier had a solid alibi, but it seemed he still held a grudge against her and her department. Understanding his point of view didn't make it any easier to be around him. And now her baby cousin had been kidnapped right under her nose.

She wanted the city's trust, and gaining the confidence of community leaders was a big part of that. Ruiz had a great deal of influence, considering the number of people in his employ and countless others who carried out work here. His poor opinion of the police could trickle down as a result of his doubts and fester until she had a real problem.

She returned to the chair next to Troy. "Can you think of anyone else who benefits if Everleigh Emerson is exonerated?" she asked, keeping her voice low.

Troy shot her an incredulous look. "You're serious."

"I am."

"Melissa, all due respect, you're off base. It's too soon. If the logical assumptions—relatives and friends eager to clear her—don't pan out, *then* we can dig deeper. I think it's a waste of our limited time to look at long shots this early."

She gripped the pen in both hands. "Thank you. I needed to hear that. Walk me through the closest relatives first. Who do you like? Who has the ability to pull this off?"

Troy sat up straighter. "We're assuming the kidnapper was in disguise?"

"Safe bet. But disguise or not, it was a woman, not a man dressed as a woman," Melissa said.

"Why are you so sure about that?" Troy challenged.

She reminded herself this was the rhythm of working a case—idea, debate, next idea. "I've seen all the available footage of our kidnapper entering and leaving the hotel. I don't think it was a man's walk or a man's way of carrying a toddler."

"Fair enough."

"As you said," she reminded him, "we can explore secondary options once the first and most obvious suspects have been cleared. As fast as she disappeared, I want to conduct interviews based on the proximity to the hotel."

"Divide and conquer?"

She shook her head. "Just you and me. If we divide and conquer, we'd have to segment the list and then we're stuck wondering if someone got played."

"Understood," Troy said. "I'll get our route planned."

Due to the nature of the ransom note, she hoped they could bring Danny home before she had to issue an Amber Alert. Melissa addressed the officers Sergeant Joseph hadn't sent out yet. They'd been trickling in from the reception and the search, each one of them wanting to help. "No one speaks to the press," she began. "I'll give a statement to the media in just a few minutes." She looked around at her team, most in wedding attire, others in their GGPD uniforms. "Thank you all for stepping up. I'm confident we can bring Danny home safely to his mother. Tonight."

She assigned two officers to stay at the hotel to handle any further developments, and another team to stay with Desiree at her house. "If you see anything, call it in, no matter how trivial it might seem. At this point, everything is a possible lead."

When she had everyone's agreement, she walked out,

taking a moment in the restroom to freshen up before she faced the media waiting outside. By some miracle her hair was fine. All credit to her stylist for that. Wishing she could do this in her uniform, she added a bit of color to her lips. She clipped her badge to the sash cinching her waist, just to make it clear she was on duty and in charge.

Taking one last deep breath, she headed for the hotel entrance and walked out alone, to the flash of lights and barrage of questions. It was all she could do not to duck and cringe.

"Your attention, please…" She waited for the voices beyond the extended cell phones and microphones to quiet. "Earlier this evening a child went missing from the hotel. My officers began a search immediately. At this time, the Grave Gulch Police Department is working every possible lead and we are confident the child will be found soon. If we feel that help from the public is warranted, we will distribute more information. Thank you."

A chorus of "Chief!" and "Chief Colton!" nearly knocked her back as everyone vied for her attention.

"Is the child a boy or girl?"

"Where are the parents?"

"How old is the child?"

"Did the search dogs find anything?"

Melissa waited a beat. She had to find the balance that would stem the tide of rash speculation and still protect the integrity of the search, as well as her cousin's privacy.

"The child is eighteen months old," she reported. "A boy. That is all I am willing to share at this time. I'm asking you to give us room to work so we can bring this crisis to a safe and swift conclusion. Thank you for your time."

She ignored questions about ransom demands, time frames and suspects. A question about her attire nearly stopped her in her tracks, but she ignored that, too, relieved to slip back into the warmth and steady lighting of the lobby.

"Nicely done," Troy said as she returned to the conference room. He'd removed his suit coat and tie, and rolled back his shirtsleeves to his elbows. Though the dress shirt was a step above his normal attire, he resembled the expert detective she saw most days at the station. He shot her a quick grin. "Thought you were going to snap at the comment about your dress."

"Me, too," she admitted. Melissa longed for her uniform and the plain pearl-stud earrings she wore to work every day. A hairbrush would be appreciated, too. As much as she'd enjoyed the French twist, she longed for the familiar bun or ponytail.

The uniform was more of a signal to others. Neither her authority nor her confidence was tied to her wardrobe, as the people she intended to question would soon find out.

"Tell me you have an interview plan for the Everleigh Emerson connection."

He tapped the notepad on the table. "All charted out. We can take my car," Troy offered. He stood and put on his suit coat, stuffing the tie into a pocket.

His sedan was more subtle than her official SUV emblazoned with the GGPD shield. "The media will catch up with us, anyway."

"Your call."

She wasn't sure it made any difference. Word was

out and whoever had kidnapped Danny and sent that ransom message would surely use the advantage to refine the plan or hiding place. "Your car," she decided. "Let's get rolling."

"One more thing. I asked your mom to drop off a uniform for you." He tilted his head toward a garment bag draped over one of the empty chairs at the table. "Just in case you want to change."

She stared at Troy. "Seriously?" Her cousin was a lifesaver. "Give me five minutes." Grabbing the garment bag, she hurried down the hall to the restroom to change.

IN THE SURVEILLANCE OFFICE, Antonio's cell phone rang nonstop. Reporters, picking up on the crisis from social media and Melissa's brief statement, continued to crowd the hotel entrance. He gave strict instructions not to allow them inside, and to be clear that any and all information would come from the police department. With luck, they would migrate there as soon as it was clear there was no search happening on the grounds.

The press was as necessary as the police department, but that didn't mean Antonio enjoyed their presence. His guests deserved privacy when they stayed at his properties and he did everything in his power to ensure they got it. The poor bride and groom had been through enough. At least the bridal suite was at the back of the hotel, with a view of the lake.

It would always be a balancing act, and in this particular instance, they might eventually need everyone in town on the lookout to find that little boy. As of right now, though, Melissa had refrained from sharing a picture and asking for community help.

He set his phone to vibrate only and returned to his

research while the other two men searched for anyone who had interacted with the kidnapper. He was certain the woman who had carried Danny away from the wedding had been in the hotel before tonight. There was something in the way she moved, the way she carried her head, that struck him as familiar. It wasn't enough to take to the police yet, but he wasn't giving up. Melissa and the department were focused on facial features to make an ID, but Antonio had years of practice and experience in recognizing people by their mannerisms as much as appearance. Reading body language helped him serve a businessman whose deal fell through, or do something special for a couple newly engaged.

He reviewed the few seconds of footage of the woman in the blue dress and hat entering the hotel, comparing her to others in the crowd, assessing her height and slender build. He couldn't be absolutely sure, but he felt as if there was a small hitch in the woman's gait. Maybe one leg was slightly shorter than the other, or maybe she had a knee or hip problem. He rubbed his eyes. Or maybe she'd simply been trying to avoid stepping on the heel of the man in front of her.

Although Antonio didn't have Ken's footage handy, he was certain he'd seen someone with that same uneven stride recently.

On a sigh, he thought about the ransom demand the chief had received. Tonight's wedding had been on the hotel calendar for months and was definitely an event known to the police. In a small city like Grave Gulch, that made it public knowledge, too. There was no way this was a spur-of-the-moment crime; it had gone too smoothly.

The kidnapper knew just where to be to avoid the

best camera angles. What she couldn't avoid, the hat blocked. And despite that imperfect stride, she'd gotten away swiftly. He muttered an oath under his breath as he accessed more video from the weeks leading up to the wedding. He focused on the routes they knew the woman in blue had taken, but it was still too many hours for him to review on his own.

His phone sounded off again and he sighed at the text message from his manager on duty that the GGPD chief wanted to speak with him. Smothering a sigh, he headed toward the conference room they'd turned into a staging area.

Looking for Melissa in her deep green dress, he did a double take when he saw she'd changed into her dark blue uniform. Her hair was still the same, and her vivid blue eyes were accentuated with the more intense makeup, but the stern expression indicated she was all business.

"Thank you for the space," she said. "We'll be clearing out and moving all of this to the station. I've assigned two officers to remain here at the hotel, just in case the kidnapper returns Danny here."

"We'll make sure they're accommodated," he said. "Are you planning an arrest?"

She frowned at the query. "In time," she answered. "We're just beginning this investigation. There are several people to question about their possible involvement." She stuck out her hand. "Again, the department appreciates your assistance."

"I'm going with you," he blurted, ignoring her offered hand. "I can recognize the woman who took Danny."

"You found footage of the kidnapper's face?" She

glanced at his empty hands. "Where is it? Did you send it by email?"

"Not her face," he admitted. "Her stride, the way she moves. Let me come along. I *will* recognize her. I can help you rule out suspects faster."

"No. Absolutely not."

He paused. "You need my help," he insisted.

"This is *police* business," she stated, her lips as firm as her tone. "If you find anything helpful, please contact the department." She handed him a business card.

Now he was annoyed on top of everything else. Folding his arms over his chest, he blocked her path to the door. "Witnesses can identify perps in the field." He couldn't stop the wave of sarcasm. "I've heard it's something that happens regularly in police business."

"You're not a witness, so there's no cause to ride along. If—*when*—we make an arrest, I'll invite you to the station."

Invite him? What a useless line. "Without me, you will likely arrest the wrong person and waste valuable time." He saw the jab land and he didn't regret it. The GGPD had made mistakes time and again. With a baby's future hanging in the balance, he expected her to be smarter than this. Though his hopes of fatherhood had been dashed, he couldn't help identifying with the distraught mother. He wanted her to have a happy ending.

"I have the means to haul you in for obstruction."

"What's the holdup?" Troy asked, entering the room. "I pulled the car up to the kitchen entrance."

Antonio turned. "You have room for me?"

Troy arched his eyebrows, his gaze moving to his boss, who was also his cousin. "Yes?" he replied slowly, gauging Melissa's reaction.

She caught Antonio's elbow firmly, holding him in place. "You're staying right here, Mr. Ruiz. Someone will be in touch if you're needed."

Her hand was warm, but the contact sent a bolt of unwelcome awareness through his system. More intense than the shock when they'd been in the surveillance room together. Without her heels, she had to look up at him more. Although, in uniform and wearing that air of authority like a cloak, she didn't seem any shorter.

"You do need me. Right now." He turned to the detective. "I'm riding along to help you identify the kidnapper."

The man's eyebrows climbed higher toward his hairline. "That's—"

"*Not* happening," Melissa interjected. She maneuvered around him, clearly hoping to leave him behind.

"Why fight good help?" he said, but she ignored him. "I should've known the GGPD wouldn't change, not even for one of their own," Antonio said loudly. He didn't care who overheard him.

Melissa stopped short. "What did you say?"

"Should I repeat it?" He wasn't afraid to state his opinion or call out their mistakes. "The GGPD is in no position to turn down any assistance, no matter how small. You don't need facial recognition or an immediate confession with me along. I *will* recognize the kidnapper."

Troy stared at him. "How, exactly?"

"He can't." She shook her head. "This is absurd. Let's go."

"Can you really afford to blow off my help?" he asked. "What does it hurt to take me along?"

Storm clouds moved through her blue eyes, but behind her, he could see Troy relenting. "What we don't have is time to waste arguing," the detective said.

"Fine." She planted her hands on her trim hips, arched an eyebrow in challenge. "Keep quiet and keep up."

He fell into step beside her as they moved down the hall and through the kitchen to the delivery area.

"You're in back," she said, holding the door for him.

She sat up front and let Troy drive. When they were on the move, she swiveled in her seat to face him. "You *will* keep quiet while Troy and I handle the questions. If you recognize something or someone, you speak to me about it, not the suspect."

"Yes, ma'am."

She rolled her eyes. "And if we get into any trouble, you will follow my orders. I don't need civilian injuries complicating this case."

"Do you have a safety waiver you'd like me to sign?" Antonio queried.

"In the glove box," Troy said, shocking him. "Always have them ready for media ride-alongs or school career shadow days."

Melissa found the form and pulled a pen from her pocket. "I suggest you hurry up and sign before we reach our first stop."

"I was joking," he said.

"Well, I'm not," she retorted. "We have the forms and policies for a reason."

And yet somehow they kept messing things up. Orr was surely responsible for Wendy's death, but the man wasn't in jail. Antonio was admittedly biased, but he wouldn't be the least bit surprised if they'd messed up things in the Emerson case, too. Melissa was devoted to her work and the community, but somehow she had to lift the rest of her department up to that same high standard. He felt as though he had an obligation to prevent another blunder with the kidnapping. His stomach churned at the thought of a mother and son being separated forever. He signed the paper and thrust it back at her. She looked at his signature and, apparently satisfied, folded the sheet, then tucked it into her pocket.

Troy turned off Lakeview Drive into an older neighborhood. Streetlights glowed over cleared sidewalks and small, snow-covered lawns. He parked on the street in front of a Tudor-style home and cut the engine. For a moment no one moved. Melissa was reviewing some information on her cell phone.

"This is Janet Carlisle's residence," Melissa said. "She worked with Everleigh at Howlin' Eddie's bar prior to the Fritz Emerson murder. She could possibly be our kidnapper and she wasn't at work earlier this evening."

"You have the still shot?" she asked Troy.

At his affirmative nod, she opened her car door. "Let's go."

Antonio obediently followed, keeping his thoughts and opinions to himself as they approached the house. The woman who answered the door confirmed she was Janet, but she was shorter than the kidnapper and her hips were wider. She left them on the stoop instead of inviting them in and he noticed that roused the suspicions of the cops in front of him. But when she walked away to ask her roommate to come and verify her alibi for the time of the reception and kidnapping, Antonio was sure she wasn't the right woman. Her gait was too even.

Troy showed them the picture of the kidnapper. Neither of them recognized anything about the woman or offered any information that would move the search for Danny forward.

Antonio was surprised when Melissa shifted gears and asked Janet a few additional questions specifically about Everleigh.

"I know she didn't cheat on her husband," the woman said with unwavering confidence. "That girl is loyal to the bone. Fritz probably started the rumors about Everleigh as an excuse to leave her. That man was a class-A jerk."

"How so?" Melissa queried.

The woman rolled her eyes. "Sometimes he'd come in while Everleigh was working. He was a big tipper, especially if the waitresses gave him extra attention. And he would flirt with other women in front of Everleigh all the time."

Sounded like a jerk to Antonio.

"Did you ever see Fritz get physical with Everleigh?" Troy asked.

"No," the woman admitted. "That doesn't make him less of a creep. However it went down, I say the world's better off without him."

Antonio expected Melissa and Troy to blow off the claims in a rush to get back to their search. Instead, they continued to ask intelligent follow-up questions, waiting patiently for the replies and taking notes. The thoroughness earned a bit of his respect.

They repeated the same thorough process at their next stop with an old high-school friend of Everleigh's and he was grudgingly impressed by their steadiness, neither of them jumping to conclusions.

After each interview, Melissa checked in with the teams watching Everleigh's relatives. So far no one was acting strangely. At their visit with Everleigh's aunt, Antonio realized Melissa deliberately asked for a glass of water to give him a chance to evaluate the woman's stride. But the aunt was far too short to be the kidnapper. On top of that, when asked to send a text, she fumbled through the test. No way she'd sent that ransom message.

"How did you decide the order of interviews?" Antonio asked when they were back in the car on their way to speak with Everleigh's mother.

"Proximity to the hotel," Troy answered.

"Based on the timing of the ransom note and the swift disappearance of the kidnapper," Melissa added. "The scent dog lost the trail at the parking lot. Do you have a suggestion?"

It was the last question he'd expected. "No. Not exactly. I wondered because it appears we're talking to a cross section of Everleigh's associates. A coworker, an aunt, a good friend from high school and so on."

"None of them strike you as the woman under that hat?" Melissa asked.

"Not so far. I think we might be dealing with an older woman."

"Why older?" Troy asked.

Antonio explained the issue he'd noticed with the woman's stride. "I'm not one-hundred-percent convinced it's permanent," he admitted. "But it was too consistent not to be real."

Melissa didn't respond, her gaze on the street in front of them.

"I haven't given you enough credit," he said. "Watching you tonight, you're a solid cop, Melissa. You're both good with the people and the investigation." This peek

Regan Black

Regan Black 49

behind the curtain had given him a better appreciation for the delicate line she walked.

"Thanks. I appreciate that," Melissa said. Troy shrugged.

"But you still don't want me here."

"Not really," she admitted with a faint smile. "This situation has become enough of a circus already."

They'd picked up a bit of an entourage on the way, as reporters caught wind of the questioning and followed them in a grim parade, hoping to be there for the baby's rescue or a big nasty takedown.

"Chief, you want to go out of order and visit Emerson's grandmother?"

"Stick with the plan," Melissa said. She checked in with the team outside the grandmother's home.

Was that doubt in her voice? He was all in to help find the little boy, but the more people they spoke with, the more he wanted some kind of confirmation that the GGPD would take another look at the evidence against Everleigh, who was on trial for murder. If Melissa was open to that, maybe he could eventually convince her to investigate Orr again, too. So far, no one bad-mouthed Everleigh outright and no one exhibited any stress over being questioned.

"Hard to believe a woman this widely adored did something as nasty as kill her husband," he mused into the heavy silence in the car.

"Tonight, my primary focus is finding Danny," Melissa snapped. "Be alert," she warned as Troy parked again. "From the pictures, her mother fits the build of the woman who took him."

Troy glanced at Antonio through the rearview mirror. "You good?"

He nodded and climbed out of the car, hoping with

everything he had that this would be the last stop of the evening. He needed to see a happy ending for baby and mother, but for his own peace of mind, as well.

Technically, he could walk away. Melissa would surely approve that choice. But he was too invested. Despite the old pain and loss dredged up by the situation, he wouldn't let another parent suffer if he could help it.

Chapter Three

All of the interviews without results were wearing on Melissa. It was as if the January weather grew colder with every stop. Troy's stoic reserve was in place, but she'd caught him gripping the steering wheel with extra force as they headed to Everleigh's mother's house. They had to find Danny, then they could sort out why the kidnapper resorted to such drastic measures.

Compounding the stress were the consistent denials from the family and friends. Not only about being involved with the kidnapping, but also about Everleigh. No one they'd interviewed so far seemed completely convinced she was a murderer, but they weren't convinced of her innocence either. The DNA evidence and witness statements had resulted in her arrest and anchored the prosecutor's case. Obviously someone with significant doubts had kidnapped Danny to force the department into action. When Melissa found her little cousin, she would take action, but it might not line up with what Everleigh's ally intended.

"Maybe we've gone at this the wrong way," Troy said quietly as they paused on the walk.

Behind them, Antonio snorted. She wished the man was anywhere else right now. Recent compliments aside, he got under her skin, whether he was voicing his opinion or keeping it to himself. So far he hadn't recognized anyone's build or seen a similarity in their movements, and he sure wasn't behaving as if he noticed her efforts to give him a chance.

She knew he wasn't pleased with how GGPD handled his statement about Drew Orr being involved, but she couldn't just toss one man in jail on the word of another. The system wasn't perfect, but it was in place for a reason. Evidence had to back up theory or it would be chaos.

"Want me to get another team started with questions to cover more ground?"

She heard the urgency in his voice and was so tempted to agree. "No," she said after thinking it through. "I'll worry about missing something. And Mr. Ruiz can't be in two places at once." She didn't make a habit of micromanaging her detectives and the investigation had led directly to Everleigh, supported by the evidence reports.

"That's true," Antonio said.

His deep voice rolled over her. In another time and in a better context that voice might make her shiver with anticipation.

Right now, she could barely tolerate him. She sensed his frustration with her methodical approach, yet he'd been the one to forcefully offer his assistance and supposed expertise. His improving opinion of her as a cop shouldn't matter, couldn't impair her own assessment of the situation. He hadn't been pleased with anything about the GGPD for months now. She could practically feel him looking for a chance to contradict or challenge her every decision.

Ignoring his presence as much as possible was her best option until they found Danny. Then she could address his lingering frustration with her, her work and her department.

"We can't abandon a plan because it takes time to execute," she said, reinforcing that fact for her sake as much as for his. "We planned this search in a logical manner. Based on the timing and the tone of the ransom message, the kidnapper doesn't want to hurt Danny."

"You're assuming a female kidnapper will nurture the boy and keep him safe?" Antonio asked.

More like she was praying, but wouldn't admit it to a civilian. "I'm not assuming anything," she stated. "I am working a case with one of my best detectives. If you're not happy tagging along, you're welcome to walk back to the hotel."

"Wouldn't be much of a walk," he said. "Any one of those media outlets would give me a lift."

He was right. Several cars had parked behind Troy on the street. Melissa turned to the porch of the sweet craftsman cottage. It felt a mile away from where they stood, though it was only a few yards. By now word had surely traveled through the family that the GGPD was convinced a relative or friend of Everleigh's had taken Danny, so any element of surprise would be gone. That didn't bother Melissa. All she needed was a clue. One lead or reasonable cause and she could bring in Ember and search until she found her favorite cousin.

Amie McPherson, Everleigh's mother, was waiting on the porch when Melissa, Troy and Antonio reached the stairs. Amie had a medical boot on her right foot. If it was real, Melissa didn't need Antonio to tell her that she couldn't be the woman involved. Unless she had taken it off for the duration of the kidnapping. The only way to find out was to start the interview.

"I know why you're here," Amie said, dabbing a tissue to the corners of her eyes. "I don't have that little boy."

"We understand," Troy said. "Are you here alone?"

"For the moment," she stated.

"We just have a few questions," Melissa explained. "Would you be more comfortable inside?"

Mrs. McPherson glanced to the media clogging up the sidewalk. "Fine."

"How did you hurt your foot?" Melissa asked as the three of them followed the woman into the house.

"I tripped over the cat and twisted my ankle," Amie said glumly. "Two weeks to go in this contraption."

"Do you have the doctor's report?" Troy asked.

At the woman's indignant gasp, Melissa intervened. "It feels intrusive, but it would speed things along," Melissa said.

Mrs. McPherson muttered under her breath. She flipped on the light over the dining-room table. Thankfully their conversation would be blocked from view by the drawn curtains over the front window. "Wait here. The physical-therapy instructions are on the refrigerator—will that be sufficient?"

"Yes, ma'am," Troy said. He followed, keeping an eye on her, then she returned and they all sat down.

"Mrs. McPherson, we have a photo of the person who did take the baby," Melissa began. Just because Everleigh's mother wasn't the woman under that hat didn't mean she wasn't involved somehow. Melissa imagined it would be torture for a parent to have a child accused of such a violent crime.

Troy showed Mrs. McPherson the picture while Melissa continued. "The only ransom demand for the return of the little boy is for the police to exonerate your daughter." Melissa steered the questions, much as she had with Everleigh's friends and aunts. "Could you please tell me where you've been this evening since five o'clock?"

"Here. My husband and I did the grocery shopping this morning." She sniffled. "I put a stew together when we got back and we sat down to eat around six. I don't know what else to tell you."

"Please take another look. Do you have any idea who this is?" Troy slid his phone closer, urging her to take a good look at the image on the screen. "Do you recognize anything about the outfit?"

Melissa gave the woman credit for studying the picture. Beside her, she could sense Antonio taking in the details of the woman and the home. She wondered what he was thinking now.

"No. I don't recognize anything or anyone," Mrs. McPherson said.

"Where is your husband?" Melissa asked.

"Andrew went out to watch the hockey game with his friends."

When Melissa asked for the information, Amie provided the name, address and phone number.

"On it," Troy said. He stepped away from the table to make the calls to confirm Amie's story.

"Do you have any idea why someone would do something so drastic to help your daughter?"

To Melissa's dismay, Mrs. McPherson broke down crying. "I'm s-so sorry," she stuttered through the sniffles. "So, so sorry."

Melissa's instincts went on high alert. "Why are you sorry?"

"For my daughter. The family. His, too. I—I can't

believe she killed Fritz. She is such a good person. Big heart. Gentle." She lifted her gaze to Melissa, her eyes red and swimming with tears. "I didn't want to believe it. But she must have done it." Her gaze darted between Melissa and Antonio. "Her attorney told me they have her DNA on the murder weapon." She cried into her tissue for another few seconds. "Her DNA," she repeated, shaking her head. "Why did my sweet girl snap and smash her husband over the head with that paperweight? I didn't want to believe it, but the facts…" Whatever else she wanted to say was lost in another crying jag.

Melissa sympathized with the overwhelming grief of a disillusioned parent unable to comprehend a child's actions. Amie McPherson was conflicted and emotionally distraught because she was sure her daughter was guilty.

Standing, she extended a business card to Mrs. McPherson. "If you hear anything about the kidnapping or the people involved, please give me a call." She stopped just short of apologizing.

Out on the porch, they joined Troy. "Husband is with the guys. They say he arrived just before seven. I sent a patrol car to verify. Based on the physical description and the pictures on the dining room wall, no way that man packed himself into the blue dress we saw."

"You're grasping at straws now," Antonio muttered on the way to the car.

"Hush," Melissa ordered. She didn't want any of the reporters hovering nearby to pick up any dissent between the three of them.

Once they were in the vehicle, though, Antonio started in again. "That poor woman. Her faith in your system has torn apart her family," he said.

"Save it," Troy barked. "We work within the system,

or it's chaos. We build a case from evidence and facts, like Mrs. McPherson said."

"After everything we've heard so far, you still think Everleigh's a killer?" Antonio persisted. "You're convinced everyone who knows her well *must* be wrong because the evidence is king."

"Stop," Melissa ordered. "Arguing gets us no closer to Danny. And besides, her mother apparently does believe her to be guilty." She twisted in her seat to glare at Antonio. "If you can't be helpful, you can't stay."

"You need me," he grumbled.

"Doesn't mean I'll tolerate you making matters worse." Melissa took a breath as he quieted, then indicated Troy should head for the next name on their list, Hannah McPherson, Everleigh's grandmother.

The woman was in her eighties, but they couldn't leave any stone unturned. They were running out of people with enough motive to carry out this stunt. Melissa had been so sure they'd have found Danny by now.

In the quiet of the car, her thoughts raced. Antonio made a valid point about Everleigh's friends and family. No one they'd spoken with this evening credited the rumors of her cheating on her husband and no one believed her capable of taking a life.

But the most pertinent question was, who among her friends or relatives might be capable of taking a baby away from his mother? Who could justify causing a mother that much pain? She understood parenthood was a rollercoaster, but this was a low point no one could anticipate. And still, she longed for a family of her own someday. Melissa promised herself that no matter when they found Danny, she would revisit the evidence in the Emerson murder case.

Hannah McPherson lived just over a mile from her son and daughter-in-law and her two-story home was in excellent condition. The walk and steps were clear of snow and the brass light fixtures flanking the front door gleamed. If she handled the maintenance on her own, Melissa and Troy had probably underestimated the widowed grandmother.

"Good evening, Chief," Hannah said when she answered the door. "I just put on a pot of coffee."

Melissa introduced Troy and Antonio. "You were expecting us?"

"Of course." She gave a nod to the media circus arriving on cue. "News travels fast in a town this size. And, of course, the girls called."

Melissa assumed "the girls" referred to Everleigh's mother and her aunts. According to the profile, Hannah was eighty, but she looked much younger in slim jeans and a bulky wool sweater. Her short cap of silver hair framed her face, and behind rimless glasses, her gaze was polite and curious. Not the least bit wary.

"Come in out of the cold," Hannah said. She led them inside and back to a cozy den off the kitchen. A fire was going strong in the fireplace and the television mounted over the mantel was tuned to the news, the volume muted. "Would anyone like coffee?"

"No, thank you," Troy said for all of them. "We have a few questions and we can be out of your hair."

"Of course. I can't imagine how that poor mother is coping. So dreadful."

Hannah settled into what was surely her favorite chair. Troy took the chair closest to her. Antonio and Melissa were stuck with a love seat on the other side of the coffee table. The cushions sagged toward the center and her thigh rubbed against his from knee to hip. Heat flashed through her system. Again, in different circumstances she might enjoy being close to him.

Apparently oblivious to her internal struggle, Troy extended his phone, sharing the picture of the woman in the blue dress and large hat.

Melissa was watching her face for any reaction when Antonio bumped her knee with his own. "It's her," he said as he cleared his throat to cover his words. "I can tell from the way she walked inside just now."

Melissa struggled to accept the revelation, even as Antonio smiled genially when Hannah looked his way as if they were lifelong friends, here to catch up over a plate of lemon bars.

While she answered questions about her whereabouts and her granddaughter's case, Hannah's gaze darted again and again to a dark doorway. That small tell, along with Antonio's certainty, had Melissa's instincts prickling. Did the woman have Danny stashed in that room?

Standing, she moved straight for the doorway, braced for anything. She pushed through the door and found herself in a small room. She turned on the light and looked around.

"What are you doing?" Hannah called after her. "We built that for my husband's hip replacement, rest his soul. These days, I use it when my knees are too sore to get up the stairs at night."

The small bedroom was empty right now, the twin bed neatly made and covered with a beautiful quilt. Melissa checked the big armoire and under the bed, but Danny wasn't here. Discouraged, nearly defeated, she turned around and saw a navy blue dress and spectator hat hanging on the hook on the back of the door. She drew her weapon while she was still out of sight and kept it low as she returned to the den.

"Troy," she said, "cuff her."

Hannah's eyes went round. "What is this?"

Troy was already in motion, snapping handcuffs over the woman's wrists with care.

Melissa called for backup and then turned back to Hannah, summoning every ounce of self-control. "What have you done with Danny Colton?"

"This is outrageous." Hannah's eyes started to tear up. "You've got this all wrong."

"Keep an eye on her, Troy," Melissa ordered. "I'll start the search."

"Wait, please," Hannah begged, interrupting Troy. "The boy is safe, just listen to me. Let me explain. *Please.*"

With her weapon trained on the elderly woman, Melissa paused. "Where is he?"

"This isn't necessary." Hannah raised her cuffed hands. "I'll cooperate. The boy is perfectly fine. He's a lamb. I'd never hurt a child."

Troy finished reading Hannah her rights, then Melissa demanded again, "Where is he?"

"Upstairs, first bedroom on the left."

Antonio leaped up from the small sofa and rushed out before Melissa could move. Damn it, he might inadvertently contaminate the scene. She hurried after him, leaving Hannah to Troy.

"I never would've let anything happen to the boy," Hannah insisted, her voice carrying through the house. "He was tuckered out," she continued, digging a deeper hole for herself. "He fell asleep watching *Tom and Jerry* cartoons."

Melissa felt the space between every heartbeat when she reached the staircase and saw Antonio at the top, his arms full of her little cousin. She returned her weapon to the holster, relief coursing through her. The pressure in her chest eased as Antonio started down the steps. Her arms trembled as she waited to hold the little boy again.

"Got him," he said quietly. Danny was tucked up against his shoulder as if Antonio held children all the time. "Sound asleep." Tenderly, he transferred the sleeping toddler to her.

TEARS OF GRATITUDE blurred her vision for a moment as she held her cousin, smelled his sweet curly hair. Her hand rose and fell with his steady breaths. "Thank you." When she looked up, Antonio's normally confident, self-possessed expression was gone. His dark eyes were haunted as he stared at the baby. Then he turned and walked away, and Melissa was once again trailing in his wake.

"I had to do it," Hannah said, her voice firm. Troy's phone was out and Melissa saw that he was recording the conversation. "I had to do it to get your attention. Everleigh didn't murder her awful husband. She would never hurt a mosquito."

"I suggest you stop talking," Melissa said, simply as a matter of form. Troy had already read Hannah her rights.

"I'll testify that the detective read her her rights," Antonio said. "That is, if you need me."

Support from the man that had been a thorn in her side all night was the last thing she expected. With a nod of thanks, she gave her full attention to Danny. The little guy seemed to be in perfect health. "I'll call Desiree while we wait for the CSI team."

It was over. Danny was safe and would be reunited with Desiree within the hour. But as Melissa cuddled him close, it didn't feel over. She couldn't shake the feeling that the worst was still to come.

ANTONIO SURREPTITIOUSLY CHECKED his hands, expecting to find them shaking, but they were still. So the trembling was only on the inside. That didn't make him feel much better. He kept his gaze away from Melissa and the toddler while she spoke with the boy's mother and listened along with Troy as Mrs. McPherson poured out all of the details and reasoning.

When he'd found the little guy tucked into the bed, his heart had threatened to crack in his chest. Antonio didn't do kids or family. Fate had crushed those dreams twenty years ago. And yet the sight of Melissa holding the toddler in her arms stirred up emotions he had no intention of facing again.

He walked out, aiming for the front door, half tempted to call the hotel car service to come pick him up. The flashing lights of the police responding to the scene and the slew of reporters kept him rooted in place. He'd come along to help and he would see it through.

Besides, this chaos was nothing compared to the night his pregnant wife and their unborn baby had died. He didn't have any stake in this, no real ties to the people most affected, so it shouldn't be this hard to distance himself.

He opened the door for the crime-scene unit and again when Desiree arrived with a police escort. Although he was happy for her, he couldn't bear to watch the reunion. It cut too deep, left him staring at the aching emptiness of happiness he'd been denied because life wasn't fair.

It seemed like a lifetime ago. It was, in fact. He'd been twenty-two when Karen and the baby had died due to a complication with the pregnancy. If life was fair, he'd be headed home to a house filled with love and a busy, happy family. His oldest would be almost twenty now, leading a pack of younger siblings in Antonio's dream world, and Karen would be more beautiful today than the day he'd fallen in love with her.

"I had to do it," the grandmother said again. "You didn't give me a choice."

She hadn't stopped that litany since they'd found out she was the kidnapper.

"Everleigh's own parents gave up on her. I had to do something," Hannah wailed. "She's the sweetest of all my grandchildren and would never hurt a fly. All her life, even crickets or spiders that wander into the house, she scoops them up and carries outside."

Antonio wondered if Melissa and Troy were even listening anymore. Worse, he feared it wouldn't make any difference for Everleigh. With his mind still circling the what-ifs of family dreams long gone, he struggled to sort out his feelings and opinions of the entire mess. He was angry that anyone in this city felt the need to go to such lengths and he was equally angry that Hannah had made an innocent mother suffer.

It was past time for Melissa, as the chief of police, to take a hard look at what was going wrong in her department.

She appeared abruptly, as if his thoughts summoned her. "We're heading back to the station," she said, her gaze moving past him to the swarm of reporters crowding the path to Troy's car. "I can't order you to keep quiet, but I would ask you to please be careful if you choose to give a statement."

"Careful?" Was she serious? "Will you be careful with this case?" She flinched and he almost regretted his hard tone. "That woman is the personification of desperate. What are you going to do to help her?"

Melissa's mouth flattened, her blue gaze going sharp. "The kidnapping is a police matter," she said. "The GGPD is grateful for your help in the rescue of a child." She cleared her throat, her eyes still locked with his. "*I* am grateful for your help, Mr. Ruiz."

"Antonio," he said.

She acknowledged that with a nod. "Would you like us to drop you at the hotel?"

"I'll ride along to the station," he decided. "Someone should make sure Mrs. McPherson is treated fairly until her legal team arrives." He would personally see to it that she didn't have to settle for a public defender. "I have personal experience with not being heard by your officers."

"It's regrettable that you feel that way," she said. After exchanging a look with Troy, they headed out and Antonio followed.

Questions pelted them from all sides behind the lights of cameras and cell phones. Both Melissa and Troy repeated the no-comment line while Antonio just followed, fuming in silence. For now.

In the car, Troy slid his phone toward Melissa. "Worse is waiting," he said.

From the back seat, Antonio had a clear view of the short video clip of local and regional media blocking the front doors of the police station.

"Guess it's a good night to use the back door," he said.

"On the contrary," Melissa replied. "I'll take that mob head-on and make sure they understand the three of us rescued Danny."

"And when they ask if you'll take another look at the Emerson case?" It seemed he'd lost all his normal tact and diplomacy.

"The whole mess is a police matter and will take some time to sort out," she replied. "But, yes, we're already taking steps to verify Hannah's claims. Contrary to your opinion, I *do* care about the people in this city. It disturbs me more than I can say that she resorted to kidnapping because she felt it was the only way to get our attention."

No one spoke the rest of the way to the police station. Troy parked in the space reserved for the chief and cut the engine. The only visible indication of Melissa's state of mind was the quick swipe of her palms across her slacks before she stepped out of the car.

The media were kind enough to give them a path as they climbed the steps to the front door of the station. Antonio didn't know there were so many reporters and cameramen in Grave Gulch. In front of the doors, Melissa paused to give her planned statement about the co-operative effort to rescue Danny.

"Does this mean Everleigh Emerson is innocent?" someone shouted.

"Is it true an elderly grandmother took the toddler?" asked another unseen reporter.

Variations on those two questions rippled through the air as several reporters simultaneously vied for attention and answers.

Troy kept his mouth shut, while Melissa paused at the top of the steps. "At this time, I can only reassure you that the toddler taken from a family event earlier this evening has been reunited with his mother. No injuries were immediately apparent and we expect his pediatrician will give him a clean bill of health."

"Chief! According to the ransom note this kidnapping occurred because the police made some sort of error. Will tonight's events affect the trial of Everleigh Emerson?"

Antonio was close enough to see Melissa's breath catch. Who could've fed the media the details of the ransom note? As far as Antonio knew, not even Desiree had seen it.

"Please…" Melissa held up a hand. "This an active investigation. We will be handling every detail thoroughly and with the utmost care. That's all I have at this time."

"Mr. Ruiz, do you blame yourself for tonight's kidnapping?"

He was so shocked, he replied to the media question without thinking. "No. The hotel is not at fault in this matter."

"What measures will the hotel take to prevent such a tragedy in the future?" another reporter called out, heedless of his first answer.

"The hotel systems and security protocols in place were instrumental in recovering the boy swiftly," Melissa interjected. "If you'll excuse us."

Her praise caught him off guard, but he acknowledged it with a nod. "I was glad to be of help tonight," he said simply. But he had to wonder if he'd helped find a little boy only to wreck a grandmother's life. No, he couldn't take that on. Hannah McPherson had made her own choices. "Please excuse me."

He turned to follow Melissa and Troy into the station. Not his favorite place, but it would be an instant improvement over the media crush. Raised voices chased the trio.

"Do you still believe your partner, Drew Orr, murdered his girlfriend?"

To name Orr and not the victim annoyed him immensely. "Her name was Wendy Paxton," he snapped. "Orr and I were never partners. And yes, I believed he killed her."

"Chief, will you reopen the Paxton case, as well?" The follow-up question was no surprise to any of them.

"You can be sure we'll do everything necessary to see justice served in Grave Gulch."

A chorus of questions about "Granny" McPherson's fate chased them into the station.

Rather than make a beeline for the back door, Antonio followed Melissa straight to her office, pausing in the doorway. After closing the blinds at the window, she tugged the pins from her hair. One by one, they plinked to her desktop, then she finger-combed the deep red mass into loose waves. His fingers tingled with an urge to take over that task, to learn the weight and texture of that fiery hair. He dragged his thoughts to more appropriate territory.

Her eyes rounded when she realized he was still there. "You don't need to stay," she said.

"You defended me out there," he said, and entered her office.

"Of course I did. The hotel didn't make any mistakes and you were instrumental in finding Danny quickly."

Was she trying to flatter him so he'd forget the department's previous errors? A few hours ago that would've been his assumption. Now, after seeing her in action, he wasn't so sure he understood her as well as he'd first thought.

The potential error bothered him. He took great pride in assessing people accurately. If he was wrong about her, that would bring his current tally to two big mistakes in the past year. His skill at reading people should be improving, not faltering.

"Are you okay?" She tilted her head. "You seemed a little…"

"What?" he prompted when she didn't finish.

Her auburn eyebrows flexed. "I don't know. Be careful with the reporters. You know how little it takes to breathe life into an old story."

"But you may not have the right killer on trial for Fritz Emerson. No one was ever even arrested for the Paxton murder, either."

She shook her head, her hair rippling across her shoulders. "You want me to reopen the Paxton case? All because a heartbroken grandmother did something drastic?"

"I saw you out there."

She stared at him, her gaze cold and hard. Here was the unyielding law-enforcement officer he was used to seeing. Although he appreciated confidence, a person had to be open to changing course when necessary. Melissa didn't seem at all that way and it lit his temper.

"You have doubts." He drummed his fingertips against her desk. "If something went wrong in the Emerson case, is it such a stretch to think something was off with the Paxton one? So, yes. I do want you to look at Orr again for that murder."

"Antonio—"

"There was blood on his hand," Antonio said. "The man was frantic, chattering like a loon about what he'd done and what he should do next. And somehow your department can't find any evidence tying him to Wendy? How is that possible? They were in an intimate relationship." He was pressing hard and he didn't care. "That woman's family deserves real justice. Closure." If Melissa couldn't handle the criticism, she shouldn't be the top cop in town.

"I couldn't agree more," she said at last. "Why do you think I got into police work?" She pressed her fingers to her temples for a moment before meeting his gaze again. "I promise you I'll closely review both cases, but Emerson's, being an active trial, takes precedence."

"All right." She'd surprised him again. "I thought I'd have to push harder."

"Harder?" One eyebrow arched and he would've sworn her lips twitched with amusement. "You've made it clear time and again how little you think of me and my department," she said.

"It isn't personal," he said. "I told you seeing you in action changed my perspective on the quality of your work. But I still think something's off, in both cases."

"And you won't stop pressing until you see me personally take some definitive action?" she asked, folding her arms over her chest.

"Something like that." He tucked his hands into his pockets. It rattled him how much he wanted to touch her, to take some of the burden he could practically see piled high on her shoulders. "I'll give you some space."

"And time," she said as he started for the door. "This kind of thing isn't managed instantly, no matter what you see on television."

He smiled. How was that even possible when facing off with her? "I'll keep that in mind."

After walking out of the office, he studied his surroundings with fresh eyes. The classic stone exterior of police headquarters fit in with the age and architecture of the city center. Inside, it was clean and modern. Brighter than he remembered from the days he'd been in here dealing with Orr's mess. From the front desk to the back doors, the desks seemed to be laid out for efficiency, with her office and a few conference rooms in view on the perimeter. He saw the sign for holding cells and wondered if Hannah had been tucked away already.

He would see if there was anything he could do for her before he left. It wouldn't earn him any points with Melissa, though. And why did that matter? He was headed down the hallway to the holding cells when someone called out Melissa's name.

Turning back, he saw Clarke jogging toward her office. "Mel! You need to see this."

"You found something?" she asked, stepping into view.

"Yes." He paused to catch his breath. "Look at these lab reports. I think Everleigh's grandma might be on to something."

Chapter Four

"Show me," Melissa said. She couldn't decide if it was good news or bad that Clarke had found something so quickly. She had to remind herself to breathe. As a private investigator he rarely helped directly with active GGPD cases, but she'd officially authorized his assistance in this instance and was grateful for her brother's skills tonight.

Clarke flipped a couple pages in his notebook. "First off, the CSI report from the scene and the forensic scientist's report are in conflict. Originally no hair and fibers matching Everleigh Emerson, GGPD's prime suspect, were found at the scene. None were processed at the lab. But in a report that was filed the next day, signed by our forensic scientist, Randall Bowe, he states that two hairs and three fibers previously overlooked were a DNA match for Everleigh."

Melissa swore. "Her attorney didn't catch the discrepancy?"

Clarke shook his head. "A poor excuse for a public defender. They had a stack of cases, one of which is also being tried right now. According to the court transcript, didn't even address it on the cross-examination."

"Conflicting evidence? That sounds a lot like what happened in Orr's case."

Melissa followed that unmistakable voice to find Antonio leaning on a nearby desk, his long legs stretched out and crossed at the ankles. Her pulse hummed in a purely feminine reaction that was the epitome of bad timing. She jerked herself back to her senses.

"What are you doing here?" she demanded. This was *her* station and he should've been on his way back to his hotel.

"This is a public building, right?"

"Yes," she said, curbing the urge to snarl at him. She had no real expectation of privacy out here, but even the media respected her boundary within the building.

When would she escape this nasty spiral of a bad day? This was supposed to be a night off, a time to relax and celebrate with friends and family at Mary's wedding. And yet, here she was, back in the station, butting heads again with the one man who simultaneously stirred her senses and infuriated her. "This doesn't concern you," she responded.

"But it does." He advanced, as if daring her to throw him out. An action she might've considered if the media wasn't still flocking outside.

"The witness—*me*—saw one thing and your lab couldn't manage to corroborate it."

She supposed she should be grateful he didn't mention how they'd interviewed him as a suspect based on Orr's statement. "As I said earlier, I will look into both cases." He didn't seem inclined to leave. "Surely you're needed at your hotel."

"I doubt it." He sent her a slow smile. A hot energy

simmered through her system. "My staff is remarkably dependable."

Aggravated by the heat in her cheeks and unwilling to give him any more of her attention tonight, she asked Clarke to step into her office. She turned to Antonio, keeping her voice low. "You said you would give me time and space."

"I've changed my mind," he stated. Another smile.

She barely contained her sigh of exasperation. "About what?"

"Time. I want to speak with you about the Orr case tonight."

No. No, no, no. This unending day was exactly why Martin had given up on their relationship. He hadn't been the only one… "No," she said. "You are keeping me from handling my top priority."

"Threatening to charge me with obstruction?"

She didn't like the way he seemed to see right through her. "If that's what it takes to make it clear." She took a half step closer, regretting it immediately. His masculine scent, a clean, woodsy spice, zipped along her senses. "You are not *qualified* to interject yourself here. I will be in contact when I've reviewed the Orr case. It will *not* be tonight."

"I'll wait." He dropped into the nearest chair.

He wasn't the first man, officer or civilian, to believe merely being present or persistent would change her course.

She was a woman in a typically male-dominated field. While it wasn't quite as much of a boys' club as it had been for her sixteen years ago at the Michigan Police Academy, female officers in general consistently faced uphill battles with sexism, or worse. Antonio couldn't know how the general ribbing between officers, outright sexist jokes and sheer tenacity had focused her on her path to become the chief of police. From her first day on the job, she'd met and overcome every single obstacle with patience, humor and tenacity.

His stubbornness wasn't the same thing, but she was up to the challenge. Doing her best to forget him, she returned to Clarke, closing her office door. She would deal with any complaints from Antonio later. "Continue, please."

"Is he a problem?" her brother asked under his breath.

Yes. To more than just her work… On levels she wasn't about to explain to her older brother tonight. "He believes we mishandled a case he brought to us last summer. I'll address his concerns after we sort this out."

"Mel, if you need something—"

She cut him off with a smile. "We both know I can fight my own battles."

"True. But I'm your big brother. The offer never expires."

"One more reason you're my *favorite* brother," she joked. This wasn't the time or place to get mushy on him. Her emotions were too close to the surface, had been nearly out of control since Danny had disappeared from the wedding reception. And though mother and son had been reunited, she felt edgier than ever about the role her department might have played in this. Mistakes happened, but they were not the norm here. She'd been part of this department from her first day as a rookie cop and working her way up; she had a unique perspective on the strengths of her people. An error like this was unthinkable and she was determined to root out the truth.

She gestured to his notebook. "Getting back to Everleigh. Her grandmother's actions are compelling. Adding in what you found..." Her voice trailed off. "I'll need to speak with the DA. There has been some turnover in the forensics department. It would be maddening if something fell through the cracks with Bowe, because of the personnel changes."

Clarke scowled. "So how will you figure out who made the mistake? Was it the CSI on the scene, or did something get misfiled in Bowe's lab?"

Neither scenario gave her any comfort at this point. "I'll do what we both do well—investigate." She tried to smile.

Overwhelmed didn't begin to cover it. Inside, she felt as if she'd been squeezed too tightly, every emotion twisted up and wrung out from the moment Danny had been taken. Unfortunately, finding him hadn't set everything right. She had no idea how the errors that led to Hannah McPherson's desperate move had happened, but she would not allow a blatant miscarriage of justice to stand. As a department, they would retrace their steps in the Emerson case until they found the answers.

"Who was the CSI at the scene?" she asked, ready to make her own notes.

Clarke pulled a face, looking pained. "A rookie."

That was all the information she needed. "Jillian," they said in unison.

Their younger cousin was new to the department and, as with all rookies in any capacity, she wouldn't have been attending a murder scene alone. From everything that drifted up the grapevine to Melissa, the woman was good at her job and eager to prove herself. Jillian had made some mistakes—nothing on the level of suddenly finding forensics where there'd been none before—but minor errors were part of any learning curve. "Who else?"

"No other name is listed," Clarke said.

Something had truly gone amiss. "That's my starting point," Melissa said, checking the time. "Is Ruiz still out there?" she asked, picking up her phone to call Jillian.

Clarke shifted just enough to peek through the office blinds. "Right where you left him."

She rolled her eyes, waiting for Jillian to answer the call. When it went to voice mail, Melissa left a message and requested a call back as soon as possible.

When she'd told her parents that she'd applied to the police academy, they'd worried about the dangers of her confronting violent offenders. Once on the job, Melissa had discovered that, personally, waiting for a case to develop was a big hurdle. Good investigations required patience for evidence to process and leads to play out.

But the really low points were those instances when justice was elusive.

Melissa carried vivid memories of the overwhelming shock and sadness when Aunt Amanda, mother of her cousins Desiree and Troy, had been shot and killed in a home invasion. She'd been only six years old and remembered those early days as feelings and grieving faces that eventually faded to resignation. The case had gone cold and remained unsolved.

From day one on the job, she worked to bring justice to her community, even knowing it wouldn't always be possible. And right now there was a man waiting outside her office eager to remind her that was becoming a distressing norm within her department.

She rolled her shoulders and took a long, slow breath. Good cops out there were counting on her to guide them through this crisis. The anger and frustration had to take a back seat to unraveling what had gone wrong and where so justice could prevail. "I'm authorizing you to stay on this," she said. "Keep pressing the public defender for anything else he may have missed. Being overworked isn't a sufficient excuse."

Clarke raised an eyebrow, but agreed to do it.

"Thanks." She felt like a fugitive when she peeked through a slit in the blinds to check on Antonio. Still there, stubborn man. "Do you have any idea how the media got wind about the ransom message?"

Clarke's eyes went round and he swore. "I didn't share it."

"Troy wouldn't, either," Melissa said. She didn't want to accuse Antonio, but it was possible. "Do you think Hannah McPherson could have sent it out?"

Clarke nodded slowly. "It would certainly fit with everything else she's done."

Melissa hoped Hannah McPherson had been working alone, as she'd claimed at the house when they arrested her.

And would the evidence they gathered hold up? Both Antonio and Hannah McPherson insisted the evidence on two different cases was wrong. Was there an issue with her forensics team? She knew her department—her investigators, officers and detectives in particular—was excellent, but she could not afford incompetence at any level.

There was no choice. She had to call in someone at the state level to help her investigate these discrepancies. She reached for her phone when it rang under her hand. "Chief Colton," she answered.

"It's Jillian. I just saw you called."

"Thanks for the quick response," Melissa said. She sank into her chair and pulled a notepad within reach. Not a chance with Antonio lurking nearby.

"Is this about the Everleigh Emerson case?" Jillian asked.

"Yes." Melissa exchanged a glance with Clarke. He'd pulled a chair around to hear as much as possible. "I've always felt awful about missing that evidence," Jillian said. "I'm sure you know that they teach us some hairs and fibers aren't obvious to the naked eye. It's why we bag everything for the lab."

"Right," Melissa said. "So there isn't a mention in your report of any hair visibly different than the victim's hair on the paperweight—the murder weapon—because it wasn't visible to you at the scene?"

"That's right. I took pictures and worked the scene, but obviously I must have missed something big. The goal is to put the right person behind bars."

"I understand what happened," Melissa said. "It takes all of us, especially on a murder case. From this end it seems you did everything right," she assured her cousin.

"I'm glad you think so, Chief. I am trying to be careful out there. And I'm glad I brought in everything for the lab to process."

Melissa appreciated her humility, but she just wasn't convinced this was all on Jillian's shoulders. She made herself a note to check on the new CSI's other cases later this week. Rookie issues like this one rarely needed a chief's attention. The forensics teams had an internal management structure that dealt with scheduling and the day-to-day.

"Did Bowe reprimand you for the oversight?" Melissa asked. Clarke nodded his approval of the question.

"Not officially. But when the final report came in, I had to do a few hours of coursework review. I didn't mind," she added quickly. "I want to learn from my mistakes. Since then, I've done everything possible to be more diligent."

Her earnestness warmed Melissa's heart, made her want her cousin to get better at her job. "And this was the first crime scene you worked alone?"

"I wasn't alone," Jillian replied. "Billy McClusky was there with me."

Clarke shifted, then pored through his notes and eventually shook his head.

Another discrepancy to add to the growing list. A chill slid down Melissa's spine. "Jillian, you can't share this conversation with anyone," she began. She lowered her voice. "I'm not convinced you or Billy made any errors on this case."

There was a long pause. "What?" her cousin asked, incredulous. "What are you saying?"

"We're just digging in, but we're finding some inconsistencies with the Emerson case as a whole. Until I sort that out, would you please take extra precautions on your cases?"

"How so?"

"Please back up your notes, pictures and copies of your final reports in a separate location. Whatever system you choose, make sure it's somewhere different from the official department database."

"You're serious?" Jillian breathed.

"I am. Again, none of this is for public knowledge."

"Understood," Jillian promised. "If I can help you sort out anything else with this, please call."

"I appreciate that." Melissa ended the conversation

and cradled the phone in her hands. She looked up Billy's personnel record and dialed his cell phone, despite the late hour.

He answered immediately. "Hey, Chief."

"Sorry to bother you so late," she began. "I just have a couple questions about the Emerson case."

"I figured, after the mess at the wedding," he said. "Fire away."

"Were you Jillian Colton's supervisor at the crime scene?"

"Yes, I was. She did a great job, everything by the book. She's a real asset."

His confidence gave Melissa a much-needed boost. "And you filed your report as usual?"

"You bet. We delivered everything to the lab all at once, same as always."

"Just what I needed to hear. Thanks so much, Billy."

She sat there for a moment, dumbfounded. Her cursory search didn't show any evidence logs or reports from Billy at that scene, though there were records from other cases he had worked that same month.

What on earth were they up against here?

"Want me to go back to the defense attorney tonight?" Clarke asked.

"You've done enough tonight," she replied. "Tomorrow is Sunday. They won't be in court and we can use that time to get a better picture. I'll add this as part of our official investigation of the kidnapping case."

"Sure thing," Clarke said, standing. "Be careful."

"Always."

She followed her brother out of her office, pausing to lock the door. It was no shock that Antonio was sitting right where they'd left him. "Closing up without giving me a chance to talk?" he asked.

She bit back a scathing reply. It wasn't entirely his fault that she was antsy. Picking fights wouldn't help anything. Before she could form a polite response, her stomach rumbled.

"I'll remind you this was supposed to be my day off." It was so strange to be the person complaining about her demanding job. "Since Danny was taken before I got my dinner, I'm willing to hear you out as long as food is involved."

His expression softened the hard angles of his chiseled features as her words registered. "My place or yours?"

"Neither." She couldn't imagine having this striking man, the owner of several opulent hotels around the country, in her very average three-bedroom, two-bath, single-story home. "I was thinking that Paola's Pizza sounded good."

"That works for me," he said.

It dawned on her then that her car was still at the hotel. "Let me just get the keys to a cruiser. Unless you'd rather walk?"

The restaurant was only a few blocks away and the chilly night air might be just the thing for the heat building under her skin when he was near. Her professional distance seemed to evaporate around Antonio.

"For the record, I wasn't just sitting here doing nothing," he said with a heart-melting smile. "I asked one of the hotel drivers to deliver your SUV."

She didn't know what to say to that.

Antonio chuckled. "Is there a law against that kind of peace offering, Chief?"

"Probably. But I'll let you off with a warning tonight."

She'd always found him handsome, but that twinkle in his eyes made him too sexy for any safe association. It was going to be an interesting conversation, assuming she could concentrate on what he had to say and not all the things he made her feel.

ANTONIO HAD TO work a little too hard to smother his amusement. Melissa was one surprise after another, starting with the lovely dress she'd had on earlier all the way through the competent search-and-rescue. He didn't want to be attracted to her and yet he didn't want to avoid it, either. Best to chalk it up to bad timing and keep the boundaries clear.

Especially when he wanted her to reopen the Wendy Paxton murder case.

He'd used the time she left him cooling his heels to sort out the bits and pieces of information he'd picked up tonight. He didn't condone Hannah McPherson's actions, but it sounded to him as though someone in the forensics department had made a big mistake on that case. Didn't that make it more plausible that the evidence against Orr had been overlooked or mishandled, too?

"Did you ask the driver to leave the car out front?" she asked, pausing as they approached the back door.

"Nice of you to assume the worst of me," he replied, not the least bit offended. He'd thought about doing just that so she would have to face the press one more time. But after all they'd gone through tonight, the move felt petty, so he'd instructed the car to be parked behind the police station.

"It feels like our pattern."

And there it was, that simmer of attraction, nudging

him to shift their pattern toward more amicable terrain. "I double-checked with another officer and had the valet leave the car out back. I can't promise a complete absence of press, but with luck it won't be as bad as earlier."

"I appreciate that." Sincerity shone in her blue eyes.

He shrugged into his coat and then took the coat she had draped over her arm, holding it for her.

"Thanks," she said, clearly surprised by the gesture.

"My dad told me good manners make the man."

"Is that so?"

He watched, mesmerized, as she buttoned the dressy wool coat over her bland uniform. The effect was a strange illustration of the two parts of her life: the hard-nosed chief who worked diligently for her department and her city, and the lovely woman underneath those responsibilities.

"Mom said it lulled her enough to fall for him," he added.

"So after hours of giving me grief tonight, your new plan is to lull me into whatever you want with chivalry? Interesting approach," she quipped as he held the back door of the station for her to walk out ahead of him.

He wasn't accustomed to letting a woman drive on the way to dinner. Then again, he usually spoiled his dates with one of the property cars, sometimes a chauffeur, depending on the occasion. Besides, this wasn't actually a date. The police chief was undeniably beautiful and his perspective about her had shifted since seeing her in that dress and later, with the little boy in her arms.

Didn't matter, though. He wasn't about to let his old memories throw him off. He had two decades of practice keeping his old baggage locked down. Now that he had her full attention, he intended to make the most of it: for Wendy's sake.

"Why did you go into law enforcement?" he asked as she parked the car in the lot behind the restaurant.

She cut the engine and gave him a long look, her face a study of contrasts between the dark car and the glow from the tall parking lot light overhead. "Why did you start buying properties?" she countered.

"Money," he admitted easily. "Security and profit." *To support my new family,* he thought, pleased he'd stopped himself before that slipped out. "I doubt that's why you joined the police."

"Well, no, I'm not in it for the big payday."

Her smile was slow and edged on exhaustion. For a moment, he considered giving her a break and putting off this conversation. The search for her young cousin had taken a toll. On both of them.

She pulled the key from the ignition, tracing the jagged edge with her fingertip. He was mesmerized by the movement and too curious about how those long, slender fingers would feel against his skin.

"My aunt was murdered," she said, capturing his full attention. "The case was never closed. I guess the effects lingered."

"I'm so sorry for your loss."

Another faint smile. "You don't have to say that."

"It was sincere," he assured her.

"Thanks," she said. "The loss and all of the unknowns rippled through the family in different ways. I wanted to catch the person responsible, to learn why they decided to hurt her. You might say an initial morbid fascination matured into a hard line about the meanings of justice and fairness."

And yet a killer was walking around free. Orr should be in jail, but he wasn't. Antonio supposed the count was actually two killers on the loose, if Hannah McPherson was right about her granddaughter's innocence. If the buck didn't stop with Melissa, then who could the city count on to handle the problem?

Her stomach rumbled again. "Let's take care of that." He got out of the car and rounded the hood, not quite in time to open her door for her. Instead, he offered his hand.

"I'm good," she said, avoiding his touch.

"Habit," he explained. But he had to wonder if he would've helped her with her coat, held the door or shown her any such manners prior to this evening.

The answer was a resounding "no" and for some reason that annoyed him. The sidewalk from the parking lot to the entrance had been cleared and salted, and she was in sturdy shoes now with thick treads. He was the one more likely to slip on an icy patch than she was.

"While I was waiting, the wedding coordinator called and told me the newlyweds were settled into the bridal suite. I thought you'd be happy to hear they took the abbreviated reception in stride."

"I'm glad." Melissa tucked her hands into her pockets. "I should've checked in with her when we got back to the station."

"Plenty of people around to handle the bride. You had other priorities."

Melissa's lips were moving, but the whine of a car engine blotted out her words. They both turned into the glaring headlights of a small dark car, fishtailing through the slushy side street.

Antonio barely registered that the window was down

as the car came closer. Was the driver not paying attention at all? The streetlight illuminated the person's face at the same time Melissa shouted, "Gun!"

On reflex, he dragged her to the ground and blocked her body with his. He heard the pops of gunfire, expected pain to follow any second. Instead, there were only sounds. Bullets ricocheting, the engine revving, the tires spinning as the driver fought the conditions and sped away. Antonio jerked around to look, but snow blocked the license plate.

His pulse slowed and he picked out details, one by one. Freezing cold wetness seeped through his slacks and his leather gloves. A line of bullet holes marched along the wall of the building. Fine dust and bits of paint from the wall had landed on her coat, in her hair. Her hands fluttered up and down his arms, across his chest, even over his hair, but her voice was calm.

"Are you hit?" She helped him sit back and lean against the wall of the restaurant. "Antonio, answer me."

"I'm not hurt," he said. It felt like he was shouting with the echo of gunfire ringing in his ears. "Are you?"

"I'm good."

He listened to her make a phone call. Could hardly believe it when she said the words *drive-by shooting*.

"What?" He tried to stand, but she held firm. "What the hell was that?" Her eyes were so big and her cheeks pale. She looked almost as scared now as she'd been when the ransom message had come through. Only this time, she hadn't melted—she'd taken charge.

"Thanks for the cover," she said, as the sounds of emergency sirens grew closer. "Keep breathing."

He followed her gaze back to the wall. He counted seven holes before he gave up and closed his eyes. It was too much. Too close. "No promises," he said, rubbing his chest. He would never just stand back and do nothing when a woman or child was in danger. "It was Orr."

"I beg your pardon?"

"The driver. I couldn't make out the license plate on the car, but I saw his face." He pointed up at the streetlight. "It was Drew Orr."

"You're sure?"

"Absolutely." And he had inadvertently put Melissa at risk with his comments to the press. Unacceptable. His throat was tight, his hands curled into fists. He had to fix this.

"All right," she said, standing. "Glad one of us got a good look."

GGPD patrol cars already blocked both ends of the block. He hauled himself up out of the wet snow to stand with her. The shooting had brought out a few bystanders, too, searching for the source of the noise.

"Why would Orr show up now?" he wondered aloud.

She rubbed his shoulder and even through the layers of his coat, he felt the comfort she offered. How many new facets of her personality would she show him tonight? "We'll talk about it in a minute."

He was ready to argue when he spotted the blood. A thin line of red trickling from behind her ear and down her neck, disappearing into her collar. Not serious, but enough to make his stomach cramp. "You..." He pulled himself together, away from the memories of Karen's body, lifeless... This was hardly the same thing. "You. There's blood." He gingerly turned her chin to the side so he could see how bad it was. He reached inside his coat, pulled out a handkerchief and folded it, then pressed it to the small wound, while holding her face still. So fair and fragile. "I pushed you down." Too hard, clearly.

Her fingers curled around his hands for a moment and her lips parted. He wanted to kiss her, to breathe her in and know they were both okay.

"You saved my life," she said. "Thank you." Easing back, she kept the cloth in place, her gaze intent on his.

He didn't have time to respond as the officers descended on them. At her encouragement, he gave his statement first while she and another officer and the CSI team examined the damage to the wall, then started collecting evidence.

He watched, detached from it all as the cops moved like a well-oiled machine around him. "Maybe this should wait until tomorrow," Melissa said when she was done with her official role as chief and as a witness. A paramedic had cleaned the small wound behind her ear, declaring it a scratch that didn't need stitches.

"You still haven't eaten," he replied. He felt weak and shaky as old losses and near misses twisted and tangled up in his gut. Fortunately, after two decades of practice, he hid his emotions well.

"I'll grab a sandwich at home," she said. "Come by—"

"You can't go home!"

He didn't realize he'd shouted it. Her vivid blue eyes had gone cool under arched eyebrows. The other officers turned toward them, clearly ready to leap to her defense. Later he might admire that devotion. "Pardon me," he said, scrubbing at his face. "I'm more rattled than I care to admit."

"It happens," she said in the way that professionals dealing with a volatile, inexperienced public did.

Her steady calm scraped against his jangled nerves.

The doctor had used that carefully modulated tone when reporting the death of Antonio's wife and baby...

"I'll take you home," she began. "And then—"

He shook his head. "You can't be alone." He leaned closer. "It isn't safe. That was *Drew Orr*." He was certain of it. Who else would have the audacity to take a shot at the chief of police?

"So you've said."

"He's already killed one woman," Antonio said, struggling to match her cool detachment.

"We'll handle it." She opened her coat and tapped the emblem on her uniform shirt. "If you're worried for my safety, you should be worried for yourself, as well."

He might be pushing his agenda to make sure Orr paid for killing Wendy, but Melissa was the real threat to Orr's freedom now. Antonio might be a thorn in the man's side, but his statement was already public record. Only Melissa had the authority to give Orr real trouble. Until she understood the danger, Antonio wouldn't leave her alone and vulnerable. A badge didn't make her invincible. "Come with me to the hotel. I can feed you and explain it all."

"Antonio. We have this under control."

"Do you?" he challenged. "Orr is free to drive around and shoot at people because *you* didn't do your job."

She wrapped herself into her coat, cinching the tie. "Or maybe it wasn't Orr—he's just on your mind. Maybe the shooter is connected to the Emerson case," she snapped. "Either way, you're leaving now so I can do my job without any distractions."

"I'm not leaving without you. You were nearly a victim. Aren't there rules about that?"

"Spare me." She rolled her eyes. "Am I driving you home or is someone else?"

"You, please. And the hotel instead of my house."

If he could get her to join him inside, he might have a chance at making her understand the risks of underestimating his former associate.

Chapter Five

Melissa had never been more grateful for silence or the distracting task of driving. Neither of them spoke on the short drive to the hotel. She'd promised him a conversation, but she needed space. When Antonio was close, she nearly forgot herself, her focus. And they'd never been closer than during those moments on the sidewalk, his long body sheltering hers.

That hum of awareness whenever he was around had been pervasive long before tonight. It went back further than the day he'd walked into the police station last summer to file a report against a business associate.

It was as if the sight of him sent her back to the days of her awkward high-school crush on the star basketball player. Antonio was a walking sexual fantasy. One of the most desirable bachelors in the state, if not the country. She'd seen the splashy photos and gossip columns that proved how many women succumbed to that sharp smile and smoldering gaze. Galas, charity events, local and around the world. In addition to his powerful presence, each picture had one thing in common: a different, beyond-beautiful woman on his arm every time.

The man was an expert at dating and clearly averse to commitment.

Although she couldn't argue the appeal of a no-strings, blow-off-some-steam kind of fling, for her, in her position, the gossip that would light up the city wasn't worth it. As attracted as she was to Antonio, she was really after more than a one-night stand. She was in the market for a partner who wanted to be there for the long haul, even with the hours she worked. A husband, kids and the kind of happily-ever-after bliss usually reserved for fairy tales…

Big dreams? Sure, but she wasn't quite ready to settle for less.

She followed Antonio's directions around the hotel and parked in a small paved strip that must have been reserved for his personal use. "Take care of yourself," she said.

He turned, frowning. "You need to come in."

"I think it's best—"

But he was already out of the car and rounding the hood. Resigned, she stared him down as he opened her door.

"You need to eat," he said. "I have kitchens full of food. And I need to talk."

"Fine." She cut the engine. It wasn't as if she had a better offer at home. He guided her up the short walkway, tapped a card to the security panel and then held the door for her.

This man didn't quit. She couldn't recall the last time a date had held the door for her…although this *wasn't* a romantic encounter. For that matter, she'd be hard-pressed to remember her last real date. Attending the wedding with Martin didn't count. For the most part, her boyfriends had been few and far between. Unending days like today made it easy to understand why they usually gave up on her. No one wanted to feel ignored in their personal life.

"This is my job," she murmured, thinking aloud. "My life is one interruption after another."

Antonio didn't break stride as they continued down the hallway. "You were quite focused this evening while we searched for Danny."

"Crisis of the moment," she said. "You were a big help," she added. She had to admit his actions at Hannah McPherson's home were downright heroic. She and Troy had picked up on the older woman's nerves, but having that confirmation from Antonio allowed her to take swift, decisive action.

He used the card again and she found herself in a commercial kitchen. It felt way too small to manage the demands of his hotel. And it was empty even though she knew the restaurant was still open. "Where are we?"

"One of the events kitchens," he explained. "We allow caterers to stage from here. It's also available if we need to accommodate a guest with severe allergies."

"Wow." The kitchen was still and the air cool. The stainless steel gleamed from every angle. Counters, coolers, racks with empty trays ready to be put to use.

Antonio opened a refrigerator and pulled out two platters covered in plastic wrap. After setting them on the nearest counter, he paused. "Would you like coffee, plain water, infused water, or lemonade?"

"Water, please. Plain," she clarified.

He returned with a tall glass pitcher filled with clear water and ice. "Can you carry those?" He dipped his head to the platters.

"Of course." What was he up to? "Is feeding people your thing?" His eyebrows arched. "Does it settle you down? My mom is like that," Melissa rambled on. "She cooks when she's upset, delivers food when she knows others are hurting."

"Are you hurting?"

"The question was about you," she said, picking up the platters as he started toward the door.

"I won't deny being shot at shook me up," he admitted. "And I wouldn't be in the hotel business if I didn't enjoy people."

"Enjoy caring for people?" Why was she pushing? They didn't need to be friends. She wasn't sure she even wanted a more in-depth understanding of the man who sent her body into overdrive with just a look.

"Sure."

So much for an in-depth answer. She told herself she was relieved. "Where are we going?"

"My office," he said. "It's the best I can do to guarantee your safety and privacy."

He'd relaxed bit by bit the farther they went into his hotel. "You're confident about your security," she observed.

"I am." He glanced at her, his gaze serious and sincere. "And I'm sorry that they failed to see the threat Mrs. McPherson posed before she took Danny."

Melissa shrugged that off. "She was determined. If not here, she would've managed it somewhere else."

"Because she's desperate."

"True," she agreed as they entered his second-floor private office. She'd never been up here and yet she immediately recognized his personality and standards in every feature and fixture. The decor was sleek and masculine without being stark, thanks to a neutral color palette offset with pops of deep colors. Accents were placed with care and she'd bet most of the pieces were personal, either family heirlooms or from his travels.

She noticed a blue-and-white ball vase on the corner of his massive desk with a smaller arrangement of the fresh flowers from the lobby. A live-edge coffee table anchored a conversation area; the contrasting color of the wood grain gave the pretty piece the suggestion of movement like a river.

This was a luxury condo compared to the chief's office at the station. The gap between his work and hers, his life and hers, felt as big as the dark expanse of Lake Michigan outside his windows.

"We can eat here." He set the water on the glass-top table centered in the bay window. He turned and relieved her of the platters, then set them down on the table.

She unbelted her coat and discovered Antonio was right behind her, ready to ease it from her shoulders. For a split second she wished she was back in the dress she'd worn to the wedding instead of her uniform. The reaction was so unexpected she shook her head. Clothes did not make the woman.

"Something wrong?" He'd moved off to a tall cabinet built into the wall near the table, and was taking out glasses, plates, utensils and napkins.

"Just a little awestruck." She watched him fill each glass with water, admiring his steady hands. His world was so different from hers. "Our, *um*, *offices* are night and day."

"As they should be. If you had Baccarat crystal in your break room at the station, I imagine taxpayers would come after you with torches and pitchforks."

"And they'd be right to do so," she said with a laugh.

"Please, sit down," he suggested. "Be comfortable."

His smooth baritone slid over her skin and she had to suppress the urge to lean in to him.

Ridiculous reactions. This was not a date. Not even a prelude to a fling. She was here because of the case he thought she'd screwed up. There might even be a new case if that had been Orr behind the gun.

It was the sobering reminder she needed as he took the seat across from her. She sipped her water while he unwrapped the platters of cheeses, fruits and various meats and cold vegetables. "Beats a plain sandwich, right?"

Her stomach growled again and they both laughed. "This is a thousand times better. Thank you."

He smiled and she was glad to be sitting down when her knees went all weak. Again, it would be nice to blame her fascination and attraction on stress, but it was all him. They dug into the food, the silence companionable, and she enjoyed the peaceful reprieve while it lasted.

He seemed to fill up faster than she did, reclining and stretching an arm out across the back of the banquette, peering at his water glass as if wishing for something stronger. But he didn't speak until she pushed away her plate.

"That was delicious," she said. "Thank you again."

"You're welcome." Now he sat forward and despite the table between them she felt crowded. "That *was* Orr in the car."

She blotted her lips with the napkin and shifted into the cop she was. "All right. Let's start with that. Was he shooting at you or me, do you think?"

"I've been giving that some thought," he admitted, a

troubled expression brewing in his dark eyes. "I think he must have been after you."

"What?" She was too tired to completely hide her surprise. "Why?"

"Because I reported him over six months ago. He was furious, but he managed to turn the police on me and eventually go on with his life as a free man. He's aware I've given the police all the information I have. I think he's afraid you really will start digging into the Paxton case."

"You were never a serious suspect," she said.

"Apparently neither was he."

The words cut deep and she struggled to stay professional. "We recovered the body and evaluated the evidence, Antonio. I'm sorry it didn't line up with what you saw and what he told you."

He opened his mouth and snapped it shut again. "He killed her. I know it."

It bothered her, deeply, that he might be right, despite the fact she'd gone by the book. "The timing feels coincidental," she admitted. "Was there a business deal you'd originally planned to discuss this time of year?"

"No, our business ended about a year ago." His gaze drifted to the window as he thought about her question.

"Have you seen him in town again prior to tonight?"

"No," he said with a sigh. "Once he got away with the murder, I never expected to see him again."

Another solid blow, but she held her ground. "Tell me why you're so sure he's a threat to me, rather than you." She studied him as he gathered his thoughts and caught herself leaning forward. He often spoke at city-council meetings and other events around town and she always appreciated his sharp mind and flawless logic.

"Because you said earlier today you'd reopen the Paxton case. He can't let you do that."

"I said that in private," she countered after mentally rewinding the events of the past few hours.

"Not just in private. You said something about justice for Grave Gulch."

He was right. "I wasn't specific. I'm not sure I was even thinking about Orr directly at that moment."

"But you were standing right next to me when I said I believed he was guilty."

"Even so—" she checked her watch "—he must have been close to take action that fast."

"Orr isn't one for patience," Antonio said with aggravating certainty. "I know him better than you do. He had me fooled for a long time."

"I'm listening."

He ran a fingertip around the rim of his glass. "Drew started as a casual acquaintance. Looking back, I'd say he worked me over systematically. He stayed at the hotel a few times. Introductions were made and we found common ground as property owners. He asked my opinion on a couple of developments he was kicking around." He finally raised the glass and took a sip of water.

She was nearly distracted by what should've been uninteresting motions. With Antonio, even something as mundane as swallowing had her temperature rising. She'd been tucked under his body when the gunfire started and she now knew the scent of his skin near his collar.

"Eventually, he proposed a joint venture." He shifted in his chair. "It looked good at first, nothing out of the ordinary with a serious profit margin. Then I saw the bids and the list of contractors he planned to use."

"Red flags?"

He snorted. "Plenty. But it was the timeline that put a spotlight on the problem. The only way to make his proposed grand-opening date was to take shortcuts on the foundation and swap out the finer details with cheap finishes."

"You balked."

"I tried to talk first. It's not my nature to bail without reason." Another sip of water, followed by the glide of his tongue over his lips. "Fortunately, I hadn't invested any serious money at that point and we hadn't finalized the contract. As his friend, I didn't want to leave him hanging, so I confirmed he had the capital to get started. Told him not to worry about what I'd given. Once he got started, it would be easier to find investors to carry him to the finish line. About the same time, one of my Florida hotels took some serious hurricane damage. I couldn't responsibly spread myself so thin."

"And he understood all of that?" she asked.

"I thought so." He took a deep breath. "I dealt with my projects. Drew dealt with his. We had dinner once in a while or went out for a round of golf. And then another friend in Canada called me, wanting insight on Drew after a questionable interaction they'd had with him. Suffice it to say, either he'd always been shady, stealing from one project to pay off another, or he'd made some significant mistakes after we parted ways."

"Does it matter which?" she queried.

"No to me. I didn't talk to him for several months until the day he turned up with blood on his hand, frantic about what to do now that 'she was dead.'"

"*She* being Wendy Paxton."

He nodded.

"I'll pull the file and read the statement, but can you refresh my memory?"

He drank some water, taking his time. "Drew said, and I quote, 'I killed her. Oh, God. I don't know what to do.' He told me he tossed her body in some area of the city park. When he asked for my advice, I suggested he turn himself in. Repeatedly."

That was concise, but not quite what she was after. She could see he wasn't enjoying the conversation, but she'd never spoken directly with him about the case. "Where were you when he turned up that day?"

"I was helping my elderly neighbor with yard work..."

His voice trailed off as she burst into laughter, too tired from everything else to stifle the automatic reaction.

His gaze narrowed. "That's funny to you?"

She fanned her face. "I'm sorry. Blame it on fatigue or—"

"Being shot at?"

"That, too." The drive-by *had* rattled her. It seemed as if she'd climbed onto a never-ending roller coaster of emotion and drama since the moment Danny had disappeared. She tried to catch her breath and, noticing the amused sparkle in Antonio's eyes, she started sputtering all over again.

"Seriously," she said at last. "Forgive me for having a hard time picturing you up to your elbows in dirt and mulch." She bit her lip. "You're always so...you."

He stared at her and then tapped the table. "I will take that as a compliment. And, yes, I was getting my hands dirty. One more reason I didn't shake Drew's hand when he showed up."

"The blood was on his right hand?"

"Yes," Antonio replied immediately. He turned his own hand palm up and showed her where he'd seen the blood. "My first thought was he must have been in an accident. He had that frantic, shocked energy."

She knew exactly what he meant, having been on scene for emergencies ranging from fender benders to domestic violence. Adrenaline was a powerful chemical reaction and the rush manifested in many ways, depending on the person and the situation.

A prime example was that moment on the street when she thought Antonio was going to kiss her. When she would've kissed him back.

"The more he talked," Antonio continued, "the clearer it became that he'd done something terrible."

"You didn't offer to help him?" she queried.

"How? By covering it up? Not a chance, even if I had still considered him a friend. He showed up, distraught and close to a panic, and I told him to go to the police."

"No one else overheard this conversation or recognized him?" she persisted.

He shook his head. "He wore a hoodie, pulled up and shading his face. He called me over to him near the curb. Looking back, it becomes clear he was avoiding as much contact as possible."

She had to give him credit for delivering details without embellishment or speculation. "You didn't tell him to get a lawyer?"

"The man was not my friend." He leaned back, propping an ankle on the opposite knee. "I have no idea why he even came to me. I went straight to the police after he came to me and your department let it go."

She bristled at that—they hadn't let it go, but had investigated and not found sufficient evidence to charge

Orr—but contained her reaction. "Did he tell you why he killed her?"

"He told me she'd been cheating on him. He was a wreck," Antonio replied. "I'd met her a few times, over dinner. They weren't what I'd call a stable couple."

"How so?"

"They argued over dumb, irrelevant things. He kept tabs on her phone location, checked her messages. They fought once in front of me when she and my date bonded over their latest sexy celebrity crush."

"So he was the jealous type." It shamed her to feel a pang of envy for the woman who had been his carefree date that night. She couldn't imagine thinking of another man, celebrity or not, while spending time with Antonio.

"He was the unstable, criminally negligent, fiscally dangerous, murderous type." Antonio leaned forward. "I don't have psych evaluations or a rap sheet to show you, but Drew Orr is as shady as they come in business. He takes shortcuts, makes payoffs to smooth his way."

"In other words, he's nothing like you."

"That's right." The cool, slightly aloof mask she recognized from city-council meetings dropped over his face. "I'm confident you were his target, not me. I can't do anything more to him. You can. His past actions prove to me there is no limit to how low he'll go. He wants to prevent you from taking another look at Wendy's case."

It was a logical argument. If Orr wanted to get to Antonio, he could've been more aggressive at any time in recent months. Still, the timing of tonight's attack bothered her. "Are you aware of any other connections between Orr and the police department?" She assumed his arched eyebrow meant no. "Never hurts to ask." It was something she'd have to dig into as soon as the Everleigh situation was handled. "Any idea where Orr spends his time when he's not shooting up Grave Gulch?"

"You aren't taking me seriously," Antonio accused, pushing to his feet and pacing away from the table before turning around. "I underestimated him once and nearly lost a fortune. I won't repeat that mistake. Lives—yours, mine, Wendy's—are invaluable."

Fortune. She briefly wondered how a man like Antonio defined that term. She didn't ask, as that detail was irrelevant to the case and wouldn't advance the situation with Orr.

"Thanks for the meal," she said, standing. "Can I help you clean up?"

"I can manage. If I get stuck, I'll just call Housekeeping."

She really had offended him with the laughter over him working outside. "All right." She went to the coatrack for her coat and folded it over her arm. "I'll let you know when I have news."

"Haven't you been listening?" He scowled and stalked closer. "You can't go home. Stay here. At the hotel," he added in a hurry.

"No, thank you." The city would never approve that kind of expense and she wasn't in the mood to toss away money on a pricey room when she had a perfectly good house a few miles away.

"Melissa." There was an ache in his voice that struck a chord deep inside her. She caught the flash of pain in his eyes, the clenched jaw. "Tell me you're taking precautions. Please. This man is dangerous."

"I'll be careful. I can defend myself, you know."

"I've had more contact with him than you. He won't

hesitate to hurt people close to you." He stepped closer. "Wasn't the trouble with Danny enough of a scare?"

"Any trouble is always too much," she said. He was pleading with her. "I'm on high alert. You might not trust my department, but we are good people. Smart and reliable, too, though I understand why you would doubt me." She managed to get her coat on by herself this time.

He scrubbed at his face, then shoved his hands into his pockets. "There's a penthouse suite with private access and impenetrable security right upstairs."

She gripped the ties of her coat. "You have a safe house."

"Yes. I build at least one into every hotel. It's yours," he said. "No charge. You'll have everything you need and Orr can't get to you."

The urgent worry was a wave crashing over her. Where was this coming from? "That's very kind." And *definitely* too much. "*You* should use it."

"But he's after you."

She tried to smile. "Your opinion. The smart cop in me says we're both at risk."

He blew out a breath, muttering something in a mix of languages she couldn't decipher. "There's room for both of us in the secure suite."

"Stop." She held up a hand. The idea of hiding from her responsibilities was bad enough. But sharing a private suite with Antonio was far too tempting. She needed a clear head if she was going to bring her department thought the problems with the Emerson and Paxton cases.

With deliberate steps, she moved to the door. "Thank you again for your assistance tonight with Danny and…" It was suddenly difficult to mention the drive-by shooting. "I will keep you updated on the Orr case as things develop."

"Nothing I can do will change your mind?"

"No." She wanted to touch that whisker-shadowed jaw, to smooth away the worry creasing his forehead. She couldn't recall another man outside of her family ever being so concerned for her safety.

"Then I'll have to settle for walking you to your car," he said.

Ever the gentleman, she thought as he stuck by her side from the office to her vehicle. He waited for her to get in, buckle up and start the engine. But it was the tilt of his mouth, a little sad, a lot frustrated, that left her second-guessing her decision.

BACK UPSTAIRS IN his office, Antonio finished clearing the table but he couldn't relax. Tension gripped his shoulders in an unrelenting hold. Had she made it home? He should've insisted that she call one of her officers to escort her. Why hadn't he asked her to call him when she got to her house?

He knew she could keep herself safe… But Melissa was out there alone with a killer on the loose and there wasn't a damn thing he could do about it. His supposedly legendary charm and influence had no effect on one stubborn police chief. Who would help her if Orr struck again?

He tried work, his preferred method of distraction, but he couldn't concentrate on the work that had been interrupted when Victor stormed in with news of Danny's abduction. More than once, he caught himself with one hand on his cell phone, determined to let Orr know he'd been seen driving that car.

Firing that gun.

That would pull the jerk's focus off Melissa.

Well, to be fair, he hadn't seen Orr's finger on the trigger. And now he was thinking like Melissa. Facts only, no guessing allowed. In Antonio's mind it was the only logical conclusion. They'd been shot at by the driver of that black car and the driver had been Drew Orr.

He went back to the table and discovered the lingering scent of Melissa. She'd worn a soft, unforgettably feminine fragrance tonight. Instantly, he was back on that sidewalk, wishing he'd kissed her.

His gloves had been torn, but his slacks had survived. They were nearly dry now. His heart worried him more. The feel of her hands skimming over him, searching for any injury...well, he wouldn't be forgetting that anytime soon, either.

He enjoyed dating and was always clear about his short-term philosophy. It was a rare woman who gave him enough sparks to remind him of the joy and affection he'd shared with his wife.

Melissa had done that, and they didn't even like each other.

Maybe he liked her a *little*. She was undeniably attractive. He'd definitely gained more respect for her while she'd worked the rescue operation, too. Her sense of justice needing to prevail resonated with him, too. A normal man might enjoy that connection, but it only made Antonio twitchy.

He shouldn't be looking for common ground. Not with her. Nothing could erase the mistakes made by someone in her department. Where and why those errors occurred wasn't his concern. Orr should be held accountable for his crimes.

Antonio stretched his neck and stared out across the dark lake. Yesterday, he might not have cared if that pursuit put Melissa at risk. Somehow, tonight, he couldn't stop worrying for her safety.

Aggravated with himself, he walked to the closet he kept stocked with a few key items and changed into worn jeans, a thermal shirt and a thick flannel. Melissa would probably laugh all over again if she got a look at him now. Well, if everything went well, she wouldn't.

He donned thick socks and a pair of boots in case he had to keep watch for any length of time and then grabbed his heavy coat and another pair of gloves. If she had a patrol team posted, watching her back, he could go home with a clear conscience. If not, he'd stay until morning just to make sure she didn't get hurt by Orr's violent tenacity.

Melissa's home address was a matter of public record. And even if it hadn't been, she kept her official car parked in the driveway in an understated attempt to deter crime in the neighborhood. That kind of subtlety would hardly stop a man who'd opened fire on her once already.

As he waited for his car to warm up, he told himself he should just head to one of his southern hotels for a few weeks. He could let winter blow itself out without any more frigid nights or worrisome drama. Then he recalled the stark relief on Melissa's face when he'd come down those stairs with her little cousin in his arms.

Who was he kidding? He'd stay the course, do everything possible to protect her from whatever Orr had planned.

Maybe if he'd told her the whole story she would've stayed in the secure suite. He really shouldn't have held anything back. Once she finished the urgent matter of the Emerson case, he trusted her to dig into the Paxton case.

Based on comments and conversations with his friends in the last few months, it seemed Orr had moved on, leaving Antonio and Grave Gulch behind. It made him twitchy to think of Orr returning to this area, being close enough to react so swiftly to a throwaway comment during a media crush.

Antonio drove slowly down Melissa's street. She lived in a neat cottage with craftsman details and a wide front porch. It was similar to the house he'd grown up in just a few blocks away. When his dad retired, his parents had sold the house to him and moved back to Florida. He'd lived there and made some updates while he built his home on the lakefront. A home big enough for his parents, siblings and their families to visit anytime.

It was a double-edged sword to see Melissa's official SUV in the driveway. At least there was a GGPD cruiser parked at the curb across the street. He took a deep breath, inordinately relieved that she wasn't taking anything for granted. She'd pegged him when she observed that he enjoyed caring for people. With her, though, he didn't *want* to feel anything except professional courtesy. Unfortunately, he couldn't put a lid on the emotions surging through him and the streak of overprotectiveness that reared up in him.

Maybe it was the kidnapping that brought back all of the grief and angst with such a vengeance. Much as he wanted to blame that situation, he knew there was more to it. She was more.

Melissa Colton threatened his peace of mind. Even when all he'd known was her quiet, calm professionalism, something about her tempted him. Now that he'd seen her in action, that tough competence broken up by the flashes of vulnerability when she'd seen the ransom message or worried he'd been shot, he was utterly fascinated.

It wasn't good news.

At the end of the block, he turned and made his way back toward the hotel. He'd spent more time in this neighborhood of the city tonight than he had in years. It pressed in on him, and he gripped the wheel. At one time, this was the very heart of his biggest goals and dreams.

"I can't do this, Karen," he said, addressing his dead wife. "Not with *her*."

She and the baby she'd carried had been gone for two decades, both of them dead in a complication during delivery. Every so often he felt as if she was still by his side. A breeze would brush his cheek and he'd be right back in those days, reaching for her. They'd been inseparable from the first moment they'd met, happily married before they could legally drink and worrying both of their families in the process.

"She's smart, but she takes risks. I'll never be able to protect her," he continued. "I can't get close to a woman like that."

She could make you happy.

The words echoed in his head, so clear he wanted to believe the light of his life was right here in the car, listening to him vent about another woman.

"I'm happy enough," he told himself. He had more than enough money. As a property owner, he held substantial influence in this city and others. The only thing missing was his wife and the half-dozen kids they'd dreamed of raising. But he'd lost her and the baby in one dreadful afternoon. They'd gone to the hospital together, full of hope and wonder, and he'd left a shell of a man, lost and haunted.

"I'm happy enough," he repeated with more determination this time. Widowed at twenty-two, overcome with loss and grief, he funneled all of his energy into business as a property developer, working day and night to reach a substantial net worth by a young age.

And you keep pushing.

For the first time ever, he was annoyed with the memory of his wife's voice.

"How could I quit?" He parked in his reserved space at the rear of the hotel and rested his head on the steering wheel.

In those early days, if he stopped for more than a few minutes the loss caught up with him, knocked him down and threatened to keep him there. So, hell yes, he kept going. He let the media dub him an eligible bachelor and took hold of that moniker with both hands.

By the third year of grieving, his mother tried to set him up, urging his siblings to bring female friends to family events. He put up with it, knowing they loved him, but he wouldn't let anyone close again. The day he'd buried Karen and the baby, he'd buried his broken heart with them.

He stared up at the Grave Gulch Hotel. This was the first major undertaking in his real-estate venture, his only true passion now. His joy. He poured everything he would've given his wife and children into the businesses. Life had given him another shot at happiness. It just looked a whole lot different.

Back in his office, his cell phone chimed with a text message from an unknown number. Not unheard of, but at this hour it usually meant some kind of emergency. He was tempted to ignore it, and then realized he couldn't.

Antonio looked at the screen and the text in the preview sent a chill across the back of his neck.

Call her off or else.

Should he respond or ignore it? He took a screenshot. Antonio wanted something solid to add to the police file tomorrow.

Annoyed and in a contrary mood, Antonio texted back.

Or else what?

For several long minutes he waited for a reply that never came. He gave up on Orr and stretched out on the couch to get some sleep when his phone started ringing. Seeing the caller ID for the alarm company that monitored his home, he picked up and gave his security code.

"Mr. Ruiz, we have two alerts at your home. An open back door and the smoke detector in your kitchen. The fire department is on the way. Are you in the house, sir?"

"No," Antonio replied, his blood thundering in his ears. "Is there video footage?"

"No, sir, not at this time."

That was zero comfort. "I'm at the office, but I'll head over and meet the fire department."

"Just stay clear of the house, sir."

With a promise to cooperate, he ended the call and headed back out into the freezing January night. When he reached his home he could see smoke rising into the night from the rear corner of the house. Exactly where his kitchen windows overlooked the lake.

Antonio parked as close as he could and jogged the rest of the way to join the first responders. The fire department seemed to have everything under control and there wasn't anything he could do about it, anyway.

He recognized one of the police officers who'd responded to the drive-by shooting. "Busy night, Officer Warren."

"Mr. Ruiz, I'm glad you're not in there. Your security company informed us the house was empty at the time of the fire."

Antonio glanced around, but most of the homes on this street were nestled back into wooded lots. His nearest neighbor probably wouldn't notice anything amiss until tomorrow.

"Is there anything we can do for you?" Officer Warren offered. "Anyone we should call?"

The generosity surprised him. "Me? No, thanks. I was planning to stay at the hotel tonight, anyway, to catch up on work."

"That's good, that you have a place to stay. I meant to say thank you earlier. Everyone in the department is grateful for your help finding Danny."

That explained the new heights of friendliness. The GGPD officers who responded to calls at the hotel were always polite, but not always this warm. "You're welcome." It came out more like a question that it should have. "I was happy to help."

"That little guy means the world to all of us."

They both turned as the firefighters emerged from the house, sparing Antonio from further praise or conversation.

"Wait here," Officer Warren said, then jogged over to

converse with the firefighters. When he returned, he was shaking his head. "The fire's out, Mr. Ruiz, but please don't enter the premises until further notice. We'll need some time to investigate."

"Do you suspect arson?" If that was the case, he had a good alibi, right up until the point when Melissa went home. Then again, swiping in and out of the various areas within the hotel would confirm his whereabouts. Not to mention he'd have no motive to burn down his own house... "What concerns you?"

"The damage around the sidelight at the back door," Warren explained. "As I said, we'll look into it and co-ordinate with your security company."

After leaving details of where and how to reach him, he drove back to the hotel. This time, he stopped by the security office to let them know he was moving to the secure penthouse. "Unless this particular building is coming down, I am not to be disturbed before nine o'clock tomorrow morning."

That gave him time to get some sleep before he took Orr's text message to Melissa...or before she came looking for him once she heard about the fire.

Apparently, Melissa was right. It seemed he was the target after all.

Chapter Six

Sunday morning came far sooner than Melissa had hoped for. On top of her derailed Saturday night, she wasn't in the best of moods when she rolled out of bed the next day. She set a cup of coffee to brew and walked to the front window. The patrol car was still in place. When she sent the officers a text to check in, they confirmed they were fine, and coffee and breakfast had been dropped off by another team.

Satisfied, she checked for any new messages while she let the caffeine kick her brain into full function. A run would be nice, so she could breathe out the last of the tension from the chaos of last night, but she changed her mind when she saw a voice mail from Desiree.

Her cousin had called and left a whispered message that she couldn't stop watching Danny sleep. All of the sincere thank-yous and I-love-yous held a sharp edge that sliced through her frazzled nerves. It was wonderful to hear the love, to know two of her favorite people in the world were content and safe. But it was tough to swallow that the GGPD was the reason they'd been subjected to the trauma and nightmare to begin with. She needed to track down the forensics reports in question today and set up a face-to-face with the CSI on the Orr case.

She sent a text message reply to Desiree, just in case mother and baby were sleeping in. Her phone rang immediately when Desiree called her right back.

"Good morning," Melissa greeted her cousin.

"It's a *fabulous* morning," Desiree gushed. "Say hi, baby. Say hi to Mel."

"Hi." It was Danny's sweet voice.

Her heart swelled to bursting with love and relief all over again. That bright greeting intensified her longing for children of her own, despite all of the chaos with her career as chief of police. If most of her department could juggle family and work, surely she could figure it out.

"Hi," Melissa said through the guilt that chased the happier emotions.

Desiree came back on the line and talked about the weekend plans and the newlyweds for a few minutes. "Do I have to press charges?" she asked abruptly.

At last, the crux of the call. "We've already charged her," Melissa replied. "Right now, it's out of your hands. First-degree kidnapping is the tip of the iceberg. I'm not sure what else the DA will pile on."

Desiree sniffled. "Forgive the waterworks. I just want it to go away, Mel. I saw her face on the news this morning. She looks like the sweetest grandma. And she did it to help her own granddaughter."

More guilt wound around Melissa's heart, although she knew she had to hold firm. "Hannah McPherson struck me the same way. Caring and devoted. I know you can relate to that. Although I don't believe she ever would have hurt a single hair on Danny's head, she did steal him."

"To get your attention."

"Trust me, that's clear," Melissa said. "I'm following up on everything we learned last night."

"I just want it on record that I forgive her. And then I want to forget it all happened."

Melissa understood completely. "We'll sort it out," Melissa promised. "No guarantees, because the DA is in control, but I will let you know if there's anything you can do for Mrs. McPherson."

"Thanks. Swing by anytime if you want some fresh air and sunshine with a handsome guy today."

Antonio's face flashed into her mind before Danny's and she felt the heat rise in her cheeks. Good thing she was alone. "I'll call first," she promised. "One more thing." She took a deep breath. "There was some additional trouble last night."

She explained the drive-by shooting with the fewest details possible. Calming Desiree's initial concerns about her well-being, Melissa continued, "As much as I'd like to believe it was random, chances are high that this is a problem. We don't have a definite ID on the shooter, but if our best guess is correct, it's *possible*— not likely, just possible—that the person involved will try to manipulate me by going after my family. So please take extra care in general. I'll let the rest of our relatives know, too."

"Mel, it's me," Desiree said. "Do you think this is connected to Everleigh Emerson?"

"No. This is about a different case, but it is the potential indicator of another GGPD error and that worries me."

"Oh."

There was a wealth of meaning in that single syllable. "Just be careful," Melissa said. "If you see or feel anything that makes you uncomfortable, report it or tell me right away."

"I will," Desiree promised.

One down, Melissa thought, ending the call. What a way to start a Sunday. She dialed her parents next. They were the most vulnerable, not just because she enjoyed a close relationship with them, but because they weren't tied in any way to the GGPD themselves. Travis, as a businessman, had a good handle on his surroundings at all times. Clarke, as a private investigator, and Stanton, owner of a protective detail agency, were always ready for anything. Not invincible, but sharp. Still, she had to call each of them about this new risk. While she spoke with her immediate family one by one, she finished her second cup of coffee of the morning.

It was past ten and bright sunlight made a run irresistible. She pulled on layers to ward off the cold and laced up her running shoes. Stepping outside and breathing in the bracing winter air was an immediate improvement.

Striding to the police car, she made sure they could track her phone and gave them her planned route. "Just keep an eye on the house," she said. "I've got pepper spray and a whistle with me, too, if something happens."

"Are you wearing any headphones, chief?"

"Not today," she assured him with a smile. "I promise, I'll stay alert. It's just a two-mile loop."

Broad daylight and a Sunday morning when most people would be home made it a bad time for Orr to take another swipe at her. Didn't mean he wouldn't, but it did increase his chances that he'd be seen or caught in the act.

She'd be okay with that. And maybe, in the back of her mind, she was silently daring Orr to take another shot. As she found a good pace, her mind wandered while her ears and eyes were aware of every detail. No, she wasn't impervious to bullets or fear. Though she didn't relish being shot at again, the fact remained that they had to get the man off the street. And that meant doing whatever it would take—even putting herself in the line of fire—to bring in a bad guy.

And she felt an obligation to her officers to behave with confidence despite the sudden onset of problems. She absolutely believed that as a team, the GGPD could get to the bottom of these issues together.

Antonio was certain his former associate had killed a woman last summer and equally certain he'd fired at them last night. She needed a last known address for Drew Orr and then to get eyes on him. Thanks to Antonio's statement at the scene, one of her officers would be working on that already, making time to speak with Orr and confirm his whereabouts.

As a near-victim of the incident the night before, she had to allow the responding officers to handle it. She was fine with that, too. That freed her up to dig deeper on the Emerson and Paxton cases.

Wrapping up her run, she waved to the officers in the car, just as she'd done with the neighbors she'd seen, and headed inside. Her cheeks were cold and her body felt rejuvenated and loose. She took the time to stretch out the last of the aches before her shower.

Feeling warm and edging toward starving, she wrapped herself in a towel and walked into her bedroom. She tensed up at the realization that someone was in the house and reached for her phone. Relief followed immediately as she recognized the voices drifting from the kitchen. Her parents were here.

Mildly exasperated that they'd enter when she was already on high alert, she quickly dressed in her favorite jeans, fuzzy socks and a cozy half-zip fleece with the GGPD logo embroidered on the shoulder. In the kitchen, her mother whipped up eggs at the counter while her father sipped coffee at the breakfast table, a travel magazine in his hands.

It was always a joy to see them, although she had no idea why they'd chosen to surprise her today. "What are you doing?" she asked. "We just talked about keeping your distance for a few days." Hadn't they heard a word she'd said? "This... I didn't even hear the door chimes."

Last night, she'd adjusted her security-system settings so she'd hear the chime if a door was opened.

"You were in the shower. We called out and sent a text," her mother said, as if she showed up to cook every Sunday.

"And then she just got to it," her father explained. That was the way it had been for as far back as Melissa could remember. Either Frank Colton or Italia Vespucci Colton would start a sentence or a thought and the other would finish it. Frank had met his wife during a vacation to Italy. When asked, they both claimed it had been love at first sight and Italia swore there had never been a moment's regret making the move to Michigan.

They were so adorable and content she didn't have the heart to kick them out. Shoving her concerns down deep, she kissed her mom's cheek. "Can I help?"

"Go talk to your dad," she said. "I've got this."

Filling a glass with water, she did as she was told. Thirty-six and still a child, even in her own home.

"Desiree and Danny doing all right?" Frank asked.

"They are. I, *um*, put her on notice, too, that she

should be alert and careful of the person I mentioned to the two of you."

"We're fine," her mother said. Forty-one years in America hadn't dulled her Italian accent. "Obviously." She dipped slices of bread into the egg wash and placed them on the skillet. "Get the plates out, sweetie," she directed. "This will be ready soon."

French toast was Melissa's favorite. She couldn't stay upset when her parents were going to such lengths to offer their support.

"Sounds like quite a bit of drama in the department," Frank said.

"Unfortunately true," Melissa confirmed. "We'll sort it out," she replied. And if there were errors, they would find a way to put the right killers behind bars.

"Will any of these unpleasant things jeopardize your position?" her mother asked. "You are a good chief of police."

"Thanks, Mom." She appreciated the love and the faith. "As I said, we'll sort it out." She carefully filled a small dish with powdered sugar for her dad and set out butter and syrup for her and her mom.

"Is that fire last night connected to any of this?" Italia asked, bringing over a plate piled high with piping hot slices of French toast.

"What fire?" Melissa looked from her dad to her mom and back again. "I haven't heard anything about it."

Her dad speared two slices of the bread with a fork and dropped them on his plate, adding butter and powdered sugar. "The news reported it as Ruiz's place. Said no one was home at the time and there were no injuries."

Melissa's pulse thundered. Was Antonio okay? Had she missed a message? She popped up from the table to grab the cell phone she'd left on the table behind the sofa in the front room. She scrolled through the local news sites for more information as she returned to her seat. Someone should have told her about this.

Irritation prickled like a rash over her skin at the lack of messages. This wasn't the time for her department to get protective. She needed all the information to do her job to her best ability.

"So you and Mr. Ruiz *are* close," Italia asked.

Her mind on the fire and Antonio, Melissa couldn't make sense of the comment. Her mother could not be matchmaking. She looked to her dad for an explanation.

"She saw the two of you during the search for Danny," he said. "Thought you looked like a good team."

"Mom," she scolded gently. Melissa took a bite of her breakfast to smother her annoyance. Not every man she spoke to was a prospective suitor. Her mother never pressured Melissa, but she was fully aware of her daughter's dreams of motherhood. "We're not a team or together or anything. Danny was taken from his hotel. Mr. Ruiz felt obligated. And he had skills that helped us," she explained.

"He's single."

"Mom."

"And handsome and wealthy, too." She reached over and patted her husband's hand. "Never discount that winning combination."

Melissa diverted the conversation to happier topics to get through breakfast.

Before her parents headed out, she pulled her mom into tight hug. "I love you," she murmured. "Love you both." At her dad's quizzical expression she forced a confident smile. "Please be careful. I can't go into detail…"

"That's all you need to say." He gave her shoulders a squeeze. "We'll stay sharp."

"Thanks, Dad."

It was one thing when she took risks for her job and something altogether different when her job threatened her family. She wouldn't use the department as her personal security, but she could ask them to help her be vigilant.

Her mother sensed her lingering distress simmering under the surface and wrapped her into another hug. "We'll be fine, my love. You and your siblings are the ones we worry over."

"Thanks, Mom." She embraced them as they left. She would always be the only girl. That fact wouldn't change. It didn't matter that she could hold her own with any of her three brothers, or all of them at once. Of course, her parents were frequently concerned about her brothers, too, but there was that inherent assumption that they were a little less fragile. Fifteen years ago she would've argued or been snarky about it. Today, with some life experience under her belt, she knew she didn't have to prove a thing. Not to her mom and dad, not to her brothers.

Only to her department. Critical mistakes had been made on her watch and it was up to her to sort it out and restore confidence in the community.

She waved from the porch as they drove off and then stepped back inside, locking the door. With moms and children on her mind, maybe she should go over to Desiree's place. She could see Danny in his element, no worse for last night's excitement. It might make her feel better, might even be worth the inevitable longing for a baby of her own that resulted from every visit.

But if she did visit, she might lead Orr straight to someone she loved. Better if she went to the station and got some work done. There was no guarantee that the judge would grant any delay in the Emerson trial based solely on the discrepancies Clarke uncovered.

With fresh determination, she swapped the cozy socks for practical footwear and prepared to leave for the station. Officially off duty, she didn't change into her uniform today. Her plan was to lock herself in her office and study the evidence reports in the Emerson and Paxton cases.

And she wanted details on the fire at Antonio's house. Why hadn't anyone called her? She supposed it technically wasn't her business. And she should *not* be curious about where he'd spent the night. After pulling on her coat, she dropped her phone into her purse and pulled out her car keys. She was just setting the alarm at the side door that opened onto her driveway when she heard the doorbell out front.

Not her parents then, she thought with a rueful smile. She paused at the SUV to put her purse on the front seat and then continued around to the front of the house. Antonio suddenly appeared on her front steps.

He was safe. Here. Everything inside her seemed to go loose and bubble to the surface. She clamped her lips together before a ridiculous giggle could escape. "Should I be worried you know where I live?"

"Yes. I mean, it's public record." He seemed to lose his train of thought and then his lips tilted to one side. "Hi."

"Hello." She gave a thumbs-up to the patrol across the street. He'd shaved, the stylish scruff neatly trimmed this morning. But there were shadows under his eyes that implied he'd had a short or stressful night. "Are you okay?"

"Okay enough," he replied. "You look...refreshed."

"Thanks. I had a good run and then Mom's French toast."

He frowned, opened his mouth and then clamped his lips shut again. "Sounds nice."

"I have leftovers that will reheat easily enough if you're interested." She hadn't planned on making that offer, but something indefinable inspired her to reach out. Loneliness, she realized. The man who was always polished and quick with the charming smile seemed uncharacteristically isolated today.

Oh, it was hard to see under the overall presentation. His hair was perfectly styled and he managed to make basic blue jeans, boots and a puffy jacket the height of fashion, but she could see he felt off. She wanted to gather him into her arms in a big hug, but sharing food was a safer choice. "I heard about the fire," she said. "How bad is it?"

"Bad enough." He rocked back on his heels. "They found signs of a break-in and are investigating for arson." His gaze darted from her to something behind her and across the street.

"Come on inside," she said. Whether or not he was hungry, he obviously didn't want to have this conversation out here.

Her mouth went dry. She'd invited him inside and it was too late to back out. She loved everything about her house. Though it was more space than she needed right now... She'd bought it with that potential family in mind.

"Where were you headed?" he asked.

"To the station. It can wait." The files weren't going

anywhere, and perhaps she could glean more information from him in this conversation. She motioned for him to follow her around to the back door. It was easier than trying to maneuver around him on the narrow front walk. She could see it now, making the wrong step on a slippery patch and ending up in his arms. It was too appealing to take the risk.

"I take it they haven't found Orr," he said when they stepped inside. "Or whoever was driving the car last night," he added hastily at her sharp look.

She disarmed her security system and was struck again by the vast differences between them. He'd shared a meal with her in his posh office with furnishings that had probably cost more than her entire house. Here she was, about to offer him leftovers on a table she'd picked up at a summer flea market and refurbished herself.

The hotel offered a Sunday brunch buffet with mimosas and prime rib every week, along with a made-to-order omelet station, a waffle bar and anything else a person could think of. Melissa had been several times through the years with family and girlfriends. Her mom's leftovers were bound to be a disappointment for Antonio, but it was too late to back out.

She draped her coat on a hook in the utility room and did the same with Antonio's. He wore a light brown sweater that brought out the golden hues in his skin and eyes. As if the man needed another layer of sex appeal.

"Coffee?" she offered as he ran a hand across the top of one of her ladder-back chairs. She'd collected them two at a time, so while the basic style and new cushions were the same, the six chairs were slightly mismatched.

"Did you inherit this set?"

To her surprise his tone was friendly and the little knot in her belly loosened. "No. Flea-market finds."

"And you refurbished them on your own?"

She nodded. "Coffee?" she asked, hoping to shift the focus from her secondhand breakfast table.

"I've had my share today," he said. "This is excellent work, Melissa."

How did he manage to make her name sound like a caress? "Just time and elbow grease," she said. "And video tutorials online."

That earned her a genuine smile and her stomach tightened for an entirely new reason. She really needed to get a handle on this persistent attraction to this man. "Have a seat," she said as her pulse skipped, "and tell me why you came by."

Antonio knew he shouldn't have come here. Driving by last night was silly enough. He'd meant to do the same thing today. Cruise by, make sure someone had her back and keep right on going.

Instead, he'd parked and walked right up to her front door. Damn the ghosts in his head.

She wasn't family that he needed to worry about or an employee he felt obligated to keep an eye on. She wasn't *his* at all. She was the chief of police, clearly capable of taking care of herself. No one had handed her the job, which he'd learned by watching her; she'd worked hard to earn that office and the weighty responsibilities that came along with it.

Still, if there was any chance to keep Orr's attention on him and away from her, he had to try. His reckless comments to the press last night had made her a target and the ache that left in his gut was unbearable. He waited until she joined him and pulled out a chair for her. When they were seated, he didn't waste any time. "I think you should leave the Orr case alone. I'm sorry I brought it up last night."

Her body went still and she stared at him with those big blue eyes. "Did you hit your head last night? Inhale too much smoke at the fire?"

"That was mostly out when I arrived. You can check with Officer Warren to confirm."

"Count on it," she said.

He didn't think she was kidding. "I think Orr set the fire." She had to understand the gravity of the threat his former associate posed. He pulled out his phone and turned it so she could see the screen shots.

"Unknown number," she noted as she studied the screenshot. "Doesn't explain your sudden change of heart."

"It does if you accept Orr sent the message. I asked 'or else' and within fifteen minutes my house was on fire."

"All right. We'll add this to the case file for last night. Help me out a minute. Did your security company get a visual good enough for facial recognition?"

He shook his head. "Too dark. The security company only has a vague image of a man...*person*," he amended at her slight scowl. "Someone in dark clothing, further blurred by shadows. There is a motion-activated light that didn't work for some reason. I've hired a couple of people from the hotel security team to keep an eye on my place around the clock in case this *person* comes back."

"Smart," she said. "It would be helpful if they coordinated with the GGPD."

He started to protest, but that was pretty much the reason he was here. "I'll make sure and set that up."

"Good." She sipped her coffee. "Thank you."

"Am I wasting my breath asking you to stop looking into the Paxton case?"

"Yes." Her eyes narrowed. "But you had to know I wouldn't back down. I don't even believe you want me to do that."

"It kept me up all night," he admitted. Dropping his head back, he rubbed his temples. He faced her again. "I've made no secret about my displeasure with your department in that situation, but the idea of you or one of your officers getting hurt because of me—"

"Him," she said.

"He's only here because of *me*, even if he also had you in his crosshairs last night." He couldn't let her forget that. He didn't know exactly why Orr had gone on the attack, but it was clear he was furious with Antonio.

"Now this text is threatening you, specifically. Wendy's parents have waited this long," he said. "So why not hold off on the Paxton review until he leaves?"

"Because if he is behind the drive-by and the fire, I intend to catch him. Then we can work on holding him accountable for the murder, too, if he is, in fact, the killer."

"He is." Antonio sighed. "That day, when he showed up with blood on his hand, he said it was an accident, but he often went hunting and I think he was too good for that kind of mistake."

"You didn't say that last night."

"It's in the first report I gave at the station, though." He didn't know why he'd held back. "Makes me queasy to think about it."

"For the sake of debate, if he's that good with a gun,

I have to consider someone else could have been shooting at us last night."

And that was the other reason. "I know I'm asking a lot, but please drop this," he said. "Focus on the Emerson trouble until he goes away again."

"You're frustrated and hurt and overtired," she said. "He tried to use you and took advantage of your good nature. Every conflicted thought and feeling you're having is understandable, Antonio."

"I don't need you to soothe me like I'm some shaky victim." He shoved back from the table, too restless to sit and handle this politely. It stung that his behavior only proved her point. Taking a deep breath, he pulled himself together. "He's a risk. I *don't* want you to drop it. Not really. But I can't let you get hurt, either."

"I know how to do my job."

"And still, you went for a run. Are you trying to bait him?"

"The officers sitting outside knew my route and were tracking my phone the entire time. I had pepper spray and a whistle with me. I didn't have my earbuds in. And today is a day when most of my neighbors are home."

"So that's a solid 'yes.' He shot at you yesterday."

She looked at him as if he'd sprouted horns. Maybe he had. "You were there, too," she said. "If he set the fire at your house, then I'm inclined to think you're the real target."

"Did you know about the fire when you went for a run?" he demanded, arms folded over his chest. Recognizing his defensive posture didn't help him correct it.

"I did not."

The admission made it all worse. "I just don't want you taking chances."

"How I do my job isn't your concern," she stated.

He wished he could be okay with leaving her to do her job her way. "He asked me to call you off. I've tried. Be careful. This city would suffer if something happens to you."

She stared at him, incredulous, her lips parted. He ran a hand through his hair. No horns. But that expression made him want a taste of her. He *was* overtired. Kissing Melissa was the worst idea, especially after flipping out.

"Thanks for your concern," she said stiffly. "I understand it. But I won't let a man I suspect is responsible for three violent crimes dictate my caseload."

He couldn't put everything rolling through him into words. Not in a way that would make any kind of sense. "Can you assign the case to someone else?"

"No. I'm taking the lead on this. It's my job to figure out where the Paxton case broke down and find a solution."

"I knew this was pointless," he grumbled. "I didn't even want to come over."

"Then why did you?"

He slumped into the chair he'd vacated. Probably not a good idea to tell her the memories of his dead wife were pushing him into actions he would normally avoid. "Doing my civic duty for Grave Gulch," he said, lamely. "That man's a snake and whatever he's been doing since he was last here, it doesn't seem to have made him a better person."

"Does it help to know I'm more concerned about *you*?"

"No." He cleared his throat, uneasy with her statement. He didn't need her or anyone else worrying over him. Too many expectations went along with worry and concern. Managing that with his parents and siblings was enough.

"I'm a grown man..." He left that sentence unfinished as her blue eyes sparked with a challenge. "I'm not being sexist. I only meant that I value my independence."

"Same." She sat back, crossing her arms over her chest. "Go on and keep digging."

"I have a security team."

Her toe started tapping. "Same."

"You can't blame me or anyone else for worrying if you are the real target," he said in a desperate attempt to drag himself out of the verbal pit he'd created.

She froze, as if time had come to a screeching halt, and then burst out laughing. After she caught her breath, then dried the tears gathered at the corners of her amazing eyes, she said, "The fire implies *you* are the target. Just as I told you before."

"Maybe he just couldn't get to you."

"A fact which only underscores that my precautions are enough."

But how long would those precautions hold up? "He can't get to me now. I'm in the penthouse. Join me there." He caught himself before he reached across the table for her hands. "Please, Melissa. Orr must be coming unhinged if he's back in town and raising hell."

"No. Thank you." Her answer, delivered in that cool, calm tone, only aggravated him more. "And you're still assuming Orr is behind all of this. I can't make assumptions."

"Once again, one eyewitness isn't enough?"

"Your account from last night is a good start. Reliable. Valued. And you will need to give a formal statement at the station, preferably today. Many eyewitnesses are not as reliable as you, which is why the justice system relies on evidence. I have to operate within that system."

"And if the evidence in the system is compromised, like Hannah McPherson claims?"

"Again, I am working on it. For both of you. I can't give you details—"

"The news reported that the DA dumped Hannah in the county jail. That's pretty rough for a woman her age."

"It is," she agreed. "My cousin, Troy, wrote up the report, took her statement and handled the transfer. You don't like it, talk to the DA."

He shook his head. "Seems extreme for such a sweet old lady."

"Sweet old *kidnapper*, you mean." She held up a hand and he had a ridiculous urge to draw those long fingers to his lips. "The case is out of my hands. I just had the same conversation with Desiree," she added.

"Danny's mom is furious, I bet."

"You'd lose that bet," Melissa mused. "She's far more relieved. Maybe it's motherhood."

He waited, but her gaze drifted somewhere he couldn't follow. "How so?" he prompted.

She shifted in her seat. "I won't explain it well."

"Try," he urged.

"Desiree almost condones the grandmother's actions. It's bizarre. As if she can't cast stones because there's no end to how far she'd go for Danny."

"And you can't relate?"

Melissa's nose wrinkled. "I think I'm more worried that I can." She looked up at the ceiling, her hair, long and loose today, falling back in a river of red fire. "When we were talking to Everleigh's mom, my heart cracked at her loss of faith in her daughter. And when we were at Hannah McPherson's place, the desperation was palpable.

"Three moms last night facing the darkest times in parenthood. And... I don't know. My heart ached for all of them in turn."

Not the darkest times, he thought. They each still had the child they loved. Maybe out of reach for a time, possibly in danger or in trouble, but alive. Where there was life, there was hope. Death was irreversible. Insurmountable. No going back, no hope for a brighter tomorrow.

"All of them heartbroken, if only in the short term," he said quietly.

"What do you mean?"

He avoided a direct answer. "I believe your ability to relate to each of them last night and today is part of what makes you a good cop."

Whatever he expected, it wasn't another laugh. "Since when? The rumors eventually get back to me, Antonio. The entirety of the GGPD is aware that you believe we're incompetent and that it starts at the top."

"Surely you have to agree letting Drew Orr roam free isn't a shining moment. Maybe if *you* had taken my statement, it would've been handled properly."

"You're unbelievable," she said. "Just when I think I've figured you out, you change gears. That kind of comment is as much of an insult to me as it to the detective who led the case. It's six months now, right?"

"Pretty much."

"The statements and reports wouldn't change anything unless the evidence backed it up. I don't tell you how to be hospitable. How about you stop judging my work until you have a degree and more than a decade of experience in law enforcement?"

"You're right," he said, stung. He rubbed the spot where his chest ached, standing again. "Forgive me." He would not burden her with the ghosts of his past. They were irrelevant, anyway. "I really didn't come to argue, only to report the text messages and that's done. I need to get over to the house to meet with the insurance adjuster."

"Would it be a problem for me to join you?"

Until she mentioned it, he hadn't realized how much he wanted her there. "Two cars or one?" he asked, reaching for her coat.

She didn't even roll her eyes this time as he held it for her. She did pull her keys from her pocket. "Two cars."

"I thought there was safety in numbers," he teased.

"Call it an experiment," she replied with a grin that set his pulse skipping. "This way if someone opens fire, we might be able to sort out the real target."

But Antonio was starting to believe neither one of them was safe with Orr on the loose. He had to let her handle things her way, but he struggled with the overwhelming urge to protect her. His fingers tingled and he shoved his hands deep into his coat pockets. The last woman he'd been willing to slay dragons for was his wife. He swallowed an oath. What if Orr won? What if the worst happened and Antonio lost Melissa too?

Chapter Seven

The fire damage was worse than Melissa had anticipated. She'd called the station on the drive over and
according to the report the officer on duty read to her,
the fire hadn't had much time to grow. The officer also
told her the firefighters now suspected arson. Antonio's
kitchen told a far more graphic story.

The sidelight at the door that connected the deck to the
kitchen had been smashed. She agreed that the broken
glass allowed the arsonist to reach through and unlock
the door, tripping the first alarm. Glass fragments had
been trampled by firefighter boots, crushed against the
beautiful travertine tiles. Scorch marks bloomed from
two corners of the cabinetry. Two accelerant devices
had been placed and ignited, according to the fire chief.

He was lucky he hadn't lost the house, she thought
for the umpteenth time since walking into the scene.
She didn't bother to say it; she was sure he'd heard the
words enough from the others.

There was no sign that the intruder had moved beyond
the kitchen, though the insurance adjuster and Antonio
had walked the entire residence, inside and out, to be
sure all the damage had been documented.

"Your security system did the trick," she said when

they stood side by side on his deck that overlooked the lake. "The alarm must have rushed him."

"I don't believe he wanted the whole house to go," Antonio said. "Yes, I'm *assuming* it was Orr, and based on that assumption, I can tell you that he has a good idea how I'd react if he burned down the house."

"Maybe you shouldn't share those details with the chief of police." She smiled, softening the reminder of her position. "Tell me why the house is so important and how it is Orr knows you so well."

He pushed his gloved hands through the snow on the deck rail. The man was always in motion. "He knows it's my pride and joy even if I spend most hours at the hotel. I told him how I designed the house from the front door all the way to this deck. How I wanted it to sit on the site so I'd have the best views of the lake from the right rooms."

"The right rooms?"

"Sure. The most inspiring views shouldn't be visible only from the master bathroom or whatever."

"Got it," she said, amused. "Is there an architecture degree in your long list of accomplishments?"

"No. And the list isn't all that long. I just knew the end result and worked backward. Once I decided Grave Gulch would be my primary base, the land came first. After that I found the right architect, had the plans drawn up properly."

"Well, the kitchen was beautiful." That had been obvious despite the glaring damage.

He rolled his shoulders, tucked his hands into his pockets. "It was."

"It will be again," she assured him. "Do you enjoy cooking?"

"A man must eat. Once I left home I quickly realized

how smart my mother was to insist that I learn how to cook for myself and the family."

"My mother is Italian. Same philosophy. Sounds like the two of them would get along."

"Or possibly fight over the counter space," he joked. "Do you think *this* crime will stick to Orr?"

"I'll do my best to find out who did it," she promised. There was no point in debating the accusation. Antonio was convinced and although she'd manage the investigation with impartiality, she had a hunch he was right.

Frankly, she was hoping to break their current pattern of being almost friendly only to wind up arguing again. There were people in town she adored, more people she got along with and a few people she avoided because, like oil and water, they didn't mix.

Antonio had been in the last category before now, a man she was happier avoiding. Oh, he was handsome as sin, but they didn't agree on anything... Until last night. The look on his face when he held her baby cousin had convinced her there was more to him than luxury hotels, increasing his net worth and his next gorgeous date.

"Why this particular piece of land?" she asked as she stared out toward the lake. Deep snow pressed up against the waterline, stretching out in white sheets over the water. Icicles dripped from the trees, jagged beauty that transformed the view. If she lived here, she might never be persuaded to leave.

"You're making my point for me," he said, bumping her shoulder with his. "It's the view. You should see it from the loft. You'll have to come back for the full tour."

The unexpected affection made her skin tingle all over. "I'd like that," she said without thinking. It was too easy to imagine waking up to these views after a night in his bed. Now she'd have to create an excuse if he ever did offer.

Seeing more of his house would wreck the happy little fantasy she'd spun up last night. The one where she was his date to some gala, leaning close enough to breathe in his cologne. The woman within his reach, able to stroke his arm or accept a caress in return… Would that woman ever be *her*?

"Melissa?"

She snapped back to the present, feeling the color rising in her face. If she was lucky, he'd blame it on the cold wind blowing off the lake. "Tell me more about Orr. You've told me he can shoot and I'd imagine he enjoys it. For now, we'll assume he isn't afraid to start a fire."

"He can kill," Antonio said, his voice grim. "And get away with it."

She wouldn't argue that, either, right now. "Any other dangerous skills I should know about?"

"He believes he can outthink and outmaneuver anyone," Antonio said.

"We have a know-it-all like that on the CSI team. He annoys everyone, but he's almost always right. Which is good, but adds to the annoyance." She turned her back on the lake, leaning against the rail while she studied Antonio. Not her smartest move. He wore dark sunglasses against the glare of sunlight on the snow. Unable to enjoy that gaze, her eyes focused on his mouth.

Big mistake. His somber expression didn't dull the appeal of his sensual, firm lips. The temptation to kiss him was overwhelming. Desire pooled low in her belly, sweeter than the syrup she'd poured over her French toast.

"That's not what I mean," Antonio said. "He craves

knowledge. At first I thought it was to compensate for a lack of formal education, but he has a master's degree in political science, of all things."

"And he's a real-estate developer?"

"In name only. He's a con man. Always has an angle in play using other people's money. He makes big promises backed only by creative excuses to keep investors from cashing in before he has the next mark lined up. From what I could tell, his education is the only legit thing about him."

"Unless it's fake, too."

"No, I looked him up. He went to Northwestern. The pictures in the yearbook match up. The longer we were associates, the more convinced I was that he lied about everything *but* that."

"So he's proud of his education." How would that change her approach when they found him? "Is he arrogant about it?"

"He wasn't with me and I only have a bachelor's in business."

Only? He had a bachelor's and a mind that turned one hotel redesign into a massive net worth and portfolio. "I should let you have your Sunday," she said, straightening. "I have a full plate and several interviews to prepare for."

"You have a master's in criminal justice, right?" he asked.

"Yes." It wasn't a secret and it was actually preferred for advancement. "I wish that and determination was enough to solve every case."

His mouth curled into a sexy grin. "If it was, then your work might be as easy as I've implied. I am sorry for my bad attitude."

"Hardly the first time. I've felt the same way," she admitted. The wind caught her hair and she shook it out of her face, wishing for a hair tie. "Way back when I was a kid and my aunt was murdered, I couldn't comprehend why the police couldn't find the killer. Learning it all, working my way up to chief, I think the only silver lining in that entire mess was my ability to empathize with victims."

"I think your empathy is rooted deeper than an unsolved crime." He tugged off his glove and tucked her wayward hair behind her ear. "Not that my opinion matters much."

Her ear and cheek blazed at that light touch, then he put his glove back on. For a long, awkward moment she was speechless. Tenderness and Antonio didn't go together in her mind. Until recently.

She licked her lips and, before she made a colossal mistake and followed her urge to kiss him, she repeated something about how busy she was and scooted around him.

"Be careful!" he called after her.

She urged him to do the same as she hurried to the safety of her car. But his voice and the conversation lingered in the back of her head. It turned out his opinion mattered to her more than she expected.

That was completely new. And the worst possible timing.

In front of the station, she passed protestors braving the cold, waving signs and chanting "Free Granny." They weren't blocking the street or access to the station, so she decided to let the cold dictate how long they stayed out there.

She closed herself in her office and forced her full

attention on the Emerson case. If there was a chance the DA had an incomplete or inaccurate picture of the evidence, Melissa needed to find the truth as soon as possible.

She pulled up the case file on her computer, then read through all of the notes on the Fritz Emerson murder from transcript of the first emergency call to Everleigh's arrest and arraignment. The investigation looked textbook, right down to the witness who put Everleigh near the scene. Things started falling apart with the evidence. As Melissa read the final forensics report, she could understand the logical conclusion that Everleigh had struck that fatal blow.

Wanting to discuss it with an objective person, she stuck her head out of her office to look for Troy, but he wasn't in. She wasn't about to call him after last night. He deserved some rest. Her next visit was to the forensics lab downstairs, but Randall Bowe wasn't in and neither were Jillian or Billy, who had worked the case.

So she returned to her office, took a deep breath and called the district attorney, Arielle Parks. The DA would not be pleased with what Melissa wanted to discuss. After bringing the lawyer up to speed, she waited for the reaction, pen tapping against her palm.

"Her defense attorney should have found this," Parks said.

Melissa agreed. "I wish there wasn't anything for her attorney to find. Can you ask for a continuance?"

Parks sighed heavily. "How much time do you need?"

"I need time to speak with Bowe," she said. "He's not in the lab today, but I'll track him down at home if necessary. I'm hopeful he can shed some light on this when we talk."

"Be quick," Parks said, her voice stern. "After all the press last night, I spoke with the judge. Neither of us wants a mistrial or hung jury due to public sympathy for Hannah McPherson. I'll call him back. He won't want to risk having a conviction overturned on appeal for a technicality you should have caught. At the same time, Emerson has a right to a speedy trial. I expect he will only grant a continuance through Monday and we'll be back in court on Tuesday."

Just about thirty-six hours. With the clock ticking in her head, Melissa ended the call. At least she'd bought a little time. Next, she dialed Bowe's home number, but it went to voice mail and she left a message. She tried his cell phone too, but he didn't answer. She left another message, hoping her frustration wasn't too obvious. The last thing she wanted was to be here spinning her wheels when time was short.

As a rookie, her training officer had taught her that when she bumped up against a brick wall, sometimes it was best to take a step back and look for a window or a way around. She wasn't making progress on the Emerson case, so she shifted focus and pulled up the Paxton files.

The pictures of the area in the park where the body had been found were comprehensive and she remembered Ian Elward had been the CSI on the scene. The man always documented everything in excessive detail. The body had been located off a remote section of the hiking trail, hidden by natural underbrush. The photos were a bright green contrast to the weather outside today; the trees' foliage would've given the killer excellent cover, even if someone else had been around.

She studied the crime-scene photos, specifically those showing any blood, but nothing at the scene gave her a close enough view to independently corroborate Antonio's story about Orr's bloodstained hand. The victim had been shot, and it had been messy, but what she had here wasn't enough to take action.

She switched over to researching the county park website, identifying the placement for any wildlife trail cameras, but it seemed that section of the park was completely blind. The detective on the case had noted the same thing at the time of the investigation. Being thorough, she called the Parks Department, verifying that no other cameras were in that area.

Had Orr known about the lack of cameras on that trail? Antonio said the man believed he could outthink anyone. If not, it had been awfully good luck to have chosen that particular section of the trail.

The questions plagued her as she left the station, planning to drive out to Grave Gulch Park. She changed her plan, going by Bowe's house first. If he was home, he didn't come to the door. Frustrated, she left another message on his cell phone and then drove out to the park. Walking back to the site where Wendy's body had been found didn't lead to any new revelations and she eventually climbed back in her car for a long drive to think through the troubling situation.

Time was of the essence, and it bothered her immensely that Bowe had not returned her calls. When the sunny day faded to twilight, she turned for home. She'd fix something to eat and, as the best option, study the original Paxton and Emerson files in preparation for the Monday meetings. Contrary to Antonio's opinion, she was not ready to hang herself out like bait for Orr.

She rose with the sun on Monday morning. Rolling into the station early, she was surprised to see Free

Granny signs in store windows all along the central boulevard. She knew those store owners and wouldn't have expected them to become protestors, but the media was drumming up community sympathy for the elderly Hannah McPherson.

She doubted most of the people behind the movement had even heard of Hannah McPherson before Saturday night, though. They were simply upset over an apparent injustice. Those who did know Hannah were likely even more upset because the woman was kind, thoughtful and clearly determined to defend her granddaughter.

Melissa went in through the back door and greeted the officers on duty. In her office, she set her travel mug of coffee on her desk and reached over to boot up her computer. While she waited for the machine to come online, she called down to the lab and left a message for Ian Elward, the CSI on the Paxton case to come to her office first thing. She wanted his take on that scene before she spoke with Bowe about it.

She couldn't say that she'd made any real progress or found a glaring error, but she felt confident about the entire case file from Antonio's initial report to the recovery of the body. She went to the break room to top off her coffee and saw Ian striding in.

"Good morning, Chief," he said.

She'd often wondered if he used that clipped tone all the time. That perfect diction made everything out of his mouth sound like he was reciting an academic paper to people who had no hope of understanding the findings. Ian wasn't the most popular of people in the GGPD, due to his constant need to prove he knew everything, from the science behind a blue sky to the newest method of processing evidence.

"Thanks for coming in," she said, and they went to her office.

"Of course." Ian sat in one of the visitor chairs in front of her desk. "How can I assist you with the Emerson case?"

The query caught her off guard. After closing the door, she took her time settling into her chair. "I actually wanted to discuss a different case. One you processed last summer."

His thin eyebrows snapped together over his nose and she could almost see gears turning in his head.

She clarified quickly, before he could toss out details on every crime scene he'd worked. "It's a cold case. Wendy Paxton. The body was recover—"

"Recovered in Grave Gulch Park. Early July. The second or third. Everyone was gearing up for the Fourth of July, but it was definitely before the barbecue contest."

Melissa pressed her lips together, then said, "That's the one. The victim—"

"Midtwenties. Female. Blond hair, slender," Ian interrupted. "Two gunshot wounds, one in the shoulder. Fatal bullet entered back to front at close range and went through the heart. Do we have more evidence to reopen the case?"

She ignored his question. "That's right. I've read your field report. There were light scratches on her arms and legs consistent—" She held up a finger to prevent another interruption. "Consistent with walking through that part of the park. No defensive wounds."

"Correct. She really should have worn more appropriate clothing for hiking."

And this sort of tunnel vision was why she was glad Ian worked on the scientific side of criminal justice. He wasn't suited to a public-facing role where a careless comment could alienate a grieving family.

"Reading your report from the scene, you made note of scratches that might also have occurred postmortem." She tapped her pen to her palm.

"That's right. Skin damage, but no blood. Not many, but they were consistent with the victim being moved through that environment."

Which led her to believe that Wendy's killer might have wrapped the body before moving it. She checked her computer monitor, where she glanced at the final forensics report signed by Randall Bowe, complete with pictures of the body.

"Anything else you can recall about the case?" she asked Ian.

"Yes, Chief." Ian took a breath and she settled in for a long monologue. "At the scene we were all agreed that the body had been moved to the position in which we found it. A small amount of the victim's blood was discovered less than one hundred yards away. Not enough for it to be the location of the fatal shooting, by my assessment."

He paused, a frown on his face. "Feel free to speak your mind," she prompted. As if anything would stop him.

"I work the scenes I'm sent to. I file my reports, and most of the time, I hear that the officers take that information to close cases. In this case, no arrests were made."

"That's correct."

"Chief, there was a clear thumbprint on the body." He pointed to the corresponding area on his throat. "Right about here. A print in the blood and based on the position and bruising around her neck. It appeared the person, presumably the shooter, had started to strangle her before shooting her a second time. I took pictures of that print and documented the findings in my report. That should've been enough to compare to any suspects questioned in the case."

She shot him a look, enough to have him blanch and back down from doubting the work of her officers. Ian loved to overstep, believing he alone was responsible for finding the evidence to help them do their jobs efficiently. Most of the time he was right, but because he was so snobby about it, no one wanted to listen.

On the other hand, more amiable CSIs, like her cousin Jillian, were easier to work with and were always better received because they maintained confidence balanced by a dose of humility. There were layers to police work and, as Hannah McPherson so vehemently pointed out, evidence wasn't always the whole picture.

Especially if mistakes had been made.

Melissa knew her own triggers after years of experience as a police officer and testifying in various cases from traffic court to felonies. The attorneys didn't like to call Ian to testify because juries never warmed up to him, no matter what he said. She had to fight the same urge to dismiss him now, simply because he was too sure of himself, what he had found.

"The only pictures from the crime scene—"

"You mean the scene where we found the body," he corrected her. "I wasn't aware the actual scene of the shooting had been identified."

"You're right." He was lucky she'd had two cups of coffee before this conversation. "The pictures in your report from the area where the body was found do not include any clear views of the print."

"That's impossible. I took the pictures. I documented each one and filed it appropriately." Without any invitation, he popped up out of the chair and came around to peer at her computer monitor over her shoulder.

She resisted the urge to shove him back, out of her space. Instead, she slowly clicked through the available photos.

"Where did they go?" Ian was clearly perplexed and his expression indicated he was rushing headlong into being furious. "I know what I saw and how it was documented. There's an error."

"Relax and take a breath," she suggested. "No one is blaming you. Didn't you and Bowe argue about the state of that print?"

"He was wrong." Ian snapped upright, bracing his hands on his hips. "That print was clear at the scene and in transit, and I documented it accurately."

"I believe you," she responded. "However, none of that documentation is with the file. Only a picture of a smudged print in the area you indicated." She pointed to the monitor.

"That's the same case?"

Was he actually accusing *her* of manipulating the file now? "It is."

"That's not at all what I saw then." He started to lean in again, to reach for her keyboard. At her hard look, he backed off. "Check the database."

Each word was delivered with razor-sharp precision, and though she didn't comment, she took note of his lack of a "please."

"I've checked the database," she assured him. "I even

pulled the hard copies, but the photos you describe are not part of the digital or physical case file. Please take a seat."

"You're going to tell me I've confused facts, mixed up this case with another. That simply isn't true."

In fact, she wasn't going to tell him that, because she didn't want to deal with the fit she knew he would throw at hearing it. "No." She sipped her coffee, holding the mug in both hands, doing her best to put him at ease. "I was going to ask if you kept a backup of your files anywhere." At his blank stare, she continued. "The cloud, a private computer, anything?"

"No." He blinked slowly. "Police business stays here, on the official servers. Any other precaution would be a breach of security."

An answer she appreciated as it implied he had the same confidence in the GGPD database as he had in himself. But if he hadn't misfiled the photographs, where were they? His written report referenced a clear print, but in the lab, Bowe contradicted that finding, claiming the print was smudged, useless. This put Bowe at the crux of two questionable findings in two different murder cases.

"Did you know Wendy Paxton?" she asked.

"Of course not. If I had, I would've recused myself at the scene."

Because Ian followed every protocol to the letter. "Great. Thank you for your time."

"That's it?"

He didn't look any happier than she felt. "One more thing," she said. "Did you review or process any evidence in the Fritz Emerson murder case?"

"No. That was Jillian. In my opinion, a rookie should

never be on a murder call." He cleared his throat. "I understand she is a relative, Chief Colton. I still stand by the statement."

She didn't react. Ian would always be arrogant. He'd always believe he was right. There were several people who shared her last name on the GGPD. Nepotism, contrary to Ian's inference, had nothing to do with it. Other than Grace, she hadn't hired any of the Coltons currently on the GGPD.

"You were on the team that processed the evidence for the kidnapping case at the McPherson home Saturday night?"

"Yes, I was. I'm filing my reports this morning."

"Then I'll let you get to it. Please send me a copy directly."

She stopped short of asking Ian to back up his information and photos somewhere other than the GGPD as she had with Jillian. Though Ian had never been a gossip, she wasn't in the mood to listen to his opinion on the security risk of cloud services. Nor did she feel that being candid with him about a potential problem within forensics worked in her favor.

She might not like Ian much personally, but she was confident he wasn't the problem downstairs. Bowe was the common denominator in the Emerson case and the Paxton case and she needed to speak with him immediately.

She scowled at her cell phone. Bowe still hadn't returned her calls and she'd been clear that she expected him to call her back at the earliest opportunity. His silence raised her suspicions, though he was a stickler for keeping to business hours barring his presence at an active crime scene. It seemed as if he was the only person in town who didn't realize they were a department in crisis.

ANTONIO SET ASIDE his cell phone, having completed another call with his insurance adjuster. He appreciated how quickly they were processing his claim. Now all he needed was confirmation from the police that he could start cleanup and repairs.

That made him think of Melissa and the resulting smile was a pleasant surprise. He could always drop in and check on the progress personally. Her interest in the fire was likely just a courtesy after he'd helped them find Danny. Still, he enjoyed talking with her, watching those blue eyes blaze with humor or intense interest.

He picked up his cell phone, already anticipating her smile for his unexpected arrival, when his desk phone rang. "Antonio Ruiz," he answered.

"Mr. Ruiz, this is the front desk. Desiree Colton is here, requesting to speak with you for a few minutes."

Antonio smiled again. "Is her son with her?"

"Yes, sir."

"Let her know I'll be right down."

Since moving to the secure suite, he'd been borderline paranoid about security, but he was confident his staff could keep Orr away from the hotel. Antonio regretted every tour he'd given Orr, every drink they'd had in his office or meal they'd shared in the main restaurant. He felt like a fool to have called the man a friend at any point in their history.

He reached the wide, sweeping stairs that curved into the lobby and spotted Desiree and her son right away. The little boy was gripping her finger and dragging her around the central fountain, giggling with every step.

Antonio's stomach cramped, his heart in a cold vise as the sadness of what he'd lost washed over him. Karen would've glowed like that, a combination of pride and exasperation, all tangled up with endless love for their child. He'd never even allowed the doctors to tell him if she'd been carrying a boy or a girl.

"Ms. Colton," he said, approaching the pair. "It's a pleasure to see you again."

In a smooth, practiced motion, she scooped Danny up into her arms and settled him on her hip. "Mr. Ruiz." She extended her hand to shake his. "We came over to say thank you."

The little boy stuck out his hands and threw all of his body weight at Antonio.

Desiree rolled her eyes. "And now you see why Mrs. McPherson had no trouble sweeping him out of the wedding reception. He doesn't know the concept of strangers."

"May I?" Antonio asked. He'd been so excited about becoming a father before he'd lost everything. It had taken years for him to be comfortable around children again, knowing he wasn't strong enough to bear the risk of attempting to have a family with another woman.

The sweet hands were already grasping his fingers and the little guy was making it clear he wanted out of his mother's embrace.

She picked up on his intention. "Yes, of course, you can hold Danny," she said clearly.

Her son didn't seem to care that she was trying to send him a message about safety and strangers. Danny beamed and patted his new friend's face before dropping his head to Antonio's shoulder, much as he'd done before he'd gone into Melissa's arms at the McPherson home.

The gesture didn't last as long. The boy wasn't at all sleepy right now. He sat up again and touched Antonio's close-cropped beard.

Touch. Giggle. Touch again.

Desiree started to laugh and Antonio joined in.

"He's a goofball sometimes," Desiree explained.

"All children should be," Antonio agreed. He started to walk, just meandering through the lobby, and pausing when something caught Danny's eye.

It surprised him to feel so relaxed with a child. Sure, he'd had similar experiences with nieces and nephews, but today there seemed to be soft buffer between the past grief and the present moment.

"So, as I said, thank you." Desiree beamed at her son. "I was out of my mind with worry. Melissa said you were instrumental in finding him."

"Instrumental is overstating it." He wasn't comfortable with the high praise. "I'm glad I could help, though I don't believe your son was in any danger."

Her eyes widened for just a moment before she averted her gaze. "Melissa didn't say it in those words, but I think she agrees with you."

He wisely withheld comment on that. "Mrs. McPherson was quite desperate for the chief's attention."

"Clearly," Desiree said. "There's another reason I came by. You were there and, well…" She pressed her lips together. "I'd like the DA to drop the case against Mrs. McPherson."

Antonio stopped moving and the toddler strained against his hold. An orchid, swaying in a nearby floral arrangement, had captured his attention. It was just out of reach, but he was determined to touch it.

Antonio took a step away and the toddler fussed. He

tickled his round tummy, effectively distracting him. "Maybe we should discuss this privately," Antonio suggested.

"That's not necessary." Desiree looked around the mostly empty lobby. "I just wanted your opinion. Do you think that sweet old grandmother should go to jail for taking Danny?"

"She committed a crime. You're part of the GGPD," he pointed out.

"Part-time sketch artist," she said. "Full-time mom. My son's never been accused of a crime and let's hope it stays that way. But if I knew he was innocent? Well…"

"What exactly are you asking?" Antonio queried.

"I thought maybe if we both wrote to the DA she would consider dropping the charges."

Antonio was astounded by this woman's capacity for forgiveness. In her shoes he was sure he would want to throw the book at the kidnapper, no matter how benign the appearances. "That may not be the best precedent," he cautioned. "Or even the right thing for the city as a whole. As I told your cousin, I'm prepared to testify to what I saw and heard at Hannah McPherson's home. The hotel has already received an official request for the security footage of any suspected instances of her on the property."

"You have to turn that over," Desiree said, nodding. "I'm not asking you to impede the investigation or anything." She sighed, then smiled when her son blew her a kiss. "I should be angry."

"I imagine you would be still if we hadn't found him so quickly."

They neared the fountain and the boy wanted to scamper. "So much energy," Desiree said. The three of them walked the circle, Antonio making sure Danny couldn't dash away, and Desiree close enough to be sure he wouldn't find a way into the water.

"Melissa assured me Mrs. McPherson's fate is up to the DA. But," he added when Desiree started to protest, "I will add my support to your request for leniency. In my opinion, the woman was not happy that she caused you stress."

"She just didn't feel like there was another way," Desiree said. Danny leaned on her legs and she picked him up.

"We could both be wrong," Antonio pointed out. "Melissa is being cautious about looking into the Emerson case. She can't afford to be seen condoning this method of bullying the police department."

"Oh, trust me, I heard it all from my brother," Desiree said. "Part of me feels like a traitor for feeling sorry for Hannah."

"You have a good heart, Ms. Colton. And a beautiful son."

"Thank you." She brushed her nose to Danny's.

The tender moment melted through him, right up to the cold ball of fear that protected his heart. Everything had turned out all right for these two, and though Hannah McPherson was in jail right now, her concerns were being addressed. Someone needed to find justice for all parties involved. Justice beyond the obvious legalities.

"We'll let you get back to work," Desiree said, smiling up at him. "Again, Danny and I will always be grateful."

He gave her a friendly smile and send-off, unable to find a more personal sentiment. The outpouring of gratitude shook him more than he wanted to admit, even to himself. For the better part of two decades he'd focused his energy on building his business. There was nothing else for him after losing Karen and the baby.

Heading back up the stairs, he knew he'd done the right thing on Saturday night. Eventually the emotional upheaval would quiet down again. He caught himself rubbing his sternum as he walked into his office. A man didn't make it to forty-two without a few regrets. There was nothing he could do about the past except allow the painful memories to fade away again.

A distraction was in order, and what better option than helping the police figure out where Orr was hiding?

What could possibly have brought Orr back to the city *now*? Antonio had been sure he was working a new angle on investors in Chicago. The possibilities whipped through his mind. After almost falling for Orr's con, he'd spoken with friends and investors, letting them know his opinion on Orr had changed and why. He refused to let people he trusted and respected be pulled into Orr's shady net.

No way to know how much had that cost him. Could Melissa be right that Orr was targeting him and not her? She had to prioritize the Emerson case since Everleigh Emerson was on trial. But maybe he could give the police something more to go on when she could take another look at the Paxton murder.

The text that had come through just before the fire wouldn't help much. It didn't offer a location or even confirmation that it was actually Orr behind the threat.

Sitting down at his desk, he opened the archived file with the communications and notes he'd taken while planning a project with Orr. There had to be something in here the police could use to show a pattern of behavior.

The old emails creeped him out in hindsight. The

golf outings, double dates, regional charity events. Antonio stopped skimming emails and retrieved his journals from those same months. He'd been so focused on the business potential, had he overlooked something worrisome about Orr's personal nature?

Everyone made mistakes, but this was a big one, letting himself be fooled. Well, if there had been anything obvious, he would've parted ways with Orr sooner. Other than an awkward argument between Orr and Wendy during a double date, Antonio hadn't noticed any red flags. He needed to give Melissa something more substantial than an easily dismissed personal account and a few random moments of intuition.

He called the firm that provided security for the hotel and asked them to run down anything they could on Drew Orr, past and present. The company had built a file for him, the same as they did for any person or business he planned to partner with. It hadn't raised any red flags back then. Hopefully, this time around they would find an issue the GGPD could build a case on.

It gave Antonio chills to read through his journal entries of those first meetings with Orr. This time, he saw it as the setup Orr had intended. The man was good, but by killing Wendy, even getting away with it this long, he'd burned his bridges with Antonio and Grave Gulch. It made no sense for him to come back.

Discouraged that he was letting down Melissa, Antonio tossed aside the journals and turned his attention to current news and websites that discussed markets and investors.

When he saw a headline, he swore, having completely forgotten about his call with a friend in San Antonio last month. They'd discussed a joint venture that involved the restoration of a sizeable segment of the River Walk. They'd been approached by a third company, new to both of them, that was eager to jump on board. To make the numbers work, the corporation needed three buildings but had a hard cap on the purchase price. The seller hadn't wanted to accept their offer and the new company had offered to make up the difference just to push the deal through. Orr's name hadn't shown up in the background search Antonio had ordered at the time, only a list of lawyers representing a real-estate group.

It was a stretch, but still possible, that Drew Orr was behind that company. If Antonio had inadvertently botched another deal for Orr, that would certainly explain the man storming back into Grave Gulch for revenge. He sent the real-estate-group information on to the security company. If they could connect the dots, it could put a quick end to this pervasive sense of danger.

The thought of spending time with Melissa without looking over his shoulder for Orr sent a zip of anticipation through his veins. He needed to know she was safe, but more than that, he wanted to see those blue eyes sparkle with curiosity as they worked toward a common goal of justice for Wendy Paxton.

Better yet, he was looking forward to teasing a smile out of her. One that had nothing to with a case and everything to do with just the two of them.

Chapter Eight

Following her chat with Ian, Melissa had to put out a few bureaucratic fires that included calls from the mayor and the DA about Hannah McPherson. Since there was nothing concrete to share on the case, she could only listen, and it wasn't fun. With still no response from Bowe, she had no choice but to ask the state police to send her a forensic scientist to review the evidence.

When she finally escaped her office at a quarter past nine, she went straight to Troy's desk, pleased to catch him. "Sun's out. Can you take a walk with me?" She often did better thinking when she was on the move. She'd been stuck in her office all morning and she didn't want to be interrupted again.

He squinted toward the window. "Sure?"

"Thanks." She went back for her coat and gloves, and then caught up with him in the break room. Shrugging into her coat, she was surprised to miss Antonio holding it for her. She had a problem where he was concerned, a problem that had nothing to do with police work. It had taken her all of five minutes to appreciate his thoughtful manners. Less time than that to lose herself in his dark gaze. She wanted to keep thinking of him as oil to her water. They would never mix…and yet she really wanted to try.

"Are we just out here for the sake of frostbite?" Troy asked, dragging her back from the brink of those dangerous thoughts.

"No. I need a fresh viewpoint and some scenery before I tackle a delicate interview."

"All right, I'm listening."

"What do you recall about the body we found in the park in July?"

"Paxton?"

She nodded. "That's the one."

"It was memorable in the lack of details. The crime scene didn't give us much to go on."

"Body location," Melissa muttered.

"What?"

"Oh, I said 'crime scene' when talking to Ian about it this morning."

Troy laughed. "And he corrected you." He chuckled again when she nodded. "He was the first to propose it was only a dump site, but we were all thinking it. Not enough blood for two gunshot wounds."

"Ian told me about processing the scene, finding the victim's blood in another location."

"Right. Blood and nothing else. Nothing much to go on except her tie to the boyfriend, Drew Orr. We cleared him, despite Ruiz's concerns, and then cleared Ruiz, too, after Orr pointed the finger at him."

"And that was okay with you?" she queried.

"Not at all. Orr was squirrely. But the evidence…" His voice trailed off. "Man, do you remember that blowup Ian and Bowe had over the evidence?"

She couldn't recall a fight like that. "What do you mean? Where was I?"

Troy squinted, thinking back. "Probably at Danny's birthday party," Troy said. "I got over there just in time for the cake. And before you get all guilty about it, you don't take enough time off as it is. There was no need to call you in over a personnel dispute. Especially not for those two."

Troy was right. Bowe and Ian had frequently butted heads since Bowe had come to Grave Gulch three years ago. Two know-it-alls in one lab didn't always make for a peaceful environment. Ian hadn't mentioned a fight, though he had been indignant and upset earlier when she'd told him his pictures and report weren't included as he'd filed them.

"What if it was more than the typical fight?"

"Over what?" Troy countered. "Ian and Bowe get on each other's nerves. You know how Ian is."

"Randall Bowe isn't much better," she commented.

"No, but he has the last word since he's in charge."

Melissa prompted Troy for the details on the fight.

"Ian asked about the results on a fingerprint he'd seen in the blood. Bowe said the print was smudged, unusable. Ian yelled about photographs, Bowe showed him the body. There were insults and insinuations about who smudged the print and how the angle of the only photo that had been uploaded rendered it useless for identification. They nearly came to blows."

She had a moment envisioning how that fight might look. Both men were slim, but Ian was taller, giving him an advantage on reach. "How did you separate them?"

"Carefully," Troy said, joking. "Took two of us to haul

Ian out of the lab. He's tougher than he looks when he's having a tantrum."

She turned all of that over in her mind. Would it have changed anything if she'd known this at the time? Probably not. They couldn't process evidence they didn't have. Had the fingerprint been smudged on purpose? If so, why?

"Wait a minute. Ian railed about having photos of the print and told me he'd uploaded all of that properly. Where did those photographs end up?" Her stomach knotted at the mere thought of anyone in her department tampering with evidence. She trusted her people. But something was off in these two murder cases.

"No one found a connection between Paxton and Ian or Randall, right?"

"No," he replied slowly. "I didn't look for a connection to Orr." Troy looked at her as if her brain had frozen. "What are you thinking?"

She stopped, her gaze scanning her town, fully aware that there were eyes on them from every angle. "Clarke found discrepancies in the evidence against Everleigh Emerson. After a man, identified by Mr. Ruiz as Drew Orr, shot at Mr. Ruiz and myself, I think there is reason to believe evidence is off in that case, too."

Her stomach rolled and the chill on the back of her neck had nothing to do with the bitter-cold January wind. No matter how she studied the cases, it came down to serious trouble in the forensics department.

"The fingerprint." He stared at her, horrified. "Melissa, you have to be careful."

"I'm aware." She pressed the toe of her boot to the snow gathered at the edge of the sidewalk. The grid pattern of the sole reminded her of the mullioned arched windows at Antonio's home. Not where her mind should be. "For the life of me I can't come up with a motive. I don't want to alienate good people, but we have to get to the bottom of this. Will you come with me to talk to Bowe?"

"Absolutely. It won't be fun, but it could be entertaining."

She tried to laugh, but couldn't quite make it work. She might as well be walking across thin ice, but the only way to the truth, to real justice, was to keep going.

"And, of course," she added as they started back, "you can't breathe a word of this to anyone."

He lifted his chin toward the central intersection where a dozen people were milling about in front of the station with Free Granny signs. "Anyone other than them? They were listening when you said you'd take a second look at the Emerson case. They're counting on you to keep them updated until McPherson is free."

He was right. "So let's go find something worth an update."

"You know if we do reveal an error in the evidence, defense attorneys will be filing appeals right and left."

"They do that anyway," she said, wishing she felt as cavalier as her tone implied. "The only way to know if we managed to get it right the first time is to look again."

Melissa and Troy deftly avoided the milling protestors, entering the basement lab directly at the rear of the building. They found Randall Bowe, GGPD forensic scientist, in his office. The slender man was a few inches shorter than Troy, with brown hair brushed back off his forehead and brown eyes currently glowering at his computer monitor.

Maybe he didn't appreciate the email she had sent

last night on top of her other calls and voice mail messages, asking him to see her as soon as he came in today.

Or possibly he was aggravated by the media coverage following Saturday night's events and the implications made by Hannah McPherson's new attorney. More than one outlet had picked up the story and #FreeGranny had become the social-media hashtag of the moment. Several writers and bloggers were happily pointing fingers at the ineptitude of the GGPD. It was discouraging to have lost the community's faith, but it only made her more determined to set things right.

"I got your messages. I went upstairs but you were out," Bowe said. "Of course, you'd interrupt me now when I'm in the middle of a new report." He switched off the monitor and tucked his hands into the pockets of his lab coat.

"We won't take much of your time," Troy assured him.

Melissa kept her opinion on the timing to herself, letting Troy's cool demeanor lead the way.

"Could we discuss your report on the Emerson case?" Troy asked. "We need to be sure everything lines up."

"It's all in the database," Bowe snapped. "Go on and dig around. Look all you like. There's nothing to discuss. I processed the evidence delivered to me, no thanks to the rookie CSI."

Melissa swallowed an automatic defense of Jillian. Her cousin hadn't worked the scene alone and Billy had backed up her report, though she had yet to find that record in the database.

His arrogance had always irked her, but she'd done her best to take the high road. The man had an excellent reputation in his field and she'd put that above the challenges of communicating with him. "We're here because of discrepancies between the reports on the evidence gathered and your findings. The DA wants us to confirm the details before the trial resumes tomorrow."

Bowe pursed his thin lips together until they all but disappeared. "As if I don't see the great Colton family uniting against me. Look in the mirror, Chief. It was one of your precious relatives who screwed up at the Emerson crime scene.

"They bag and tag whatever they like and take hundreds of photos."

"As they're trained to do," Troy interjected.

Bowe's lip curled. "And then I must use my education and experience to sort it into something viable for a case. Give me better field investigators and you'd get better results."

Her jaw nearly cramped, but she clung to her fraying patience. "I don't believe the discrepancy originated at the scene," Melissa stated baldly.

Bowe puffed up his chest. "Are you suggesting *I* made a mistake?"

"Surely everyone makes one now and again," Troy observed.

"Not in *my* lab." His arrogance was appalling. "I take my duty seriously and I am thorough, focused and meticulous about it."

"You're implying any discrepancy happened at the scene," Troy said.

"No. I'm stating it outright," Bowe snapped. "Whether or not you believe it, your precious cousin is a weak link in this department. I could list ten mistakes she's made in the last month that could've been disastrous for your cases." His glare raked across both of them. "This particular police department would benefit from less nepotism and more expertise."

Melissa bit back a retort and Troy tensed up beside her. It seemed there was one thing Ian and Bowe agreed on. Clearly, she needed to do a better job rooting out that misplaced resentment. She would add it to her task list once they had answers for the Emerson case.

"The explanation is simple, Chief," he sneered as he used her title. "As you know, not all fibers are visible to the naked eye, which is why my role in the process is imperative."

She'd had enough lectures for one day. "I understand your role," she said through gritted teeth. "It's past time you understood my role as the chief of this department. A woman went to extremes to get our attention. Please review and process the evidence again and get me a new report as soon as possible."

Bowe sputtered. "That's preposterous! I can't—"

"Noted," she barked, cutting him off. "The state is sending someone to handle it. You will show whomever arrives the utmost professional courtesy."

"You *cannot* do this," Bowe said with startling conviction.

She stared him down. "I can. In this case, with a woman on trial for murder, it seems the prudent move."

"You're afraid of those sign-toting fools on the street." He snorted. "Of all the Coltons in this department, I thought *you* had guts."

Troy whistled low and long, but Melissa refused to sink to Bowe's level. "Mr. Bowe, for the sake of department unity, I'll blame your poor attitude on the Monday blues. I expect your cooperation and compliance on this matter moving forward. Be a leader in your department,

Mr. Bowe, before I'm forced to conduct a job search for your replacement."

She walked out, giving him no time to anger her further.

"If he didn't like you before, he hates you now," Troy murmured when they were in the stairwell.

"*Us*, as Coltons," she amended. "He can pull himself together or get out, though."

"You think he's at fault?"

"My opinion isn't the point. We need to be sure," she replied with brutal honesty. She pulled open the door to the main floor, letting Troy go in first. "I need to be able to trust our team," she added fiercely. "Even when their personalities annoy me. This is all about getting justice for victims—not ego."

If she'd been forced to point a finger at who made the error, she'd choose Bowe, but only because she was mad right now. She'd had a similar reaction, if far less intense, when Ian had made his insinuations against Jillian. She would need more information before drawing further conclusions.

What was *happening* in her department? A week ago, she would've said her family included everyone on the force, not just those named Colton. She remembered feeling part of something bigger from her first day as a rookie. There had been so much to learn and so many good, trustworthy people to guide her.

Now, she was chief of police and her unspoken goal was to honor that legacy, to build on that foundation. Everyone tied to her department was her responsibility, even the few who regularly got under her skin like a road rash.

What a nightmare. As the chief it all flowed back

to her. Any problems within the department ultimately rested on her shoulders. It was hard to convince anyone, even herself, of the good work they did day in and day out when she didn't have any real answers for this dreadful situation.

She signaled Troy to follow her to her office. By the time she'd closed the door her mind was made up. "I'll call the state lab for another forensic scientist to examine our evidence," she said. "I need you to *quietly* dig into the Emerson investigation. Revisit witness statements. Go see Everleigh at the county prison if you need to. Be fast and accurate. Parks only guaranteed us today. Sift through every detail we have on the deceased. You saw McPherson. Whatever we find will likely affect the kidnapping case, too."

Troy shook his head. "She didn't waver, not once, about taking Danny. She was remorseful about causing the family grief, but she did *not* back down about why it was necessary."

"That's what scares me," Melissa admitted. "Get moving. We both have work to do."

Alone in her office, she draped her coat over the back of her chair, but she was too restless to sit down as she made her phone call. They needed the truth, even if it made things worse. She thought about the protestors on the street and the media milling out front, not wanting to miss another update.

Hannah McPherson had kicked over a hornet's nest and Melissa had no idea how she was going to guide her department through the stinging fury.

With the Emerson case in Troy's hands, she returned to the cold case she wasn't ready to hand off: Paxton.

The woman's family deserved answers. Justice. Melissa understood how it felt when those things never came around. A memorial service might offer closure, but peace was elusive when a killer was still out there somewhere, alive and free.

Thinking about the Paxton case inevitably led her mind to Antonio. It would've been nice to enjoy a simple, brief daydream about the man. She knew he'd keep pressing her for answers and she really shouldn't be looking forward to those exchanges on a personal level. Yes, he made her pulse race and stirred up more than a few fantasies.

But he should have answers, too, and she harbored plenty of guilt and worry that mistakes—or worse— made in her department last summer were coming back to plague him now.

START-OF-THE-WEEK MEETINGS, CALLS and emails kept Antonio engaged through Monday morning, but his mind never wandered far from Melissa. Was she getting anywhere on the Emerson issues that led to the kidnapping? Selfish or not, he had to hope the case was resolved quickly so she could shift gears and focus on how Orr slipped through the cracks.

The anonymous text messages prior to the break-in and fire were still on his phone. Clearly Orr wasn't worried about being caught. Was it simply because Orr didn't care if the police found him? Not the latter. Antonio crossed that off his list. Orr's intention to stay out of prison was the only thing that made sense.

He found himself starting at the "or else" message. There was no way Melissa would drop this, especially not after the drive-by and the fire. She was in serious danger just because she was good at her job. He had to find a way to protect her.

Suddenly, his cell phone rang. The caller identification showed the number had been blocked and the icons on the screen suggested spam. Antonio answered, anyway.

"I told you to back her off." Orr's voice, low and tight.

His grip tightened on the device as adrenaline pulsed through his veins. What new threats would Orr toss out today?

"Hello, Drew." Antonio leaned back in his chair, grateful he'd installed the feature that allowed him to record incoming calls. "I'll say it again, turn yourself in. The cops have you dead to rights for the shooting and the break-in at my place."

"Spreading more lies about me. My attorneys will bury you in slander and libel lawsuits."

"Whatever firm is foolish enough to take you on will cut you loose before that happens," Antonio told him. "I gave the police a positive ID about the shooting."

"That won't hold up."

"Take some advice from an old pal," Antonio said. "Breaking and entering isn't your strong suit, either. My security system caught enough that night for facial recognition." He hoped this lie provoked Orr into a mistake.

"My friends in Grave Gulch told me you've been dragging my name through the mud. I've been in Texas for weeks. Michigan is too damn cold in the winter. Whatever you want, I'm not afraid to tell everyone how *you* backed out of our deal, Ruiz. You broke the promises."

Antonio wasn't buying in to any of this. All he'd done was turn down a business opportunity, and he knew Orr must be in Grave Gulch, looking for revenge or trying to save his skin. Likely both. "I changed my mind before anything was inked," Antonio clarified. "I did nothing illegal. You, on the other hand—turn yourself in. If the cops have to come looking for you, it won't go well."

"You first. Tell the truth," Orr said in a mean hiss. "Go on and tell your pretty cop friend what you did with my girl."

"Nothing." That was a line Antonio had never crossed. He didn't mix business with pleasure and breaking up relationships wasn't his thing. "You and Wendy had issues that didn't require interference from anyone else."

"Shut up. You have no right to speak her name after what you did."

Finally, Antonio understood the real motive for the call. Orr assumed that Antonio would be reporting this call or possibly even have the police listening in after the fire. He'd tried to pin Wendy's murder on Antonio before and here was the next attempt.

"Are you done?" he asked as if he didn't care. As if he wasn't the least bit sickened by Orr.

Shady, reputation-wrecking business deals were more than enough cause to part ways. When they'd met, he'd never imagined this affable, charismatic man was capable of taking the life of someone he'd claimed to love.

"Don't worry. You'll know when I'm done."

The call ended and Antonio shut off the recording app with a quaking finger. It would be nice to blame the unsteadiness solely on his anger, but it was fear, too. The sunlight pouring in the window felt all wrong, completely at odds with the dark tone of the call.

He had to take this to Melissa—whether or not she could use it, she needed to hear Orr's threats for herself.

Maybe then she'd take her safety more seriously. He started for his coat and keys and paused. Orr had urged him to "go" and tell Melissa about the call, implying Antonio and Melissa would be in the same physical space sometime soon. If he invited Melissa to the hotel, it was basically the same thing, with one primary street between the two locations.

All Orr had to do was wait on that route and the police chief would be easy pickings.

He sat down again, forcing himself to think and anticipate what Orr might do. Taking a deep breath, he reached for the phone on his desk, giving a start when it rang under his hand.

"Ruiz," he barked.

"Hello to you, too," Melissa said. "I'm heading your way—"

"No!" he shouted, leaping out of his chair. "Sorry. How close are you?"

"What's going on?"

"Turn around," he pleaded. "Wherever you are, turn around and go back to your office."

"I actually haven't left the office yet." Her voice shifted so that she sounded like the consummate professional she was. "What's the problem?"

"Good. Stay inside. Close your blinds," he said. "Please."

An image of the drive-by shooting flashed through his mind only this time it ended with her lifeless on the sidewalk, not checking him for injuries. He couldn't bear a loss that heavy. It terrified him to care this much.

"Give me a reason why."

He caught his breath and pulled the chair back so he could sit down again. He was jittery from head to toe.

"Drew Orr just called. Making threats. I recorded the conversation. I'm not sure which one of us he wants to kill more."

"We can sort it out," she said, her voice cool. "I'll come over."

"No. That's just what he wants—another chance to hurt you. I was going to come to you."

"All right. I'll wait."

"Don't do that, either." He scrubbed at his face, aggravated with his indecisiveness. "I think Orr has set a trap for me. Us."

"Mr. Ruiz—" she began.

Her suddenly formal tone was so absurd he started laughing, though it felt bitter. "Stop it." He took another deep breath. "I'm not paranoid, but he is pushing me in that direction," Antonio allowed. "When you hear the call, you'll understand."

"And when will I hear the call if you won't let me come to you?"

"I can send the audio file as an email attachment," he decided as clearer thinking prevailed. "And you should know I've got my security firm researching Orr's whereabouts over the last six months. On the call he claims he's in Texas, but I'm sure that's another lie. I'll share whatever they find with you."

"Great." She didn't sound too happy. "My department is working the drive-by shooting," she replied evenly.

"And doing a great job, I'm sure. I mean that sincerely," he added, regretting that the clarification was necessary.

"Thank you," she said softly. "I'll keep you in the loop as we make progress."

"You haven't reopened the Paxton case, have you?"

"Not officially. I've spent most of the past twenty-four hours reviewing it, though."

Was that the only reason she sounded tired? "You said it would take a back seat to the Emerson situation?"

She sighed. "This would be a better conversation to have in person."

Not if it meant Orr getting a clear shot at her. Another wave of panic threatened to swamp him. With the hotel situated as it was on the lake, there was one primary drive in and out. Of course, there were access roads for service and deliveries to the property, but Orr could park himself at the main intersection and wait for one or both of them to roll on by.

"Is there a way for you to ride over with someone else?" Once he had her here, they could discuss all of the details and then he could convince her to move into the safe suite.

"Let's start with the easy pieces," she said. "Send me the audio file. Once I listen to it, I'll be in touch about the next steps."

"Just stay alert." He tucked the handset between his shoulder and ear so he could send the file from his cell phone. "He isn't going away."

"You be careful, too."

"I'm taking precautions. His picture has been circulated to all the staff." Melissa should be here, behind the layers of expert protection he'd implemented. "There, the file's sent."

Over the phone he heard a faint ping. "Got it. I'll call when I can."

"Melissa—"

But she'd hung up and the disappointment was sharp and uncomfortable. What was his problem? After losing

Karen, he hadn't allowed himself to get this involved, to get close enough to be consumed about anyone's welfare. General kindness and compassion were fine, but this swirling thing growing inside him for Melissa specifically... No. He had to find a way to stop it.

His days of sheltering someone precious were gone. He'd buried all of those tendencies with her and the child she'd carried. Independence was what life had decreed for him. Frequent, lighthearted dates were the ideal situation and he could dote on his nieces and nephews. All the fun, and no real risk of deep heartache.

By rights, Melissa should've stayed on the periphery of his life. She epitomized independence. Just being the chief of police, despite the pitfalls and potholes that must have riddled her path to the office, illustrated her ability to watch out for herself. She wasn't his business, yet he couldn't get her out of his mind. Couldn't stop feeling some responsibility for putting her in danger.

He checked his watch, then his cell phone. He'd sent the email almost five minutes ago. The conversation with Orr hadn't lasted even that long, had it? Maybe the file hadn't gone through or the recording was garbled.

He started to dial the station's phone number and stopped himself. If he'd learned anything the night of Danny's kidnapping, it was that Melissa was thorough. And while he viewed police work as reactive, once she got over the initial shock, she'd never been rash or in a hurry during their search, though they'd been searching for her defenseless nephew. He had to give her time.

Antonio went to brew himself a cup of coffee and realized it would only make him more restless and impatient. He poured a tall glass of water instead, then strolled to the window, determined to be calm. He'd done everything he could do to protect his property. Though he'd tried to protect Melissa, he had to trust her to protect herself *and* the town.

His office, on the second floor, offered good sightlines down the main tree-lined drive. This time of year, with the limbs bare, he could see most of the intersection. Was Orr out there somewhere lying in wait?

A dumb question. He had to be. He'd all but told Antonio he would strike again soon.

He glanced back at his desk. What was taking her so long with the audio? He really should be there to explain some of Orr's comments, give her the whole story about Drew and Wendy.

He realized, belatedly, just how successful Orr had been with his phone call. Antonio's focus was gone, derailing the tasks on his agenda. Plus, the entire mess dredged up his old frustrations and doubts of his dealings with Orr. Not a good place for a man who made decisions involving millions of dollars at a time. If Antonio let worry and fear edge out common sense, Orr had the upper hand. He couldn't live that way. Wouldn't.

If he couldn't convince Melissa to move into the hotel for her own safety and his sanity, he would hire a team to shadow her. This seemed like a situation when it was better to ask forgiveness than permission. He would not stand back and allow Melissa or anyone else he cared about to get hurt or die when he had the power to prevent it.

Chapter Nine

In her office, with the blinds still open, Melissa played the recording repeatedly. The first time through, she only listened. On the second pass, she started making notes through the brief phone call, trying to gauge mood and motive from both men.

Antonio had clearly urged him to do the right thing, making it easier to believe he'd done that on the day Orr had shown up with a bloodstained hand. The ploy to point a finger at Antonio was too weak to take seriously. She paused and checked herself. She shouldn't be making assumptions because she found one man warm, helpful and too attractive for her peace of mind.

Yes, Antonio had been an asset in saving Danny quickly. That didn't make him a saint. Far from it. Plenty of criminals inserted themselves into cases for a variety of reasons, all of them self-serving. Just because they didn't get much of that here didn't make the possibility irrelevant. But it was unlikely, since Orr's statement against Antonio had held no weight.

She wanted another opinion of the recording to make sure she wasn't accepting Antonio's side simply because he'd helped find Danny and she liked him. She needed someone objective who could listen to this conversation without any bias. But who?

Officer Warren and his partner came to mind, but they were working on the drive-by shooting and the arson. This recording could skew how they worked the cases, inadvertently point them to Orr at the expense of other suspects.

The department couldn't afford to have another case go awry for any reason.

She didn't want to pull Troy from his review of the Emerson case and she wasn't sure he could be impartial, either. Not after they'd rescued Danny as a team. Should she call Ian? No. He'd worked the Paxton case. Once he identified the men speaking, he'd have opinions that might turn into conjecture or, worse, rumors.

As she gazed out over her department, she realized there was only one person she wanted to speak with about this. She called her older brother, Clarke.

"I'll buy if you'll bring lunch for both of us," she said when he answered.

"Pretty late lunch," he countered. "It's already after two."

"Blame it on a long Monday morning," she explained. "I really need an ear that can be objective on something."

"All right. How about I bring over your usual from Mae's Diner?"

"Yes, please." Her stomach rumbled in anticipation. "Thanks, Clarke."

With help on the way, she opened up every file in the database that involved both Antonio and Drew Orr. She didn't expect any big revelations, but she wanted the full context. She was in the middle of a similar search through local media archives for any articles and interviews involving the men when Clarke walked in.

Her office was graced with the savory aroma of juicy cheeseburgers and salty, thick-cut fries. "Did you bring onion rings?"

"Of course." He set the white paper bag and the drink tray on her desk.

She grinned at him. "Thanks for coming." He hadn't closed her door, so she hopped up and handled that detail herself.

"So it's a working lunch," he observed, unpacking the bag. "No milkshakes on the menu today," he explained. "It's a root-beer float instead."

"Perfect." And it was. For a few minutes they ate in companionable silence. When she finished the last onion ring and he was down to a few fries, she told him why she needed to talk.

Clarke sat back, crossed his ankle over his knee and motioned for her to hit Play on the conversation Antonio had sent. A hard scowl creased his face as he listened.

"Well?" she prompted.

"Still wondering why you called me."

"I need someone objective."

"Then you missed the mark," Clarke said. "He saved Danny and then saved you, too, Saturday night. I'm not inclined to be objective. Why are you?"

She picked up a pen and tapped it rapidly against her palm, searching for the most expedient way to explain. "There's the outright lie about the facial recognition at the house. Plus the hesitation in his voice after Orr makes his vague accusation about Wendy."

Clarke motioned for her to play it again. Reluctantly,

he nodded and pointed at the pad of paper on her desk. "You made a note to ask him about that, right?"

She nodded.

"I think he's trying to provoke the man." Clarke bounced his heel. "Did Antonio see the shooter on Saturday night?" Clarke asked.

It took her a half second to recover from the unsettling idea of Antonio provoking a man who had likely already killed a person. "He says he did. Gave a description at the scene. He's sure it was Orr."

"But you can't confirm?"

"No." She drummed the pen on her palm. "Antonio blocked my view of the car."

Clarke leaned forward. "On purpose?"

"No." She forced herself to think it through. "Not even a little bit. He was operating on instinct, I think."

"Brave man."

"Or sure he wouldn't be hit?" she asked, for the sake of argument.

Clarke gave her a knowing look that reminded her too much of their dad. "Now you're just thinking the worst of him to be contrary, instead of just considering both sides to be impartial. What would he gain by scaring you?"

"If Antonio did kill Wendy, blaming Orr for the drive-by raises a whole lot of reasonable doubt," she pointed out.

"Come on, Mel. Your own detectives cleared the man when the crime was fresh last summer."

"I know." She swiveled her chair from side to side. "See why you're here?"

"Yes, I think I do." Now his expression turned sly. "You like him," he accused.

"You sound like a twelve-year-old."

Clarke grinned. "And there's the confirmation," he crowed.

"Exasperation isn't at all the same thing."

"Isn't it?" He held up his hands in surrender. "Before you toss me out on my ear, let me say this." He stood up, bagging the trash. "My take is, Orr called to provoke Ruiz and mess with his head. A solid revenge strategy. Yes, Antonio has voiced disappointment for your department recently, but he isn't sowing discord outright. He could've let us flounder in the search for Danny, but he didn't."

"True," she allowed.

He sank back into the chair. "What's really going on with you and Ruiz?"

"Nothing," she assured him. "The Emerson and Paxton cases just leaped out and tossed him into my path."

Clarke smiled, clearly not convinced that was the whole story. One of the detriments of having a private investigator for a brother. "Good thing from this side of the desk," he said. "I owe him a big thank-you for saving my sister from a random bullet. He did the right thing when it mattered. That puts me on his side until something real proves me wrong."

"All right. Thanks." She dropped her pen to the pad. "That gives me a lot to think about."

"You've always had good instincts, Mel," Clarke said. "Don't undermine yourself or your officers."

"Easy for you to say. I have two cases getting picked apart by vultures."

"From what I saw in Everleigh's case, those discrepancies were in the evidence, not the police work itself."

It was a nice affirmation. Now she just had to find a

way to determine if the cause was simple human error or if she had a bigger problem. "Thanks for the insight." She stood to give her brother a goodbye hug.

"When you talk to him, ask your questions and then *listen* to the answers," he suggested, giving her a shoulders a warm squeeze.

"I promise."

Her brother's words hovered in the back of her mind while she continued working, her door open again for anyone who might need to check in. She'd invested in herself and her career from the moment she'd applied to the police academy. The road hadn't been easy, especially as a woman. The digs that bordered on mean, the sexist remarks and the assumptions that her heart was too soft or her body too weak for the job hadn't been easy to overcome.

But she'd done it. Her eye had always remained on the goal of helping her community. That coud be one person at a time or as a whole; she'd always wanted to make a positive difference in the city she loved. It didn't always work out in a courtroom, but until recently, she'd been confident in the police work.

The prosecutors and defense attorneys could theorize all they wanted in front of a jury on a case like Paxton or Emerson. Evidence separated one person's account from another, illuminated the situation and led investigators to the right perpetrator. It was interpretation that was fallible.

Knowing the implications and dreading the fallout of making an announcement, she had to accept that the evidence had been mishandled in those two cases. Whether it was done purposely or not would raise more questions, create more problems. Either way, she would be held accountable. She needed to get Internal Affairs involved. The most important thing was cleaning this up for the victims and families involved as well as the department.

One step at a time. She left her office and asked the dispatcher to send a unit to cycle through the area near the hotel. The only instructions were to look for the black car that matched the description from the drive-by shooting. She didn't give Orr's description. Not yet.

Picking up the phone, she finally called Antonio. This wouldn't be an easy conversation to have over the phone. The man had been right to be frustrated with her department.

He picked up on the first ring, as if he'd been waiting on her call. "Well, did the recording help at all?"

She stifled a sigh. "It possibly shed some light on motive," she allowed. "Before I say anything more, the conversation we are about to have is not official."

"I understand," he said too quickly.

"Drew Orr clearly wants to get under your skin," she said. "It seems like he also anticipated that you'd record the call and hoped to make reporting it a challenge for you."

"That was my thought, too."

She didn't bother to ask about whether Antonio had had any interest in Wendy. It just didn't serve any purpose. Her officers had cleared that potential minefield last summer—Antonio told the cops Orr blamed Wendy for cheating, but denied any involvement with his former associate's girlfriend. And the investigation supported his claims, finding no instances of Antonio and Wendy ever communicating or being together outside of Orr's presence. "Based on the drive-by, the fire, the text messages and now this call, it's obvious that we missed something in the Paxton case. I'm sorry we didn't bring Orr in successfully."

"Melissa—"

"The family will get a public apology later. I hope to reach out when we have her killer in custody."

"Did you find something new?"

This was the tricky part. "Not yet, but we're working on it."

"I figured as much." He swore softly. "What are you going to do?"

"We'll keep working the drive-by, the fire." She wanted to swear now, too, because of how thin the evidence had become in both cases. "It will take some time." And she would be hands-on, working with her team until this was resolved. She would be the active leader her department needed.

"You may not have time. He's not happy with me, but *you* are the bigger threat to him."

The urgency in his voice rattled her. "Antonio, please trust me."

"You can't stick with routine," he insisted. "A woman living alone is an easy target."

She bristled at the incorrect observation. "I'm *not* weak and I know how to take care of myself."

"No one said you were weak." His voice cracked. "He shot at you. *Us.* He set my house on fire." Another muttered oath. "Please move into the hotel. Everyone needs someone to watch their back on occasion."

Melissa felt how her body and mind were at odds when it came to Antonio. The idea of tucking herself safely away from danger went counter to her nature. Her role was to lead by example, to protect and serve. She couldn't do that from his hotel, no matter how her skin warmed when she was near him. That simmer of undeniable attraction wouldn't help her drop a net over Orr and bring justice to the Paxton family.

"It's a generous offer," she began.

"Do you want me to meet you at your house to help pack your things?"

"What? No. I can pack by myself."

"Good. What time should we expect you? The front desk will have instructions, of course, but it's best to give the kitchen a heads-up."

He was steamrolling her. "Antonio, *stop*. I didn't say yes." She understood his inherent need to step in and protect, but he had to respect her boundaries and the demands of her job.

"In fact, my answer is *no*, thank you." The silence went on so long, she thought the call had dropped. "Please, don't worry about me."

It seemed she was always saying those words. First to her parents and brothers, later to boyfriends who lasted more than a few dates.

"I'm frustrated," he said. "And, yes, worried."

She wished she'd closed the door. "Because I'm a woman?" she asked under her breath.

"In part, yes."

The admission was so unexpected she stared at her phone, incredulous until she heard him speaking. "...because you are a woman I care for. Who is important," he said. "To the community."

She should be mad, but she wanted to understand why he kept saying things like that. More that she wanted to dig a little deeper into the man she found so captivating. What would he be like on a normal date? Did he need galas and paparazzi or did he enjoy simpler things?

"Melissa?"

She yanked herself away from an unwise and impossible fantasy of getting involved with a man like Antonio. "Yes. I'm here. I appreciate the kind words."

"Kind words? I asked you to have dinner with me."

"Oh. Pardon me. I, was, *um*, distracted by a message." She couldn't go to dinner with him. Not out where they'd be seen publicly. People would start to speculate and that could blow back unfavorably on the night he'd helped them search for Danny. "Do you trust me?"

"Yes," he replied, wary.

"Then let me cook for you tonight. At my place. There's a security system just like at your hotel."

"Hardly the same."

She refused to be offended. Especially not when she caught what might be amusement in his tone. "And armed police stationed outside the house."

"I can add another security team at any time. In fact, I already have."

That sharpened her focus. "You have?"

"Yes." That lone syllable was packed with intensity. "They'll be on-site within an hour."

"You really should clear that kind of thing with me."

"Why? The hotel is private property. I'm telling you now, Melissa. Orr's call emphasized to me that there's one primary way in and out of the hotel. There are service entrances, but that singular intersection is a prime place for him to lie in wait for us. So I would ask you to come via the back entrance."

"That's why you didn't want me to come to you," she said as the revelation clicked for her. "I sent out a patrol car to keep an eye on the area."

"I noticed. They've been by twice already," he said. "Thank you."

"You're welcome."

"What will it take for you to see reason and move into the hotel until the search for Orr is done? You know I can create a command center for you."

She could hardly admit she was afraid her resolve would fail her if they were in the same building all day long. "Why don't we discuss it over dinner at my place?" she asked.

"Why not cook for me here at the hotel?" he countered. "The suite has a full kitchen, or you can choose one of the catering kitchens."

"Not the same," she replied, hearing the flirtatious tone. "Come by—" Her buzzing intercom interrupted her. "One second."

She cringed, grateful he couldn't see her as she set aside the phone and answered the summons. Hopefully they'd found Orr's car.

"Chief Colton, the patrol team at your house has a situation." The rookie on the front desk filling in for Mary sounded nervous.

Remembering her own days as a rookie, she smiled. "Go on."

"On the last perimeter walk of your house a photo was found on your side door, but the officers didn't see anyone suspicious in the vicinity."

The smile and fond nostalgia vanished at the dangerous implications. Someone would have had to cut through the backyards to reach that door unseen. "I'm on the way."

"Um, no, ma'am. I—I mean, they asked me to tell you to stay here at the station. *Please.*"

Not a chance. She looked at her cell phone. Antonio was still on the line. "I'll call you back," she said and then ended the call.

Shrugging into her coat, she grabbed her keys and pocketed her cell phone. She would not allow Orr to have his way in her city.

HAVING SOMETHING TO look forward to this evening didn't erase the worry over how she'd ended that call. Something was wrong and Antonio knew he'd only caught a snippet. Had Orr made another threat already? The little he'd heard indicated Melissa was taking precautions. He wished she would just give in already and agree to move into the hotel.

In her shoes, he supposed he would be offended if a civilian thought they could do better. He would have to keep that in mind when they talked at dinner.

He had to find a way to illustrate that the hotel was safer due to the additional personnel. Her department couldn't devote as many people to her security because they had a broader mission of maintaining the peace. Antonio struggled to believe that would be sufficient against Orr's threats.

Control issues were the root of his worry for her, but understanding that was only half the battle. Maybe less. He'd been unable to help his wife and baby. He couldn't see a way to steer Orr off this violent course. And, apparently, he had no influence over Melissa, either. It was humbling and awful and completely unacceptable.

And yet he eagerly anticipated their next meeting.

She was making him dinner. With a different woman, he might consider it an overture. With Melissa, he felt she was merely trying to prove a point. There had been interest in her voice, almost a teasing tone when she refused his offer to cook in the hotel. It had sparked a warmth under his skin he should resist. With so much chaos and danger swirling around them, this was the worst time to be thinking of Melissa in a personal way. Her focus should be on the needs of the community, not him. And yet, he didn't just want her attention; he also wanted to help, to be her safe haven when things were difficult. Dangerous territory.

As the patrol car she'd sent out cruised by again, he wondered what had drawn her away from the station in such a hurry. He called her, but the call went to voice mail. Picking up the house phone, he called his security office.

"Hotel security, Charles speaking."

Charles had been with him for several years. "It's Antonio. Have you heard about any sort of crisis or emergency in the area?"

"Not near the hotel, sir. But several units were dispatched to a neighborhood in regards to a disturbance."

"The address?" Charles rattled it off and Antonio's breath backed up in his lungs. That was Melissa's home. "Thank you," he said before he hung up the phone.

Antonio paced his office and then went upstairs to the suite. He should let her handle it. She'd call if she needed him. Then again, she would likely downplay any crisis to prevent worry or protect him.

No. That wouldn't fly. He was going over to see what had happened for himself. If the incident wasn't related to Orr, he'd back off. If it was... Well, she couldn't expect him to sit back and let his former associate run roughshod over everyone in his quest for revenge.

Though caring for her had blindsided him, he was invested in her safety and would do anything possible to protect her.

Chapter Ten

"Chief, you need to think about moving out." Sergeant Joseph drummed his fingers on the clear plastic evidence envelope he held. Inside was an eight-by-ten collage of candid photos of Melissa. All taken within the past forty-eight hours.

Melissa stared across her kitchen at the sergeant, momentarily speechless. She'd trusted him for the entirety of her career and now he was suggesting she hide?

Joseph seemed to take her silence as consent to press his case. "Just until we find this bastard. Those boys out there feel terrible."

"They didn't do anything wrong," she said, finding her voice. "Whoever put that on my door was careful about it." *Whoever.* As if it this wasn't Drew Orr's handiwork.

The man was sneaky. The door on the side of her house was hard to see from the street, which was why the team on guard walked the perimeter at regular intervals. Orr had taped the collage to the glass, timing it perfectly so he wouldn't be caught.

When word got out about the images in the collage, nearly everyone on duty had come to help look for clues. Most of them had already left, or were widening the search through her neighborhood, but she didn't expect any helpful results. She braced against a telltale shiver as she looked at the collection of images.

The photographer had snapped a picture of her with Antonio on his deck the day after the fire. There was an image of her at her office window, another in her car. And whoever it was worked quickly, since there was also a picture of her out on her walk with Troy this morning.

"He didn't get inside," Melissa stated.

"Not yet," Joseph said. "Come on, Chief. It's the smart thing to do."

Joseph was right. Adding patrols only put more people in the way if—when—Orr escalated. But where could she go that wouldn't create the same trouble for civilians or cost the taxpayer a fortune? Antonio's suite was *not* a good option, especially when he needed it himself.

Her best bet was to reach out to her youngest brother, Stanton. He owned Colton Protection, a small protective-detail agency that catered to high-end clients. While she didn't expect him to part with one of his bodyguards, he surely had a safe house she could use for a few days.

Resigned, she picked up her phone to make the call when a scuffle broke out on the front porch. Melissa turned toward the raised voices, peering through the front window.

"What now?" she muttered. Striding toward the door, the sergeant cut her off, blocking her path. "This is my home," she reminded him. It took a few seconds longer than it should have, but he finally stepped back. The chime sounded as she opened the door to see Antonio arguing with the two officers standing guard. Warmth spread through her system, a burst of summer sunshine in the heart of winter. She worked to suppress a smile and maintain her professional demeanor.

"Mr. Ruiz? Is everything okay?" Why was Antonio here? Granted, she'd been interrupted before she'd given him a time for dinner and she'd ignored his calls, but she hadn't expected him to just show up. Twice in two days, she realized.

"I could ask you the same question." His gaze was sharp, impatient, his mouth tight with worry as he studied her. "I didn't realize dinner was a group event."

She appreciated the attempt at levity. "Come in." She turned to the sergeant. "Thanks for handling this mess, but I've got it from here."

"You'll call Stanton for extra security?" Joseph asked.

Melissa gritted her teeth. "Yes. Please keep one unit on the street. I'll let them know when I'm leaving."

Joseph faced Antonio. "She isn't to be left alone, Mr. Ruiz."

"I understand," he promised.

"That's enough," Melissa guided Joseph to the front door. "We all have things to do, right?" She aimed a meaningful look at the evidence envelope. "I'm counting on you."

With a nod, Joseph walked out and she locked up behind him. A few words were exchanged and then the officers vacated her porch. She'd just taken a breath when Antonio began demanding answers.

"What happened?"

"You get your wish," she said, walking around him to secure the side door as well. "I'm being forced out of my home for the sake of security."

"Why do you think that's my wish?" he queried.

Again, she was speechless. "You've been pushing

me to hide out in your hotel. What would the city have to pay for that?"

"Melissa, charging you would be absurd. I've been pushing you to protect yourself," he corrected.

Exasperated, she picked up her phone to call Stanton, but suddenly she was wrapped in Antonio's arms. "What are you doing?" No one was shooting at them; there was no reason for him to shelter her here in her kitchen.

"Making myself feel better."

"Oh." She wasn't sure what to do with this abrupt show of caring. But it felt so good to be held, as if she was a treasure, that she gave herself up to the gesture. She wound her arms around his lean waist, resting her head on his shoulder.

He sighed, as if something settled perfectly into place. Her pulse quickened imagining the pleasure of tipping her head up for his kiss. She wouldn't linger, but she wasn't about to reject the moment, either.

"Tell me what happened," he said into her hair.

"I don't want to." Under her cheek, she felt his body stiffen. She sighed. "You'll only get mad and spoil this." And she needed this respite, needed him, more than she wanted to admit. She wanted a sexy, fascinating and interested man in her life. Not just any man. *This* man. Her persistent attraction to Antonio was growing into something deeper with this constant exposure. She had to pull herself together.

She released him on that disquieting revelation and stepped back so she could watch his expression as she explained. "Yes, Orr was probably behind this stunt. No one was hurt, unless you count the pride of my officers. He, or someone, got close enough to put a collage photo on the side door."

His hands dipped into his coat pockets, but she could tell his fingers had balled into fists. "Where is this collage?" The soft menace in his tone was worse than shouting.

"Sergeant Joseph took it into evidence." Seeing his jaw tighten, she relented. "I took a picture of it."

He swore as he enlarged the image on her phone, studying each candid picture in the collage. "We'll move you into the suite tonight. Let's get you packed."

"Not so fast." He was acting as if they were a couple and he had a vote in her decision. "I was about to call my brother."

"The private investigator?" His eyebrows flexed into a frown.

"Don't be obtuse. I'm well aware that Colton Protection has done business with your hotel guests through the years. Stanton can get me into whatever safe house he has in town."

"So you'll go between this safe house and the station just as you've done from here?" Antonio rubbed his temples, as if she was the simpleminded one. "How is that better? At the hotel, the suite is one-hundred-percent secure and if you won't let me set up a new command center for you, I have the cars and staff to escort you between the residence and the station."

"I can't just move in with *you*!" She threw up her hands. "The optics would undermine my position." She'd never dated anyone as recognizable as the wealthy hotelier. Well, she wasn't actually *dating* Antonio. In one night he'd become a hero to her family and saved her life, but they weren't a real couple.

They'd had exactly one hug. About one minute ago. She couldn't deny wanting more. Her lips felt feverish whenever she thought of the times they'd been close enough to kiss. The hug was a perfect example of another missed opportunity, but the way they'd been thrown together in the midst of the cases she was juggling wasn't a healthy start for any potential relationship. Definitely not a good start for two prominent figures in the city.

If she moved into his hotel, word was bound to get out, assumptions would be made and her reputation would take a worse beating when the relationship fizzled.

Except Antonio wasn't a relationship man. Recalling that detail cooled her down in an instant.

"Melissa."

She glared at him, willing herself not to melt into a puddle at his feet at that sultry tone. "No."

He spread his hands. "Explain a better option."

She didn't have one. "Your way could cost me my job."

"Orr has shown he's willing to take your life," Antonio said. "Don't put your family through that worry. Don't force me to bear that guilt. I'm the one who brought the bastard into our city."

His gaze was haunted. She'd seen that look time and again. Through interviews and town gossip, she'd heard his wife had died when they were barely more than kids themselves, but she didn't know the details. He was a man who'd taken on significant responsibility in his career choices. Did he carry survivor's guilt or feel responsible for losing his wife, too?

The notion turned her soft and, sensing it somehow, he pounced. "A move to the hotel limits Orr's options.

Plus, my security team and your officers are close. It's a sensible decision."

Sensible, sure. Right up to the moment when she was surrounded by everything Antonio. That was the more personal, imminent danger. Unfortunately, it was logical. Combining forces, along with the potential of bringing down Orr with less risk to the community, held tremendous appeal.

"Fine." She scooted around him and down the hall to her bedroom. She wrestled a suitcase from the back of her closet and unzipped it. She reached for extra uniforms first, then paused, wondering what else to take. Did she pack the oversized T-shirt she slept in most nights or something more feminine? Ruthlessly, she popped the bubble of hopeful lust and threw the T-shirt into the suitcase.

All she knew was there was *one* secure suite at the Grave Gulch Hotel. With a kitchen. She could assume it was luxurious, but that was about it. Was there one bedroom or two? Did they have a rollaway option or a sleeper sofa?

She closed her eyes. She should *not* move in with Antonio.

"We have an excellent laundry service." Antonio displayed an appealing confidence as he leaned a shoulder on the door frame. "Along with every other amenity or item you might need. And we can come back anytime."

"*We* again," she murmured.

"Yes." His voice took on an edge she could relate to. "Would you advise anyone else in your shoes to handle this situation alone?"

"No." More logic. She opened the dresser drawer

where she kept her workout gear. "Would you be standing here if I were a man?"

"But you're not," he said.

She tossed the leggings and layers for winter running into the suitcase. "That's a cop-out."

"I disagree."

Her entire body went on alert as he entered her room. This bedroom would surely fit in the suite with room to spare. Possibly the entirety of her house. They were so different and she was getting tangled up in thoughts and feelings that could never come to pass. Stress, adrenaline, whatever it was, she needed some space, but he kept closing the distance. One deliberate step at a time.

The sensual heat in his eyes sent her heart rate into overdrive. Like a cornered rabbit, she looked around for an escape even as her traitorous body quivered, eager for contact.

"Melissa."

Her knees went weak and her gaze locked with his.

"You are the chief of police, and man or woman, I would offer my assistance either way. Especially since a former associate of mine is the one causing trouble." His hands skimmed up from her fingertips to rest at her elbows. "However, if you were a man, I would not be here." He gave her arms a light squeeze, then stroked higher to her shoulders. His thumbs brushed the sensitive skin of her throat. "I fear, even if you were any other woman, I would not do this."

Slowly, he leaned in, giving her plenty of time to say no. She shifted into him, touching her lips to his, her hands resting at his hips as if they did this every day. Sensation rocketed through her, taking something simple into uncharted territory from one heartbeat to the next. His hands moved into her hair, then he changed the angle and deepened the kiss.

He tasted of heat and dark, enticing promises, and her mind blanked. They were the only two people in the world in this moment. She moaned, her fingers clutching the fine fabric of his shirt as she hung on for dear life. His mouth moved along her jaw, his breath at her lips casting a spell. Her head fell back, caught safely in his hand, as he trailed kisses along her throat.

When he eased back, she rested a hand on his chest, delighted to find his breathing was as rapid as hers. She didn't know what to say, only what she wanted to do next, starting with more kisses.

But his gaze dropped to her suitcase and he frowned. "There's a full gym at the hotel. You don't need outdoor layers."

The momentary intimacy broken, she had to agree. As much as she loved running outside, it wasn't smart while Orr was tracking her. She reluctantly moved away from Antonio's touch, removing the outer gear and choosing other pieces instead.

"I promise you I won't be in the suite for long," she said, striving for her professional voice of calm command. "The GGPD will capture Orr and make sure he's sent away for a long time for the crimes he's committed in this city."

"I appreciate that," Antonio said. "And I believe you."

Why did those words strike her as far more important than a hot kiss or the size of his suite? She should keep packing, should definitely not be hanging on his every word like an awestruck teenager face-to-face with her crush.

"I'd like to be clear," he said. "You're very good at

your job and passionate about safeguarding this community. I apologize for ever questioning your commitment."

"Thank you," she whispered.

Heat flared in his eyes as his gaze dropped to her mouth, fanning the flames deep inside her that lingered from that kiss. She ducked into the bathroom to pack her toiletries or they'd never get out of here.

The moment she added the small tote to the suitcase, he caught her hands with his. "I want you to be comfortable at the hotel. *Safe* and comfortable. But, also, I want *you*. Those two facts stand independent of each other."

That was definitely crystal clear.

She laced her fingers through his, tipping up her face. She thought she was ready for the next kiss, but when their mouths met, something exploded. Need. Longing. A promise of satisfaction right here, literally within her grasp.

Pressing her body to his, she gave in to the roar of desire. Shoving his coat off his shoulders, she protested when he released her to shake it off, sighing as his arms came around her again.

But the embrace lasted only for a moment. He untucked her uniform shirt with an urgency that matched the pounding in her bloodstream. His hands trailed up and over her ribs, higher, to her breasts, and she arched into the touch, wanting more. Craving everything he was willing to give.

His hands dropped to her belt and she nudged him aside to deal with her service weapon properly. Once her gun was secured properly in the portable safe, she turned back, shocked and delighted by the stark desire in his dark eyes.

Were they really doing this? Here? The questions

went up in smoke as he dragged his sweater up and over his head, then tossed it over her open suitcase.

He was mouthwateringly fit, his skin hot under her hands, the crisp hair on his chest adding more texture to those deftly carved muscles. She stroked his chest and he caught her hand under his, right over his thundering heart.

"You do this to me," he said, not sounding pleased about it.

He cupped her backside and brought her flush to him. Body to body, she flexed her hips instinctively against his arousal. It was too fast and yet somehow not fast enough as they fell to the bed, tangled in each other. His kisses blazed across her skin as he dispensed with the rest of her uniform and boots. And the wicked grin on his face as he stripped away the last of his clothing filled her with an ache only he could soothe.

She reached for the nightstand and pulled a condom from the drawer. Rising up on her knees, she kissed him where he stood, letting her hands wander and finding joy in his reactions. On an oath, he put a halt to her explorations. Grabbing the condom, he covered himself and then prowled over her, leaving a trail of blazing kisses until his mouth met hers again.

At last, they were joined and the world seemed to stop, giving her time to savor every sensation, every pulse arcing between them. Through them. Her next breath, her very existence, was summed up here and now with him.

His every touch amplified her pleasure, as if he knew all her secret desires. She breathed him in, already addicted to his masculine scent. Joy sparkled through her like stars over the lake when he purred his approval as she stroked his arms and back. His body was a masterpiece and she couldn't get enough. When the release crashed over her, his body went taut a moment later, her name on his lips.

As he shifted to stretch out beside her, she stroked his hair back from his face. Though she tried, she couldn't come up with adequate words to express this wonderful blend of physical satisfaction and inner contentment. Sex had never felt this…involved. It was as if he'd answered a question she didn't know her soul had been asking.

He got up to dispose of the condom, pausing at the edge of the bed. "Your pants are glowing," he said with a wink as he reached toward the floor.

Her whole body felt aglow after Antonio's thorough attention and she appreciated that he didn't mention it if he could see that, too. She covered herself with the sheet, taking her cell phone from his hand. Their fingers brushed, but the soft sizzle disappeared when she saw Troy's name and personal number on the display.

Braced for the worst, she answered.

"Bowe is gone," Troy said without preamble.

"I beg your pardon?" She scooped her hair back.

"Randall Bowe didn't go out for a long lunch after we talked with him," Troy explained. "He took at least a year's worth of files and his hard drive, too."

Shocked and furious, Melissa dropped the sheet, modesty forgotten along with Antonio's presence as she dressed. "Tell me everything you know."

The implications struck like hammer blows, one after another, as Troy listed the details he had. The hard copies for both the Paxton and Emerson cases were missing. No surprise since those were currently under a microscope. Bowe had vacated the lab and it seemed he'd fled town, as Troy couldn't get an answer at the man's house.

"Cell phone goes straight to voice mail. And nothing is showing up on tracking so far."

"Keep trying," she said. "Is Ellie around?"

"Yes." She heard the squeak of Troy's desk chair.

Ellie Bloomberg was the technology expert at the GGPD. If anyone could help them find a way to restore or recover the files Bowe had stolen, it was her.

"You're on speaker," Troy said. "Ellie's here."

"Hi, Chief," Ellie said.

"Hi, Ellie. Troy will give you the details." How to say it with Antonio hovering nearby? "We need you to start a recovery operation. When files are uploaded to our system, we back them up, right?"

"Yes, ma'am."

Her instant confirmation gave Melissa hope that they hadn't lost everything. She wouldn't know how to tell Antonio they'd been pushed back to zero on the Orr case. "As I said, Troy will fill you in and I'll be in as soon as possible."

She ended the call and scrambled for clean socks, avoiding Antonio's gaze. From her peripheral vision she knew he was dressed, but that was about it.

"Trouble?"

"Always." She aimed a smile at him without really making contact. "Just a technology glitch," she fibbed as she tied her boots. "We'll sort it out, but I do need to go back in."

"All right. I'll drop you off and take your things on to the hotel."

"Oh." She hadn't thought about that. "I'll need my car." She looked up and his cool, assessing gaze was such a contrast to the earlier open warmth, she shivered. Once more, her career was taking precedence over her personal life. "I guess dinner will have to be another time."

"No worries, I'll handle it." His smile seemed sincere as he knelt in front of her. "Have your patrol car follow you to the station. My security team is out there waiting for me."

Embarrassment flooded her face as she imagined what his people and hers might be assuming, but Antonio didn't seem flustered at all. He kissed her and helped her to her feet, pulling her close. If they kept this up, she'd never get to the station.

Would that be so bad? Tonight, yes. She removed her gun from the safe and blushed again. "This has to go, too."

"Sure."

He was taking this too well. In the past, when she changed plans or hurried away from a boyfriend, there'd been friction and bruised egos. Antonio, unfazed, carried her suitcase and the empty gun safe while she picked up her purse and coat and then set her alarm system.

On the porch, he hesitated, standing just a little too close. "Call me when you're on the way to the hotel. Please."

"I will," she promised.

He gave her fingers a squeeze and then carried her things down the steps to the waiting car.

She felt effervescent and hoped the bliss coursing through her veins wasn't too obvious on her face to the patrol team as she explained her plans. Worry was a lingering storm cloud in her mind, but not even Orr's threats and antics could blot out the glory of being with Antonio. She watched him leave and mentally doubled down on her determination. The sooner she sorted out the current crisis, the sooner she could get back to Antonio and start defining whatever was blooming between them.

IF ANYONE HAD ASKED, Antonio wouldn't have been able to explain what was going on in his head when it came to Melissa. When she'd let him hold her and finally wrapped her arms around him, he'd felt an electrifying connection he'd assumed he'd lost forever. Melissa's kiss had been fresh and exhilarating, and it scared him more than a little how perfectly they fit together.

One big perk about being the boss was no one questioned where or how he spent his time. As he took her things straight up to the suite, he hoped her officers extended her the same courtesy.

Something about her just struck a chord deep inside him, dredging up thoughts and feelings he preferred to avoid altogether. Did lust count as a feeling? There was plenty of that when he was around her and that scared him. At the taste of her lips, he'd forgotten all about Orr's threats.

Not smart for either of them, and even more proof they needed the security his suite provided. If they lost focus when Orr could reach them, it could be a disaster.

Antonio had had enough disaster for a lifetime.

Surely it was the unexpected attraction and the constant togetherness that was throwing him off. Seeing her in that dress at the wedding had cast her in a different light, moving her out of the professional-associate category. He understood Melissa the Cop, or thought he had. Until the wedding that's how he'd always seen her, whether she was on duty or just around town.

He smiled, imagining her reaction if he told her any of this. The clothing didn't make the woman, but apparently, he was just primitive enough that the clothing changed his perception. Now that he knew what was underneath those clothes, he couldn't wait to have her in his arms again.

Restless and hungry, he headed downstairs to his office. Waiting for her to call wasn't going to bring her back any faster. He thought he'd demonstrated admirable restraint not asking about the call she'd received, but he couldn't help wondering if it had something to do with Orr.

The man was planning something. That collage was a message and he hoped Melissa and her department were up to the task.

Antonio scrolled through digital media for any local news and checked his phone and email messages. Everything seemed quiet this evening, but he couldn't shake this impatience simmering inside him. He wasn't exactly worried about Melissa, but he needed an outlet, a more effective distraction.

No one in his employ had found Orr and no one in the local media mentioned his name. Was that good or bad? There was a brief story on the trouble at the chief's house, but no real details. That was good news in his book. If he was going to protect her, or attempt a relationship with her, he wanted to make sure no one could criticize her choices.

Was he after a relationship?

The answer had been "no" since the day he'd lost his family. The answer had to remain "no" until he understood why Melissa stirred up those long-buried emotions. Until he could say "yes" without any doubts, he wouldn't open himself to that kind of pain again.

Chapter Eleven

Melissa was running out of time and the DA needed answers about the Emerson case. She'd missed two calls from DA Parks and one from the mayor while she'd been in bed with Antonio. Not that she had any real regrets about that.

Unfortunately, the trial would resume tomorrow, based on the current reports. If Emerson's defense attorney tried to call Bowe, that would be another black eye since he'd fallen off the radar. Naturally the man who processed evidence knew how to avoid leaving a trail. She didn't want to believe the worst about Bowe, but his abrupt disappearance on top of the discrepancies made it nearly impossible to remain neutral. It stung to have relied so heavily on a man apparently capable of manipulating cases.

She'd spoken with Ellie and Troy upon her return, but they didn't have anything to share yet. She'd skimmed through the initial reports of the officers who'd responded to the incident at her home. None of her neighbors had seen Orr or anyone else approach her side door.

Something had to give, and soon, or an innocent woman might go to jail and a presumed-guilty man would continue raising hell. She'd known the job would be a challenge, but this had to be a low point for anyone in her shoes.

Her stomach rumbled, reminding her she was supposed to be fixing a meal for Antonio right about now. He'd been so accepting of her running out, she wanted to make it up to him somehow. It had to be more than infatuation that made her want to go the extra mile for him. Although, maybe he wasn't offended by the change of plans because they didn't really have anything deep going between them beyond a common interest in catching Orr.

She bit her lip, impatient with her own uncertainty. It wasn't like her to get swept away in a moment. She worried that talking about it would only make her look clingy. As resistant as she was to a conversation about feelings, it would help if she understood the expectations while hiding in his secure suite.

When her cell phone hummed against the desk, she rushed over, grinning like a girl in the throes of her first crush, hoping it was Antonio. No luck. Clarke's face filled the screen. She answered, eager for some good news on any front.

"Melissa," he said, his voice low. "I'm in the rear parking lot. I found someone who would like to speak with you. If your office is clear, I can bring my friend in through the back and avoid the media."

"What's this about?"

"We just need to have a casual conversation, that's all," he said.

That cleared up nothing. She glanced out her window, but Clarke wasn't parked where she could see his car. Wary, Melissa thought of the protestors and media camped outside the station. It would be nice to give them some kind of positive update. Her brother rarely asked for favors, and when he did, he had good reason. "I'll be waiting in my office."

Clarke ended the call without another word. Melissa wondered what she was in for and found herself wishing it was news on Bowe. Hard to believe Troy would've reached out for Clarke's help at this point. Whomever he was bringing in, if this casual conversation helped her put any open case into the solved column, she'd take it.

Clarke walked in with a woman that struck Melissa as being vaguely familiar. She appeared to be in her mid-to-late twenties. Petite, with a short cap of dark hair and light brown eyes in a round face. "Come on in," she said, standing as Clarke ushered the woman into the office.

He closed the door. "You might want Troy to join us."

That set off more warning bells, but she called in her cousin and they waited in an awkward silence until he joined them. Troy's eyes widened in recognition when he saw the woman with Clarke. "Stephanie Dunn." His gaze locked with Clarke's, then shifted to her, questions in his hazel eyes.

The name finally clicked for Melissa and she faced their guest. "You were the eyewitness in the Emerson case," she said to Dunn.

"Yes," the younger woman replied. "I was supposed to testify today, but court was delayed."

Thanks to Hannah McPherson, Melissa thought.

"Mr. Colton…" Dunn's eyes darted nervously between both men. "This Mr. Colton," she clarified with a nod to Clarke. "He called me this morning about the case."

"Why?" Melissa asked the room at large. She had a

sinking feeling that no matter who replied, she wasn't going to enjoy this conversation.

"Stephanie, just tell the chief and the detective what you told me," Clarke encouraged her. "It'll be all right."

He really shouldn't be making any promises on behalf of the department, but she held her tongue until she learned what they were dealing with.

"When Mrs. Emerson was accused of killing her husband, I told police that I saw her near the crime scene around the time of the murder," Dunn began.

"I took your statement," Troy said leaning against the wall, arms folded over his chest.

"Yes. I'm sorry. Th-that wasn't true. I'm so sorry."

Melissa's stomach cramped and she swallowed hard as her gaze dropped to her desk. The apology was practically useless. How had she let this happen on her watch? Anger slowly burned through her disappointment and her chin came up. She pinned Dunn with the hard gaze that left her most-seasoned officers quaking. "What *is* true?"

"I did *not* see anyone around the Emerson home that night. I lied. I wasn't even outside." She squeezed her hands together tightly in her lap. "I'm really sorry."

"Why did you give a false statement?" Melissa snapped.

"Someone gave me a thousand dollars. I needed the cash. He said I wouldn't have to lie in court."

"Who?" Melissa demanded.

"I don't know. A man..." Dunn looked at Clarke. "I gave Clarke a description of the man a-and the transaction."

Melissa handed Dunn a box of tissues as she started weeping. "Sum it up for me," she said to Clarke.

He jumped in. "She was approached, *after* Everleigh's arrest, by a man she's never seen before or since. No names were exchanged. Payment was handled online and she used the money to cover expenses on a recent fender bender. The man who approached her, however, was *not* the same man driving the car she bumped in a grocery-store parking lot."

During Clarke's recitation, Melissa watched Dunn nod along while blotting tears from her eyes.

"A setup?" She looked to Troy and Clarke. "From the fender bender on."

Both men murmured in agreement. They were all thinking the same thing. Someone, likely the killer, had gone to great lengths to keep Everleigh in the hot seat.

"Payment was through an app," Clarke said. "I'm looking into it, but so far nothing helpful."

Melissa swallowed a curse. "They wouldn't have made a mistake at that point." She picked up a pen and drummed it against her palm, thinking.

"What happens to me?" Dunn asked, her voice small in the heavy silence.

Melissa exchanged a look with Troy. Her cousin shrugged. The decision on how to proceed was all hers. She pulled up Bowe's department headshot and showed it to Dunn, ignoring the raised eyebrows from her cousin and brother.

"Is this the man who bought your testimony?"

Dunn studied the image. "It could be. He was pretty average in height and build. He had on a hat and sunglasses the one time he spoke with me."

It would've been nice, but confirmation was a definite stretch. If she charged the woman, it would be public record and Stephanie could become a target of the person who actually killed Fritz Emerson. She wasn't willing to put anyone else in jeopardy.

"I won't press charges against you at this time," she said at last. Dunn sagged with relief. "And you haven't perjured yourself in the courtroom." The woman should send Hannah a thank-you card for that alone.

"However, we will document this meeting," she continued. "It sounds like you were targeted with deliberate intent. You will stay in town and I advise you *not* to discuss this with anyone else."

"Yes, ma'am."

"If you feel tempted to go against those two directives, I suggest you reach out to Clarke first."

"Okay. I will. Thank you, Chief."

Melissa held her breath, afraid to speak until Clarke led Dunn out of the office.

"You all right?" Troy asked.

"Are you?" She stood up, antsy and searching for the right direction. "This all but confirms Everleigh is innocent and there's a killer out there on the loose." In all her years on the force, she'd never expected to deal with something like this in Grave Gulch. "Has Ellie found anything?"

"She will," Troy said. "I'll spare you the techno-speak, but she's confident she can recover the files Bowe stole."

"Good." She'd had tough days on the job, but she'd never felt quite as ill-equipped as she did right now. Something was critically wrong with her forensics team. "I've only dealt with cases like this in a hypothetical ethics scenario." She paused to take a deep breath. "How is it we've missed the right killer in two cases?"

"We were deliberately misled," Troy said. "Now that

we can see the facts and evidence clearly, we'll make progress in the right direction. On both cases."

"I hope you're right."

"What are you going to do?" Troy asked.

"The only thing I can do," she said. "Make the calls." He walked out and she closed her office door, keeping the blinds down for complete privacy. Her pulse pounded in her temples, but aspirin wouldn't help this headache. At her desk she rested her head on her folded arms, waiting for the pain to recede. An innocent woman might have been convicted without her grandmother's rash actions. What would it take to recover the community's trust?

When she was sure her stomach and head were settled, she picked up the handset and dialed the DA's number. The conversation with Parks was remarkably brief and, once more, a case was officially out of her hands. Next up, the mayor. No surprise that discussion ended in a summons to his home office for a private meeting. As she drove out to the mayor's house, a patrol tailing her as a precaution against Orr, she wondered if this would be her last act as the chief of police. Her foot eased off the gas pedal as the possibility of being removed from her post sunk in.

What would she do? Being chief of police had been her ultimate goal. Invested in the community and career, she'd never thought she might lose the job. Not like this. Unshed tears burned in the back of her throat and she continued to the meeting. Job first, emotions second.

WHEN ANTONIO GOT the call that Melissa was finally on her way, he gave instructions for the staff to set up the dinner he'd ordered in the suite and open the wine.

Whatever had happened after they'd left her house, he wanted to pamper her a bit. He doubted she took enough time for herself in general, but definitely not when she had two killers on the loose in her city.

He refused to overthink it and simply followed his intuition about wanting to end the day on a happier note. They didn't know each other well on an emotional front, but he was looking forward to rectifying that tonight. He'd had a few hours to think it through, and he wanted to see where all these sparks led them.

He was downstairs in the lobby, eager as a kid on prom night, when her SUV pulled up in front of the main doors, followed by a patrol car. Good. He would've been frustrated if she'd put herself at risk.

Her smile for the valet was warm and a little weary when she handed off her keys. He thought that curve of her lips brightened a bit when she saw him. She walked straight to him, then seemed to catch herself, sticking out her gloved hand as if she was here for an official meeting. He couldn't stop the laughter. She was adorable.

"Is your long day over?" He guided her toward the elevators on the far side of the lobby, his hand barely touching the back of her coat. That wisp of contact sent a tingling hum of anticipation through his system.

"Finally."

"I can't wait to hear all about it," he said.

"Seriously?"

"As much as you want to share." Apparently that wasn't a common response. Good. He didn't have any intention of being a common occurrence in her world.

At the elevator reserved for his elite clientele, he pressed the button, helping her out of her coat while they waited. When the car arrived, they stepped in and he entered the code to access the secure suite on the top floor of the hotel.

With her hands full of her coat and purse, he brushed his lips across hers. "It's good to see you."

She stared up at him, her blue eyes a bit dazzled. He kissed her again, pleased that he could, savoring the easy connection.

The chime sounded, announcing their arrival at the suite. The doors parted to reveal a marble foyer and Melissa's gasp was a sweet reward to his ears. The staff had set out a vase of fresh flowers on the table by the door, giving the air a hint of spring.

"Welcome to your home away from home," he said, grinning. He threw open the door to the suite and she walked in ahead of him.

"This is..." She turned a slow circle as he closed the door. "Wow. It's wow."

Her eyes were huge and he took great pride in seeing her so impressed. "And completely secure." He took her coat and hung it in the front closet. "Make yourself at home. Your gun safe is right here," he said, pointing to the console table near the door. "I wasn't sure where you wanted to stow it."

"Thanks." She stowed her weapon and then didn't seem to know what to do with her hands. "Your office is stunning and completely you," she said. "This is just layer after layer of luxury." She ran her hand over the distressed leather sofa. "In a really comfortable way."

"That might be the best compliment I've ever received." Her cheeks turned rosy. "And this suite has the best view of the lake for miles."

"Seriously?"

He gestured toward the double French doors. "See

for yourself." She dashed over, as delighted as a kid in a candy store. Her excitement gave him a rush of happiness he hadn't felt since...well, not since Karen.

The women he dated now expected the luxury, the indulgences of spending time in his world. Melissa seemed overwhelmed, as if every bit of polish, from the crown molding to the antique rug under her feet, was a miracle to be celebrated. Since when was refreshing so damn arousing?

While she delighted in the view outside, he knelt to start the fire. Gas logs, but the warmth and ambiance were real enough.

"Where did my suitcase wind up?" she asked, turning back to the room.

"Bedroom." He gestured toward the open door across the room. "Dinner is in the oven and the wine is breathing, but it'll keep if you aren't ready to eat."

"Oh, I'm starving," she admitted. "Just let me get out of these boots."

He'd noticed everything had its place in her house and she seemed to maintain that habit here, as she tucked her boots under the console table by the door.

She joined him at the table, where two places were set. A pitcher of water was within easy reach, as well as a basket of the hotel's famous rolls and a fresh salad. "I'm in trouble now," she said on a laugh. "Those rolls are addictive."

"You want the recipe?" he asked, with a heavy dose of flirting. "I know a guy."

"I bet you do." She sipped her wine and then filled the water glasses while he served up the spicy chicken casserole he'd requested for them tonight.

"This is amazing," she said after the first bite. "I don't recall seeing this before."

"Family recipe," he said. "Sometimes I just want the flavors I grew up with."

She hummed in agreement. They chatted about their favorite comfort foods as kids, promising to exchange a couple of recipes.

"More wine?" he asked when they'd had their fill of the food.

She covered her glass with that fine-boned hand. "On one condition."

"Name it."

"Tell me what we're doing. Please. I really enjoyed, um, earlier," she said, color suffusing her face. "And I appreciate the safe place, I do. It's just… I'm not sure what's going on with us."

He gathered her close and just held her for a moment. "I don't know if I have all the answers," he said, leading her toward the chairs in front of the fire. If he sat with her on the sofa, he wasn't sure he'd keep his hands to himself. That would only blur the lines when she wanted clarity. Returning to the table for the wine, he brought the glasses to the table tucked between the chairs.

"You surprise me," he admitted. "Yes, the suite is for our protection, but I want to spend time with you, apart from the crisis that brought us to this point. I want to give you a more normal evening. I think we could both enjoy more time together, if you're willing."

"This is so far from normal for me," she said with a light laugh. "But it's wonderful, too. Thank you. For the protection, and what seems to be a friendship with superb benefits."

He couldn't stop the grin. "If you'd be more comfortable with the whole thing, I can move downstairs to the office."

"No. I'd feel awful if you did that." She peered over his shoulder. "Worst case, I'll sleep on the couch."

"That's absurd."

She arched an auburn eyebrow in challenge. "Is it? Emergencies happen at the most inconvenient times."

"So I discovered this afternoon." He reached over and touched her hand. "Do you want to talk about it?"

She wrinkled her nose, pursed her lips and then nodded. "You're aware we found discrepancies in the evidence against Everleigh Emerson," she began. "I have a forensic scientist coming in to review our original findings. Troy called because of developments involving Randall Bowe, our forensic scientist. He signed off on the Paxton case *and* the Emerson case."

"Progress?"

"Not the direction I'd hoped for," she replied. "I believe in my people. I trusted Bowe, and he's run for the hills." She wound her sleek ponytail around her hand. "It's hard for me to accept that he's made unforgivable errors, or worse, been actively manipulating cases. That's caused you tremendous grief, and without Hannah, Everleigh might have wound up in jail."

His fingers tingled, ready to feel that glossy hair in his hands again. "Might have?"

"More developments," she said. "That's why I was so late. The DA and the mayor had to say their piece when I gave them the updates."

He fought the urge to bluster in her defense, but when she smiled he realized that wasn't what she needed.

"I expect the DA to release Everleigh tomorrow."

"And her grandmother?"

"No idea, though I hope they work it out soon. It's only a matter of time before me or someone else in the department bumps into one of those protestors."

"I heard she was moved to the prison infirmary." To his shock, her eyes welled with tears. "My mistake, I shouldn't have mentioned it."

"Of course, you should have. I caught the news on the drive over." He reached for her but she waved him off. "I'm okay. Really. The guilt just gets heavy. Everleigh was nearly convicted and her grandmother was only trying to help."

He clasped her hands. "Melissa, let me be a friend."

"None of my friends have all of this."

"I guarantee if they did, they'd share it with you."

Her blue eyes were wide and full of emotion when she lifted her gaze to his. "That's a lovely thing to say."

"Trust the expert observer." He stroked the back of her hand with his thumb. "You have the loyalty of your department."

Her gaze slipped to their joined hands. "We'll see if it lasts. Staying up here with you feels like hiding."

"To me it feels like hope." He heard the words, felt the rightness in them. "Come here." He drew her over to sit with him on the sofa, caving to his need to touch her. He traced the smooth line of her jaw, watched her lips part.

This time her lips tasted of wine and an essence that was uniquely hers. As she relaxed into the embrace, he eased back. "To me the police department in any town is a vague necessity. I valued the work and the officers, but it never clicked for me how much each of you do. When the GGPD let Orr walk, I was angry in part because his violent behavior proved I'd misjudged him.

It was easier to lay all the blame on the police and not take any on myself.

"Seeing you in action these past days has opened my eyes. Not just to you, but to what you do." He tipped up her chin so he could look her in the eyes. "You don't change the rules to fit the person."

"Of course not."

He smiled. "You lead with knowledge and balance it with compassion. Up close, it makes you even more beautiful."

"Antonio."

This time when she kissed him, he didn't let her stop.

Chapter Twelve

Melissa had been a coward, waking early and slipping out of Antonio's arms, out of the suite, before he woke up. She'd left a note, claiming an urgent meeting and suggesting they meet for lunch, but now she wasn't sure that would be enough.

If there was a protocol for how to behave when a sexy man was going over and above to protect his latest romantic partner, no one had shared it with her. She hoped she wasn't giving him a reason to move on too soon.

It would be so easy to count on Antonio, to get used to conversations over wine and kisses in the dark and his body keeping her warm through the night. But she couldn't read too much into this interlude. He didn't do long-term and he hadn't made any promises.

"You're in early," Troy said, sticking his head into her office.

"Same to you. Any lead on Bowe?"

He shook his head. "His phone hasn't come back on. Probably ditched it by now."

"Have you found anything linking Bowe to the victims or any suspects in the Paxton or Emerson cases?"

"Not so far. I'm digging into his financials today and Ellie's been here all night reconstructing deleted files from the server. She says she'll have enough for the forensic guy from the state to start on soon."

"That's some progress," she said. They had to keep working the cases. "The DA's office will drop the charges against Everleigh soon. Today, probably," she told him. "I want to get through some paperwork before Parks gives me the go-ahead for the press conference. Then I'm going over to County."

Troy frowned at her. "You want to be there for her release?"

"Yes. We owe her an apology and if I can do that without a media circus, maybe she'll believe I'm sincere."

"Mel, come on," Troy protested. "We worked the case we were given."

"You think Bowe will show up and apologize for nearly destroying her life?" At Troy's grunt, she responded, "Exactly. I'm going. You don't have to like it. Go find Bowe."

"Yes, Chief."

She read through the summary of overnight calls and checked for updates on the search for the black car Orr had been driving the night he'd taken shots at Melissa and Antonio. So far, no one had spotted it, not even in her neighborhood. They'd just have to keep searching. If he was close enough to leave photos on her door, he was too close. And too cocky.

It was midmorning when Parks finally called, reporting the release paperwork for Everleigh was in progress and her family had been notified. "What about Hannah McPherson?" Melissa asked. "The protests are getting louder every day."

"I'm aware," Parks said. "I'll let you know when we make a decision on that one."

For several minutes, Melissa debated how to handle it. She wanted to apologize to Everleigh before the media swarm began, which meant the press conference had to wait.

She had her coat on and was nearly out the door when Desiree appeared, Danny on her hip. The little boy pushed away from his mother, reaching for Melissa. She happily accepted the sweet toddler hug.

"How is my little man today?"

"Happy and healthy as ever," Desiree replied.

"Good." Melissa looked at Desiree. "Did someone call you in?" The last thing she needed was a new case.

"No. I wanted to ask if there was anything I could do to help Hannah."

Melissa rolled her eyes and tickled Danny's tummy, making the boy giggle. "Your momma is silly."

"I can't imagine being so desperate for someone to listen," Desiree said.

"You wouldn't have resorted to kidnapping," Melissa stated. Melissa sympathized with both women and she couldn't say she knew what she would do in either situation since she wasn't a mother. She seemed to be locked into the role of doting aunt with her young cousin. That status wouldn't change as long as she was with Antonio. But what would a family with him be like…?

She handed Danny back to his mom. "I'm sorry I can't talk longer, but I'm on my way out. If you want my advice, write a letter to the DA on Hannah's behalf. As the victim's mother, that will carry the most weight."

"I'll write the letter," Desiree said, her voice sad as

she kissed Danny's hair. "I just didn't want to cause trouble between us."

"Not a chance," Melissa said. "As a friend as well as your cousin, I think it's a great idea. You've got a big heart, Desiree, and I think Hannah is lucky to have a sympathetic mom in her corner."

"You're the best." Desiree gave her a big hug.

But Melissa didn't feel anywhere close to the best at anything as she drove out to the county jail with a patrol car behind her as protection. She gripped the steering wheel as another wave of frustration washed over her. Thanks to Bowe's betrayal, the GGPD's reputation might well be shattered and she didn't even understand why he'd tampered with evidence. On top of that, she was more than halfway in love with a man whose personal goals didn't line up with the commitment and family she craved.

She really should put an end to this fling before it dealt her heart a fatal blow.

But when her phone rang and his handsome, smiling face filled her screen, she knew she couldn't walk away from him. Not yet.

They spoke for a few minutes and made plans to have dinner together. Melissa felt as if she was glowing from the inside out every time she thought about Antonio. There was plenty going on around her, more than enough unpleasantness, but having something to look forward to in her personal life put all the rest into perspective.

With all the talk of work-life balance, maybe it was more about outlook and emotions than a true balance of actual hours on a calendar. It scared her more than a little that she enjoyed his company so much. Yet she didn't feel dependent on him. More like supported, encouraged. Of course, by their own agreement, whatever they were doing was more of a fling than the start of a lasting commitment.

Regardless, determined to enjoy the interlude, she was in a good mood when she reached the county jail. Thankfully, there seemed to be a distinct lack of media presence in the area surrounding the prison. She didn't want Everleigh to mistake this for some kind of feel-good publicity stunt.

Inside, she checked in with the guard and was told Everleigh was nearly through processing. A few minutes later the woman walked out wearing dark jeans, black ankle boots and a purple long-sleeved T-shirt with the Howlin' Eddie's logo from the bar where she'd worked. She had a coat over her arm and a simple, small black purse. Her short, blond hair had grown out and she had it tucked behind her ears.

Melissa wondered what she would do first now that her ordeal was over.

"Mrs. Emerson?" Melissa stepped up, her hand extended. "Chief Colton."

"I know who you are," Everleigh said, a wary edge in her hazel eyes. "My lawyer said he was sending a cab."

Melissa lowered her hand and refrained from sharing an opinion about the public defender. "I'm not here to harass you." She took a deep breath and squared her shoulders. "I wanted to see you and personally apologize on behalf of the GGPD."

"My lawyer said something about a problem with the evidence."

"Unfortunately, we didn't discover the issues earlier." Melissa opened the door for Everleigh. "Again, my apologies. I hope to regain your trust, in time."

Outside, Everleigh looked up to the sky. The door clanged shut behind them. Tears sparkled on her lashes when she turned to Melissa. "It's hard to care about what happened to me when Gram is still locked up. Is there anything you can do for her?"

"It's out of my hands." Melissa was getting tired of saying that. "The DA hasn't made any decisions about your grandmother's case, but I can assure you the community is rallying around her."

"Really?" Everleigh's eyes brightened for a moment and then her gaze fell to the pavement. "I can't believe she did that. Your family must be furious."

"Actually, no. The baby's mother wants Hannah released." She smiled a little. "Again, it's up to the DA." She watched the cab pull into the parking lot and walked over with Everleigh. "I won't keep you any longer. Take care of yourself."

What a mess, Melissa thought as she drove back toward town, followed by the patrol car. She hoped common sense would prevail in the DA's office and Everleigh's family would find a way to heal.

Her phone rang, interrupting her thoughts. She used the hands-free option to answer the call from the station.

"Chief, we found the black car."

Finally, a break. She flipped on her emergency lights. "Where?"

"In the employee parking lot at the hotel."

Her heart dropped to her stomach. Orr was after Antonio after all. She sped up and hit the siren. "I'm on the way."

The press conference would have to wait. Everything would have to wait—she needed to get to Antonio as soon as humanly possible.

ANTONIO HEADED DOWNSTAIRS and out into the courtyard he'd been working on recently. The day was bright, as sunlight danced across the snow-covered landscape. And the temperature was cold enough he really should've brought his coat and gloves. He didn't plan to stay long, he just wanted a moment to himself and a breath of air, no matter how cold.

He shoved his hands deep into his pockets and walked the narrow path the groundskeeper had cleared. In the summer, flowers bloomed within the circle of the low boxwood hedge. It was a knotted pattern he'd seen in an English garden on his honeymoon. He and Karen had decided they'd re-create the garden when they had a house and yard.

It had taken him years to work up the courage to build it here, but this was for her. A promise kept. When his mother had seen it, she'd asked why it was so easy to keep a promise to his dead wife and so impossible to make any kind of commitment to a new woman.

He'd given her some flippant reply about keeping dates and not breaking hearts. His mom, missing nothing, tapped a finger to his chest and told him that Karen would want him to find love again.

Loving again terrified him. The next right woman, if she was out there, would understand that he couldn't be open to that kind of pain again. Losing Karen and their growing family had all but destroyed him. If he took another chance and history repeated itself, he'd be no good to anyone in his family or his business interests. Too many people relied on him, on his ideas, his insights, and the jobs his hotels created. That's why he didn't cut corners and that's why he was happiest on his own. Until now…

He hunched his shoulders against a gust of wind and turned around, coming face-to-face with Orr.

The man was bundled up in a basic blue parka, his hair hidden by a knit cap and sunglasses over his eyes, a colorful scarf wrapped around the rest of his face. The outerwear didn't conceal the way he carried himself or the aggressive stance. This was definitely Orr.

No one else had cause to aim a gun at him. The threatening gun was no match for Antonio's rising fury. His mind raced, calculating how to put an end to this ordeal.

"I guess I'll tell my security team they can stop searching for you," Antonio said.

"They'll forget about me once they find your body. Everyone will want to know why the most eligible bachelor in Michigan killed himself."

Antonio's pulse hammered. "You can kill me, but that story won't fly."

"It will," Orr countered. "You're consumed with guilt for killing Wendy."

"*You* did that," he said, scrambling for a way out of this.

"No, you let your control issues and jealousy ruin a friendship and end her life."

Curses raced through Antonio's mind. His cell phone was in the office. He couldn't call for help. He'd chosen the most remote courtyard to wander through and his hands were stuffed in his pockets. No way to make a move without drawing notice.

He took a step, shifted one hand. "Let me call someone for you, Drew."

"Hold it." Orr aimed the gun at Antonio's chest. "You're not making any calls. You'll sit right here in the snow and shoot yourself. With my help."

"Get out while you can," he said. "I've increased security across the property." He had to drag this out until the next patrol came through. "Everyone is looking for you now."

"Not everyone," Orr sneered. "And when I leave, they'll have all the evidence they need to pin two murders on your sorry ass. Wendy and your pretty cop friend."

Antonio's thoughts crystallized. He was not letting this maniac hurt Melissa or anyone else. "When exactly did you lose your mind?" he challenged, taking a step closer. Orr held his ground. "How can I do anything to the chief if I'm dead in this garden?"

"The elements will make it hard to determine time of death," Orr said. "I've done some homework. You set a trap for the chief, then came here and, full of remorse, shot yourself near the ashes of your wife and baby."

How did this useless, false friend even know about that? Antonio's vision hazed red. "You expect me to lie down and let you stage a suicide? No one will believe it. You need to turn yourself in."

Orr's lips twisted into a sick imitation of a smile. "Why? The world is about to know I'm innocent and you're the killer."

A big boom sounded nearby and a plume of black smoke pierced the clear day. "Huh. That was early," Orr said. "Should've watched that tutorial one more time."

The explosion gave Antonio the window he needed. He threw himself at Orr and took the man down into the hard, icy hedge. The gun flew out of his hand, landing out of reach and sliding across the cleared walk.

Antonio, with the advantage, punched at Orr's face.

He knocked away the sunglasses and reached for the scarf, planning to use it as restraint. Orr bucked Antonio off him and rolled, throwing elbows and fists in a wild attempt to get free. He got to his feet, but Antonio caught the hem of his jeans, and Orr went down, face-first this time.

With a scream, he rounded on Antonio, kicking as he scrambled backward, toward freedom. Antonio curled away from one kick aimed at his gut, taking another in the shoulder. He rolled up to his feet, but his shoes slipped on the icy ground and Orr got up and over the low wall. Antonio gave chase, shouting for help from anyone nearby, but Orr had planned his escape well. He jumped into an idling pickup truck and floored it, driving away on the service road. This time, Antonio had a clear view of the license plate. He repeated it over and over as he ran back toward the hotel.

One of the surveillance cameras should've caught a good view of Orr's face during the fight. If not, there was another one where the access road met the cross street. He looked around the courtyard, torn between picking up or leaving everything where it was.

He had to leave it, but he also needed to get someone out here in a hurry to bag the signs of the fight. What a time to forget his phone.

On the other side of the hotel, he could see that plume of smoke and he heard the sirens now. Was anyone even in the security office, monitoring the cameras? Antonio wanted to blame Orr for his clever tactics, but the only reason the bastard knew when and where to exploit the system was because Antonio had trusted him too quickly.

He blew into his hands and noticed the evidence of the fight. Maybe he had somehow gotten Orr's DNA on him, but he doubted it—he hadn't scratched his former associate with his nails. He picked his way across the cleared path to the door, relieved to see one of his security guards jogging toward him.

"Sir, are you okay?" Charles asked.

"Alive is better than just okay," Antonio said. "I don't have my phone on me, so can you please call the police?"

Charles pulled out his radio and made the call.

"Tell them my attacker was Drew Orr and he left in a dark green pickup with Illinois plates." Antonio recited the plate number, waiting for Charles to repeat it for the emergency dispatcher. "He threatened the chief of police."

"The chief is on-site, here," he assured Antonio before relaying the warning to the dispatcher. He lowered the radio. "What happened to you?"

"Orr was hoping to frame me for a bunch of crap and fake my suicide. What's that about?" He lifted his chin toward the black smoke.

"Car explosion," Charles said. "We noticed a black car matching a BOLO in the employee lot and reported it. The police were pretty sure it was the car you described during the drive-by shooting on Saturday night. Not sure why it blew up."

His blood chilled, and it had nothing to do with being outside in the January afternoon. "Was anyone hurt?"

"No, sir," Charles replied. "One of ours was in the car, unconscious but alive."

"One of ours," Antonio echoed. "He's okay?"

"Yes, sir." Charles shuffled his feet. "When they

opened the door to check on him, a charge blew under the engine. Other than the smoke it was mostly noise."

"Hell of a diversion," Antonio muttered. Melissa had asked him about Orr's skills, but there was no way he could've predicted something like this. "Let's block off the arca and—"

The security guard's radio crackled a moment before he saw Melissa striding up. Emotions surged too fast and high for him to name them individually. The general theme was relief that she was safe and he was alive to appreciate it, underscored by a current of gratitude, desire and the softer sense that she was here. Right here, within reach.

Her face was pale, her gaze sharp, as she approached. All that motion and intensity came to a quick stop when she entered the courtyard. "Are you okay?"

"Nothing a bag of frozen peas won't cure."

Her gaze swept over the scene and he knew she saw it all. The gun, the scarf and sunglasses, the flattened snow from the fight, the footprints leading to the wall.

"He left in a green pickup truck. Got the plate number this time," he said.

Her eyes locked with his and he didn't know whether to step back or close the distance between them. He could sense the fire blazing under the calm exterior.

Much as she'd done at the wedding reception, she gave directions to everyone present, including him. "I'll take you to the hospital."

"I'm fine," he said, though it was obvious she wasn't interested in his opinion on his health.

"Come on." She turned, clearly expecting him to follow. He didn't want to be anywhere else, so he obeyed without comment. It took all his willpower and focus to not wrap her up and kiss her in the sheer joy of being alive.

Chapter Thirteen

Melissa didn't trust her voice, didn't believe the first questions out of her mouth would be the slightest bit professional. As they walked to her vehicle on the other side of the hotel, she called in the K-9 teams, giving orders for them to sweep the area for Orr. He'd been waiting out there somewhere and she wanted his hiding place. But she wanted to touch Antonio, to clean his battered knuckles and the cut over his eye herself. Now that he was warm, the swelling had set in. The bruising was sure to be colorful.

He was wet from the snow, his slacks plastered to his long legs, his sweater torn. Must've been one wild fight.

Time seemed to slow and everything snapped into sharp focus. She was in love with Antonio. This wasn't mere attraction or lust or a relationship she could explore after the crisis passed. She was in it, living it. Her breath backed up in her lungs. She loved him. Now she had to figure out how to deal with it.

At the intersection where the main hotel drive met the street, the light was red. She gripped the steering wheel tight in her gloved hands. "Tell me what happened," she said, tackling the official work first. "Why were you out there without a coat? It's January."

He reached over and covered her hand with his bare one. She stared at those raw scrapes, looked past them to admire his lean hands. It was all she could do to keep from lacing her fingers with his. The offered comfort and connection were so tempting, so dangerous to her peace of mind. She couldn't deny wanting to feel those hands gliding over her skin again.

"I was worried about you, too," he said. "That explosion, the smoke."

"Not a scratch on me." The light changed and he pulled back so she could drive. She missed his touch immediately. "Don't make me read this in a report, Antonio."

"I needed some air," he began. "Only meant to go out for a few minutes."

She listened, questions taking shape in her mind as he walked her through Orr's approach, his threats and the fight that ensued.

"Wait," she said as they pulled up at the emergency-room entrance. "You stepped closer to an armed man who has killed before."

"So you believe me now?"

She shook her head. "I've never really not believed you. We just couldn't prove his connection to the Paxton crime scene."

"Right."

"I'm not going to tell you how to run a hotel, so don't tell me how to be a cop."

"Right," he repeated.

"You need medical help."

"For agreeing with you?" Antonio had the audacity to chuckle. "This isn't a concussion talking," he said. "Orr is a serious threat."

"I'm aware." The GGPD had to get him into custody before anyone was seriously injured. She hopped out of the car and came around to open his door. "Let's get you checked out."

"This isn't necessary," he said, keeping his seat. "I can deal with it at the suite."

She leaned across him and unbuckled the seat belt, took his chilled hand and tugged him just enough to get out of the car. "It helps the case if we get your injuries, minor or otherwise, documented." She could rattle off the growing list of charges she planned to bring against Orr as soon as they found him.

Antonio and the security guard who had been trapped in the car when the explosion happened were the only patients in the ER at that time. Melissa didn't have a long wait, but it was enough time for her to start second-guessing their dinner plans and her presence in his secure suite.

Just when she was working out how to postpone and move to a different safe location, he was wheeled out into the waiting room, a mildly annoyed expression on his lean face and a trio of butterfly bandages over his eyebrow.

It hit her then, at the worst possible moment, that she might easily have found him dead in that courtyard. Only the combination of Orr's desire to trash Antonio's reputation and Antonio's quick thinking had saved him.

As a cop, she was no stranger to crime scenes or physical violence, but the idea of Antonio becoming a statistic made her stomach drop. Her hands went cold and she fought off a dizzy spell. If anything happened to him it would destroy her. One more good reason to put some distance between them, and fast, she thought.

Annoyance shifted to concern in his warm brown eyes when he saw her. "Melissa? You're pale."

"Just what every woman wants to hear," she said, exchanging a glance with the nurse. "Don't worry about me." She forced her lips into a bright smile. "Everything's good."

It was obvious he didn't believe her, so she spoke with the nurse. "Any precautions or follow-up?"

"Oh, you're together? I'm sorry, Chief." The nurse handed Melissa the paperwork. "You should've said something and we would've let you back with him."

She blanked at the nurse's assumption that they were a couple. Her heart gave a hopeful kick, but being in love with him didn't erase that they wanted different things. "It's okay. I had calls," she fibbed.

Beside her, Antonio collected the paperwork. "Thank you."

"Take care of yourself, Mr. Ruiz," the woman said with a starstruck smile. "Those butterfly bandages will itch in a day or two," she warned. "Don't pick at them."

"The chief will make sure I behave," he replied, urging Melissa toward the exit.

"I'm parked over here." A fact he surely knew since her marked vehicle stood out from the others.

"Don't," he said, stopping short and catching her arm. "Let me call a car from the hotel."

"You can't be serious."

"Have they found Orr yet?"

She sighed. "Not to my knowledge."

"I'm not taking any chances that he did a better job with a second explosive than he did with the first."

She tried to reason with him. "No one has been near the car."

"You can't be sure," he accused, backing away and tugging her along.

"I can be. The patrol is right there." She pointed to the police car parked at the end of the row with a clear view of the ER entrance and her SUV. She understood his hesitation, recognized the signs as the reality of what he'd escaped settled over him. "We're safe," she promised.

The temperature was dropping as the sun dipped lower on the horizon. "You need to get into warm clothes. A hot shower wouldn't hurt," she told him concernedly.

He glanced at his watch. "I guess I have time for that before our dinner date tonight."

She dropped her keys. He thought of it as a real date? What was between them was more than just friends who had great sex? Her blood simmered and she felt her cheeks color. She gave all her attention to backing out of the parking space.

"We should probably reschedule." There, now she sounded like herself. Reasonable, calm, steady.

"Why?" he asked.

"Because you're hurt and your brain needs to rest."

"I don't have a concussion."

"They put it on your discharge papers," she said. "Under signs and complications to watch for."

He unfolded the paper, gave a grunt. "Orr has snapped," he said. "Maybe the man I knew was the mask and this is the real him."

"Either way, we'll find him soon. Rest is probably the better choice for both of us tonight." They needed a break from the talk of Orr. It would be nice to sit in front of the fire with him and just relax…and back off any talk of real "dates."

She drove around to the side entrance of the hotel and parked, determined to walk him in and make sure he got inside safely.

He grumbled a little when he spotted one of her officers standing next to one of his security men at the door. "Team effort," she reminded him. "At least until we have Orr in custody."

"Smart," he reluctantly agreed. "You don't have to feel obligated to hold my hand."

She had a sudden wish that they were holding hands. "I'll be back around seven."

"You won't be alone, either?" He twisted around, looking for the car that followed them from the hospital.

"They have my back," she assured him.

"I suppose I have to trust that's enough."

"It would help if you did." She heard a vehicle behind them. The engine and tires sounded way too fast for the parking lot.

She turned to look, but everything blurred as Antonio grabbed her by the coat and spun her around, all but tossing her into the shrubs planted around one of the light poles.

She used the momentum to roll to her feet, then pulled her gun, but the truck careened around the end of the parking row and sped away.

The men near the door had pulled their weapons, too, and both fired. The rear window shattered and the tailgate bounced open as the driver hit a pothole, but the truck didn't stop.

Antonio caught her around the waist when she started after him. "You're not going anywhere," he declared. "Not until that maniac is under control."

"That was Orr?"

"Same ugly face. Same truck he escaped in earlier," Antonio confirmed.

She holstered the weapon she'd never had a chance to fire. "You saved my life," she said on a shaky breath. "Thanks." She pressed her fist to her pounding heart. Melissa sucked in another deep breath, afraid to close her eyes and see that truck bearing down on her. "Thank you," she said again.

He was holding her, giving her far more support than she should be asking for. But she couldn't get the image out of her head, just how close she'd come to being run down. A hard shiver ripped through her and he just held on, keeping her steady. Without Antonio's quick reaction she would be headed for a hospital at best.

The officer assigned to support the hotel staff jogged over, followed by one of Antonio's security guards. "I've called it in. We have a BOLO on the plates and driver."

"Should've had that earlier," Antonio grumbled.

"Easy," she said, automatically defensive. "They put out the order and everyone has been combing the streets." She looked around, though there wasn't anything to see. "To be this much of a pest, Orr is hiding somewhere close."

"Pest?" Antonio glared at her. "That's the second time he's tried to kill you. He's a menace."

She straightened her shoulders, pulling herself together. A jagged ache started in one shoulder and ran down her back to the opposite hip. She wasn't seriously hurt, but she'd feel this for a few days. She turned to Antonio's security guard. "Please make sure he gets upstairs safely. And have someone check on him periodically."

"Where are you going?" he snapped.

"Station," she replied, willing the quivering in her knees to stop. "Need to write this up. Keep the search rolling."

"You need a hospital."

"I do not." She tried another smile. "You made sure of that."

He stepped closer, lowered his voice. "Melissa. Take a minute for yourself."

"I'm okay. Really." She'd be better once she got back to the station. The familiar surroundings and the routine of the paperwork would be a comfort.

He touched her elbow and she hissed in pain. His eyes flared. "You're not. I hurt you."

"No." She rested her hand on his shoulder until he met her gaze. "I've taken worse in training classes. Please don't give it another thought."

Nothing she said eased the worry in his gaze. As she studied his face, her eyes lingered on his lips, and she wished she had the right to kiss him. This wasn't the time or place to stir up that kind of gossip. She tried to back away, to get to the safety of her car. A little distance would restore her sanity and put this all into perspective. "Thank you again," she said. "I'll call when I'm on my way back."

"Melissa."

She took another step and tripped over the curb, or possibly her own feet. But she didn't tumble. Antonio had caught her. How was it a man that was such a threat to her peace of mind could make her feel so safe?

"Humor me," he said. "Come inside."

"But there are reports to file."

"You're the chief of police. Surely we can handle all

of it here," he insisted. "You want me to get into warm clothing? To rest?"

"Yes."

"Then come make sure I do."

"That's low," she said, despite being inexplicably charmed by the tactic.

"But it worked." He smiled.

His arm was still at her waist, but she couldn't pull herself away from that support, that persuasive warmth. He just kept guiding her. Into the hotel, down the hall, to the private elevator.

"Happy to be of service."

ANTONIO GAVE IN to temptation and kissed her in the privacy of the elevator. To hell with shock, a possible concussion and his busted lip. He'd come too close to losing her out there. When he paused to breathe, her blue eyes, still appearing dazed from the near miss, landed on his lips like a touch and he had to start over.

He wasn't sure his heart rate would ever settle again and he doubted he'd get any sleep tonight. Every time he blinked, he saw that truck mowing her down.

But she was here. Alive and breathing, if pale. She was warm against his side. Thankfully, she wasn't shrugging off his touch. It was irrational, but he was afraid to let go, afraid if he did he'd discover Orr had succeeded after all.

First, they went to his office, where they could speak to her officers in person or by phone while he cleaned up and changed into dry clothes. He refused to allow *anyone* up to the suite where they would be staying until Orr was in custody.

At the knock, he opened the door to two of her officers. "Make yourselves comfortable," he said. "I'll just be a few minutes."

"Take your time," she said, giving his fingers a squeeze. "I can fill them in."

He shot her a look as he retreated to the small bedroom behind his office. "I'll be right back." A fast hot shower—he was mindful of the butterfly bandages— did wonders for him. And hearing her voice in the other room smoothed out the last rough edges.

He felt almost normal as he dressed in a pair of jeans and a thick cable sweater. He slipped his watch back over his wrist and sent an order for food and wine to be delivered to the suite. Opening the door, he paused, just taking in the sight of her in one piece. A weight lifted from his shoulders and a peacefulness he'd nearly forgotten swept through him. She was here, safe and alive, and they would find their way through this together.

"Please..." She motioned him in. "They're ready for your statement if you feel good enough to give it now," she said.

She wasn't at the table tucked into the bay window. She'd settled her team in the conversation area that was situated away from the glass. He didn't think she'd made the choice solely because there was more room. The two incidents had clearly left her on edge. Him, too.

"Better to do it while it's fresh in my mind." Maybe getting it out would clear the horror. He sat down next to her on the couch, keeping his hands to himself when he desperately wanted to reach for her.

She poured him a glass of water and he sipped gingerly around his busted lip as he answered each question. At last it was over, and the two officers got up to leave. "Do you still have a detail watching your house?" he asked.

All three of them nodded. "We'll keep it that way until Orr is caught," Melissa explained.

"Good." He didn't want her to suffer any more for his poor choice in associates. He added his thanks to hers.

When they were alone, he took her hands in his, staring into her pretty eyes. "How are you feeling?"

"Sore," she confessed. Her gaze swept over his face, lingering this time on the cut over his eye. She lifted a hand, caught herself. "May I?"

"Of course." He craved her touch, anywhere he could get it. "You can have your way with me."

Whoops, too far. She stopped, her fingertips a hairbreadth away. "Glad you have your sense of humor," she said, pressing gently at the edges of the bandages. "You shouldn't have gotten this wet so soon."

"Hard to avoid it when the rest of me needed cleaning up." Her lips were so close, peachy and full. He stole a quick kiss, happy to see it bring color into her cheeks. "Warm clothes do make a difference."

She smiled, but it was a faint imitation of her usually vibrant expression.

"Hell of a day," he said.

Her stomach rumbled and he chuckled. "I've ordered food and wine. It should be delivered upstairs soon."

Her gaze fell to their joined hands. "It sounds wonderful, but I should stick with water since I have to keep tabs on you and that concussion."

"I'm fine," he insisted. "A glass of wine will be good for both of us."

Her lips tipped up in a half smile. "I don't know whether to be impressed or intimidated around you."

"How about just pleased?"

She met his gaze and the half smile blossomed. "I think I can do that."

"Excellent."

Holding hands, they left the office behind for the safety of the suite upstairs. She went to clean up and change clothes, stepping out of the bedroom a few minutes later in faded jeans and a beautiful green turtleneck that hugged her curves and set off her red hair to perfection.

"I'm sorry about the mistakes we made last summer," she said as she joined him at the table. "They won't be repeated when we bring him in again."

"We've let Orr steal enough of our time." He wanted her to be able to relax and rest in the awareness that they were safe. "Let's talk about anything else. We could even not talk at all."

He stroked a hand along her spine, bringing her closer. How could a woman so trim be so strong? She was steel wrapped in supple silk. Her hair was down and he let the gleaming fire sift through his fingers. "You're beautiful."

Resting his lips gently on hers, he took his time with the kiss, enjoying the gentle torture of resisting the urge to drive and rush and plunder.

"Wow," she whispered into the charged air between them. "What was that?"

"Just about perfect," he said. "Should we try again?"

She gave a tiny shake of her head. "I think I need a minute."

He let her step away, though it cost him. "You're going to blame all of this between us on adrenaline or shock."

She cocked an eyebrow. "It has to factor."

He didn't believe in making excuses, but maybe she was right. Seeing the pickup bearing down on her, he hadn't thought, only reacted. Save *this* woman. He could do something to protect Melissa when he'd had no power to save his wife. He wasn't a monster; he would've done his best to help anyone in the same situation. But he wouldn't have needed the personal touch, the affirmation, afterward. He had no desire to replace his lost wife with this woman. Melissa was not Karen; she was a wonderful person in her own right.

"I suppose you're right. But recent events don't explain away everything between us."

"No?"

"No." He pulled out a chair for her, relieved when she sat down. Room service had delivered a cart full of food to the foyer, even popped the cork on a bottle of wine. He'd loaded the table with bowls and platters with a fresh green salad, stuffed mushrooms and pasta with two sauces, as well as traditional meatballs and grilled chicken. It was wonderful to care for someone again. To take these steps for Melissa. "I tried to cover all the bases," he explained as he poured the wine.

He raised his glass. "To our health."

She touched her glass to his and sipped. He'd ordered extra rolls, but tonight she didn't seem all that enthused.

"Do you remember the roofing project on the east side of town?" he asked.

Her gaze narrowed. "Last September, right?"

"That's it." He'd donated supplies for several homes in need of new roofs before winter set it. "You weren't afraid of any pitch, you said yes to every request."

"We were there to work," she said, finally cutting into her chicken.

"It sure contradicted my theory that you were lazy and less than invested in this city." He placed a roll on her plate. "I'd like to apologize."

She laughed, the sound tired and merry at the same time. "Accepted." She broke the roll in half. "You were right to be upset with the department." Those blue eyes locked with his. "With me."

One thing he'd learned in business was never to go into a discussion without having a clear outcome in mind. "I brought it up, the roofing project, because I think I owe you an apology."

"For what?"

"Ogling you. You have amazing legs." He wiggled his eyebrows. "And everything else."

The blush stealing across her face, the incredulity in her gaze—it was all worth admitting his less-than-honorable behavior that day.

"But it also proves that this amazing chemistry isn't just shock and adrenaline."

He wasn't sure why it mattered so much. He wasn't a long-term man. Not anymore. He didn't want anyone relying on him, didn't want to wind up devastated if something happened. And Orr coming after her today only illustrated his less-than-stellar track record with relationships. The last person he needed to care about was a woman who might rush into a dangerous crisis on any given day at work…the risk was too much. He couldn't lie to himself, he did have deep feelings for her, but he didn't dare admit it.

"All right." She leaned forward. "If we're exchanging confessions, I should tell you that we didn't run out of water right after lunch."

"No?"

Her hair swayed with the tiny shake of her head. "There were two cases in my trunk. But then you took off your shirt." She licked her lips, her gaze raking over his chest as if she could see through his sweater. "I knew I'd embarrass myself if I didn't get out of there for a minute."

"Lying about water is a serious offense," he said with a smile, tracing her fingertips.

"Just a misdemeanor," she corrected him. "And no one suffered from dehydration."

He laughed and she joined him, and then, somehow they were kissing and the meal was forgotten as they indulged in each other, proving that adrenaline had nothing to do with this undefinable, thoroughly wonderful chemistry between them.

Later, when they were reheating the food for a snack, she tasted the red sauce. "*Mmm*. That's good. My mom would be impressed."

"I'll take that as the highest compliment," he said.

"One hundred percent," Melissa said. "She is the best cook I know. Dad was on vacation in Italy and it was love at first sight. When it was time for him to return to the States, she came along with him."

"How romantic." It was the safest response. He'd felt that wild rush of love at first sight with Karen. And he could admit he'd been attracted to Melissa from the get-go, too. Was it happening again? He'd never expected his heart would heal enough for another true love. With Melissa, the thrill he remembered was brewing, along with a new sense of deep alignment.

"It's pretty much a family legend. They raised my brothers and me in a home full of laughter and love. Lived the example of devotion, commitment and abiding love."

"Tough standard," he said.

She sighed. "The right partner is worth the wait," she said, her eyes on her plate. "Your parents are still married, right?"

He set down his fork, wondering how she knew that. Then it dawned on him. "How much digging did you do last summer when Orr suggested I killed his girlfriend?"

She wrinkled her nose. "Just the basic, standard rundown. Plus, you're local, so your family history is local, too. Grave Gulch isn't so big."

It certainly felt small right now. "My parents moved to Florida ten years ago. But you must know that, too."

She avoided his gaze, studiously creating a perfect bite of her salad greens. Reluctantly amused, he waited her out.

"There are trends in criminal justice," she said in a rush. "A basic history can reveal circumstances that might lead to delinquent or outright illegal behaviors."

"I've never broken the law." Though he wouldn't hesitate to take whatever action was necessary if he ever laid eyes on Orr again after today.

"I'm aware of that," she said, matching his level tone. "But Orr did throw suspicion on you and I did my due diligence. You can't run around town accusing me of being lazy and then get aggravated when you feel challenged because I'm good at my job."

"It's not about feeling challenged. And I already told you about the moment I realized you aren't lazy."

He felt too many things at that moment, and he wasn't

eager to discuss any of them. If she knew about his parents and his lack of criminal activity, it was logical that she knew he'd been widowed. He couldn't decide if that was good or bad.

"So tell me about your stable home," she suggested, ending the awkward silence.

For a split second he thought of Karen and their house, which hadn't been too unlike Melissa's. The first piece of new furniture they'd purchased had been a rocking chair for the nursery.

"My mother's parents are originally from Cuba but she grew up in Florida," he began. "My father is from Puerto Rico. They met in college and followed his career as a commercial real-estate developer until they settled here, raised the family."

Should he mention his wife or would it be old news to her that he'd met Karen in college? How should he feel if she already knew? Did he want her to know? Antonio was unsure.

"Like your parents," he continued, "they're still wildly in love and happier on the beach than dealing with snowstorms." *Or killers*, he thought, grateful they were out of harm's way.

"I don't suppose you'd be willing to take a vacation and let someone else deal with Orr?" he asked.

"Not an option." He caught a flash of deep sadness in her eyes, though she tried to hide it by starting to clear the table. "I do take vacations," she said. "I know how to relax."

Was he supposed to gain some insight from that? Unsure, he loaded the room-service cart with the serving dishes and pushed it out to the foyer for the staff to pick up when they had a chance.

When he returned, she was on the phone, pacing in front of the balcony windows. She moved with such a lithe grace, and his body responded to her with an intensity he hadn't experienced in a long time. Until she noticed him watching. Then her cheeks turned rosy and she forced herself to be still.

It was adorable.

Antonio felt the realization click like a lock opening. Melissa Colton had come to mean everything to him. She was part of his life now and he wanted her to stay that way, forever.

Chapter Fourteen

While Antonio dealt with the cart, Melissa was debating another glass of wine when her cell phone rang. "Chief Colton," she said, picking up.

"It's Joseph. They found the truck Orr was driving."

"Where?" She darted into the bedroom, tucking the phone between her ear and shoulder while she gathered up her clothes. She could hardly answer a call in the plush hotel robe. "Did you call the others?"

"They're on the way."

"So am I."

Antonio, seeing her dressing, started to grab his clothing, too.

"I'd advise against that, Chief. Let us clear the scene. After what happened at the hotel, I think staying away is the smarter play."

"Sergeant," she began and stopped herself. He made a good point and if she ever wanted to find a balance, she had to be willing to step back and change up her patterns. "I don't like it, but you're right."

"I'll keep you in the loop."

"Every step of the way, please," she said. "We need to drop a net on this guy."

"Sure thing," Joseph promised.

Ending the call, she looked up at Antonio. "They found the pickup truck," she said. "No sign of Orr yet."

"Are you staying or are we going?"

That use of "we" sent butterflies swarming in her belly. "Staying."

He straightened his robe and crossed the room to her. "Good." He kissed her, his lips soft and sweet against hers. "I suggest more wine, in front of the fire." He bumped her nose with his. "I'll show you my pecs."

It was impossible to argue with a man who made her laugh.

"It's not forever," he said, his voice low as he nuzzled her neck. Was he talking about her staying up here, out of the way, or was he referring to their amazing sexual connection?

Her heart picked apart every syllable, searching for meaning and significance. The fact was, sex didn't make a relationship. Attraction and chemistry and some crazy near-death vibes could be all he wanted.

She wanted so much more from life. For her life. The thrill of hauling in bad guys wasn't enough anymore. When she went home, the house had a stagnant feel, as if it was merely holding its breath for a real family to walk in and liven up the place.

At one time, she'd dreamed of filling a home with children. One of four, she was used to the noise and camaraderie and sibling shenanigans. Then she just kept getting older, and while she was healthy and fit, her job wrecked every relationship.

Her mother had told her if the man was right, her career wouldn't matter. In Melissa's experience there wasn't a single man in Grave Gulch willing to play second fiddle to the police work. Except Antonio had said "we" as if he planned to accompany her to the call if needed.

How did she interpret that?

She shot him a sheepish smile, shaking free of her troubling thoughts. "Wine and pecs, it is."

She accepted the glass he handed her and took a sip. "That's smooth."

"One reason it's a favorite. It's from my brother's vineyard."

She felt her chin drop. "Your brother has a vineyard?"

"Up in Traverse City." He winked. "That didn't show up in the background check?"

"I'm a police officer, not a snoop," she said.

"You say tomato…"

She knew he was joking, but it was often close to the truth. "Come over here." He held out a hand. "Sit with me and enjoy the fire."

He pulled two chairs closer and moved an ottoman, urging her to prop up her feet and relax "You make it easy to put work away," she said with a sigh.

"Years of practice," he admitted. "At least a decade before I found any balance. You have a demanding career."

"The same could be said for you."

"Until Orr, the fatality risk was minimal."

She wanted to laugh, but it was a little too soon. "Is that why you built this suite? To manage risk?"

"It's good to be prepared. We cater to high-end clients and they can be paranoid."

"I've always admired people like you who can be casual, have fun and not hurt themselves or others."

He paused, staring at her. "Is that a compliment or a dig?"

"Compliment," she said in a rush as her cheeks heated

with embarrassment. "I get accused of being too serious, too focused."

She rolled the wineglass between her palms, sipped again. "Sorry. I admire your balance. My personal and professional goals have been at odds lately," she blurted out. "It creeps up on me when I'm tired or stressed."

"And you've had plenty of stress these past days," he said.

"With more to come." But the wine and the fire and the man beside her were helping.

He leaned forward, elbows to knees, his wineglass held loosely in his hands. "Melissa?"

"Hmm?"

"What is it you really want, sweetheart?"

You. By some miracle, she managed not to blurt that out. "The balance you've found," she said after a moment. "From over here it looks fabulous."

"My balance isn't all that great." He sat back, scrubbing a hand through his hair. "You know why I was in the courtyard when Orr found me?"

She shook her head, half-afraid of the pain in his gaze.

"I go out there to think. It took me twenty years or so, but I built that garden last summer based on a plan I made with my wife. Her ashes, and the ashes of the child she carried, are scattered there. They died due to a complication with the pregnancy."

Her heart cracked for him. His choices suddenly made more sense. No commitments or emotional ties meant he couldn't be hurt like that again. "I'm so sorry." She set her wine on the table and just held his hand, offering comfort. Her love for him and her longing for a family might well be more of a burden than Antonio could bear.

"Some balance. When I lost her, I poured myself into work rather than face the empty house." He squeezed her hand, tried to smile. "Orr figured out that she inspired that garden. I should've said all of this to the officers earlier, but I couldn't. He said he would kill me and make it look like a suicide."

"No one would've believed that," she said. "We would never have let that story stand."

His smile was sad at the edges. "I told him the same thing." He pulled her up into his lap.

She ran her fingers over the soft bristles of his beard. "An empty house is a hard thing sometimes." They watched the fire for several quiet minutes as a contentment filled her. "Being here with you is nice."

"And more fun," he said.

She appreciated his attempt to lighten the mood. "And more fun," she agreed, her gaze on the fire. "You know what you want, what's important," she murmured. "I admire that. There are days I go home alone after a shift and the satisfaction I felt on the job fizzles when there's no one to share it with. Does that ever happen to you?"

"The views take the sting out of it," he said.

She started to get up, to leave the melancholy behind, but his arm around her waist held firm. "What is it you want, Melissa?"

With her fingers in his hair, the answer just tumbled past her lips. "What my parents have. That partnership and closeness. Kids." She caught herself. "I don't mean to trample on a sore spot."

"You aren't trampling anything. Tell me more."

He was easy to talk to in this moment, with the darkness outside and the glow of the fire and warmth of the wine. "I want it all, and no one wants it with me. The police gig gets in the way."

"Wait." He brought her face around to meet her gaze. "Men have said that to you?"

"Yes. And I do understand no one wants to be the runner-up to a city all the time." She sighed, moved back to her own chair. "I had three years under my belt with the GGPD when I met the guy I thought was the one."

Antonio smiled. "I remember that feeling."

"That's the whole point, right?" she said, keeping it light though jealousy of the woman he'd loved prickled like a rash under her skin. "He was a contractor. He understood the ever-changing schedule. For over a year we managed the missed dates and cold dinners and had a great time.

"Then one morning I went into the bathroom, peed on a stick and while we were waiting for the results, he'd drafted my resignation. I wanted a husband and family. He wanted a wife and children. In his head, that meant I'd quit the force and stay home."

"That's not a partnership," he said.

Agreeing with him, she almost let out a cheer. "It does work for plenty of families."

"But you weren't done with your career."

"Not even close back then. I'm still not," she admitted. "It's probably time to stop wishing for the impossible and make a new dream."

"Were you pregnant?"

His question made her heart ache all over. "No." Although the negative result still stung some days. "Good thing, too, since those three minutes made our conflicting goals crystal clear."

She stretched her toes toward the fire. "I know we

weren't expecting any of this to happen. I do understand it doesn't mean anything in the way of serious commitment."

"Melissa." He sat on the ottoman, stroking her leg from her ankle to her knee and back again. "I care for you, in and out of bed." The sparkle in his eyes was irresistible. "I enjoy spending time with you, though I wouldn't mind fewer crises. But I don't want to hurt you. I want to be clear that I'm not built for relationships anymore."

Melissa watched the fire reflected in Antonio's eyes. She caressed his jaw, the texture of his trimmed beard teasing her palm.

She should say no. A fling with Antonio would only delay and derail her goals of husband and family. Although...who was she kidding? There wasn't anyone on the horizon willing to compete with her career. She deliberately released those intangible dreams for the very real and present pleasure sitting right in front of her.

Whatever had brought her to this point, she couldn't resist the desire Antonio created. Tomorrow would have enough problems of its own.

She touched her lips to his, let herself go into his arms. Giving all she had to him, to this moment, she forgot goals and threats looming outside the suite. He was all she needed right now and she wanted to be all he needed, as well.

Taking things slow, as if they had nothing but time in this safe cocoon, they made love in front of the fire, desire cresting in soft waves. Content and sated after, she cuddled close while he told her about purchasing the original Grave Gulch Hotel and turning it into this exquisite property that brought tourists to town. When she shivered, he carried her to the bedroom while she giggled at the two of them.

Laughter faded to sweet sighs as they snuggled under the covers, his strong body at her back, his arm heavy across her waist as she listened to his even breathing.

But she couldn't sleep. Her mind went round and round on why Bowe had manipulated evidence in at least two cases, the cycle interrupted only by ideas on how to catch Orr. This city relied on her to keep order and peace. She wouldn't let them down.

Antonio started to snore lightly. This time with him might be temporary, but it was good for her. Not just as a distraction. It was nice to have a friend, someone who knew her as she was right now. Someone with his own expectations and goals. Yes, they were wonderful together, not just in bed. She vowed she would stay his friend, even after they were done.

Their conversation gave her hope that if he could understand her career goals, someone else might, as well. Someday. Her heart wished for today to be the day and Antonio to be the man, but that was a dangerous wish that could bring this all crashing down on her head too soon.

Careful not to disturb Antonio, she slipped out of the bed. The plush hotel robe was cozy around her body as she left the bedroom. Her phone was charged and she checked her messages, finding two from Troy.

It was just past midnight, but only an hour had passed since his last attempt to reach her. He often worked as obsessively as she did when following a case. She called him back, prepared to leave a message.

Waiting for the phone to ring, she carried the empty wineglasses to the dishwasher in the kitchen. The space was so well-designed that a person really could be at home here for an extended period of time. If she dared to imagine life with Antonio, suites like this one would be a decadent perk, but she would want a true home to return to. Immediately the view from the deck of his lakeside home popped into her mind and she willed it away. Growing more attached would only make it harder when this ended.

"Melissa?"

"Did I wake you?" she asked.

"Not even close," he replied. "How are you doing?"

She felt remarkably refreshed, considering she couldn't sleep and had nearly been run over. Not that she could say any of that to her cousin. "About as well as you think," she hedged.

"I saw the other officers come back after they lost Orr's trail. Everyone wants this guy off the streets."

"He's clever, but unraveling. He'll make a mistake soon," she said with confidence.

She just hoped it wouldn't mean more pain or further injury to Antonio or his hotel. They needed to find the right draw to lure in Orr. Maybe it was time to use the press sticking close to the station for word about Hannah McPherson to prod Orr into acting before he was ready.

"So why did you call me earlier?" she asked.

"It's Bowe." He sighed. "The more we dig, the worse it looks for the GGPD's forensics department."

Goose bumps raced up her arms. "So Ellie found something."

"An understatement. Now that she has recovered the files, it confirms the evidence against Everleigh was both circumstantial and falsified."

Melissa swore.

"I said the same thing," Troy agreed. "The fibers Bowe reported finding on the murder weapon were originally from the apron used at the bar where she worked. Not anywhere close to something found on the bloody paperweight used to kill Fritz Emerson."

That matched Jillian's claim.

"The real issue is some of the evidence is right," Troy continued. "Only the pieces that tie Everleigh into the crime are not."

"What about the hairs they found on the paperweight?"

"Those were originally logged as 'potential suspect DNA.' An unspecified number of hairs appear to have been pulled from a hairbrush in the residence."

"I guess I'll get back with Jillian. She'll be relieved to know she didn't make a mistake."

"Already done," Troy said. "The hairbrush was collected to rule out or match other material at the scene."

"Standard procedure," Melissa mused, thinking out loud.

"Everything Ellie found backs up Jillian's work and report. Why in the hell would Bowe deliberately falsify those results? There is nothing I can find that connects him to anyone involved in this case."

"The same question is keeping me up at night," she admitted, pacing in front of the hearth. Bowe had manipulated evidence from the Emerson crime scene, which only lent more support to Ian's allegation that Bowe had smeared the fingerprint on Paxton's body.

"Mel," Troy began, "what if this is only—"

"Don't you dare finish that sentence," she snapped. "Yes, it's a safe bet that Emerson and Orr weren't the only cases Bowe tampered with, but let's keep a lid on that can of worms for now. If we learn *why* he manipulated evidence in these two cases, we can narrow down our search to similar incidents."

It tested her confidence in her own judgment that Bowe had done this right under her nose. The entire GGPD would be dealing with the fallout, likely for years to come. Attorneys would be filing appeals left and right, and soon the lawsuits would roll in against the department. Her officers hadn't specifically done anything wrong, but Bowe's actions would blow back on them, anyway. Most citizens lumped all the aspects of law enforcement together...not to mention however many miscarriages of justice had been perpetrated as a result of his misconduct.

"Do we have any leads on where he's hiding?" It might take five minutes or five days, but she would make Bowe talk when they caught him.

"He's in the wind," Troy said. "The last time he used his credit card, it was to fill up with gas just outside the city, on the south side. Not a trace of him since that transaction.

"Assuming he's outside the city, maybe we should put Clarke on this. I'll give him a call in the morning. Go get some rest."

"Is that an order?"

She heard the smile in his voice. "For both of us."

ANTONIO WALKED OUT of the bedroom, thrilled to find Melissa hadn't disappeared early on him this morning. She was sipping coffee and watching the local news. He went straight to her for a kiss, refusing to dwell on why that was more important than anything else.

Then she smiled and his heart soared.

Love was the reason.

He'd known his feelings for her were growing deeper than the remarkable physical intimacy between them. And he'd already decided he wanted to find a way to keep her in his life. But love? He didn't expect it to feel so wonderful.

More than a little bewildered, he poured coffee, considering how he wanted to proceed now that he knew for sure. Should he tell her? No, he should wait. He knew his reputation and it would take time to overcome it. Besides, there was too much going on. When he told her, he wanted it to be special. Memorable. *That was it.* He wanted to start creating new memories with Melissa that they would cherish for years to come.

She made an incomprehensible sound. "If I see one more 'free Granny' hashtag I might start writing citations."

He glanced at the television and winced. Sure enough, they were reporting on the protests all over the city on behalf of Hannah. "You can do that?"

"No," she admitted. "But it's a nice fantasy."

"At least they're showing the crowd in front of city hall, too, instead of just the police station."

"True." She carried her empty coffee to the sink. "Given the choice, I'd let her go," she said, rinsing the mug and loading it into the dishwasher.

He wondered how long it would take her to get used to Housekeeping handling those chores. Then again, Melissa likely wouldn't drop a good habit.

"You can't recommend that to the DA?"

"I have." She turned to look at him and her red ponytail spilled over her shoulder.

The sunlight from the French doors caught that fiery

silk, striking some strands gold, others deep copper. He wished he could just take her right back to bed.

"You don't have to look so surprised." Her scolding brought him back to the moment. "I know the woman only did the unthinkable under duress. And it worked," she said with another grumble.

Her gaze clouded over and he wondered what else was on her mind. "She kidnapped a toddler. Sent the entire town into a panic," he said. "There should be consequences."

"And we got him back right away, thanks in part to you." She smiled and walked to his side of the counter and hugged his shoulders.

"Most people are stuck on the image of you arresting her," he said, wishing he could erase all her distress. "It'll pass eventually."

She checked her phone and dropped it into her purse, pulling out her keys. "I have to hope the story that blots out 'Free Granny' is good news, but the odds aren't in my favor. It seems the city is suddenly rife with killers."

"Rife?" he echoed.

"Orr is at large. Whoever really killed Fritz Emerson is out there, too. Bowe's actions have eroded the public's trust and I'm not sure how long it will take to pull things back together." She wrinkled her nose. "Sorry to dump on you first thing in the morning."

"I don't mind." Another sweet wave of emotion toward her coursed through his system. For all the times he'd been frustrated with her and her department, he understood now just how hard she'd tried to find justice for Wendy last summer.

Antonio topped off his coffee, smiling to himself. He could see mornings like this tomorrow, a week from now, next year, setting up for the day in the familiar peace of each other. After avoiding this kind of intimacy for so many years, he wanted it all. With her.

"I have a hotel in Chicago that I need to visit soon," he said. "Why not come with me?" It would be the perfect place for romancing her, and over champagne and strawberries he could tell her how he felt. "A few days away might be the break that reveals the solution." And he'd consider it a happy coincidence that the trip would take her out of Orr's reach for a little while.

"The department is already working on a solution," she said absently, lacing up her boots. "This morning we're officially reopening the Paxton case and moving Drew Orr to the top of the most wanted list."

"You are?"

Her auburn eyebrows knitted and she frowned. "I promised you I would."

"Well, yes, but you've had your hands full." And she'd nearly been run over. It had been six months since Orr had killed Wendy; surely a few more days wouldn't matter now.

"The department is in agreement that we have to be deliberate and provoke a reaction to put an end to his harassment. I can't be effective if he's taking shots at me at will."

Antonio's pulse stuttered. "Deliberate how?" She couldn't mean to make herself a target. He couldn't let her even think about it. To lose her now, after realizing what she meant to him—life couldn't be that cruel.

She walked over and kissed him. "We're still working on the details," she said. "I'll check in with you later, okay? Have a good day."

He trailed her to the door, pulling her in for one more

kiss. "Be safe," he said, too shocked by his roiling emotions to add anything more.

"Don't worry." She squeezed his shoulders. "The GGPD isn't nearly as inept as recent events suggest."

"I wasn't thinking that," he began.

The small huff of skepticism was followed by a quick laugh. "That wasn't aimed at you," she said. "Bowe's actions have put a spotlight on the GGPD. It hasn't been our finest hour. We need to close a case, the right way, and soon."

He couldn't argue with the logic of starting with Orr. The man was a clear and present threat to her. "Use me," he said as she opened the door to leave. "I can lure him out, lure him here." It was the perfect plan and it kept her out of danger. "Then your officers can haul him away."

She paused in the foyer, her blue eyes full of affection. "Antonio, you've done more than your share already." She rested a hand on his chest for just a moment. "There's no way I'm using you or any other civilian for this. Leave it to the GGPD."

If only he could. Leaving it to her meant relinquishing control and sitting on the sidelines while she took all the risks. Not happening. He squeezed her hand, feeling the strength, yes, but also the fragility. To lose her would destroy him. Orr was a liar, a cheat and a killer. He'd nearly succeeded in killing Melissa twice already. Antonio would not give his former associate another chance.

"I can't do that," he murmured.

Her body stiffened and her hand fell away. There was a sudden chill in the foyer.

"Of course, that's too much to ask." Melissa's voice was as brittle as the winter ice edging the lake. "I'm sorry, Antonio. For all of it." She punched the button for the elevator. "If I could, I would fix the past."

"What?" He'd made a misstep, but wasn't sure just where he'd gone wrong.

"And I can't rewrite procedure to suit you," she snapped. The elevator arrived and she stepped farther away from him.

"Melissa, wait." He stuck out his hand, keeping the doors open. "Talk to me."

She shook her head. "I'm already late. I'll stay at the station tonight. It's safe enough."

"Like hell it is."

Her face went pale, her eyes full of a pain that he couldn't put into context. He would suffer if something went wrong, too, not just her.

"Safe enough," she repeated. "I'm the chief of police. An entire community counts on me."

"I know that." What did that have to do with anything? "People count on me, too. I understand obligations. I'm trying to help you with yours."

"No need." Her mouth set into a flat line. "That's outside your scope now, but the GGPD appreciates your offer."

What was he missing?

The elevator chimed, an alert that the door had been open too long. "Thank you for your hospitality. Please have my things delivered to the station." Her voice cracked as she pushed his hand out of the way. "Someone will be in touch if we need the hotel for the Orr capture."

The doors closed between them and he struggled to make sense of it. She'd left him. No, it didn't make sense. What had set her off? He replayed the conversation in his head, struggling to identify his mistake so he could fix things.

He would not accept that he'd lost her just when he'd figured out she was the woman he wanted with him forever.

Chapter Fifteen

Melissa was almost grateful for Drew Orr. With her heart caught in an ever-tightening vise after walking away from Antonio, setting a trap for a criminal was the perfect distraction.

She wasn't looking forward to spending another awful, lonely night on a cot in her office, even if it was the right move. The station was the safest place in town with Orr on the loose. *Second* safest, she amended. But she couldn't have stayed in that suite a minute longer, loving a man who doubted her work. She'd thought he had started to come around, that at the very least she'd earned some respect. Her heart felt pinched and she ached from the inside out. Even focused on her work, she knew loving Antonio had changed her.

Bowe was a bad apple—he'd deceived everyone around him—but that didn't make the entire department irredeemable. She couldn't go around arresting people without evidence, even if the witness was the man she loved. There were rules, laws, procedures that kept the entire community safe.

Melissa looked at the others gathered around the table helping her plan an operation to take down Orr. Yesterday, she'd given another press conference to announce the reopening of the Paxton case. Everyone had been on their toes, but Orr hadn't yet responded. As much as she'd like to hope he'd left town, she couldn't count on it.

"What else can we do to get him to make a move on me?" she asked the room at large.

The easiest path was to offer herself as bait. A year ago, even a month ago, she might've done it, taking the chance to minimize any risk to her officers. But after refusing to allow Antonio to pull the same stunt, she couldn't expose herself on purpose. They might not have a future, but he'd suffered enough. She wouldn't pile on.

"Why not leak the detail about the fingerprint?" Troy asked.

"I think the victim's family would be impossible for Orr to resist," Officer Coleman said. He and Bear were taking more walks around the station and the hotel, under the guise of training, while searching for any sign of Orr. "We could float the news that they're coming to meet with you and discuss new evidence found in their daughter's effects."

Melissa nodded, turning that over in her mind. "Yes. That has potential." And it meant less risk to the community. She tapped her pen against her palm. She looked at the others one by one. "I want eyes at the hotel and regular updates. I'm aware Mr. Ruiz has his own security team, but I want to know if Orr goes directly at him again."

"Yes, ma'am."

"All right, let's get the word out. Who wants to pose as the parents?" She thanked the volunteers with a nod as soon as the hands shot up. With the right outerwear for the winter weather, the officers would be able to pass as the Paxtons from a distance. "The rest of us need to eliminate the places he can lie in wait." It bothered her to no end that they hadn't yet found Orr's hideout.

Troy arched an eyebrow. "We can put officers in place posing as repairmen over in city hall, up on rooftops, that kind of thing."

She walked closer to the city map projected on the screen at one end of the room. Using the remote, she zoomed in on the blocks around the station, pointing out where she wanted undercover officers stationed in anticipation of Orr's response. When she was confident they had every possible approach covered, she sent a statement to the local networks and instructed the GGPD social-media liaison to post an update online.

"Chief—" Officer Warren came skidding into the room "—we just got a silent alarm from the hotel. Orr forced Mr. Ruiz out at gunpoint."

The words hung in the air, an incomprehensible shock to her system. Her heart stalled out and she couldn't get a full breath. "Which direction—"

But there was no time to finish the question as screams erupted from the ever-present protestors out front. She swore and stormed to the front of the station, assessing the scene from just inside the bulletproof glass doors.

Heedless of pedestrians, Orr had driven right up onto the sidewalk and was shouting for the chief of police. The bastard was using Antonio as a shield. Fear and fury lashed at her. She couldn't give in to the emotions, couldn't look at Antonio as the man she loved. Yes, *loved*, despite all her best attempts to resist it. All of that had to wait until they were clear.

"Get an ambulance over here," she ordered. "No sirens. Tell them to hold back out of sight." Someone got on the radio and was speaking in hushed tones.

"Warren, I want the street blocked."

"On it," he said, rushing off.

She faced her department, steel in her voice. "I want everyone out of harm's way. One hostage is all he gets today." On the street, Orr fired into the air and bellowed for her again. She ignored him. "Troy, get someone on a roof with a clear shot. I want teams of two, but no one moves without my order. I'll keep him distracted."

Everyone leaped into motion as she stepped outside, hand resting casually on her gun. For the first time in days the steps were clear of protestors and she resented Orr for ruining the moment.

She desperately wanted to give Antonio some kind of reassurance, but she couldn't. If she looked at him, at the danger he was in, she might break. That would put them all in jeopardy and no doubt raise the body count.

"Mr. Orr, thanks for coming over," she said, as if they'd been lifelong friends. "We've been wanting to speak with you."

"I'm not in the mood to talk, bitch." He shoved Antonio forward with his gun. "I'm making a special delivery."

"That so?" In her periphery, she saw her officers drawing away the bystanders a few at a time. "Please turn over your weapon," she said. "It's unlawful to fire a gun inside city limits."

"Come on down and take him," Orr shouted. "Wendy Paxton's killer, ready to confess."

"You can't mean Mr. Ruiz." She caught sight of Troy across the street, escorting one of their best marksmen, armed with a rifle, into city hall. She couldn't let it get that far. "We have his prints on file and they are not a match to the evidence on Wendy Paxton's body."

"He did it." He gave Antonio another little shove.

"Lower your weapon," she directed, pulling her own gun. "Let Mr. Ruiz go. We can get to the bottom of this together." She had a shot, as did several of her officers by now. "This is no way to resolve anything."

"He's been spreading lies about me. He killed Wendy and ran me out of town."

"Okay. That's upsetting." She tilted her head. "Hey, is that the gun you used to fire at me on Saturday night?"

The tactic worked. Orr shifted to look at the weapon in his hand and she used the distraction to advance. He recovered quickly, though, raising the gun and taking aim at her.

Everyone moved at the same time. In a blink, Orr pulled the trigger while Antonio slammed into him and the bullet went wide, missing her and the glass doors, and lodging in the stone facade. He and Antonio were twisting around in the snow and the gun slid out of reach. Her officers closed in from both sides of the street, separating the men and guiding Antonio away.

Her heart had stalled during the scramble and seeing Antonio safe, she felt it beating again. The surge of relief would have brought her to her knees if she didn't have unfinished business with Orr.

Someone collected the gun while others brought Orr under control. She walked over and snapped the cuffs on his wrists herself. "You are done."

He screamed in outrage, making vile threats and promises of vengeance.

She let his anger roll over her, squeezed the cuffs another notch tighter as she stared him down. "Did you fire a weapon at me and Mr. Ruiz on Saturday night?"

"I was shooting at *him*," he snarled, looking around for Antonio.

"Good start." She stepped back, hands on her hips. "Did you try to run me over with a stolen truck?"

"Would've been two for one," he said. "Ruiz and a cop for a spare."

The spittle gathered at the corners of his mouth had her taking a half step back. "Did you kill Wendy Paxton?"

"Hell yes!" Orr shrieked.

"Take him to County," she said.

The officers aimed him toward the patrol car that had just pulled up.

"She had it coming!" Orr did everything in his power to shake off the officers to no avail. "Cheating on me like that. She didn't know anything."

"County," she repeated, turning away.

"You can't hold me," he screamed. "I have great lawyers. I'll be out by dinner." Orr laughed, and the maniacal sound slithered down her spine.

Why wreck his fantasy? They had him dead to rights for attempted murder today, and they would pile on with the other attempts he'd made on her life and Antonio's. Wendy's parents would have justice at last.

She started up the steps, baffled by the horror on the faces in front of her, when the sounds of a fight registered behind her. A grunt, a shouted warning and another gunshot.

Whirling around, Melissa saw one officer down, clutching his thigh, and Orr, hands cuffed, with a service weapon in his grasp, taking aim at her again. She fired, twice, center mass.

In slow motion, she watched the gun fall from his hand, watched the man crumple to the ground. Blood pooled under the lifeless body, following the bumpy pavement and staining the snow along the way.

Then, abruptly, the world snapped back to reality. She handed over her weapon, then let the paramedics confirm Orr's demise and tend to her injured officer.

Orr was dead.

Given a choice, she would rather have Orr behind bars. She looked down at her empty hands, feeling utterly disconnected and slightly out of step with everyone around her. She'd shot him in self-defense, but it was more to protect her community than herself.

Reeling with a strange sadness, she instinctively looked for Antonio, but he was gone.

Antonio's heart pounded against his ribs and his only coherent thought was to go to Melissa. He wanted to hold her until he was certain she was safe and whole. But she was surrounded by GGPD personnel and was being ushered away for whatever had to happen after an officer fired a gun.

In a fatality.

"Take it easy." Troy guided him away from the scene, around the corner of city hall. "You'll be able to see her soon," the detective said.

"Should I give a statement?" He craned his neck, hoping to get a glimpse of Melissa. Surely with so many witnesses she wouldn't be in trouble for taking lethal action. "She didn't do anything wrong."

"That's why I'm here. For your statement. Relax, Antonio. Walk me through it."

It took another few hard heartbeats to absorb the words, the meaning. He cleared his throat and explained how Orr had traded one hostage for Antonio at the hotel. "I saw Chief Colton do what was necessary to prevent further loss of life," he said to finish. "Can I see her now?"

But he had to fill in more details as Troy questioned him, until finally the interview was complete.

"We appreciate your help," Troy said. "You've been an asset to the department, to the chief in particular, and that helps all of us. Thank you again for helping us rescue my nephew."

Antonio gave a nod, but trailed after Troy. "What happens next? For Melissa, I mean. They won't force her out, will they?"

"Every officer-involved shooting is investigated and she'll have to speak with a psychologist before she can return to duty."

"But she'll return?" Antonio couldn't bear it if Orr killed her career. Melissa lived for the job, for the opportunity to serve the city and people she loved.

"I can't just say yes, because we have to follow protocol," Troy explained. "But the takedown was a group effort and there were plenty of witnesses to her necessary actions."

Nothing he could do. The helplessness burned through him. He needed a minute with her; that was all. Just enough time to make sure she was all right, but they'd led her somewhere he couldn't follow.

Returning to the hotel, he went straight to his office, making it clear Melissa was the only interruption he would allow. It seemed to take forever for his heart to find a normal rhythm again. He pressed his fingers lightly to the tender spot on his jaw where he'd taken another punch from Orr. It was begging for ice.

Would've been nice to sit beside Melissa, watch the fire together while the ice relieved the ache. Would anyone take care of her tonight or would she be dealing with all of this alone?

Their last conversation hadn't gone well and she hadn't returned his calls. Still, she had to know she could come to him, that he would be a friend, even if she didn't return his feelings. More than anything else right now he regretted that she'd gone up against Orr, unsure of how much Antonio believed in her and the GGPD. And she had no idea how much he loved her.

Chapter Sixteen

The next morning, her coffee in hand, Melissa tucked herself into her office. She wasn't in the mood for much chatter today, but she needed to be here. The department psychologist had helped her through the immediate turmoil of the shooting. Together they decided her officers and detectives needed to see the normal routine, as close as she could manage anyway, despite the questions that remained unanswered.

Studying her desktop, she searched for a silver lining amid the stacked-up files and overflowing email inbox waiting for her attention. Well, she was still the chief of police, still had her dream job, even if she had to ride a desk after firing her weapon and ending a man's life.

That hadn't been her ideal outcome, taking a life never was, although in this instance she didn't harbor any regrets.

Orr would've killed Antonio and anyone else within reach if she hadn't taken swift, decisive action.

She shied away from thoughts of Antonio. Last night, alone in her own bed at home, had been unbearably lonely. That scared her more than a little, since the beautiful peace she'd found with him had to be over. Her house had felt awkward rather than welcoming and it went beyond the differences in decor, food options and security. How many times had she started to call him last night, only to change her mind?

She wanted something he couldn't give. A clean break was for the best. Look at that, she'd found a silver lining.

She sipped her coffee and picked up a file, only to toss it back down, unread, as her concentration fractured. What was truly regrettable was that Bowe's actions had left Orr free for too long. She supposed the subsequent desk duty gave her plenty of time to review Bowe's old cases for any other signs of manipulation. What messes would they be cleaning up next?

And maybe not so silvery, but riding a desk gave her ample time to think about the next steps. For herself. Though she loved her work, she was tired of settling for only professional satisfaction. Being chief was demanding and definitely unpredictable, but her heart yearned for balance.

Swiveling in her chair, she picked up the framed photo of Desiree and Danny, a gift her cousin had dropped off after the kidnapping ordeal. Desiree was raising a child alone and doing it well. That little boy had Melissa wrapped around his tiny finger. Her heart ached in her chest as she imagined raising a child of her own. Maybe it was time to take that leap, even without a husband and partner in place. She couldn't stop the fantasy of playdates with Danny and Desiree, trips to the park, family traditions, as she and her cousin raised the next generation of Coltons.

In her mind, though, her little one had Antonio's dark eyes and mischievous grin. On a shaky breath, she returned the picture to its place of honor on her desk. Desiree's path wasn't for her. She wanted it all. Husband

and children and a career. She craved that balance, but no longer with a faceless partner.

With Antonio. The man who didn't trust her department. The man who'd vowed—with good reason—not to travel a family path again.

There were some things "I love you" couldn't cure. Her career. His past. Her obligations. His doubts.

Swiping a tear from her cheek, she turned her attention to the slew of emails she'd been ignoring during the recent chaos and set to work. She had no idea she'd left her desk to stare out her office window until someone knocked on her door.

Turning, she saw Antonio. It took every ounce of willpower not to rush forward, expecting him to catch her in that warm embrace.

"Can I come in?" he asked. "I've been worried."

"Of course." She tried to smile and gave up. "Close the door." Just in case she lost it, no sense upsetting the entire department.

He did as she asked, but didn't sit down in one of the chairs facing her desk. With his hands in his pockets, he stood there and studied her.

She assumed he saw it all. The dark circles under her eyes, the tension in her jaw, the badge that represented a system he didn't trust.

"Are you all right?" he asked.

That smooth, deep voice was a balm to her frayed nerves and she shamelessly soaked it in. "I am. It won't take them long to confirm the shooting was justified." Her gaze locked with his. Until right now she hadn't thought that maybe he disapproved of what she'd done.

"You were remarkable out there," he said, pride radiating from his eyes. "The whole department was absolutely remarkable."

She bit her lip. It was hard to accept his praise, after killing a man he'd once considered a friend.

"What do you do while waiting for the process and protocols?" he asked.

She gestured to her desk. "Plenty of work and enough time to get it done for a change."

"I see." He tipped his head. "No time off?"

She resisted the urge to fold her arms over her chest to shelter her heart from him. "Not really. We are looking into all of Bowe's cases. It will take time, but we'll figure out why he did what he did. And where he's hiding."

"That's good."

There was an awkward silence that she couldn't bear. "Antonio…" Then the words started tumbling out. "I love you. I want more time with you. But I can't settle." Her pulse steadied as the words resonated. "I want my career *and* everything else that makes a life full." He was going to walk out any second and she braced for the pain even as she rushed on. "I want a husband and children. I want family chaos and jammed-up schedules." She sucked in a breath. She wanted it all with him, despite the furrow pleating his brow. "I'm not going to be completely me, not completely happy, until I'm on that track." She stopped just short of apologizing for her dreams.

"You love me," he said.

"Yes." For all the good it did either of them.

"Do you see that love for me changing? Fading out with a fling? Maybe you'll get tired of me and the demands of my work."

No. That was the worst piece of this entire situation. She'd fallen in love with the wrong man. "No." She wouldn't lie. "Never. But that doesn't change that everything I want is at odds with what you need."

She wished she could be the one to leave, but she wasn't about to run out of her office, an emotional wreck, in front of the officers who looked up to her as the example.

Unable to read him, she turned back to the window. Just because he would leave, didn't mean she had to watch him go. She listened for the squeak of the door-knob so she knew when it would be safe to let the tears fall.

HE STARED AT the elegant line of her back and realized just how far he'd come. She expected him to walk out. He'd given her every reason to come to that conclusion.

"I'm not leaving, Melissa."

She didn't turn around.

"I love you, too." He stepped up behind her, resting his hands lightly on her shoulders. When she didn't shrug him off, he wrapped his arms around her, holding her close. Their image was a faint reflection in the window, but it was enough to confirm he was doing the right thing. For himself. For her. For their future.

"I've been scared for years. Two decades, really. Until you." He brushed a soft kiss to her cheek. "Although I suspect I'll have more reason to be scared for you in the years ahead, I am absolutely terrified of the years ahead if you're not in my world." He shifted so she was facing him. "I'm done running from a full life, as long as you're in it." He dropped to one knee, smiling when she gasped at the ring he held for her. "Melissa Colton, will you marry me and help me fill the hotel with beautiful redheaded children?"

"You can't be serious." A slow smile illuminated her face, lit up the room like a sunrise. "It's a big hotel." She caught her lip between her teeth. "Are you sure? I know what this—"

He cut her off. "I've never been more certain of anything. Marry me, Melissa." He watched her face as he pushed the ring into place on her finger. She bounced on her toes and tugged him to his feet. His heart was bursting with happiness when she wrapped her arms around him. "Is that a yes?"

She leaned back, her smile filling him with a joy he hadn't allowed himself in far too long.

"Yes." Her hands trembled as she touched his face, pulled him close for a kiss. "You're everything I've always wanted and so much more than I dared to hope for."

He felt weightless and full of light as he held her close. She was his future, his heart. He didn't want to let go, but they both had work. "I'll have the champagne on ice in the suite," he said, kissing her once more.

She beamed, her eyes sparkling brighter than the diamond on her hand. "I'll call when I'm on the way over."

And there it was, he thought—the first day of the rest of their lives.

* * * * *

COMING SOON!

LET'S TALK
Romance

For exclusive extracts, competitions
and special offers, find us online:

MILLS & BOON

THE HEART OF ROMANCE

A ROMANCE FOR EVERY KIND OF READER

MODERN

Prepare to be swept off your feet by sophisticated, sexy and seductive heroes, in some of the world's most glamourous and romantic locations, where power and passion collide.
8 stories per month.

HISTORICAL

Escape with historical heroes from time gone by. Whether your passion is for wicked Regency Rakes, muscled Vikings or rugged Highlanders, awaken the romance of the past.
6 stories per month.

MEDICAL

Set your pulse racing with dedicated, delectable doctors in the high-pressure world of medicine, where emotions run high and passion, comfort and love are the best medicine.
6 stories per month.

Celebrate true love with tender stories of heartfelt romance, from the rush of falling in love to the joy a new baby can bring, and a focus on the emotional heart of a relationship.
8 stories per month.

Indulge in secrets and scandal, intense drama and plenty of sizzling hot action with powerful and passionate heroes who have it all: wealth, status, good looks…everything but the right woman.
6 stories per month.

HEROES

Experience all the excitement of a gripping thriller, with an intense romance at its heart. Resourceful, true-to-life women and strong, fearless men face danger and desire - a killer combination!
8 stories per month.

DARE

Sensual love stories featuring smart, sassy heroines you'd want as a best friend, and compelling intense heroes who are worthy of them.
4 stories per month.

To see which titles are coming soon, please visit

millsandboon.co.uk/nextmonth

MILLS & BOON

MODERN

Power and Passion

Prepare to be swept off your feet by sophisticated, sexy and seductive heroes, in some of the world's most glamourous and romantic locations, where power and passion collide.

MILLS & BOON
True Love

Romance from the Heart

Celebrate true love with tender stories of
heartfelt romance, from the rush of falling
in love to the joy a new baby can bring,
and a focus on the emotional
heart of a relationship.

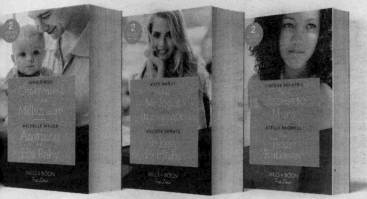

MILLS & BOON
MEDICAL
Pulse-Racing Passion

Set your pulse racing with dedicated,
delectable doctors in the high-pressure
world of medicine, where emotions run
high and passion, comfort and love are the
best medicine.

Eight Medical stories published every month, find them all a

millsandboon.co.uk